YOU SHALL SEE
the
BEAUTIFUL
THINGS

YOU SHALL SEE *the* BEAUTIFUL THINGS

A NOVEL & A NOCTURNE

STEVE AMICK

ACRE

CINCINNATI 2023

Acre Books is made possible by the support of the
Robert and Adele Schiff Foundation and the
Department of English at the University of Cincinnati.

Designed by Barbara Neely Bourgoyne
Cover art: Shedd Aquarium, Chicago. Unsplash.

ISBN-13 (pbk): 978-1-946724-59-5
ISBN-13 (ebook): 978-1-946724-60-1

The press is based at the University of Cincinnati, Department
of English and Comparative Literature, A&S Hall, Room 248,
PO Box 210069, Cincinnati, OH, 45221–0069.
www.acre-books.com

Acre Books books may be purchased at a discount for educational use.
For information please email business@acre-books.com.

For Sharyl & Huck,
my moon & stars.

& in memory of my uncle,
James Lewis Amick
(1925–2002),
aeronautical engineer & genius inventor of, among
other things, the Windmobile, the Amick Arch, & a
sailboat
that could lift off & *fly through the fricking sky.*

THIS TALE TAKES PLACE in the following times and places: Scheveningen Beach, The Hague, the Netherlands; Leiden, Wassenaar, Rotterdam; the village of Clovelly, Devon; Aceh, Sumatra; Rangoon, Burma; St. Louis, Missouri; 1882–1888; three long nights in 1889 & the months leading up to them; never & nowhere.

Glossary

(mostly Dutch & Indonesian; a little Chinese, Hungarian, & English)

Aceh—northern province of Sumatra

Acehnese—the people of Aceh

Aceh-mord—suicide attack against non-Muslim invaders

alsjemenou! —*oh my!* or *what the heck!*

alstublieft—*please*

ang mo—derogatory term for white Europeans, namely the Dutch

appeltaart—a slightly tart apple pie

bedankt—*thanks*

bérlés—rent

bib—the ideal (curved) shape of a thrown herring net

bintang kecil—little star

bitterballen—Dutch deep-fried meatballs

bohorok—dry wind on the plains in northeast Sumatra

bom, bomschuit, bomschuiten—flat-bottomed herring boat(s)

boonaken—Dutch card game

boven de hemel!—*heavens above!*

bule—Caucasian

brubru—easterly gusts

Celestial—slang for Chinese, or perhaps applied, even less correctly, to anyone considered "Far Eastern" or "Oriental"

csavargó—vagrant, vagabond

Djokjakarta—old Dutch name for the city of Yogyakarta

dūchá—inspector

einde—end

excuseer mij—*excuse me*

fruittaart (vruchtentaart)—fruit cake

gezelligheid—conviviality; feeling of coziness, warmth, pleasure in company, or a sense of belonging, depending on the context

godverdomme—*goddamn*

goedenavond—*good evening*

grappenmaker—joker

Grong-grong—small village north of Bukitkrueng, in Aceh, Sumatra

grootvader—grandpa

Gunung Abong Abong—mountain in central Aceh, Sumatra

haringbuis, haringbuizen—herring buss(es); large "factory" fishing ship(s) that could stay out for weeks at a time

Harre Jasses!—*Lord Jesus!* An exclamation conveying head-shaking surprise.

hoi—*hi*

houten schoen—wooden shoe

ijscolf—ice golf; similar to, but historically preceding, hockey

jeetje!—*jeez!*

jenever—traditional liquor of the Netherlands, juniper-flavored, known as Dutch gin

Kerstfeest—December 25 and 26

Klaas Vaak—the Sandman

klapstuk—beef rib

klewang—traditional Sumatran single-edged cutlass with a wide blade, not unlike the machete, also worn as a sidearm by the KNIL

klompen—clogs

klootzak—nutsack; a term of abuse meaning asshole or bastard

KNIL (Koninklijk Nederlandsch-Indisch Leger)—Royal Netherlands East
Indies Army

kurhaus—cure house; a seaside resort

lieve hemel!—*good heavens!*

lǎo bǎn—proprietor or headman/boss

Mahomedan—an earlier Anglicized term for a Muslim

masjid—mosque

Meneer—*Mr.*

Mevrouw/Mevr.—Madam or Mrs.

mijn hemel!—*my heavens!*

moeder—mother

mosódeszka—washboard

ondertrouw—the public notice and registry of intention to marry, which
was historically three weeks prior to the wedding

onzin—nonsense

palanquin—a covered litter; in the case of the Sumatran sultans, distinguished by an oval canopy

pappje—papa

pedang—traditional longsword of Aceh

pinda—derogatory slur for an Indonesian

picarooner—small, simple, single-masted herring lugger, peculiar to Clovelly,
in Devon, England

piszok—schmutz, dirt, filth

polder—low-lying land reclaimed from the sea or a river and protected by
dikes

redding—rescue, salvation, redemption, preservation

rentjong/rencong—traditional fighting knife of Aceh

rumah—large Sumatran traditional house

Scheveningen—beach at The Hague, pronounced *SKHEY-vuh ning-uh n*

Serune Kalee—Acehnese bamboo horn

siksaan—torture, torment

Sinterklass—St. Nicholas Day, December 5

snert—Dutch pea soup

sopo—Sumatran storage structure, often for rice

Spaans benauwd—Spanish breathless or Spanish stuffy; indicating a state of anxiety or fear, deriving from the Eighty Years' War with Spain

specculaas—a shortbread ginger cookie

spoorwagon—train

spoorweg—railway

stamppot—smashed-up potatoes complemented with whatever's at hand

sterre—*star*

strandweg—a beach promenade, boardwalk

stroopwafel—a syrup-filled Dutch waffle

't geeft niet—*it doesn't matter; don't worry about it*

Toba Batak—the largest group of the Batak people in northern Sumatra

tuchtiging—chastisement, discipline, counterinsurgent tactics in the Aceh War

vader—father

ventjager—a smaller boat that services a herring buss

wajan—wok

walvisvangst—whaling

zweefmolen—giant's stride; a chair-swing carousel, an early amusement ride

THE VERSES

Wynken, Blynken, and Nod (Dutch Lullaby)
—EUGENE FIELD, 1889

Wynken, Blynken, and Nod one night
   Sailed off in a wooden shoe,—
Sailed on a river of crystal light
   Into a sea of dew.
"Where are you going, and what do you wish?"
   The old moon asked the three.
"We have come to fish for the herring-fish
   That live in this beautiful sea;
   Nets of silver and gold have we,"
      Said Wynken,
      Blynken,
      And Nod.

The old moon laughed and sang a song,
   As they rocked in the wooden shoe;
And the wind that sped them all night long
   Ruffled the waves of dew;
The little stars were the herring-fish
   That lived in the beautiful sea.
"Now cast your nets wherever you wish,—
   Never afeared are we!"
   So cried the stars to the fishermen three,

Wynken,
Blynken,
And Nod.

All night long their nets they threw
    To the stars in the twinkling foam,—
Then down from the skies came the wooden shoe,
    Bringing the fishermen home:
'Twas all so pretty a sail, it seemed
    As if it could not be;
And some folk thought 'twas a dream they'd dreamed
    Of sailing that beautiful sea;
    But I shall name you the fishermen three:
        Wynken,
        Blynken,
        And Nod.

Wynken and Blynken are two little eyes,
    And Nod is a little head,
And the wooden shoe that sailed the skies
    Is a wee one's trundle-bed;
So shut your eyes while Mother sings
    Of wonderful sights that be,
And you shall see the beautiful things
    As you rock in the misty sea
    Where the old shoe rocked the fishermen three:—
        Wynken,
        Blynken,
        And Nod.

The Owl and the Pussycat
—EDWARD LEAR, 1871

I

The Owl and the Pussy-cat went to sea
   In a beautiful pea-green boat.
They took some honey, and plenty of money,
   Wrapped up in a five-pound note.
The Owl looked up to the stars above,
   And sang to a small guitar,
"O lovely Pussy! O Pussy, my love,
   What a beautiful Pussy you are,
      You are,
      You are!
What a beautiful Pussy you are!"

II

Pussy said to the Owl, "You elegant fowl!
   How charmingly sweet you sing!
O let us be married! too long we have tarried:
   But what shall we do for a ring?"
They sailed away, for a year and a day,
   To the land where the Bong-Tree grows
And there in a wood a Piggy-wig stood
   With a ring at the end of his nose,
      His nose,
      His nose,
With a ring at the end of his nose.

III

"Dear Pig, are you willing to sell for one shilling
   Your ring?" Said the Piggy, "I will.'
So they took it away, and were married next day
   By the Turkey who lives on the hill.

They dined on mince, and slices of quince,
  Which they ate with a runcible spoon;
And hand in hand, on the edge of the sand,
  They danced by the light of the moon,
      The moon,
      The moon,
They danced by the light of the moon.

New Friends and Old Friends (Y Cyfiall Pur)
  —JOSEPH PARRY, CA. 1886

Make new friends, but keep the old;
  Those are silver, these are gold.
Newmade friendships, like new wine,
  Age will mellow and refine.

Friendships that have stood the test—
  Time and change—are surely best.
Brow and wrinkle, hair grown gray;
  Friendship never knows decay.

For 'mid old friends, tried and true,
  Once more our youth renew.
But old friends, alas! may die;
  New friends must their place supply.

Cherish friendship in your breast—
  New is good but old is best;
Make new friends, but keep the old;
  Those are silver, these are gold.

I.

WYNKEN, BLYNKEN, AND NOD ONE NIGHT

And there it was: the crashing surf of last light [the sky shutting down for the day over the North Sea], with the herring shoals just beyond . . . Wyn helped push out onto Scheveningen Beach [trudging toward the water's edge, heaving against a ridiculously undersized fishing vessel of foreign design and doubtful seaworthiness]. This was not where he'd pictured himself being at twenty-nine, nearly middle-aged [and back in the place he'd fled], about to attempt this brutal toil all over again [without even the auspices of a properly sanctioned and registered fishing charter]. Creeping out onto the tidal sands with Luuk Blenkin and Old Ned as the night seeped over the village, he felt like a housebreaker for fish . . . but he welcomed it. He knew he was grimacing, acting gruff and annoyed about the whole lunatic scheme [as if *he* were doing the old man and the boy a big favor just by being there, by having instigated this foolishness]. Some perverted part of him didn't want them to know he needed this more than they did. So he made cracks about how he was going to have to spend all his earnings from the catch on a case of liniment and a truss [and japes about their dismal prospects, the doomed nature of their project]: "It's no matter our young friend here knows nothing about fishing," he said of Luuk [the seventeen-year-old they'd rooked into this venture]. "That's just fine, Blenkin, because we'll all drown before we can even shoot the first net."

He was thinking about the pine pitch. Even Old Ned Nodder, who had the most experience among them, had seemed uncertain they'd successfully sealed the hull of their strange little experimental boat in the final stages of applying pine tar. And unlike in a normal harbor [as featured in *normal* fishing towns], where a new boat might take on some water but its seal could be double-checked while it was still moored to the dock, here at Scheveningen, given the ridiculous condition of the beach [the entire lack of harbor], the bomschuiten were launched straight into the crashing breakers. Untried vessels like theirs were either seaworthy or sank.

"Wait—" Luuk sounded startled. "Was I supposed to—? I mean, I wasn't the one who determined whether it was watertight or not—was I?"

"That's how I'm telling it later, at the tavern," Wyn said.

It wasn't that Luuk was scatterbrained [exactly]. Wyn felt it was more a matter of his inability to stay focused. [The young man's mind reminded Wyn of a small shop he'd visited in Rangoon. Inside, it was just a room full of canaries, uncaged, flying this way and that.]

Old Ned chuckled. "Don't listen to the scamp, son. This fool, when he was your age, used to tell me he would one day buy my fine bom from me. And that thing was essentially a colander."

Wyn grinned as if he recalled this [which he didn't]. But it hardly mattered: even if what was left of Ned's family had *not* sold off what was left of *De Groot Ster* [reportedly no better than scrap after the last big storm turned half the independents' fleet into kindling, smashing them together on the beach like scattered bath toys abandoned by a toddler who never learned], they were still too few a crew for a traditional bomschuit.

Which was why they'd abandoned the standard ways [those great heaving monsters] for something downright innovative. And likely to have the same result as the Aceh-mord practiced by those Allah-crazed insurgents he'd faced back in the jungles of Sumatra [attacking head-on for the glory of the afterlife].

Well, Wyn van Winkel wasn't after *that*. He just wanted a decent haul of herring to earn a little money. [Or keep busy trying. Because in truth, he was just glad to be able to make himself useful in some way. Useful beyond his normal role as the grappenmaker, providing some entertainment.]

It wouldn't take much effort to turn all this into a joke. [An actual joke.]

He didn't think he would, but he could—he could put one together, if need be, about the grootvader, the kid, and the war deserter in a boat.

He didn't really think of Ned Nodder as a grootvader. [And Ned wasn't one, technically. But only because he got hitched so late.] By navigating back through the fuzzy chapters in his own garbled life, Wyn figured Smilin' Ned to be roughly forty-eight; the man had nineteen whopping years on him. [Even when he'd apprenticed to him, back in 1882, Ned had seemed like a well-salted mariner of the high seas.]

Of course no old salt or grampa ever lit up the way Noddie was doing now, the three of them yipping at the sight of the sparkling surf, the miracle of moonlight mixed with water, none more so than Ned. [His old friend lately seemed alive in a way he hadn't in months—at least when he stayed awake.]

At moments [like tonight, as he hooted into the wind on this long, familiar stretch of beach] Wyn thought he could just stay here, that no one would be looking for him. After the magazine explosion in his garrison in Aceh, they probably just counted him among the dead and missing.

He wondered sometimes if he *had* died. Maybe that was what was happening here; why he'd returned to Scheveningen and The Hague. [Or at least thought he had returned.] But no, Zef Kloet and Harm van Donk and numerous other local oafs were here too. [If this was the afterlife, those clowns would not be permitted—in either heaven or the other.]

The way they'd always talked about it—the plan had been to "give it a shot one night," and so—for a time—Luuk was confused. To split hairs here—it was actually *two* nights, not one—it would take them two nights to launch the thing—partly because there were only three of them, and partly because they hoped to avoid the gawkers by hauling it to the beach after sundown. But of course the time to go out and shoot the nets was *at* sundown. So the plan became a two-part plan—push it out to Scheveningen on night one, cover it with tarps and hope it didn't draw too much notice, then throw off the tarps and launch it the following early evening—night two.

And he was new to all this, of course—why shouldn't he get confused? Van Winkel had given him some advice about keeping things straight in his mind: "How do you keep all that music straight, kid? When you're doing your songs? Just think of all your assignments and checklists and duties with our boat the same way you do your verses and you'll be shipshape."

When they pulled back the tarps—the second evening on Scheveningen Beach—and began the chore of dragging it out to the surf—they actually had the beach to themselves. A few sunset gazers here and there—sparkers and strollers, the dunes painter packing up his easel—but no other herring men—no bomschuiten—they would have gaped at the puny boat—this "picarooner." Still, Luuk was a little unsure why they had to sneak around and why they couldn't have put it out in one night. He had a lot of questions—but wasn't sure about asking any of them. This was all too new to him. Plus—

☾

For Ned Nodder, it was something to just be out here . . . right on the edge of the land again . . . feeling the surf coming in . . . watching the sun leaving them, low and orangey against the far side of the sea. It was enough to make him smile . . . despite what he knew their prospects to be tonight.

"The herring are fat now," he announced . . . to himself, to the two-man crew, to the sea . . . "I'm sure of it."

The boy screwed up his face. "How do you know this? Is there some way you—I guess I'm unclear—Do you go out and *test* them or—"

Wyn laughed. "That's Agreeable Ned you're talking to, kid! Most agreeable man in all of South Holland. And maybe parts of Zeeland. And the man who puts out no argument, gets no argument. Even from the fish. I mean, what fool filet would contradict this fine fellow?"

Ned *didn't* know, of course . . . And in fact there just wasn't the bounty there had once been. Farther out than the boms worked, those outrageous Dutch busses gutted their catch and threw offal overboard right there where they fished, and it was scaring the shoals away . . . those massive factory ships . . . not thinking about how it affected anyone but their financiers, making a huge mess of it . . . He imagined the herring still living in the water, the horror they saw . . . Those sloppy haringbuis crews . . . they ought not do that . . . Plus, they cast their nets in broad daylight and left their catch . . . languishing, crowded in the nets . . . it scared the rest of the fish, drove them off . . . They were Dutchmen and should know better. They weren't *Swedes*, after all . . . The stupid Swedes had infamously scared the shoals away from their waters for sixty-nine years, all because they lazily . . . stupidly . . . gutted their catch on the beach, dumping the offal right in the surf, not carting it off for farmers to use in their fields . . . Not that Ned had anything against Swedes . . . He'd met a couple of those people and got along famously with both of them . . .

But Ned believed in the power of the grin and the upturned chin . . . "Keep it cheery," his wife would tell the young ones . . . And she didn't have to tell *him*. He'd been keeping it cheery for as long as he could recall. There was no other way to keep it.

And there was every reason to feel cheery . . . He was once again a part of a sunset launch and maiden voyage of a herring boat . . . even *this* improper little thing . . . Made proper enough, because . . . for the few who kept to the old ways . . . *this* was the hour to set out . . . shooting the nets after sunset, pulling them before the sun peeked back along the lowlands, beyond the shore . . . And some still did it . . . the bomschuit crews, at least. It was those greedy bastards farther out . . . the herring busses, at sea night and day, halfway to England . . . who were breaking the rules . . . The natural order of things . . . Shooting nets in daylight scared the herring. And entire shoals could scatter off to another, deeper corner of the ocean if they saw the nets slamming down from above, from fish heaven, in the glittery light. Anyone with sense knew that . . . That things were done the old way for a reason, and you shan't monkey with it.

For a moment there, he was off and away in the indigo deep, the gray-silver flittering of the shoals, swimming with the herring, feeling their terror . . . and then a voice was saying, "Which is why we need the man with the most *experience* here to *rouse* himself . . ." It was Wynkyn's voice . . . it always sounded to Ned like a gentle chuckle, no matter what the scamp was saying . . . and he realized they were ahead of him now . . . that he wasn't pushing the boat anymore but lying flat in the wet sand . . . dozing. Scrambling to his feet, brushing himself off, he rejoined them for the final push.

This right here was why he couldn't work the herring boats anymore

. . . not in the traditional way, at least, in a fully crewed bomschuit: this strange condition of his, this unwarranted sleep . . . The nodding off. A thing like that couldn't be kept under wraps. It didn't take the worst gossips and flop-tongued fishwives and market-mingling whisperers and bad-mouthing fenceline wags to spread around a thing like that. Who wouldn't remark on such odd behavior: *we were sitting there in the noonday sun, laying out net, and I swear, he was repairing the net, man, yet he was dead asleep . . .*

And they could like him all they wanted personally, but that didn't mean they trusted him out in the rocking sea . . . moving around in the boat, walking in his sleep . . . or slumped over, checked out, the crew now one man down . . . No, sir.

With the death of two of his brothers . . . and the third absconding to Hindeloopen to see out his days with a large dour widow named Kunigonde who kept a small inn . . . the Nodder family bomschuit was sold . . . though not for much, since it was little more than matchsticks after the last storm hit Scheveningen Beach. If he'd been a little younger . . . or not seen as a curse by potential crew afraid of his malady . . . as well they probably should be . . . he would have perhaps obtained a loan and taken on his brother's share in the bom, which they'd christened *De Groot Ster*. He would have rechristened her after his wife . . . if he'd owned it himself. But he'd needed at least eight more men, preferably eleven . . . plus being younger: he could have used that too . . . and the financing . . . So the bom was not an option . . . nor was there, he knew without trying, any chance of landing a job out on those factory ships planted way out there . . . the herring busses.

He had a small subsistence farm, of course, and did a little logging and carpentry where he could . . . whatever he could to scrounge up enough to take care of his loved ones. He kept up appearances with Fenna, smiling and telling her the Lord would provide . . . but he did worry, as his wee ones slept . . . thinking of them, thinking of the disparity in ages between himself and his mevrouw . . . She was still quite young by any standard and as fair and lovely as a cornflower. She would have his small property, and that . . . along with her great personal qualities . . . would surely be enough to guarantee a second husband in widowhood. He hoped . . . But it wasn't enough to hope.

His friend Wynkyn . . . young Wynk van Winkel . . . had teased him, upon Wynkyn's return from that awful, endless infidel war, that Ned was lucky the fishermen of Scheveningen simply avoided working a boat with him and left it at that. A few centuries back, the scamp claimed . . . or even now, among the native people of his jungle war . . . the Acehnese . . . he said Ned would have been killed as a demon or practitioner of evil witchcraft because of the odd sleeping spells he suffered. His friend had winked. "I'd count my blessings, not being burned at the stake, Noddie. Take solace in the fact we are an enlightened and humane nation."

And Ned had to laugh . . . despite his concern that he really had been left with few avenues for further income. He had to laugh because it was his nature, this need to put on a good front . . . keep his chin up for others . . . But also he laughed because good ol' Wynkyn was telling him he wasn't troubled by his spells . . . that he would even throw in with him to form a small herring crew of some kind . . . that he should go home and pat his sleeping beauties and laugh at the big old moon . . . because they were going to find a way, old friend.

And so he was all prepared . . . when he got home and told his love of the kind offer, from his loyal young friend Wynk van Winkel, to throw in with him . . . for her to point out that Wynkyn was no great catch, either . . . to question the profit in partnering with the man, considering rumors that van Winkel had returned broken, likely crazy, certainly tainted with the sinful afflictions of the Orient . . . But she only nodded as he brushed her long hair, as he did most nights, and she said, "I'm glad, dear husband. I'm glad for you both." Another man might have felt some affront that she didn't object, thinking highly of her own husband, claiming he could do better than this unhinged derelict . . . this deviant seen slinking from the Celestials' pillow-lined cellars . . . a man the villagers whispered had massacred, deserted, turned Mahomedan or smuggler . . . But Ned was not another man.

He took her nodding as quiet agreement that it was a sound partnership, and he was a man who felt great peace in agreement . . .

Sailed Off in a Wooden Shoe.—

[A little less than a year before] Wyn had written his recent traveling companion [English Van, in the Devon village of Clovelly] to ask if he could possibly supply him with plans for the so-called picarooner they'd discussed, a supposed marvel of the fellow's little English fishing cove, which [if Wyn's memory wasn't distorting the delirious yarns he and the Engelsman spun when they were holed up together] had sounded like just the thing for a short-handed crew of misfit herringmen. He took it to be a well-guarded local secret, and finding someone with the skills to draw up the lines of the vessel was a lot to ask of his friend. But on the other hand, he *had* stepped in and rescued the man on the boat back [a trader out of Rangoon] when a deck-hand had caught English Van stowed away in the cargo hold. [He would never point it out to him, of course, but] Wyn alone was probably the reason the lunatic hadn't been marooned south of the Horn of Africa [stranded and flyspecked back in French Somaliland even now].

He'd had him post the drawings to his father at Leiden University, knowing English Van could little afford the rate on his end [nor could Wyn on his]. Vader bristled, of course, but the post was covered by his department upon delivery, paid out by the clerks who handled their correspondence. [They likely assumed the long tube of shipbuilding plans was a small telescope.]

When Wyn went to the observatory to retrieve the parcel, he saw that his father had opened it.

"I wanted to determine if it was opiates," the old man said.

"Sent from Devon, England? The great Cornish poppy?"

The distinguished Professor van Winkel scowled. "Well, I have no earthly idea what you get up to, son. I never have. You're a boat-builder now, then?"

"I'm a builder of *dreeeeeeaaams*, pappje." [His father hated being called *pappje*.]

He waited the whole way back to look it over, keeping it rolled up tight while riding the spoorweg [the *clickety-clack* just a hair less tedious than the swaying he'd grown used to in his time at sea]. He waited to show it to Agreeable Ned.

It was still warm out then [the gales of autumn not yet rolling in], and he was still sleeping in public parks [which meant he had no place to examine it in private]. So he took it to the shed at the back of the small Nodder farm where they would be building the thing, and they rolled it out, placed lanterns on the corners, and took it all in.

It was sleek and jaunty, they agreed, and a thing of beauty [but smaller than even his friend had made out]. Not unlike a dogger or lugger [but smaller, much smaller].

Everything was marked and tagged: the mooring eyebolts, the grown quarter knees, sculling notch, mizzenmast housing, sternpost, raised transom, stemband, apron, breasthook, fairlead for lying to nets, rubbing strake, the side thwarts marked "shag."

It looked like something a boy would float in the reflecting pond at Malieveld. Or a rich banker's son would play with at bath.

"Appears almost Spanish . . ." Ned said.

It was a fair guess. English Van had said something about a theory that a Spanish boat wreck [perhaps even scattered from the Armada] had washed ashore, and the resourceful cliff-dwellers of Clovelly had copied the design for their own purposes.

They could build such a thing, no problem. But Noddie filled his pipe and raised the obvious question: was it lunacy how much smaller their boat was?

Wyn responded by telling the one about the Engelsman, the Scotsman, and the Frenchman in a boat.

Luuk Blenkin—though new to the task—understood—in theory, at least—why they went out at night to "shoot the nets," as they called the casting process—when they could ease the nets down over the herring and not scatter the shoal—yet it still struck him—especially once they were out there, doing it—that so much of this would be easier—and easier to comprehend—in the blare of daylight. He didn't trust his vision, his perspective and aim, in this murky moonlight.

There were songs he knew by heart—chanties of the sea he'd learned to play the fiddle to—and then the accordion—that laid out exactly this process, step by step. Though he'd never done it before tonight, he'd been over it countless times—lyrically. Somehow, that failed to prepare him. If the night—with this great sobering moon guiding them—and the calm of the two older men, to boot—weren't quite so reassuring, he'd really be panicking right now. Because he didn't have a clue what he was doing.

Preparing for this—all fall and winter, the months leading up to the big shove out into the surf at Scheveningen—he'd been thinking that he was lucky for the opportunity to try herring fishing without the complications and high stakes of the haringbuis—or even just a nine-man bomschuit. But now that they were out there he did the math and realized he was exactly one-third responsible for the outcome of this venture, and it made him all the more sure he should've stayed home. Except—

When Ned Nodder's oldest girl, the three-year-old, played with her ragdoll, she sometimes placed it inside her little klomp . . . as if it were a cart or a boat . . . directing the wooden shoe around the floor and into the air . . . He rather fancied the idea of sailing off in a shoe . . . to be free from strife . . . Only, of course, if he could take his little family with him. Or, if he must leave them and never return, at least to know that they would be safe and sound . . . Free from strife . . .

Luuk Blenkin worried about his hands—being able to play the accordion—after all this hard labor. Then again—a small injury might be worth the expression on Imke's face—what he saw—or hoped, well, *thought* he saw—earlier this evening when he confided in her what he was doing. He hadn't meant to tell her, but when he ran into her—in a hurry in the market—and glimpsed the nape of her neck—her hair pinned up in the traditional local way, with the gold hairpins—and the lumpy Scheveningen bonnet, bulbous as a full drift net—ridiculous—but her nape was exposed, and that nape had always done something to him—seated behind her in church or school—the glint of sunlight on the fuzz of her neck. It was like a secret coded message, sailing out to him, the play of sunlight on her nape—and he felt this strange feeling that if he had been carrying anything—a bundle of firewood, shirttails full of apples—he would have wanted to give them to her—to have her hold up her apron so he could pour it all overboard. Only—he wasn't carrying anything and had nothing to give her. Instead, he told about the late night fishing plan—and though he couldn't quite decipher the look in her eyes, he wanted to think it was that she was impressed. He made sure to mention that Wyn van Winkel was part of it. He couldn't figure out exactly what the people of Scheveningen thought of his new friend—Wyn—and maybe that was because opinion was mixed. Luuk knew he should just base his judgment on his own experience with the war vet, but—that was difficult. Wyn had been consistently generous and friendly to him—quick with a smile and a joke—but some folks did think of van Winkel as a bum, a reprobate, not living up to his father's standing—or at least as a scamp, a rascal—and there were disquieting whispers about the things that might have changed him when he was off fighting the heathens. *Sumatra,* they whispered—it sounded like a spell.

But the man was handsome—and wry—and never seemed to lose his ability to make the girls blush—and so Luuk went ahead and told Imke they were working together, feeling the news might impress. At least, he was fairly certain it would—it was hard to keep anything clear in his mind alongside a glimpse of the nape of Imke's neck.

Off came the shoes, then stepping out into the surf [the horizon pinking up beyond, out past the end of everything here]. *An end of strife,* Wyn reminded himself, picturing Rangoon and his ridiculous friend just on the other side of all that out there, to the west, and how *he* would say that too [Off with the shoes!] as they found comfort in some shady section of lawn in that distant land to the east.

[Taking his bearings here] it was far different from the serrated skyline of Rangoon [poky with pagodas, wetly golden like the unstable showings in the annual butter-carving contests out in those hinterlands north of The Hague, where folks lived in their windmills]. It had nearly hurt the eyes, all that glittering gilded roofing. Nodding off outdoors [under palms or near that big lake in the center of it all, or on the grounds of the Pegu Club, in full view of the limey brass] was like trying to sleep in a pirate chest open to the midday sun. But it felt relatively safe from surprise attack by some hopped-up Mahomedan swinging a klewang. The worst potential disturbance [according to his new pal English Van] would be a gentle nudge from a constable's shoe, and a polite request to "Button it down, lads. Presentable, please, presentable . . ." [if one were lounging about too loosely in shirttails, with shoes discarded, or looking too accurately like a demon of the pipe].

He hadn't stayed there long, but sometimes, when the wind picked up on that lake in the center of Rangoon, he could sleep listening to it lap its shores, and dream he was far from all of it [even from relatively safe Burma] and back on the beach at Scheveningen.

Now that he was actually home, there was [at least one] serving girl at one of the little cafés right there on the beach who sometimes took him back to Rangoon. With more women waiting tables these days, often working shifts at more than one establishment [all whisking by so quickly, bustling from kitchen to table, bent, it seemed, on proving they were as good at the job as the stuffy traditional male waiters], the source of the scent was hard to pinpoint. But sometimes he got a hint of jasmine wafting off *somebody*.

[Back in Rangoon] he'd tried [when he was able] to bunk near British gardens, where the jasmine and lily kept the pungent city bearable. It felt peaceful, that land of Buddha, but he preferred the smell of the jungles of Mahomed. When he and English Van came out of the pipe dens and were getting back on their feet [usually by lying back down, sprawled on the colonized lawns], a bad scent could make everything go horribly wrong with his guts. He'd preferred the local food back in Sumatra too. Among the Burmese, it was hard to distinguish their soupy dishes from their thick, funky river. Granted, he felt far less vulnerable [to sudden knife attack or the sight of human flesh burning], but he knew he would have to keep going, moving on.

A clear memory came to him now [barefoot in the surf] of the first time he spoke to the stranger who would become his ragtag traveling companion. This was soon after he arrived in Burma [and before he understood Van was an Engelsman]. He must have said hello in Dutch [hoi], because the first thing Van said to him [ever] was, "Hoi yourself."

The second thing he remembered him saying was, "Know what *Rangoon* means? End of strife."

There may have been other gibberish and nonsense and pleasantries in between, but those were the things Wyn recalled, and he welcomed these memories.

It was better than thinking of Aceh, of Sumatra.

The whole enterprise was a gamble . . . even back to the decision last fall, once he'd sold off most of the firewood he'd laid up and seasoned, to not restock the shed with more . . . freshly cut, an investment for the following year . . . but instead to leave the small building empty, to give them room to work . . . to leave it ready for the little foreign boat to take form. It was a longshot for Ned and his family, and if he ended up with nothing to show for it, he'd also have no wood to sell, and they'd be left in even skimpier straits . . . Yet he had to admit . . . though he would never tell his mevrouw this . . . it was a bit of a thrill, taking such a gamble . . . as if he were back in his youth and long bachelorhood . . . as if he were sailing off into the unknown . . .

The night they began the boatbuilding—in the late days of the previous year, closing in on the solstice—something very unusual happened high overhead—the so-called northern lights—a thing he'd only read about, in travel tales, but had never seen around here. He and the two older fellows witnessed it—trimming their lanterns and stepping out of the shed into Nodder's field to take in the show—the shimmering purple up toward the stars, down to a murky pea-soup fringe along the horizon—the skirts of a gypsy dancer Luuk had seen as a boy—scandalous in the marketplace—pasted up in the sky, restless.

"Is it waving at us?" he asked.

Wyn just laughed.

"Um, I mean, is it solar flares—light waves or—? What is the aurora borealis—exactly?"

"It's a good sign," Old Man Nodder said—as if that said anything.

"Maybe . . ." Wyn said. "Or maybe it's a sign we should be building a kayak instead."

They hadn't been at this project long before Luuk realized half the things van Winkel said were like this—odd wisecracks, impenetrable references. Still, the man was incredibly likable—maybe because at times there were glimpses he didn't feel half as glib as he pretended.

This was one of those times—though it was hard to be offhand about what was happening up there in the sky. He remembered too late that he should write about it—put down some lyrics—but he didn't want to make a scene—digging out his notebook right there and having to light a lamp—he wondered sometimes if the great minstrels of the world forgot what they were doing as often as he did. And he wondered if Imke was watching this—the flickering in the sky—wherever she was right then—possibly just finishing up her shift at the café. She'd said once that she was a night person. He wasn't completely sure how she meant that—and maybe would have asked her to explain further—except she hadn't really said it to him. Not directly, exactly.

What it probably meant—her being a night person—was that she was sitting up right at that moment, watching this shimmering lavender light to the north, far beyond Drempt—seemingly somewhere over Groningen province or maybe the intertidal flats of the Wadden Sea. And she would be smiling—tired-eyed, but smiling.

Van Winkel was standing close—slapping his back at the sight above like they were old pals. Wyn said he was reminded of the one about the Eskimo, the polar bear, and the Arctic explorer—"In a boat," Wyn clarified.

"Wynkyn." Ned cut the joke short, chuckling softly—lighting the lanterns again—and so they moved back into the shed to work on their secret project—the thing on which the three were hanging their dreams.

Luuk was going to see it as a good sign—these lights. Maybe.

Setting off! The westerlies [coming in at about fifteen knots, Wyn judged] gave the mainsail an admirable bunting, full with the brace of the North Sea's moonrise best. [It was early on, but she was faring well, so far.] The makeshift, repurposed sailcloth seemed to have good flex [the ladies' handiwork not yet tearing away: godverdomme impressive for amateur sailmakers!]. Between the buffeting jib and the spray off the bow, he knew he'd soon have to let out a yip and a howl, it grabbed him so, right in the breastbone [the clutching feeling there little different than the press of a young woman's hands on his chest as she leaned closer, up on her toes, to be kissed]. He had been nearly a year stuck on land, and even on Scheveningen Beach, you never quite felt that same wind [that sense of the heavens pushing you around].

Of course, this wasn't the hard blow of when he'd rounded treacherous Cape Horn as a green navy recruit, heading out to the East Indies for the first time [going the long way, to the East by way of the west]. The gales were enough to make the hardier salts weep, and they talked of the williwaw [below decks, in whispers, like it was a harpy or the banshee that soared darkly over the land of Erin]. And so on his way home [when he had more of a say in the boat he boarded] he chose the shortcut, continuing west and up through the Suez Canal [a place with plenty of scimitar-waving Arabs, of course, but none of them were a match for either the williwaw or, if he had stayed put, the pedang-waving Acehnese].

When first he was introduced to the famous—or at least well known—rogue van Winkel—Luuk realized it was not the first time they'd laid eyes on each other. During a rainy spell the previous year, when his moeder announced for the first time in his life that she could not afford new shoes for him—that his Uncle Allard was not going to unlatch his tight little coin purse for such luxury—that Luuk was going to have to go to a *cobbler*, of all things—he set off—against his better judgment, following her suggestion—to Schoenmaker's, the cordwainer's shop in The Hague—knowing full well that the man would be offended to be asked to do a lowly repair on floppy remains of footwear that should obviously be replaced—a dog's chew toy, his moeder had called them—and feeling, besides, that the shoddy shoes he wore rather fit his public presentation as a sea-dreamy world-wise troubadour—it came as a relief to find that Meneer Schoenmaker had tacked a big sign to his shop door announcing that he was gone to Drempt for four days to "see the baby"—that he was a grootvader for the first time—he'd drawn exclamation points.

Rocking directly overhead, the creaky store sign—which wouldn't last two minutes down at the beach, in Scheveningen's wind—was cut in the shape of a big klomp—though the old cordwainer worked only in the finest Spanish leather and would have been as loath to trade in wooden clogs as he likely would be to be considered a cobbler. The only other klomp customers might find anywhere in the store—by Luuk's memory—was a contraption designed to distract restless children—two massive klompen silhouettes with a bench seat and a grip bar across the front—so that if the child got to swinging his little feet, the whole thing rocked on the floor. Terribly entertaining, Luuk recalled—when he was young—at least ten years ago.

The Hague was dark from the onslaught of rainstorms, but it was still daytime—he cupped his face against the glass—out of nostalgia, perhaps—to see the big rocking wooden shoe and—alsjemenou!—saw two dark eyes in the shadows, looking back.

Sprawled across the klomp was a lean, scraggly man in what looked to be a nest of scrap leather—curling cuttings and rolls of remnants—with his legs draped over the gunwales on either side. Despite his posture, he seemed awake, staring at Luuk as if to say, *What? This is far from unusual. I'll tell you about unusual, you want to know unusual.*

Luuk backed away, and later, when Dirty Ned—the other Ned, who was the proprietor of the coffeehouse—introduced van Winkel one afternoon in the fall—Wynk was lively and clearly awake, bursting with talk of a strange little undermanned herring boat—and eventually dragged Luuk out to Meneer Nodder's small farm to show him the drawings for what they were calling a *picarooner*—neither one of them brought up the fact that Luuk had caught him napping in the big rocking klomp for kids at Schoenmaker's store.

With every soaking crash, rocking out into the great purple of it [the last bit of light chased off toward the English-speaking part of the world], Wyn felt shot through with the delight of flight [fleeing, getting even farther away from the bad, inland things of his time in that jungle. If there was anything its opposite, it was this, sailing off into the sea].

Because he often sailed straight off into sleep with no warning, Ned often woke still in his shoes. And he wondered if it was the fact that he still had his shoes on that would also . . . at times . . . send him wandering loose into the night . . . deep in slumber.

Half a dozen years ago . . . one summer morning . . . he woke still in his shoes . . . but in another's bed.

SAILED ON A RIVER OF CRYSTAL LIGHT INTO A SEA OF DEW.

This was the second night—the night of their sailing.

They'd snuck the strange craft over to the beach the night before—in the black-market hours, just on the far end of twilight. Now was the actual launch, into the crashing surf.

Rivers, he'd been on—rivers and canals—but Luuk Blenkin had never been out to sea—not even a little bit—and it struck him now how light it felt—how small and light and effortlessly their vessel swayed, like a baby's cradle, in the surf. Scared him, might be more accurate.

Ned Nodder had agreed to the plan for getting it down to the beach . . . That hadn't meant he'd been sold on the route actually working . . . Yet it did: Wynk's calculations were solid. Moving the odd little boat, slight and whimsical as a poem, took only one draft horse . . . fortunate, as Lotte constituted the extent of Ned's stable . . . and the keel rested on a stone sled he used for logging work. They skidded it there . . . staying off the cobbles, dragging it along the old farm-to-market trail that ran beside the new raised bed for the spoorweg . . . which meant there were scattered lumps of wasted coal, lost in firing the spoorwagon . . . and these clinkers made up the bulk of obstructions, so easily did it go. The Blenkin boy stood at the stern with Wynkyn, pushing . . . but they were mostly correcting the steering, steadying it after each slight bump of coal. Though they'd hoped to avoid the gogglers and comics, the grappenmakers and gossips, it looked rather grand . . . regal, even . . . the triangular silhouette of it, gliding along beside the rail bed . . . so much so that Ned found himself hoping, after all, that a passenger-filled spoorwagon might come clanking along, just to have an audience, even briefly, for this strange, sleek craft, cutting along briskly through the lowlands . . . Just to see them peering out in wonder . . .

Of course, it wasn't just ridicule they hoped to avoid. They all agreed. There were plenty of busybodies in Scheveningen who would feel very strongly that their little experiment was not the way things were done . . . The herringmen of Scheveningen, if not strictly an official guild, were all the same . . . a rigid, traditional bunch.

Young Wynkyn assured him if they got any guff from the herringmen, he'd handle it. Patting his shoulder, giving him a wink, Wyn said, "Relax, Noddie-boy. I've faced far worse, believe me. Any night when the villagers don't sneak up with pedangs and klewangs hoisted high in a mad delirium of assassin's hashish, that's an *easy* night. I'll take care of any bother up to that." He said it offhandedly, with no hint of the brag, but Ned knew, just from the several ways the prodigal young man seemed different in character now, that he would easily manage any interference . . . "We're just out for a moonlit stroll, Neddie! Just walking our pet boat to the beach . . ."

Young Luuk started laughing at Wynk's antics . . . and losing his grip on the stern.

It was a fine thing, these two signing on as more or less a lark . . . but as for him, this was serious business. This was about looking out for his family.

He didn't scold them. He gave them a smile and then a chuckle, calculating that they might not see the smile in the moonlight. Better to keep it light . . . keep it pleasant . . . everybody in accord . . .

In no time, they were at the end of the rail bed, where the spoorweg turned again, and were cutting onto the dunes that flanked the beach and protected the wetter lowlands to the east, and the little boat slipped through the marram grass, slick with dew, with a buttery susurration like the shush of a mother cradling her babe . . .

Already at the beach, Ned wondered if he'd nodded off for part of it, not leading Lotte, but her leading him.

Up ahead was the surf, the breakers shining like Christmas ribbons . . .

The Kurhaus was massive, like a grand box of chocolates with a Turkish tea cozy plopped on top. [The mosque, he thought. The masjid, in Kutaradja . . . Or the Sultan's palace, his keraton.] Certainly Wyn had been back long enough to get used to the sight of it sitting there on the edge of the sand, marring both the view to the east [of the marram-tufted land rolling back to the city center] and the coastline to the south [all along which the herringmen had regularly put in their bomschuiten, the bathers formerly working around them, scattered], but no. The thing squatting there [competing with the horizon, nearly crowding the beach] just struck him as strange and obnoxious, like a bully looming over you while you basked in the sun [some big fat boy casting a shadow over you]. The wide-open expanse of the beach, he realized now, had been something that spoke to him, perhaps even more than the wide open possibility of the ocean itself—that vast run of sand, nearly as far as the eye could see, up and down the coast, like a sandpiper's dream; that had always said *Run!* and *Let's go!* and suggested freedom and the world—all of the world. Not that he recalled ever running wildly up and down the beach. [Well, perhaps when he was quite young on a day trip with his late mother— she encouraged play and wildness in a way his somber father never cared for.]

And maybe he had run up and down a little with Fenna, the love he'd left here, before heading off to adventure in the East Indies. [Ignoring the jeers of the fellows he knew among the bom crews, sorting their tippy barges and luggers, their draft horse teams and cables and anchors.] He had some memory of that [chasing her, shrieking, along the surf, straight past where that oversized resort now loomed].

That whole expanse of sand between the crashing waves and the glittering palace was cluttered with cabanas now and an entire livery of bathing machines [like privies with wheels, so the rich and proud genteel ladies could get into the water without being seen in their bathing costumes . . .

like they were the godverdomme English]. He'd slept in some of those [the Kurhaus's bathing machines and cabanas, that is, not their rich lady guests] on a few rare occasions, when he could sleep at night. [They weren't as suited to his novel requirements, though, as the hulks of broken bomschuiten and other "bunks" he sought out during the day, his normal sleeping hours, when the Kurhaus staff was on alert.]

This hotel [with its formidable bosom of a dome] also brought to mind the dowager Rademaker's fortress of a manor house [ungainly in her private woods to the north, with every window unnecessarily aglow with crystal light]. There, too, he would never presume to curl up inside the main building, but occasionally sought shelter in one of its little satellites [the difference being that on the beach there was no cost to be extracted].

And now, at night [while grabbing his side of the tarps and working with Nodder and Blenkin to batten down and stow the little boat in the dunes, to keep it safe and hidden till the big trial the following night], the strange new place still made him anxious. Perhaps it was the fancy-pants guests in the many windows of the resort, unseen [or maybe it had nothing to do with this glittering masjid, this royal keraton], but he sure felt like the three of them were being watched.

Despite the Blenkin family history with the business of the sea—and despite the songs he wrote about the sea—Luuk had never actually served on either of the two types of herring boats that they were hopefully—moments from now—about to slyly circumvent: neither haringbuizen nor bomschuiten. That last kind had always reminded him—at a distance—of wooden shoes. Even more than this thing did—despite having christened her *De Klomp*.

Despite—so much was *despite* something else, wasn't it? He was here, stepping out into the wet edge of the abyss, *despite* his fears and lack of skills—here because of all that he wanted—*despite* growing evidence to the contrary that he would ever get it—as he could see in little flickers of clarity in his mind, just now, as the spray hit his face—

And then it was gone and hope returned.

Sure, he was disappointed Imke hadn't seen them launching the boat—the pushout at moonrise, right before sunset. A small clot of gawkers had gathered, some to heckle and snort, and in his mind, he'd pictured Imke walking by—wasn't she always walking somewhere, darting from one of her myriad jobs to the next? So many positions—all of which he would have her quit once he was a successful troubadour and they were married.

This night, he'd assumed she'd linger—just a little—and at least watch him throw his weight into the heave-ho and crashing push. No matter, of course—*this*—the fishing part of the plan—wasn't the part that would make his name for him. *This* was the part that would get him *to* the part that would make his name for him—and, soon enough, make his name *her* name.

[Since his return to Scheveningen] Wyn had been scraping by with odd jobs here and there—never enough to rent a room or to fill his shrinking belly in any way that neared steady [and *barely* enough to keep him in ale and visits to the pipe dens]. He'd find work mucking out a stable or sweeping out a store or hauling furniture. Or [when he felt particularly desperate] he'd tutor students over at Leiden [in chemistry, math, astronomy, government, world geography], just as long as the tutee promised to never let his father know. The winter months were particularly hard, and, coinciding as they did with end-of-term examinations, the tutoring was difficult to turn down.

Often [to cover up what he was doing on campus] he would combine these visits to the university with an appearance at his father's faculty-sponsored salons [so that if the great Professor van Winkel ever did spot him, Wyn could say he was there for the refreshments, continuing to pretend he was the ill-read lout his father seemed most comfortable believing in].

Sometimes he would merely poke his head in at the salons. If he lucked out [if his father was engaged, in a class or meeting or nicely distracted with his students and colleagues in the salon], Wyn would take the opportunity to grab a quick nap in his father's office, curled up on the floor, in the late-afternoon sun, behind his desk [safe and warm and indoors and *before* nightfall]. This also meant he could *seem* to be visiting yet avoid spending much time at all in his father's company; he could get away with just leaving a note on his desk and slip out without any of the awkwardness [which they'd developed into a sort of folk dance, the kind where you had to wear a very specific costume and turn and bow just so].

Vader had an ancient leaded window [in the one corner not blockaded with crowded bookshelves] faceted like cut crystal, and when the light shone through it, it cast a river of daylight stars twinkling on the Oriental rug. The times the sun shone bright and he was curled up like a pussycat next to the shaft of light, Wyn would sail off to sleep easy as a toy boat in a stream.

Luuk knew—given his youth and size—that he was *technically* the most able-bodied there. Wynand van Winkel wasn't ancient, but he seemed weary in other ways—and there were whispers among the Scheveningians about things he'd done in faraway lands. And Meneer Nodder—Agreeable Ned, as he was known to the older men of the beach—he was just plain old—at least, Luuk might guess, approaching fifty, his hair flitting out over his ears in silvery tufts.

Wyn was at the mast, untying the lines that held it there—letting the sail unfurl, getting ready to raise it—but Luuk stayed where he was—keeping low, hanging on to the middle thwart, they called it—the middle bench. Not *on* it, but beside it—squatting in the well. Strength and youth weren't reason enough to join in yanking on lines—willy-nilly, not knowing what he was doing—or to stride around the narrow boat like a corsair. His mother told him earlier, at dinner—he would have to try to concentrate and listen and learn. There was so much to learn. She often skipped her hand across his cowlick, just catching the top of his head—the way he felt compelled now to reach out over the gunwales and skim his palm across the water—to understand more, to know it. Sunset still flickered on the water—he could see it fine—so he chanced it and reached and touched it, marking that this was real—this was finally happening. The only other time he'd been in a boat was as a passenger on the canal barges, inland—braving—essentially—ditchwater—So *that* hardly counted for anything.

Fighting the sea, the crash and wash, rushing the waves, rocking out to the shoals, the boat sleek with her shallow draft: it all made Wyn grin. He knew his two friends assumed it was because he was an adventurer, a bold shit-stirrer in love with chaos. But it wasn't the buck and roll, hitting the breakers. It was the way it drowned the other sound in his ears: the rattle of bamboo stirred by wind, the *creak-creak* of its rushed growth when the heat lay unbearably still, the purr and pad of jungle cats, true tigers and Sunda clouded leopards or their counterfeit [insurgents in disguise], creeping closer, more deadly than the actual cat, about to lurch forward and commit Acehmord, to take them all down with them.

"Huzzah! Huzzah!" he shouted at the darkening North Sea as it sassed their new little boat [which was already beautiful, a humdinger, a dandy, a devil of a thing].

"Is she yare?" young Blenkin shouted, peering fore and aft, scanning all points. "I can't tell! Tell me she's fine! She's fine, right? We're doing it?"

"We're doing it!" Wyn slapped the boy on the back [opting not to tease him for loading on the nautical terms he certainly only learned in the chanties he liked to sing]. "Right, Noddie?"

Old Ned nodded to the last scar of sunset. "We're doing *something . . .*"

It was fast, this light little beauty . . . small as a shoe, but a racer, clipping along through the waves like a seabird, like a wily tern or the little shearwater, basting the whitecaps . . .

It was what they'd expected . . . that it would be quick and lightly handled, being designed to beat the big English luggers out to the shoals . . . And yet Ned had a feeling already . . . somehow it wasn't going to be quite what they expected.

A goer, though—swift as a dream . . . gliding like the cliff-dwelling fulmar petrel, with great upward arcs, as if yearning for a higher plane . . .

Luuk never knew how to interpret the winks—he'd worked with van Winkel for several months, sure—preparing for this big night—and the man winked a lot, so you would think a fellow could figure out some kind of decoding system in all that time—this wink means this, this wink means that—but he hadn't. So when van Winkel said—again, with a wink—"Well, I guess we'll see now how this English runt does in Dutch waters, won't we, boys?"— Luuk couldn't categorize the wink—and, in turn—couldn't decipher the comment: was there some big difference between the water here off the shore of their country and the water on the other side, just off the English coast?

Wyn scooted down to the stern to take over the tiller, freeing the older man up to prepare the nets—right where Luuk was in the way, so he in turn moved forward, sliding under the sail and clinging to the mast—staying even lower, worried the boom would swing around and knock him out cold—and over the side. From his position toward the bow, he could watch Meneer Nodder laying out the nets and hopefully learn—and he could ask him now about the different water

"Water's water," Ned Nodder said. "Wind's different, tidal patterns . . ."

"But the actual water—?"

"It's wet and things float in it!" Wyn shouted through the wind—and Luuk could feel the heat filling his cheeks. "Those that don't sink!"

Ned was nodding, smiling agreeably, sorting out the nets.

"Oxygen and hydrogen, kid!" van Winkel shouted. "Just oxygen and hydrogen!"

Not only swift as a dream, she was *agile* like a dream . . . *literally*, Ned thought . . . the way a dream slips in and you're suddenly riding it, immersed in it, and it deposits you somewhere wholly unexpected . . . Hard to put his finger on how exactly they had brought that out of the wood, in building it . . . They'd used standard oak and elm, nothing exotic or fairy-infested, like those dasarts believed in the lands to the north . . . Well, after a slight setback with some Caucasian wingnut wood . . . It was equally hard to explain that slight singing sound he swore he heard . . . Ned tried to block out the chatter and take it all in. It was easy enough to do: folks tended to think he was simple . . . or, lately, asleep. That misconstruction on the part of fools and others did afford him a lot of extra figuring time. And peace . . .

And in that peace . . . even if secretly awake . . . he often thought on his dreams. For all the dreams Ned produced . . . and there were multitudes . . . it was the one thing of which he had riches . . . it surprised him that there were still dreams he remembered, years later. Often he thought of the time he dreamt he was asleep beside his wife . . . then he woke up to find her there. His dreams often matched moments in the future . . . and there was often a span of time between the two, but that morning it was quite a jolt. Because waking up beside her had come *before* she was his wife . . . and before they ever spoke. It was the first time they shared a bed . . . and it only happened because of his night wanderings.

Clearly, anything could happen when he fell asleep . . . and so he hoped tonight . . . with this bright wake of moonlight dazzling before them . . . it would save him from drifting off.

So far—in the early stage of the sail—the work ran fairly close to what Luuk had expected—based merely on the countless descriptions of fishing in song—some of which he'd sung just the other night, at his debut performance as a troubadour there in town: the drowsy shimmer of the setting sun—warming them still like one last hope—trailing down to the bow of their little boat as they pushed out into the crashing surf—perhaps a bit more jarring and cold, compared to the lyrical versions, of course. And the sheer strength of the waves, slamming into their sliver of a vessel—their now silly-seeming picarooner—*that* was sobering, to say the least. He could feel in the lash of just two or three waves—how easily one could be sent to his death in the depths, overwhelmed in a world of dark water—but Luuk could also feel the *rollicking*—see why so many wanted to sing about it and write romantic songs about *me hardies* and pulling on this or that and yanking on the *whatsis*, battening down the *whoosie*—

He could observe all that—and revel in it, to a degree—because he didn't have to join in yet, being the green hand. At this stage, they were fine with him staying out of the way, and he understood now why Old Man Nodder had insisted everything be sanded and planed smooth—otherwise Luuk's palms would be pincushioned with splinters by now, the way he was hanging on tight.

Even when Wyn first apprenticed in the Nodder brothers' bom, that form of herring fishing was on the way out. They simply couldn't compete with the massive factory ships, the haringbuizen, that anchored far out in the North Sea. And so, in his second herring season [back in 1883, if he had it right], he made some glib farewell to Ned and his brothers and signed on board a herring buss [*Het Zilveren Fortuin*, by name], telling his father that ja, it looked like he was bound to become a man of hard labor [unlike Vader himself], and if that was to be so, Wyn at least needed to keep up with the times. What he didn't tell his old man was that things had grown prickly with his girl, and though he loved her in a way that felt [to Wyn's young aching bones] uncharted [somewhere between wondrous and life-dooming], the rigor of shooting those gillnets [that dropped like curtains into the black] and trawling far out at sea, under several shimmering moons, seemed preferable [to his puerile nerves] to prolonged and difficult discussions [about his "heart" and "intentions" and "constancy"].

They spent months out there, nearly to the Shetland Isles. She was a monster, with three masts, and he grew monkeylike in the rigging with this needier configuration of sails [all but the mizzen had to come down each time they shot the nets]. And the lengthy stints out on *Het Zilveren Fortuin* were harsh in a way the single-night sails with the Nodder brothers the previous season had never been. There were somewhere upwards of two dozen hands on board [the exact number was hard to pinpoint]: one clumsy man had vanished, likely tangled in the driftnet they reeled out behind them [at lengths, it seemed, as long as the river of moonlight]. It was said that another [a particularly sticky-fingered klootzak from Drempt named Panders] probably suffered the same type of accident, but Wyn knew [as most of the crew knew] that Panders had made the mistake of stealing from a few of the scarier knife-fanciers among them [*the stabbier element*, as he thought of them, with no confidant but himself with which to share this droll remark].

The standard practices out there were just the sort ol' Noddie carped about: scaring the shoals by throwing out nets in the broad sunlight, leaving fish in the net for part of a day . . . Every night, the catch was gibbed and salted and barreled right there on the broad deck of the buss. It was the least pleasant duty, and the least pleasant part of *that* wasn't the brining or barreling, but cutting out the gills and a section of the gullet and sloshing the gutbuckets over the side, and Wyn made sure he drew that duty. After the vanishing of Panders, Wyn made it a point to get noticeably handy with the filet knife, demonstrating the speed and precision with which he cleaned the tiny "silver darlings" with just a flick of his blade.

But surrounded by such disquieting men [immersed in the blood and sweat and battle of it, closer to foreign soil than home] it felt like there was no room left for thoughts of anything as tender as his girl back onshore. And so, even on those occasions when the ventjager sailed off to Scheveningen to deliver the latest full store of their preserved catch, for all these reasons and perhaps for no real reason, Wyn did not opt to go.

On still nights, though [in moments stolen between the bark of the gibbing boss], he glanced out at the trail of moonlight, rippled like a river leading back to her; to home.

Something happened when the moon rose high.

It was Luuk's first time seeing moonlight on the water—out in the middle of it, that is, not fenced off from it by the surf—and it dazzled, hypnotic—stringing out like a trail of shimmering gemstones, going—*somewhere.*

Things had seemed straightforward at sunset. But he wasn't crystal clear now what he was supposed to be doing here. Old Nodd was lighting onion lamps where he'd laid out the nets, checking the work he'd done in the gloaming—Wyn had a rope around the tiller and was bringing down the sail— which meant Luuk should really do his best to get up on his feet and help.

They'd gone over it all, of course—many times, many nights in Smilin' Ned's shed—yet Luuk really hadn't been prepared for this. It wasn't quite—

He craned his neck—to stay safe wedged against a bench—a thwart—with his back against the hull—while daring to peek out over the side. The dark void below looked cloudy now, with great white patches floating past—some sort of twinkling foam?

The sail was down, and Wyn was replacing the rudder with a long sculling oar. They would now drift slightly and shoot the nets over the shoals—drift *slightly*. But as Luuk tried to loosen his grip and rise, it felt like they were still really moving.

Something else was happening—wasn't it?

"WHERE ARE YOU GOING.

And what Wyn *also* didn't tell his father, *after* the dismal adventure on the herring buss *Zilveren Fortuin* back in '83 [though the old man certainly had to have understood eventually], was much of the cause of his *next* step: his subsequent escape to the navy [and then the infantry in Aceh] had been at his father's provocation—the constant haranguing for a "bettering" of himself [as if Wyn would ever follow him down that learned path to Leiden].

But before [his injurious, if not quite fatal, mistake in] enlisting, when he returned at the end of the herring season on the buss [bulkier and richer and probably, he knew, a little meaner in a way that made him sad], his girl was hiding from him. *Why* she was doing this, he figured he could get her to divulge [if he pressed and asked a lot of questions and really put himself out there], but the idea of doing that confused him, garbled his idea of himself, of what kind of man he was attempting to become [not the excreting silkworm of words that was his own learned father—surely not!], and so he didn't press. He left one note at her mother's, saying he very much wanted to see her and if she wanted the same she could find him on the strandweg by the tavern Klaas Vaak's, but if she didn't care to appear, she should know that he was heading to Rotterdam to join the Royal Dutch Navy.

He was young [he saw now, though only five or six years wiser]. Young and foolhardy and unkind [to both her and himself].

When he left the note with her mother, the old busybody had it open and was reading it before he'd stepped out of her dooryard. "What exactly do you want to say to her, Wynand?"

He stopped above their hedge. Years later he could picture it, glistening with dew as if in warning that the first frost might already be ready to set in.

"I said it there," he told her.

By the time he reached the Strait of Malacca, off Sumatra, he had long since wished he'd said much, much more.

They were going up into the air! Well—*maybe.* A slight, lofty incline—rising into the damp atmosphere—the breeze picking up. He couldn't be certain—never having gone up into the air in any significant way—so he wasn't sure if it was happening—

Of course, he'd never sailed before—maybe this was how it always felt to be at sea—as if you were lifting up, ramping up into the breeze.

Rare were the nights when he bothered asking himself where he was headed. The options [for bunking down] were varied enough to free Wyn of any concern. [Except on the coldest of nights.] When the wind off the sea [usually a grand thing; the heartbeat of the night] turned vicious [in deep winter, mostly] and the other bunk options weren't shelter enough, he'd have to give in and ask himself *Where* was *he going, anyway?*

Freezing to death wasn't truly a fear for Wyn. [Not because it wasn't a possibility. He just wasn't particularly afraid of such an outcome. At this point, if it happened, it happened.] But those nights, his muscles tensed against the cold [a thing that now felt foreign compared to the Aceh jungle] and made him cave in and do things he'd rather not. So it was more a concession to his weary body than it was an actual fear.

[Such were the nights he went to see the widow Rademaker.]

She kept a key [to the one-room guest cottage] hidden for him under a small white statue of a rearing stallion, so he always just let himself in. A red crushed-velvet fainting couch took up most of the room, along with a woodstove and a pie safe, usually stocked with a few slices of meats and cheeses. The only decor was a gilt-framed picture of her favorite royal on the wall facing the couch. Some nights she didn't realize he'd let himself into the cottage, or she had some social engagement and so she didn't come by. [The relief he felt was always temporary—he knew she'd keep a tally of these nights for which he still owed her "a nine o'clock."]

Paying the bérlés [which seemed to be *rent*] meant allowing her to swoop in [every night that he stayed there] and unceremoniously straddle his leg [that was it: his leg; usually his right, just about midthigh, tending toward the knee], rubbing against it with great effort.

"Have to pay the bérlés . . ." She'd singsong her entry, playing the part of the landlord [as punctual as she was unattractive]: "Just on time! Nine o'clock! Time to make Gert happy!"

She never touched him anywhere intimate, just his face, perhaps his chest. [Some nights holding his face didn't seem to do the trick, and she would rise and turn around and reseat herself in the other direction, looking up at the portrait of Archduke Rudolf, Crown Prince of Austria, Prince Royal of Hungary and Bohemia.]

The doilies began early on, after only a few of these exchanges, as she chided him about the state of his clothes. Finding "piszok," she called it, on his britches [fish scales after pickup work at the market or the briners, coffee grounds from Dirty Ned's, pine needles and duff from the forest, dune sand, or sawdust from building the picarooner at Ned's—not terribly surprising: it was his only pair of trousers], she got up and placed a doily on his pantleg, then repositioned herself and resumed her grinding.

At the conclusion of this high drama [after bearing down with a vocalization someone might make when they first suspect they're developing a toothache], she would stand and flap her skirts a little [as one would the sheets in a bed while making it in the morning], as if giving herself a little fresh air up there. She'd slap her hands together, *spick-spack,* peel the moist doily off his leg, and retire with a "ta" and a reminder that he was always welcome and he knew where she hid the key.

Along with the dreams that seemed to be visions . . . and the spells that felled him, often in labor . . . mostly then, actually . . . whether logging, suddenly slumped by a tree, his double-bladed ax abandoned in the grass . . . or sorting his nets and waking to find he'd pulled them up over him like a blanket . . . Ned was also capable of settling in to *intentionally* sleep, lying down in his own small bed at home . . . yet waking up, inexplicably, somewhere else entirely. The bomschuit aground on the beach was a common one, or in the graveyard, beside his vader . . . Pappje, the *real* fisherman . . . But sometimes he woke up in the wrong house, often on the hearth, having displaced a sleeping dog or lad, and usually he could slink out in the gray light of predawn before the owners discovered him . . . or else they walked in and saw him but knew of his malady and simply offered him breakfast . . .

It usually occurred when he was struggling with some quiet turmoil . . . and he could find no remedy for it . . . Lashing himself to the bed, piling obstacles before the door, were only inconsistently effective . . . He even tried to train himself to interject while he dreamed: *Where are you going, Ned Nodder? . . . Where are you going now? . . . Is this where you should be?*

"Where *you* going?" was what Wyn said [out loud] when he ran into Imke Holt near the Kurhaus late one night [some months back, maybe in the previous fall]. It came out all wrong. [He meant to say, *Say, you're young Luuk's sweetheart now, aren't you?* but he wasn't at his best that evening.] In fact he saw in a flash that the familiarity he'd just shown had been a miscalculation [based not on his actual knowledge of the young lady but only on the fact that Blenkin had been bleating her name like a calf for the last few months— from at least the planing and draw-shaving stage on—but that didn't make her someone *he*, Wyn, knew well enough to address in such a direct manner]. Noting the uniform, he tried again:

"How are things at the masjid?"

"Pardon?"

"The Kurhaus. Are you working there as well?" [Unless she kept getting discharged from one job after another, this would make at least three that he knew of, having seen her working as a barmaid at the tavern, plus waitressing at one other place.]

"Just started this week," she said. "What did you call it?"

It was a personal joke, referring to the new monstrosity behind them as the masjid Raya Baiturrahman, the replacement mosque back in Kutaradja. This glitzy resort [with its bulbous roof like a grand teat offered to the sky] had suffered through a fire back in '85 and been rebuilt, and [similarly] the masjid had also been a reconstruction. It was an appeasement his fellow countrymen threw up, after first invading and razing the original holy place, thinking [incorrectly] that it was the seat of the sultan's power. [Designed by an Italian in the style of India, for some reason] the new one back there was also an eyeful, plopped down as if from the heavens. Just like this thing on the beach.

He shrugged. "The Kurhaus?"

She studied him [a little too closely, he felt, to be justified by even the dimness of the moonlight]. "Are you all right, Wynand van Winkel?"

"*Wynkyn!* Or *Wyn, Wynk . . . Meneer van Winkel,* if you must . . . I think I like *Wynkyn* from you . . . My stodgy father and his ilk stick by *Wynand.*" [There was a grand moon behind her, and he felt for a moment they were on some metropolitan promenade, Edison-lit, where no one ever slept.] "My late moeder, on the other hand, called me *Wynkie . . .* unless that's too . . . ?"

"Let's say," she said, "that it definitely is."

"But indeed! Ja! I am more than all right!" [In fact, he wasn't feeling the stomach cramps today or any of the fluctuating ailments of the pipe den. And he was certain she didn't know him well enough to notice, even if it had been showing.] "Like a dream! That's how I am! Kind of you to ask . . . How are the big tippers there?"

She shrugged. "They're . . . big tippers. Those who are. I don't interact with the guests enough to see any tips, really."

He'd always felt *Kurhaus* was an odd name for these grand resorts; the idea of taking "the cure" here at the seaside. [He couldn't imagine anybody who could afford to stay there having anything really in need of curing.]

He held out his arm for her. "Come. I will escort you home. At this hour, sending you out into the dark streets . . . ! There could be orang-utans about."

She giggled. "So far I've encountered no orang-utans, but I *have* only been at this job one week . . ."

"Where I was," he told her, "there were orang-utans." Which was a lot to tell her. More on the subject than he normally divulged. [And he recognized that he was saying it like it was another joke, and that he declined to tell her the rest: that when you encountered one, lurking in the trees, you would be relieved to discover it was only an orang-utan.]

She insisted he not bother walking her unless it was on his way. He said it was, even though that wasn't accurate, since his loose "plan" was to probably go to a public park [maybe the Malieveld, where his mother used to take him, back when he could barely walk, tottering around even more than he was tonight], and then he'd try to sleep, in some sheltered edge of the great lawn, under the morning stars [for at least a little—what was left of the night]. But he didn't tell her that. He just mumbled, "My place's right around here . . ."

He didn't think he [*always*] yelped in his sleep now [not *every* time], but parks were a good place not to cause a ruckus and sleep in peace. [If a pipe den wasn't easily available, or he just didn't want to disappear for most of a day.]

He wasn't certain where they were heading, exactly, but she kept on the strandweg, heading north along the beach. [He didn't remember there being a lot of homes up that way—it was mostly herring pickling and packaging outfits in that direction.] He told her some nonsense about their good luck tonight, since orang-utans were known to shy away from the full moon. [They were not, but it was something to say.]

"Or the *old* moon, I should say . . ."

"The what now?" she asked.

Since she bit, he told her: "Even my father, who is a renowned expert on all the heavens—just ask him, if you doubt that—has no answer for this simple question: why is it a *new moon* at the start of the month but not an *old moon* later on? Is that even fair? And by extension, are we so afraid of old age that we'd rather say we're *full* than *old*?"

"Do you feel old, or do you feel full?"

"That's the limit of the options you're offering me, is it? I note the sly undercut, believe me, young miss. I feel that I'm both. Old *and* full."

"Not *so* old," she said. "You're my sister's age, I believe—Cokkie."

"Cokkie . . . Holt?"

"Cokkie Bunk now. She remembers *you.*"

"Ah yes," he said. "Cokkie." [Yet another one. Still yet another. His heart nearly broke thinking on it. There was a time when even women as fantastic as Cokkie Holt had barely drawn his gaze. What a tragedy that so much of your life is wasted on youth, the refuge of the dimwitted and callous.]

And then just like that, looming directly before them, it was she in a cowl—the big hood and lantern making her look like the grim reaper [only lovely; still lovely]. The former Cokkie Holt. [Foul disapproval on her face, but lovely all the same.]

"Little sister," she said, in a way that seemed to Wyn to both chide Imke for walking alone at this hour and to purposefully [and perversely] ignore the man who was ensuring that Imke *wasn't* walking alone. [It was a barrelful of implication to squeeze into two words, but she managed it.]

He debated whether he should speak up and explain that he was merely escorting Imke *in proxy*, on behalf of her beau and his friend [and soon-to-be fishing partner] Luuk Blenkin.

"Relax . . . *Moeder,*" Imke said, mocking her sister. "Not a child, Cokkie. I'm sure I can handle a few orang-utans and an old and bloated moon."

For a moment [as her kid sister continued on ahead], Cokkie glared back at him [as if he were clearly both of those things the younger one had named].

"AND WHAT DO YOU WISH?" THE OLD MOON ASKED THE THREE

One thing Luuk Blenkin wished—like crazy—was that he *wasn't* probably going to have to visit an optician. Spectacles wouldn't do—not for performing his songs. He'd look like one of those university beer cantus galoots over at Leiden—goggle-eyed, sloshing a mug in time to the mob racket, swaying to the beat of some worn-out tune in a student hall. They'd run him right out of the tavern.

He could see the moon just fine. He couldn't say if it was doing the talking—it appeared crisp and defined and didn't seem to have a mouth. Peering over the gunwale, looking down, he could only make out a darkness—and a glittery stirring there—but he couldn't say if it was flickering moonlight or fish—Or constellations—?

The family doctor—Goedkoop—had been saying for some time that he wasn't properly seeing things up close. Luuk did fine naming the items on the shelves on the far side of his examination room—maybe it was true that reading was becoming a blur, but he was pretty sure he didn't have this *other* thing—hyperopia—whatever that was. Seventeen was too young to have a big disease.

And the rise and fall—herky-jerky—of the boat—that wasn't helping any.

At school—for a time—they just thought he was thick and couldn't read. Uncle Allard still thought that. But then Luuk started composing

ballads, and his mama decided he couldn't be a ninny. He tried to explain
that—though he managed to scribble down notes for these ballads—the
lyrics, the musical key, maybe the tempo—mostly he worked them out in his
head. In fact, it seemed to be one of the few things that didn't jounce around
in his noggin like an egg in a milk pail—his lyrics. His best guess was it
was because the lyrics were—for the most part—inspired by Imke Holt,
who'd been two grades ahead of him in school—two pews ahead of them at
church—and now—since her vader took sick or something—worked at the
hotel and tavern—and his favorite café. Her, he could see—and everywhere.

It wasn't just the ideas in his head, of course. He tended to bounce
around *himself*. He knew that. His mama had always been on him about
that, for as far back as he could remember—or at least until the small hairs
had started, and the catty stink in his pits. He liked to think his mind had
wandered less back then, in boyhood. But Mammie thought his mind would
stay focused if he first organized his activities. "You're doing too many things
at once," she cautioned constantly. "You're too scattered!" And this was only
his lovely moeder chiming in—if Uncle Allard had gotten wind of many of
these activities—that they were shuttling small amounts of household funds
toward lessons and such things his uncle would have considered unfocused
at best and foolish and—at worst—reason enough to kick them out of
his home—certainly, he would call him worse things than "scattered." For
months now—though only Mammie knew—Thursday nights were supposed to find him trekking in to Westeinde Street in The Hague and taking his accordion instruction. Except—at some earlier point, many months
back—he'd witnessed Imke Holt flirting and smiling with a grinning crew
of herring men, asking about when the season would start, whose boms
were repaired and ready, and so now he was out here in the North Sea—or
possibly high in the air over it?—the twinkle of Scheveningen long gone
behind him—fussing with nets. So Mammie would call that—and his entire
schedule this week, for that matter—unfocused, disorganized—

True, but—

Wyn hadn't put it quite this way to the other two yet, but his only goal here
in this enterprise was to earn enough for his steamer passage across the

Atlantic. [They knew he was moving on, but if he were being completely honest, he probably hadn't stressed how quickly he hoped to scoot.] He would leave them his stake in the picarooner once he paid off that ticket to New Orleans. The price of the ticket plus a little extra to get started doing something else. It could be anything else, really, as long as it was far away. And to the west, of course. [Even farther away from those jungles to the east. *Toward the sunset,* he told himself daily now. *Never toward the morning sun.*]

His reasons for New Orleans as a port of entry were several. A, it was apparently a heavily Catholic city, and thus likely a fairly pious society [he would wager] without a lot of sinning and carrying on to drag him further off course. B, he didn't believe the Celestials had yet infused that town with much of a population, so it was less likely to offer pipe dens. [If he entered the country through New York, the comfortable familiarity he'd feel toward both the heavily Dutch communities and the Chinatown operators would ensnare him like a gillnet, and he'd never see the other side of the Hudson River.]

America struck him as the great continent of second chances and new hope, which is all he dreamed of, really. [Not a new partnership, or trade or distraction or rejuvenated respect for his family name. Just a start-over.] He even had put a little thought into his plans this time [hopefully having achieved a greater level of forethought at twenty-nine]: he would not fall into the loser's trap of sailing to New York or Boston and having to hack his way through those grimy jungles. He would go where the odds seemed more in his favor, and so he'd settled on the one port in America that got him as far west as he could go without rounding Cape Horn ever again. [Once there, he would give himself only forty-eight hours to find transport inland, and then he would head off, regardless.]

That's all he needed out of this: passage to New Orleans. Smilin' Ned and the Blenkin boy could have the rest.

Ned could hear voices out there . . . They were not yet to the shoals, but if you listened close . . . in between the lap of waves against the hull and the flap of the canvas . . . there it was: questions . . . A voice asking them what they were doing there . . . what they wanted . . . A voice that seemed to be coming from the moon . . .

His view of the miraculous was wide and welcoming enough that this part didn't throw him . . . but *small talk* from the moon? Chitchat?

He decided he was willing to accept that there was a voice from the sky asking him questions . . . just as long as the voice in the sky would accept that he wasn't planning to answer very loudly. That seemed like a fair compromise.

It was time to pass out the radishes and rhubarb his mevrouw had sent along for a snack . . . Fill their mouths and fill their ears with some good solid crunching . . .

Sometimes this Blenkin kid reminded Wyn of the red-bearded painter, Vincent [*Cent*, he'd gone by], he'd hung out with around The Hague, back in '82 [about a year before he joined up and shipped out]. The kid showed those same crests and valleys, his life seemingly pitched either toward an accession to the stars or plummeting toward despair. Maybe it was youth, though back then Cent had been the same age Wyn was now [twenty-nine, a dozen years older than this emotional jack-in-the-box of a lad]. So perhaps it had more to do with temperament than age.

Ned could see that one big reason young Wynkyn enjoyed his company now was that he didn't pry . . . And most of the folks in Scheveningen were gradually learning not to pry as well. Dumb louts were the exception . . . as well as the occasional tavern wench who saw her prettiness as a free pass to be rude . . . or at least blunt. There was one like this one night, named Ona . . . She plopped down next to Wynkyn while he had his mug raised. It was early last fall . . . maybe September 1888 . . . They'd taken one of the quieter, less drafty booths in the corner by the stove . . . where they'd been enjoying their agreed-upon ration of one ale and discussing what resources they could possibly pull together with which to build the picarooner . . . when she appeared and smooched him on the cheek before he'd even lowered his mug.

"Remember me?" she said . . . which, given the kiss, meant, Ned felt, that his friend had no other choice than to say yes.

"Absolutely," Wynkyn said.

"Ona Veenstra," she said, launching into a whole thing about how she knew he'd been fighting in Sumatra and she had all kinds of questions . . . "I have a cousin who's been there for almost ten years. We've kind of lost track of him. We know he was there in Aceh in '83, when the general reviewing the troops was shot right in front of their whatchacallit—their supposed church—?"

"Köhler. In front of the big mosque. The masjid. Sniper got him." Wynkyn sounded uninterested. "A kid, really, the sniper . . . Probably a bigger deal, really, was Teungku Chik di Tiro and his guerrillas. Nearly took the fort."

"Jan wrote us that he was there—Jan was in the ranks of men standing at attention. The general had almost reached Jan—was almost standing right in front of him when it happened! Isn't that *awful?*"

"That was just before I got there," Wyn said. "I started in the navy first— early '84, then . . ."

Somewhere in here, Ned nodded off . . . and he rose high above the tavern and the strandweg, and the indigo beach, skimming alongside a friend of his, who was apparently a high-flying gannet . . . and they kited down along the lines of the surf, right in the spray, and then . . . in a majestic banking turn . . . up over the golden glow of the Kurhaus . . .

"So you got sent home?" the seabird asked, and then it was Ona Veenstra. "How does that work? Because—like I say—my cousin— Were you wounded? Or you just didn't reenlist or . . . ?"

"I wished it so."

"You wished . . . ?"

"On a shooting star. What they call there a bintang jatuh. I made a wish."

Ned kept his eyes closed . . . Prying wasn't in his nature, in general, but with Wynkyn he wished . . . he actively strove . . . to keep the peace between them . . . a peace that clearly confounded many in the village . . . He knew they wondered why they hadn't traded blows or at least insults on the strandweg upon his return . . . given the way things had gone when the lad left.

"And that's all it took, huh?"

"Oh, no, Ona. This was the tail end of several months of wishing. *Relentless* wishing, believe me. I wished and wished and wished. And then—Allah be praised—"

"Pardon mir?"

"—this crazed Mahomedan blew up the garrison magazine. And I found myself in Rangoon, up in Burma, waiting for a transport ship home."

"You were injured?"

Ned didn't think he'd fallen back to sleep. But there was no response for a time, and then his friend said, "The only thing damaged was my sense of proportion and reasonableness."

The whole story didn't sound quite right, somehow . . . But they called him Agreeable Ned for a reason. He pretended to still be asleep . . . and then, once again, he was . . .

Luuk listened—thinking it might all be good material for his songs. All while building the boat, he listened to the tales of this jungle land where his new friend van Winkel had served—this land of Aceh. As near as he could make out, it was the marshy northern tip of Sumatra—which was a long island—and farther inland, there were high mountain areas, but that's where the danger of the Mahomedans and headhunters dwelt—plus tigers and orang-utans and who knew what. And in the lowlands, it was wetter still where they grew rice. As a Hollander, van Winkel had gone *there* from a homeland that was never quite land—that was always half sea, that was unstable and soft underfoot—especially a little farther in, just east of the coastline—where Meneer Nodder had his little subsistence farm—*that* area. For Luuk, who found he could never quite square where he stood—what was and what wasn't—he sometimes thought living in this half-wet, half-solid land of dikes and canals and shifting salt marshes and invasive seas did not fill him—personally—with a solid sense of personal stature. So why would you go—as Wyn had—to another land that was also not really land, either—*plus* had tigers? And now Wyn—that incurable adventurer—

planning to see still more of the world once he earned some real money—was talking about traveling to New Orleans, of all places. Luuk didn't know a lot about it—there were so many places in that fresh new land of which van Winkel had handed him fragments—said he'd read up on it at the library where his father taught, at the university—and the city was built on a delta, on a series of small waterways, all feeding into these half-terrain, half-swamp areas they called bayous, and the whole city was reliant on a series of levees—which sounded far too sadly close to dikes for Luuk's taste.

Luuk couldn't fathom it. The man seemed to rush from one insubstantial ground to another. He told Wyn, if *he* were making the trip, he'd head north as soon as he landed—up into the middle of America—where it wouldn't be quite so mushy underfoot. It was delta land, so there was a river there, right? Couldn't he travel up the river?

"The Mississippi," Wyn confirmed. He'd been reading some tract on it by an American named Twain. "He says the river moves around."

"Of course," Old Ned said. "Rivers are never straight."

"No. It's not just *wiggly* . . ." Wyn said. "It *moves*. It continues to meander. Maybe it storms hard one night, right? You maybe wake up one day, you're living on the *other* side of the river now . . ."

The thought really made Luuk's skin itch. Yet Wyn was laughing as he explained it. All Luuk wanted in life was a place that was *definite*—and to live there with the girl he loved. Was that really so difficult?

Getting married was never anything Ned had wished for. Bachelor fisherman would have been fine, he'd thought . . . bachelor farmer when the herring boats became impractical for him. This was just one reason he knew his union made little sense to folks in the village market, or when he brought his little brood to church . . . though he was sure they knew the story by now. The whispering and clucking that fluttered around them like chickens in the dooryard . . . back then, when it was all fresh . . . had long since subsided, but certainly they all still recalled the rumors. Ned never gave a hang about that . . . except that it likely bothered dear Fenna. She deserved better treatment from the wags and fenceline gossips, and better yet in terms of husband material. He was more than old enough to be her father. When the lads on the beach and in the taverns . . . initially, for a time . . . chose to josh and make their japes . . . along the lines of him being a cradle robber and lecher, he let it go, though . . . or pretended he hadn't heard them or even . . . once or twice . . . faked one of his dozing spells. You couldn't be hurt by snickering or chortles that you were not awake to hear. But the truth was, he *hadn't* been a leering suitor . . . not at all. In fact, immediately after the strange encounter that ended his bachelorhood, he had trouble recalling ever laying eyes on her before . . . at least not with any particular lingering. He'd known her folks, of course, though only by name . . . maybe to nod to her father passing in his cart . . . but Fenna, though a vision, sure, fair-haired and lovely, hadn't been . . . in his sights . . . wouldn't have been, couldn't have been . . . ?

What it was . . . the culprit in this . . . was the sleepwalking. His "night wanderings". . . as he thought of them . . . were an embarrassment at least, a shock upon waking, an inconvenience . . . and uncomfortable . . . Though sometimes he made it into bedrooms. And that's how he found himself . . . preposterously, in his early forties . . . waking up next to a beautiful, astonished young lady. The cornsilk hair . . . in the bright light through a garden window . . . was the first thing that was clear, but then the girl, the consternation . . . He was still in his work clothes and lying on top of the counterpane . . . and yet that didn't seem to assuage the girl's parents, standing in the doorway of her tiny bedroom . . . nor the girl's younger sister, covering her face, cowering in the adjoining trundle bed.

He proposed marriage that afternoon, before finally exiting their house . . . having sat with the father for hours at their kitchen table, negotiating . . .

He hadn't laid a finger on the girl . . . they both swore, and her father seemed to believe them . . . but there was the issue of the neighbors, the community . . . The man was insistent in a way that surprised Ned a little . . . Couldn't he simply knock on a few of their neighbors' doors and explain what had happened . . . that he'd been sleepwalking? People, he found, were generally very pleasant . . . wouldn't they understand?

Mainly, he was thinking of the girl . . . concerned she could do a lot better than an old herring man like him . . . one who sometimes couldn't end the night in the same bed where he started it . . . But the father was adamant.

Of course, he didn't regret it . . . He'd never planned to marry . . . but if he were going to do it, it would be hard to imagine landing a wife quite so lovely and young . . . And though she didn't seem particularly *un*happy all these years later, it was hard sometimes not to feel a little sorry for her . . . as well as hopeful, in an odd way, that he might find some way . . . some day . . . to make it up to her; to compensate her for the intrusion . . . and the inconsiderate turn he'd done her in making her Mevr. Ned Nodder.

Good ol' Noddie. Wyn tried not to call him Old Man Nodd to his face, though it was true he was one of the oldest people he knew [outside of his own father and his father's colleagues over on the Leiden campus]. Somehow, the halls of learning seemed to preternaturally preserve and shelter those there [in the lee of the great domed observatory] from the clutches of mortality. Wyn's father was a rickety fifty-three [and he even knew of deans of a few schools at Leiden well into their sixties]. Ned Nodder was [by Wyn's calculations] forty-eight [an impressive old age he didn't see too many hard-working Hollanders reaching]. Ned didn't seem close to death at all, unless you counted being very still with your eyes closed [which was how he was often found].

Ned was nineteen years older than him, and he remembered this number because it stirred a feeling that Ned [mathematically] could have been his father [if Ned had stepped lively about it at nineteen, rather than shuffling through life with that guileless smile, taking it all as it came]. Not that Ned had known Wyn's mother overly well [in their youth, in the village] or courted her, but compared to the stern tower of festering disappointment over at Leiden University who had given him the van Winkel name, Noddie would have been a romp to have as a dad. A seaside picnic in the stargrass and marram.

Wyn hadn't mentioned it to his friend, but he'd recently received an unexpected inquiry about Ned. While over at the campus attending one of the open salons his father hosted [grabbing a bite and hoping to catch a nap in that sunny spot in his office while the old man was occupied], he was approached by a colleague of Vader's from the medical college [Ogtrop, an anatomy man], who first asked Wyn about himself; if he was teaching "yet" or was he "still" in school. ["And perhaps you intend to join your father here at our esteemed institution? What a boon for Leiden—to double its inventory of brilliant van Winkels!"]

"Not a student, not a professor," Wyn told him [noting his father's eyebrows, already on the move, from across the room]. "Right now, I'm a herring man, I guess. Over at Scheveningen Beach."

It didn't have the intended effect. He was sure the old bird would turn up his snoot and withdraw in horror. Instead, he seemed even more interested. "Say, you don't happen to know of a man there—going by Agreeable Ned or Amiable Ned or something—rumored to be what Gélineau in Paris terms a *narcoleptic?*"

"Ned's no thief. You got bad information, doc." This wasn't strictly true. [If you wanted to get technical, they'd done a little aggressive salvage work to gather all the timber for *De Klomp*, but not straight from a lumberyard or anything of that sort.] "Maybe he doesn't believe in letting things go to waste. I call it being practical . . . Resourceful. But he's an honest man. Very honest."

"I don't understand," the doctor said, frowning. "I'd only hoped for an introduction, perhaps an examination, if he'd consent to one."

Wyn looked him over, trying to fathom his game. Then he gave him a wink and a chuck on the arm. "Only joshing, Dr. Ogtrop. Of course I knew what you meant. I'll pass it along to Ned, see how he feels." He grabbed a cheese slice as he turned to find the door, giving the professor a friendly nod. [He *didn't* know what the man wanted, exactly, but it likely had something to do with narcotics. All these brain men and alienists were so keen these days to hear all about opiates, delirium, all of which Wyn knew much about himself, but Ned Nodder did not.]

It made no difference what the old man was really asking. Wyn had no wish to ever relay to Ned that some sun-deprived graverobber over at Leiden wished for him to come in and get pinned to a velvet-lined exhibit box like a rare and specific bug.

Luuk Blenkin wished he knew what he was supposed to do here—if he was supposed to just say what he wanted, right out loud—shout it at the moon—the name of the girl he wished took him seriously? Fame and fortune as a troubadour? Just one solid shot at it, one night in one of the better taverns? *Fish?*—and if so, he wished the two older men would pipe up themselves—say their wishes. He wished he knew if this was normal—a weird but standard part of every fishing trip—being interrogated by the godverdomme moon.

Wyn wished he could care one way or the other whether this was insanity. [Wished he could muster concern.]

Ned wished, as they slid out into the sea, that he could guarantee that he wouldn't slip into one of his "spells," as the village doctor, Goedkoop, sometimes called them . . . and be rendered useless while his much younger partners did all the work.

"WE HAVE COME TO FISH FOR THE HERRING-FISH THAT LIVE IN THIS BEAUTIFUL SEA:

It *could* just be sea foam, clouding up on the dark water, witching the moonlight, creating an optical illusion. It was possible it wasn't *clouds* drifting below their boat—wasn't it? To make things even more perplexing, there seemed to be—in the breaks between what could—or could *not* be—the clouds—a glow down there—more toward what he was pretty sure was southeast—right where the heart of The Hague lay, where the gaslit streetlamps would be glowing. Luuk decided it could simply be a school of some sort of phosphorescent fish. He'd read of such things—jellyfish, krill, some of the coral, plankton—but the glowing below was only in that one spot, where The Hague would be, just inland from the coast, just east of the Kurhaus, if they *were*, in fact—Harre Jasses!—floating high above it all.

If it *was* the Kurhaus down there—and not some horrible bottom-feeder fish—his Imke would be there soon—if he had her schedule correct. She worked in the laundry in the basement of the great glowing resort, but also—on certain nights—after finishing up at the tavern or Dirty Ned's place—she was reporting back to the Kurhaus to assist the baker, preparing breakfast rolls and fresh bread for the new day.

For Luuk, it helped a little—maybe—to think of his plans regarding Imke as akin to the way they'd arrived here tonight out in the dark-blue vastness: he wasn't so great with the normal ways you courted a girl—the talking to her part, the getting to know her . . . all that. But their unusual little boat—their plan to get around the *normal* constraints of the whole enterprise of herring fishing—wasn't that a bit like what he was going to do by winning her over with his music? Getting around his personal shortcomings—including even the recent sullying of his family's name—and including personally knowing neither tip nor toe about either herring or fishing? The other fellas out there his age didn't have that sort of grand scheme—either a way to reach the herring shoals with three ill-fit men and a small craft—*or*—anything remotely nearing an enlightened approach—one that required neither social or financial standing nor personal élan—to reach that local wonder—that unreachable shoal all to herself, Imke Holt.

To be honest, Wyn van Winkel had never been able to convince himself he was truly a herring man. [He wasn't sure tonight if he even looked the part.]

His brief time in Rangoon, he'd shed all signs [belts, buckles, boots] of being soldier or sailor [he *thought*, though English Van seemed to spot it on him straight off] and disguised himself as a fisherman. He had little memory of the escape in a tiny fishing boat [across the Andaman Sea, north to the shores of Burma], but he'd kept his head down [hiding his bule face]. He felt, tonight [taking a desperate stab at a trade he'd last tried six years before], that he was *still* pretending.

This was crazy [for any number of reasons, of course, but] especially because the days of the small-crew herring industry were waning.

More than once since his return, he'd bunked in the skeleton of a storm-battered bomschuit that hadn't been hauled away but pushed naturally, by the sea, up onto the higher dunes. Its keel faced the heavens, turned over like a turtle's shell, and so though the wind and waves trespassed, it did keep him dry [more or less].

The bowplate was intact, the name, *De Heer Geeft*, as visible as in its heyday [though now reading upside down]. It was Nodd himself who caught him at it, emerging sheepishly from the upturned hulk [like a damn hermit crab] and made the obvious crack about the Lord indeed providing.

They hadn't alerted the local herring guild . . . or even looked into whether they could register their strange little boat . . . or really considered whether they were truly violating any bit of the North Seas Fisheries Convention of 1882 . . . Personally, Ned felt . . . and his dear mevrouw and his dear friend Wynkyn agreed with him . . . that the smarter move here would be to just see how it went . . . and then nod a lot and agree that they would *certainly* comply with any rules and regulations and standards of behavior for this previously untried type of fishing boat . . . There were reasons, of course, that he was known around Scheveningen as Agreeable Ned. He'd long ago learned to keep his mouth shut and just nod a lot. And smile . . . Which was why, he also knew, they sometimes called him Smilin' Ned . . .

It was better to just go ahead and do something, Wyn said, and have the authorities explain why you couldn't, than it was to ask if you could and have them dream up reasons.

The season hadn't started, true—but was there really anything legal and binding about that? *Not really* . . . And the way things were going lately . . . in terms of supporting his family . . . Ned had decided that he needed to start trading more loosely in the land of the *not really*.

They hadn't elected a captain—with a crew of only three, it hardly seemed necessary. Luuk only knew it wasn't him. Wyn was too damn flippant. Old Nodd had years of experience—it would probably be the old man, if they bothered.

But now that it seemed like the moon was calling to them—telling them what to do—and now the stars were maybe chiming in—Luuk sort of wanted to know: who was in charge here?—not only in the boat, but in the sky, too.

His instinct was to stay as close to the center of the boat as possible—low, to avoid that wobbly feeling he got every time he tried to rise to his feet—a force pushing back against his face, his chest, his whole body, pushing him down. Without the sail, the boat groaned and creaked. He stayed on the other side of the empty mast from them—out of the way. Ned had swapped with Wyn again and was back at the tiller—aft, they called it—or where the rudder had *been*—making some adjustments in their course with the oar. He was speaking softly—possibly to the moon, explaining what they were doing—?

Luuk wanted to believe the old man was at the helm—if that was the term. It had been some time since he'd felt any sense of authority in his life—with his father vanished, he wasn't sure if he should take direction from his mother or his testy uncle. And they'd also cut back on church attendance since the business with his vader—so there was no one telling him what to do there, either.

At sea—didn't they call this feeling being "at sea"?

[It was just hard to gauge *what* or *who* was off-keel when no one was setting the rules.] Wyn lounged across the midships thwart, arms on the gunwales, turned from the spray [which was strangely light, more like a dewy mist], musing on this outburst from the moon, wondering if [because they had come out here with no great plan and were simply breaking every standard and tradition for going after herring] a bit of crazy had boarded their cramped little boat.

He supposed it was [scientifically speaking] something about madness loving a vacuum. It was, he'd observed, astonishingly effortless to ease your way into crazy when it became unclear who was in charge. The Dutch East India Company discovered *that* back in Sumatra when they wrongly assumed the sultan held authority over the country [failing to grasp the spiderweb federation system of the hulubalang, sagis, and the panglima, who actually elected the sultan]. This "king" of the Mahomedan country was king in name only, and getting him in line [and his prompt death] had done nothing to repair a semblance of authority. And so the place went crazy, and crazy became the norm [to be yawned at, shrugged off, sloughed aside].

Now that he was back [from what everyone here seemed to be calling the Aceh War or "that colonial rebellion," but many back there called the Infidel War, the Dutch War, the Holy War], Wyn felt obliged for some inexplicable reason to respond to everything with a sort of careless flippancy, even though it was now met with a different reaction: back in '82 and '83, back when [as he liked to think of it] a feeling of recklessness was the beauty he sought, men like his father and his kind chalked his glib irony up to his youth. Now they clearly considered it a result of mental instability [that he had been broken in the jungles of the Dutch East Indies, shattered by the relentless Mahomedans].

In his vader's circle, the weekly campus salons were open to the public but [according to Vader] "intended primarily to encourage a collegial fraternization between faculty and the more promising students." Whenever Wyn did see his father [which was not as rare as he would prefer], the great professor would urge him to attend. And whenever he did manage to make an appearance, he knew they all assumed it was over his head. The only topic that his father and his colleagues expected would be his area of comprehension [when they moved off their respective academic fields and the general politics of the administration of the university] was the topic of King William. [Crazy Willy, some of them dared to say.] This was territory Wyn did not want to drift into with them. Not that he entirely disagreed with their views of the country's alleged leader [his own opinion had certainly always been far different from the love for William he'd seen among the hardworking men of the herring boats and the fellow grunts who served the king, back in the service]. The working class felt William had their best interests at heart. [He'd strengthened all things maritime and military and turned up his inbred snoot at the high-minded intellectuals normally caught in the gravitational pull of the royal court. He stamped around outdoors and took action.] Sure, the monarch was nuts, impetuous, forever stepping in personally and trying to run things—interfering, firsthand, with the warplay of his generals, and then moving on to the next kibitzing moment like a short-witted child. [He even sentenced the mayor of The Hague to death and then forgot about it, and no one carried out the execution, knowing he'd grow bored with it and forget.] He was humored like a doddering uncle.

The liberal-minded and political bourgeoisie despised Crazy Willy for a buffoon, but the average Hollander [in wader boots and stinking of fish guts] remained loyal. Even now that King William was essentially locked up in a padded cell, expected to die any day of liver disease. Wyn's father's friend in the School of Medicine, Dr. Ogtrop, explained to Wyn at a recent salon [over speculaas and cheese] that delirium was a common symptom in late-stage renal failure, and though William III's outrageous behavior began long ago, renal failure was likely part of the reason he was in his current state [the country being ruled by proxy].

By all accounts, he was terrible. A huge man who would act gentle and meek one moment, then explode in violence and roaring the next. Brutal to his servants [or whoever was handy] and cruel to animals. That was more than enough for Wyn to dislike him.

And yet, Wyn tried to avoid those gossip-fests about the man's sanity. [From all he'd heard, King William was indeed insane, but the derision that always arose over that specific point just rubbed Wyn wrong.] If he'd come away with any real insight from his experience fighting the insurgents in Aceh [those ungovernable people whom that same crazy monarch insisted fall in line], it was that a sense of delirium wasn't always such a bad thing to have. [And who was he to scorn anyone for simply not having a firm grip on reality; for living in a world that swam in and out of distortion and clarity, that played tricks on him like a trickster imp, like flickering moonlight?]

Hate the man for kicking his dogs, he wanted to say, or cuffing the footman or sending troops over a ridge on a whim, but don't hate him for the puppet show loose in his head. [The curtain could go up on that same puppet show for any one of us, any minute . . .]

And now here Wyn was, pretty sure it *had* [with this business of flying boats and speaking to the moon], and frankly, it wasn't throwing him as much as it probably should. [At least he wasn't kicking dogs or trying to behead the mayor.]

Luuk hoped it didn't look like he was cowering—crouching so low now his nose was practically pressed to the decking. It helped with that feeling that they were rising. He wouldn't be able to stay there soon—in a few hours, they'd be emptying their nets right there, all that stinking herring flopping around on the pristine wood. Though it was green elm—the reason, Ned said, that it smelled like manure—cut only slightly by smoke and pine tar from the sealing—still, this had to stink less than the fish.

He had never been keen on herring—pickled or otherwise. He'd never really had to be. The truth was—up until his father vanished—he'd been lucky enough to avoid such low-class fare. Haddock and whiting, maybe, but he'd grown more accustomed over the years to clams, lobster, lamb, goose, beef, braised duck—a variety that had endowed him with the hale physique—he was well aware—of the type not normally expected to be a troubadour and versifier—though the healthy muscles sure helped when it came to working the accordion.

But Harre Jasses! these poorer folks of Scheveningen sure ate a lot of bread and cheese, he'd noticed—and of course herring.

Wasn't it essentially jam-packed in this dark little sea—these fish-scattered waters that ran all the way to Denmark to the north and England to the west? How could something so puny and plentiful be prized? He wasn't out here tonight out of some love for the slippery silvery little creeps. There was money in it—he knew that. And he needed that.

[The sky to the west, at the final dipping of the sunset, was the same color, come to think of it . . . Maybe a shade darker green . . .]

Wyn never explained to the other two why he'd wanted the "pea-green" marking along the hull [just a single stripe, running below the topstrake]. It had been a compromise: he'd wanted to paint the whole thing that color.

"Let's see how it goes . . ." Noddie said. "We'll buy her a fancy coat if she works out for us."

The kid had asked if it was his "colors" from back in the war ["From the battle flag of your battalion or platoon or what have you?"], and Wyn just gave him a wry smile that said, he hoped, *You're being ridiculous, pal.* [Or even *I'm not one of your overblown sea chanties, Blenkin.*]

But the kid tried again: "This is some superstition among the herring men, isn't it?"

The reason was sillier than all that, which was why he kept it to himself [a stance he considered a good policy in general]. English Van had some drivel he kept at the whole journey back—some nonsense verse he'd committed to memory about an owl and a pussycat, sailing off "in a beautiful pea-green boat." [From the pen of one of his countrymen, apparently known for just such inanities.] This Lear fellow seemed like the sort they might run into in one their pipe dens. [He had no idea what a *runcible spoon* was, but it sure seemed like something the Celestials used to mix up a tincture.] Eventually, during the course of the rest of their voyage, following his companion's lead, Wyn relinquished the name *Sumatra* and *Aceh* and referred to it all as Van did ["The land where the Bong-Tree grows . . ."].

The final word on the matter was a [surprisingly clever] jape from Agreeable Ned. When they got to the issue of nets, ol' Nodd asked, "We're not going to have to paint the *nets* any special color, now are we, Wynkyn?"

There were big snorts all around [even the kid beaming, one of them now, it really seemed], and Wyn felt a little bad that he was going to be leaving them both in the lurch when he eventually left town.

"NETS OF SILVER AND GOLD HAVE WE," SAID WYNKEN, BLYNKEN, AND NOD.

☾

The nets they used . . . on the maiden voyage of *De Klomp* . . . were all his old nets . . . the Nodder brothers' nets. He'd spent the nights they weren't building the picarooner on sorting and mending them. It was difficult, because he didn't have a separate netting shed . . . the shed they were using for their boatbuilding was where he would normally hang his nets for repair . . . and so the work was slow and laborious but reassuring in its rhythms as well . . . in a way that made him feel there was some constancy to life . . . Nipping the mesh, bringing the shuttle around, hitching it, moving on . . . It was peaceful work, and that was all Ned Nodder really wanted these days . . . to know his family was safe and content . . . to know peace.

He did something fanciful, too . . . inspired perhaps by the lilting laughter of his wife and his little ones back in the house, carrying out over the winter-stilled plowland . . . followed, at the darkening of the window, by the trill of her lullabies . . . he wound the shuttle in such a way as to write each of their names in a net . . . the name of each of his three . . . and several nets with the name of his love . . . and even the name of the lost soul at rest at the edge of the copse in back, the one who would have been Sterre . . . the little star.

His brothers, back in the days of the Nodder family bom . . . would have heckled him plenty just for that, for the sentiment . . . even without knowing of the hunch it gave him . . . unreasonably, of course . . . illogically . . . that he was weaving in magic, weaving in luck . . .

Luuk just wanted to be clear on where things stood. There were too many things unclear in his life as it was without adding, *Am I up in the air in a flying boat right now?* These days, there were mornings he stood there stuck, unable to even decide which of his three shirts he should wear—the gray, the bluish gray, or the greenish gray. His mother claimed she'd given him too many choices—most boys didn't have three shirts to choose from at seventeen—and certainly they were now in no position to be indulging in such lavishes—and she claimed it was because he was seventeen—the hedging—and everything seemed complicated and complex at that age— not cut and dried. She assured him, with age, the fluttering focus would resolve itself.

And she claimed his deciding he was in love with Imke Holt didn't help. "All the time"—Mammie tapped his head, sweetly, replacing it with a kiss—"the gears going this way, then going that way, then back again . . . Don't let Allard see this, son—he'll see the steam coming out; he'll make you clerk in a bank!"

Uncle Allard would try to shut it down—he'd try to reposition Luuk's sights on silver and gold.

Ever since he'd been home [most of the past year], Wyn had wanted to tell his father he was sorry he wasn't able to fly [that he hadn't been able to sprout wings or cast a net over a passing shooting star] and whiz home from the Bengal Sea [to be there when his moeder was dying]. But such cracks were wasted on his father [the man found sarcasm and irony a low form of discourse; a digression and waste of time].

Of course, if he could have flown home, he would have done it long before his mother's first cough. [He would have torn out of there, at least, when he saw the ancient stone chairs, in a circle, at Ambarita, the high mountain village where ritual beheadings once occurred, with enemies roasted along with buffalo meat, stirred in as a sort of stamppot, devoured by the village's top man, and no one could quite pry out, to Wyn's satisfaction, just how far back in history this sort of buffet had occurred.]

Wyn knew there was no point going over it with his father now [whether directly or with wisecracks], because the man was simply going to resent him. That's what he did. And if it wasn't the issue of Wyn not being there to bury his mother, it would be something else [his lack of academic achievements, his prolonged bachelorhood, the fact that he hadn't provided the elder patriarch with grandchildren—or more likely, the way he saw them—further heirs]. His father didn't *hate* him, perhaps, but he certainly thought of him as a wastrel, an embarrassment, and a profligate.

His mother found him the winsome, gentle answer to his father's lofty chill. [He could have at least made her laugh a little; put her at ease in her decline.] And though he didn't want to fall into his father's finger-pointing game, if he let himself mull over the events of her death, the timeline leading up to it, Wyn had to ask himself if he *had* been there, back home in The Hague [nearby, at least], might he have noticed her symptoms earlier and insisted she go see the doctor? His father could be as distant as constellations [literally with his head in the skies, preoccupied with his cosmos and observatory telescope], so he might have missed the signs.

If they were flying now, they were flying. Fine: Ned could go along with that.

Especially since they'd started out, at least, cutting out into the sea under sail, the canvas bunting hard at full swell . . . the bowsprit, given her shallow draft, lifting like nothing he'd felt before . . . and because he'd had a dream very recently . . . the sort he had now and again in those times he would later discover he shouldn't have been dreaming . . . when he was walking somewhere or sitting in a group, seemingly engaged in conversation . . . Or even while performing physical labor . . . some of which could be dangerous, if it happened he was really asleep. This kind of sleep he had, his young wife found alarming and likely reminded her that the list was long of things she didn't sign up for with him . . . But those dreams he had in that state, at the times he later heard he was pushing a barrow or sharpening a pair of scissors for Fenna, or slumped in the tavern, sipping a beer and nodding along to Guss Visser's same old yarn about battling an English dogger with his own bare-bones bom crew, back in the hairier days, out among the far shoals, back when navies were involved and cannon fire exchanged . . . those dreams felt real and true. And as if they were not so much bits of fancy, coming from him . . . not the sort of silly puppet show starring churned-up things from his own life, nicely scrambled . . . but dreams that seemed to come from an open window, from a well-traveled breeze, a ripple in the air.

And the reason it made sense . . . that they might now be flying . . . was that he'd had one of those special-feeling dreams not long back . . . one from which Ned woke to find he was sewing a sailcloth . . . about a tall, amiable university man across the Atlantic . . . Christian name of James . . . who, in the dream, was an inventor of wind.

He was pretty sure he'd been up in the air before, back when he served as Korporaal van Winkel, back in Sumatra. That had been that wobbly time, his time in the Royal Dutch service when the pressure-relieving customs of the local natives began to draw in participants from the other side [giving in to the pipe and the poppy just as if they were no better than the wide-eyed pedang-waving terrors that filled their unmedicated dreams]. And so he couldn't swear an oath that it had happened, but he believed he'd once been invited on board an observation balloon [somewhere over a rebel-held mountain territory of Aceh, moving south toward the land of the Toba Batak]. If it was true [and not the wilted memory of long-stale dream], he'd arrived at a forward outpost in the highlands [maybe near Kutacane and the roaring whitewater of the Alas] to deliver a courier packet from his regiment, and the commandant there, noting his name and asking if he was from Leiden, back home [Wyn said The Hague, but had to concede, when pushed, that his vader was, in fact, the astronomer], announced that he *thought* he'd read a highbrow journal article *somewhere* [way over his head, he claimed] by a van Winkel at Leiden that challenged our understanding of the nature of stars. [Or that was what it seemed to be about, at least.] The conversation led to the commandant dragging him along to his next duty of the day, which was stepping into the basket of his great airship and rising above the jungle canopy [and above a rebel village, nearer than Wyn had imagined]. *Far* above, where the enemy, bent low in noon prayer, looked like rows of little field mice, nothing to terrify.

But that had been noisy [*if* it had happened]—the roar and whoosh of the bellows and burner. Here, Wyn heard nothing that dragonous, just the flutter of wind in the rigging and the creak of the hull.

Halfway to the shoals, they began to meet some cover [not quite fog, but a crystalline mug that eased in, soft as a child]. There was a change in air pressure [the wind whistled and rattled, but no longer rocked the boat, no longer buffeted them with waves, at the bow or broadside], and he could feel that pressure in his chest. It was cold, too, for June, smelling less now of brine and more of storm [metallic, chlorinated, the supply room behind a daguerreotypist's studio, where he'd once secretly taken shelter for part of a week].

The night had somehow wrapped itself around them.

"We can't be flying," Luuk Blenkin said. "Wyn, you don't really think we're in the *air*, do you?"

Wyn answered by asking if he'd heard the one about the monkey, the alligator, and the rabbi in a boat.

"I'm just trying to be clear on what's happening," young Blenkin said. "Don't you want to know what's happening?"

"We're fishing," he said. "And not very successfully. So a normal night." [Normal for independents, competing with the big, highly financed busses.]

Blenkin turned to the real veteran of the North Sea. "Ned, this is not normal, right? You've never seen anything like this, right?"

"What I've seen, son . . ." [You could hear Old Man Nodder smiling in the dark] ". . . is a lot of *never before* . . . Many times, I've heard *Have you ever seen anything like this?* And this is what I know: This world . . . the moeder planet, the whole natural world the Lord gives us, has always got a new trick up her sleeve . . . And the Lord wants it that way . . . The Lord is happy with us being filled with awe and surprise and does not wish for us to worry, and that is why I trust the Lord and know all will be well."

[Wyn stayed out of that one, leaving the Lord-talk to ol' Noddie.]

They sailed along for what could have been nearly another league [it was oddly difficult to gauge distance now, Wyn would give the lad that], until at last a wet sputter of frustration burst from young Blenkin. "Seriously. *Ned.* Can you at least say if you think we're up in the air right now?"

"Whatever's happening," Nodd said, "I'm not one to question it."

Awake, "inventor of wind" made no sense . . . but in Ned's dream, this silver-haired man James was kind and smart and chuckled at everyone's jokes, letting his eyes twinkle, letting others talk, yet all the time, he was dreaming up fantastic things that could barely be explained. He built a kind of ice yacht like the sort youth on Braassemermeer had been sailing for centuries . . . but made for sand, for a flat dead ocean out west in the New World . . . but with no sailcloth and a rigid arch in its place . . . just a great smooth arch that must have been enchanted by the wind . . . and then he rebuilt it, transforming it into a horseless wagon of some sort, for road travel, that ran faster than a horse, only on wind. Even when there was no real breeze at all . . .

And then his love of boats gave the inventor the craziest dream, and he sat by the water's edge one day, stilled by it, until he had his new invention . . . a sailboat that would keel sharply to the leeward, the bow planing, and then lift from the water entirely and take to the air, gliding up into the clouds.

Ned didn't know if this was happening now or had happened in the past or could happen years from now . . . but he felt it was that rare variety of dream that he sometimes had . . . Dreams he felt certain were true.

They didn't frighten him, this other kind of dream that felt like an open window, but calmed him . . . mostly because he'd chosen to feel good about them . . . He'd decided these dreams reassured him that life was mostly full of awe and small proofs of the universal functions of the smile and the nod: a signal that everything was . . . and would be . . . generally all right.

Of course, his first thought [as he felt the give of the hull beneath them, pulling loose of the water, heard the shiver of trailing beads showering down beneath them, running off the keel] was the opium. He'd been cutting back [he really had], and much of that was because it was more difficult to acquire here, of course. But he couldn't really blame the opium because the other two were observing all this too. He was sure they saw it [even though Blenkin was stating all his observations as questions and Noddie was claiming now that he'd dozed off for parts of the last hour or so].

Not *seeing* it so much as feeling it, really—the moonlight [shimmering at them like a wide open path] lent some perspective, but it was [for the most part] a feeling at first, not a sight. [A feeling that they were rising; that they were aloft.] And the splashless creak of the sweep oar against the sculling notch wasn't reassuring. [He just hoped ol' Neddie kept a good grip on the thing. An oar was sometimes the only way home.]

Keeping a grip was, as ever, a concern. [Always, for Wyn.] There were very few veterans of the ongoing war in Aceh who returned unsoftened, he was well aware [even though no one talked about it and little was mentioned of it in the papers]. Mental stability was at all times a barometer he must check. When he thought of *lunacy*, though, there were higher bars to use as standards, in Wyn's experience: the green recruit who got sent home when he gouged out his own eye after a "tuchtiging party" against some sleepy band of Teungku Chik di Tiro camp followers; the genius brass who came up with that theory [that if you baked enough Mahomedan babies in their own huts they'd eventually come around]; the Engelsman who thought you could stow away in a small trader from Rangoon to Europe and not get caught; and in Singapore, he watched an old stringy Celestial in the street who appeared convinced he was a rooster. [That last one paled in comparison, and anyway, he might have been a street performer. He did have a hat down and had collected a few coins. On the other hand, he seemed to actually eat the worms he found.] And of course, their very own king, Crazy Willy.

He'd heard too that Cent, the painter, was possibly another now on the edge of sanity. That redheaded maniac had always been "high-strung" [the way Fenna had put it back then], and they were both wild, even sharing the cramped room Cent had as a studio [over on Schenkweg, wasn't it?] part of that summer that he still thought of as the time when recklessness was beauty. [They were both moon-addled that summer, reveling in the rash.]

Luuk Blenkin noticed one big difference between himself and his two new partners—not their ages—a difference that was considerable, even with the youngest. And not their experience—though the two knew herring fishing and sailing and all manner of other things he did not. It was their names. He'd always admired those who had several names. Nicknames, family names, strangulations and variations: Wyn was Wyn and van Winkel and Wynk and Wynkyn and Wynand and who knew what else—Luuk couldn't imagine the number of women out there who had some other private name for him, whispered in the dark. And even Old Ned had his handful—Agreeable Ned, Smilin' Ned, Nodd . . . Wynk seemed to have a new batch of names for Meneer Nodder that he pulled from his pockets and threw at the older man all the time, just to see if they stuck—or perhaps just to wake him up—to verbally poke him in the ribs . . . Luuk worried it might be a sign of something lacking in himself that he only had two lousy names: Luuk Blenkin. It could have just as easily been *Blah Blah*—a fitting nickname if ever he heard one.

He wondered sometimes if his love, Imke, would bestow a nickname on him—when they were finally together.

She appeared behind him, suddenly . . . at their netting shed, down on the beach . . . In the few days since he'd woken in the girl's bed, he'd been looking for a way to restrain himself at night . . . to tie himself to his bed . . . and was hoping to scrounge up a few remnants of old net he could use to do just that. His brothers . . . all three of them . . . were out of earshot over by their beached bom, *De Groot Ster* . . . in the shade of the tilted hull, mending some small snag in the sails before the evening launch. The canvas billowed and caught the air and . . . along with the surf and the gulls and the rigging and bluster, of men and wind . . . covered the sound of her approach. His brothers were looking his way now . . . somewhere between grinning and gaping, clearly curious about the girl.

There was much blushing and nervous *hois* back and forth before she got to it: "Vader would become Spanish breathless if he learned I was telling you this, Meneer Nodder. He would fly into the heavens. But you have a right to know, sir. At least *I* feel you do." She lowered her voice . . . and her gaze, so that he found himself inspecting the top of her bonnet, and the nearly translucent sunshine hair that couldn't be contained . . ."I'm with child," she nearly whispered, twisting her hands into her apron. "And Vader has been in a panic, and written me off as ruined, but then *you* appeared . . . If he'd had one of these nets here, he would've thrown it over you." She smiled at this, and it was the first he'd seen her smile. "But I *don't* want to take advantage like that. It's not right."

Without meaning to, he surveyed the length of her. It was hard to tell . . . He was certainly far from expert at these things. And considering the high-waisted frocks these young women wore . . . with their layers and padding and who knew what . . . even if he were more experienced, he might not have noticed any sign of her condition. To him, she just looked healthy, red-cheeked . . .

The word *child* was a lot to take in, though.

"So just forget my vader—you certainly shouldn't feel obliged to marry me just because you got lost in the night. Tangled up in your sleep, if that's it. I know you weren't up to mischief, and anyone without the brains of a cabbage would know you're a good man and did nothing to dishonor me. It's something with your head, isn't it?" Now she looked up . . . and reached out and touched his temple . . . and he thought again of the difference in the color of his hair there, how it had once been closer to her golden color, so many years ago . . . and with the gentle way her fingers flitted there, he almost believed they could whisk away the misfirings inside . . .

It stirred something in him . . . not simply her touch, but the escape she was offering him now . . . her brave journey down here among the herring boats and profane klootzakken just to do the decent thing . . . Until that moment, he'd been hoping for some way out . . . but she was honest and straightforward and true in a way that matched the way *he* also saw the world . . .

"Well," he told her, "I was just thinking . . . how nice it would be maybe . . . to have someone around to tie me to the bed at night . . ." He saw the eyebrow arch before he could get it out. "To avoid the night wanderings again, I mean." He made sure she could see he was joking . . . and the laugh it evoked was the ripple of water over a sluicegate after a heavy spring rain.

He turned to his perplexed brothers then and called them over . . . to come meet his bride and give her a kiss and welcome her to the family.

Wyn took charge of the nets as they stood to shoot them [though by rights, young Blenkin had the longer arm and should have led the throw]. With outsized gestures, three heads nodding in time, overemphasizing the cadence they'd drilled with back at the shed [Wyn even tapping his foot to beat out the rhythm], they swung the gathered net [the novice sandwiched between him and Neddie midships] and released [hoping for the desired "bib," the halfmoon arc they'd practiced out by Ned's woodpile].

The moonlight [it had to be the moonlight, breaking on the surface] flickered silver and gold as the net played out, sinking faster than he recalled. [Hadn't they always eased down over the sides, a shimmering descent?] The first net vanished as if the cork floats had come loose or it had been balled in a bunch, though they hadn't botched the cast at all. [Even the kid had managed to keep the middle flat and untangled, casting it out in a passable bib.]

Make new friends, but keep the old, he heard in his head [as heard in the hold of the merchant ship, coming home].

He could hear the kid breathing there in the dark as they stood watching the twinkling light where the net had been. *Those are silver, these are gold . . .*

The pal he'd traveled back with from the Indies had a fondness for verse and kept several he'd clipped from various periodicals, wearied and fold-weakened, about his person. One such was some trope-crammed slop about friendship by a Welshman named Parry something. Wyn had actually preferred the really silly one [about fowl and feline dancing by the light of the moon], but Van kept his whole cockeyed catalogue in constant rotation. And now, when Wyn saw the moonlit ripples casting gold and silver [on the water: it had to be on the water], it made him take inventory of what friends he did have and which of the two slots they would all be sorted into. [He had both sorts in this very boat, Blenkin a newer friend, Nodd an old one; a gold one.]

The newer friend did have some curious quirks to him.

It was probably a month ago [maybe], if he had it right . . . It was cold and bright out, and felt like a day even earlier in the season [not May, as it had to be, if it was only a month ago, but a dry version of March, the wind whipping off the beach], and Wyn was in one of those "in-between times," as he thought of it [in terms of his stomach; in terms of the more extreme ebb and flood of the new tidal patterns his pipe den visits inflicted on his bowels], and given the vicissitudes of the elements [both internal and external], a hot bowl of lumpy, starchy stamppot [with maybe an egg, if they had it] seemed like the most reasonable thing to attempt. He needed none of the fun exotica he had to trek down to seek [at Bistro de Bintang Kecil, and the noodlier, spicier streets of The Hague] but rather a plain, homespun Dutch meal, right there, beachside at Scheveningen [at Klaas Vaak's or maybe it was at The Herring King]. Now, just a month or so later, he wasn't entirely sure which tavern, only that it was the time when Luuk Blenkin loomed into view [bounded right up to his table and stood there worrying the notebook in his hand].

"Sorry for interrupting your . . . lunch, I guess it is? Or is this your supper?"

Wyn shrugged. "Breakfast, maybe?"

The look on the kid's face [which Wyn was trying to avoid, frankly] had him all set to hear that Luuk was backing out [that he and Agreeable Ned would be left to man the picarooner all by themselves]. But the fretting was over something else [someone else].

"It's—Well, it's Imke—"

"You're eloping and don't need me and ol' Smilin' Ned anymore, is that it?"

"Not at all! I mean—jeetje, that's *so*—" He sank, uninvited, into the other side of the booth. "That's so *far* from what's happening, Wyn. I just ran into her—just now?—on the strandweg?—and well, I'm just trying to understand the *code* and—"

"The code?"

"Just interpreting what they mean—girls—*her*. I know they're not supposed to act overly interested—it's not ladylike or what-have-you—so when you're talking and they're not really responding, how do you know when to stop talking—when they're *actually* trying to move on and keep walking and, well—?"

Wyn just looked at him, dead on, hoping he'd see he'd just answered his own question. [But Luuk started up again.]

"She's *such* a mystery. And—"

"Imke *Holt*, right? That's the Imke we're talking about?"

"Right? You've seen it, I'm sure. And that's great—it is—her being so mysterious. I mean, it's part of what makes her so special—granted, but— But somehow I fear I'm maybe not up to the task."

Wyn must have twitched an eyebrow at the word *task*. Was this kid balking at the intricacies of life at *this* young stage? Because it would only get harder. But he didn't tell him that. He just chewed his stamppot.

"*Task* isn't the word," Luuk said. "I don't know the word— *This* is the problem—this right here! I'm no good putting it in words."

Wyn laughed. "You write songs, Luuk. You're at that notebook every time I look."

The kid was holding his head now, slumped on the table like a sad dog. "Totally different! It's probably *why* I write, in fact—because it comes out all wrong when I open my mouth—but . . ."

Maybe the answer was not opening his mouth so much, Wyn figured, but for this matter specifically, he couldn't help thinking that Imke Holt [in the interactions *he'd* had with her, at least] really didn't seem that complicated [or mysterious or high-strung or even remote or aloof]. She seemed like a lovely young woman [with a terrific smile] who always had a thing or two to say that was bright and engaging, even funny. [So if her reaction to young Blenkin here was puzzling, the puzzle possibly lay in the eyes of the puzzled.]

Popping the last significant hunk of potato into his mouth, Wyn slid out of the booth, dropped some guilders by his bowl, waving to the owner as he pulled on his jacket. "Maybe you're squinting at it too hard, Luuk. Things are often simpler than they seem."

[He spared him that little piece of logical gold, Occam's razor, that his vader had foisted on him since he could walk, but still, this kid probably needed it even more clearly distilled.]

Maybe he should've just told him, *If you pursue a girl and she throws down a lot of complications: then that's your answer.* But a certain amount of life had to be figured out on one's own. [Hell, he was still working on his *own* portion.]

It struck Wyn, several hours later, that he could have told the Blenkin kid a story about Lake Toba, a vast, water-filled caldera high in the mountains of Sumatra that only white visitors swam in. It was a clear, cold blue Wyn had never seen anywhere in the world [not even in the irises of the love he'd left waiting on Scheveningen Beach, back in 1883]. Because it was so crystalline and untouched, the locals thought it had to be the home of fairies and wouldn't trespass in it. But it sparkled for a much simpler reason: it was just an astounding lake, with pure, potable water. It shimmered and called to you because it was everything you'd ever seek in a body of water [not because it was inhabited by powerful underwater beings].

He should have told young Blenkin that story—how he and his men would strip down and dive in and drink from it and splash and play grab-ass while the Batak lurked on the banks [wide-eyed, sweaty, and parched].

With that story, he could hint at something the boy likely wouldn't pick up on [but Wyn found he really wanted to say to him]: *Some people, kiddo, just aren't prepared to take on what's right in front of them.*

II.

THE OLD MOON LAUGHED
AND SANG A SONG.

"My hearing's going," Ned admitted when Wyn spelled him at the transom. "You boys hearing singing?"

Wyn had been hearing it for the last quarter-hour [even over the wooden creak of the pointless sculling], but he said no. Anyway, he'd had a slight hum in his left ear since the skirmish at Grong-Grong [or ambush, really], when one of Teungku Chik di Tiro's guerrillas tried to lop off his head, but his aim was crap [or the rebel hadn't prayed enough times that day to his Allah], and so it was the hilt of this frothy-mouthed maniac's pedang that struck Wyn instead, smack across the ear. [And then the ringing began in earnest his last night in Aceh, when the garrison magazine blew.]

"Maybe," he said. "Crew on a haringbuis out there, in their cups . . . ?"

"You think they're already out there," young Luuk whispered [extinguishing his onion lamp, crouching even lower], "and they're singing to taunt us? To tell us they know we're here—that they won't let us get in close to the shoals?" [Rather shaky for a boy who'd never seen either a buss crew or real battle close up: how shaky would he be, Wyn wondered, if he actually knew of any of these things firsthand?]

"Just a drinking song," Wyn assured him, stowing the oar [which was completely dry]. "'Curaçao,' . . . one of those." Of course, he didn't recognize the melody [or whether it could truly be called a *melody*, as opposed to just a line of notes in some random order]. He'd known old salts on the Royal Navy ships who swore by Siren song [lusty sea lovelies enticing sailors to their deaths on rocky shores]. And because it wasn't a tune that could even remotely be construed as commonplace, he imagined for a moment it was the eerie Serune Kalee [which had intrigued but made no sense to his ears: all that squirming coming from a short piece of bamboo] back in the land of the fierce and crafty Teungku Chik di Tiro.

Though it was at the beach village, he knew, where many thought of him as Agreeable Ned, he privately had a little chuckle sometimes that this nickname he'd been given should apply, more than anywhere, back in his own home . . . Not only because he was happier than he'd ever imagined . . . Certainly happier than he'd imagined back in those years when he hardly imagined it *at all*, family being a thing seen through windows, or filing into church. Nowadays he felt that ember of happiness underneath it all . . . at least excluding the nights he sometimes thrashed in his sleep, worrying about the basic upkeep of this brood . . . But at home he was Agreeable Ned too, in that he agreed with his wife on everything. She was no harpy, no fishwife, no demander of *more*, so agreeing with her came with a gliding ease . . . Though she did insist on more than a few ministrations that he simply felt he had to force a smile and consent to, just knuckle down . . . chief among them being the various home remedies she tried on him in an attempt to make him sleep better, she claimed, or, lately, improve his aging hearing . . . "The two issues are connected," she'd insisted more than once, with zero in the way of a medical degree to back it up . . . But the way she pressed her little fingers, flat-palmed, lightly on his chest when she made such statements, made it sound more like a request than the demand he knew it to be . . . Her thinking was that if she could get him hearing a little better, maybe he wouldn't fall asleep as easily at those times when he wasn't supposed to, when people were raising a normal level of racket in his vicinity.

She would sit him down at the head of the kitchen table and have him push his chair back a little, then she would gently lower his head to the folded towel she'd placed on the table, and with a funnel she would pour in various solutions to supposedly clean out his ear canal—often garlic oil, sometimes seawater . . . It was messy and not entirely pleasant, other than her nervous humming and the floral scent of her and the crush of her bosom against his back, the light touch of her fingers, brushing aside what was left of his hair, touching his nape in a way that promised it would not be the last she would be touching him that night . . . She did it when the kids were tucked in, not wanting to spill the oily applications, jostled by their ramped-up silliness and running around and certain delight in watching Mammie perform such a funny prank on Pappje . . .

It never seemed to make much difference . . . Either in the quality of his hearing or in preventing his unwanted naps . . . But he was compliant in the process, mostly because there was nothing disagreeable about having his lovely young wife caress his head and administer soothing, if somewhat viscous, care . . . There were worse places he could be, he knew . . . He only had to look at young Wynkyn and see that, the places he'd been . . . Or look at himself and know where he'd be now . . . in some inn, at best, alone in a rented room, maybe in a workhouse for used-up herringmen, if he hadn't found himself here, with this agreeable girl and this agreeable family, with warm lamplight and just enough oil to light them . . .

These days, for Wyn [or nights, mostly], there was always a song [or chant or clang, whirring away] in his head.

In the jungle [even in the relative safety of the fort, but especially in a rotten canvas bivouac shelter] when the shoeless music started up [the bamboo flute and melodic, diphthonging drums of the Toba Batak] it made you want to get up and start swinging the klewangs, expanding the clearing, slashing. [Any paltry stick of flora that could provide cover for those sneaky bastards seemed to be mocking them. It got to where Wyn could feel even a strangler fig, scrawny as a rope, was taunting him.]

He'd shared a shelter with another korporaal from Assen named de Groot [who had the runs one night and made several trips to the trench latrine, later and later, until he just didn't return]. They found him about a week later, while out on patrol [nailed to a rubber tree with bamboo splints].

The visits to the pipe dens began soon after, whenever Wyn got liberty. In the larger cities out there it was hard not to recognize the neighborhoods built on the poppy, though it was said the sultan disapproved. [Even in the sticks, Wyn could scrounge up at least the weedier smoke, madak.] The rebels they fought, in denunciations to their Mahomedan followers, claimed to abhor it too. But the truth was they were all [on every side] profiting from the trade on every level and in every way.

To stand there in the dark [wishing for more moon] in the throes of that jangly jungle chime, with a sweat bead chilling your neck [and tell yourself it was only your own sweat there, not the first bite of the blade of a rentjong, rebels sliding from the leafy shadows], that was a feat all its own [never mind not escaping to the pipe dens, never mind ever closing your eyes easily at night ever again].

He wanted to get so far away from there that home, eight thousand nautical miles away, began to seem not even far enough. *Back home*, he figured [and then *keep going, keep going*...]. And the chant in his head helped drown out [*some* of] the clang of the Toba Batak.

Though he wasn't ready to contend that the moon was serenading them, Ned Nodder was willing to go along with the notion that he was possibly hearing a faint recital of *strings* ... maybe *fiddling* ... though in that, too, he could accept the counterargument ... which no one had yet raised, of course ... that it was perhaps only the power of suggestion, looking out at the moon target looming full speed ahead ... and thinking, as always, of his young wife's perfect pale face and that *hi-diddle-diddle, cat and the fiddle* she read the babies at night ... Perhaps it was only that, conspiring to make music of these thoughts, combining with the moonshine ...

But there were ghosts out here, of course. As much as he'd longed to return ... as a man, as a working herringman ... to the North Sea at the close of day ... these waters were, of course, steeped in ghosts ... not just the poor souls who met their physical demise out here, swallowed up by this narrow, rough sea ... but also just haunted by the spirits of the men who'd lost hope out here, men like his own brothers, even the one who still lived ... yet their spirits could still be buffeted about in the wind and the shimmering, couldn't they . . . raising a moan that might well pass itself off as some kind of moon music . . . a lunar lullaby . . . ?

Back in the winter months, when Luuk stole over to the shed where they worked on the strange boat, he usually told his mother he was heading to a violin lesson—even though he'd in fact put down the fiddle, deciding—or doing whatever amounted, for him, to coming close to an actual decision, which is about all he could seem to muster these days—to concentrate instead on the accordion. He wasn't sure his mother was buying the ruse, or if she'd simply decided to allow him more lead to make more decisions—or did she more accurately see them as more mistakes?—now that he was nearly a man.

The origin of this strange "picarooner," as he understood it, may have been partly Spanish, and the idea of the Spaniards made him consider, for a moment, the guitar—perhaps he needed to try that as a way to present his songs. Only where would he get one—and shouldn't he stick to the ways of his people?

When he could help out on the boatbuilding, he was extra cautious around the tools, not wanting to get a bad sliver or cut on his hands. Planing with the draw shave—for a moment—made him wonder if perhaps he should chuck all of this—the music, the songs, the fishing—and design and build musical instruments.

But—that wouldn't do. He only knew a handful of musicians in the Scheveningen Beach community—there were certainly more in town—in the downtown city center of The Hague—but he needed to concentrate on the thing that was most likely to win over his Imke—his talent as a troubadour.

And besides—the songs were what he truly loved doing. He had to remind himself of this, but he honestly believed, even if Imke had never walked into his heart—and into his head and his dreams—both waking and sleeping—he'd probably still want to pursue the songwriting anyway.

And now—in the boat—there was a song out there. Maybe.

He was keen to prick up his ears whenever he heard a tune unfamiliar to him. It was one of the few things he managed to be able to concentrate on. And so he listened hard, holding out his hands to gesture to the other two to stop what they were doing—cease the creak of the oar sculling in the stern—halt the chatter and the rearrangement of the nets in the well. But holding still, not hauling, did nothing to make the tune more clear. It felt more distant now, in fact—a realization that came with a smattering of relief—he'd imagined the mist clearing and the high hull of a massive haringbuis heaving to, unavoidable as a pirate ship, and then they'd bang into the buss, angering the no doubt nearly homicidal crew—half of them stir-crazy, half of them jail sweepings and ruckus-mongers, bullyboys—who would then bombard them with pisspots and casks and rotting offal from their last catch and anything else they could scrounge to injure and capsize their tiny, ridiculous boat. Luuk knew there were all manner of permits and jurisdictions and maritime law governing these overfished waters—rules he neither understood nor hoped to ever know well—but he suspected there was even more danger in those territorial-minded herringmen who didn't concern themselves with the prosecutorial processes at all, but would simply take matters into their own slimy, brutish, scale-covered hands.

The tune—it wasn't coming from straight out, toward the herring shoals. If you asked him, it was coming from higher up—maybe even the direction of the moon.

Wyn didn't want to laugh at the boy [not directly *at* him], so he gave him a wink when Luuk announced that he thought the singing was coming from above.

"Maybe an airship?" Luuk suggested. "A hot-air balloon? Have you ever been in an airship, in all your travels, Wynk?"

"*Probably* not," Wyn said, even though he very well might have. "Least not one outfitted with a choir . . ."

Yet . . . had he?

The boy called though cupped hands, standing now by the mast for support. "Hoi! Hoi! Someone out there? Hallo!"

Privately, Wyn was relieved when the moon failed to respond. [To change the subject] Wyn asked their young friend how his songwriting was coming, and the kid seemed, for a few minutes at least, to forget about the humming or whatever it was. He told him of the notebooks he'd filled [that he now had at least three dozen "good ones"]; he'd secured another venue that was willing to give him a showcase. The distraction worked: Luuk not only seemed to have abandoned his focus on the disembodied singing, he hadn't yet acknowledged that the picarooner had now started rocking [as if they were back ashore, on the wet tidal banks, leaning on the keel, battered rhythmically by the surf]. It was no small thing to put out of your mind the fact that the seaworthiness of *De Klomp* had not yet been tested and this rocking could capsize the thing. [Or if you accepted that they were somehow now up in the air, that they could, if the rocking continued much more, plummet to their horrible deaths.]

Wyn could make it out a little better now. It sounded a bit like that lullaby his old flame used to sing to him to loll him to sleep the few times they'd had the luxury of privacy. He didn't know the words [or if he'd once known them, he'd long since lost them back in the jungle], but the lilting melody was hers—designed for calming babies, coopted by her, in the afterglow of love, sung to a raging adventure-seeker with more nerve than brains [god help him back then, with only two dozen seasons to his foolish existence], to hold him fast in a moment of peace.

She'd sung it softly, too, the few nights they'd been allowed to bundle [when he'd pretended the knots her parents tied around him were more than symbolic and could actually restrain him throughout the night, lying right alongside her, unmarried, sharing one breath]. She'd sung it then to fool her folks that they were done with their whispering bedtime chat and were about to really fall asleep.

It was a secret Ned kept pretty well . . . one no one would suspect, he was sure . . . but for many years he had been an avid reader . . . That is . . . was how he put it to his love . . . avid for a wood-headed fisherman . . . Certainly much more learned than his brothers or really anyone he pulled nets alongside . . . Other than Wynkyn, granted, being the son of a university professor.

Back then, he'd managed, outlandish as it now seemed, to work his small farm, and fish for herring, and waste a few beeswax tapers a week over a book before bed. It had been one of the indulgences of his prolonged bachelorhood . . . not having a family had really freed up his leisure time. But now that he had four loved ones at home, he never read at all.

He'd read Homer . . . and *The Argonautica* even, years ago, and thought now of the Sirens, calling out to foolhardy sailors in uncharted waters, tempting them to their doom. He thought of boat-bustingly bad decision-making; Odysseus' crew stuffing beeswax in their ears . . . They did have radishes and rhubarb on board tonight . . . not great as earplugs, he imagined . . .

He'd even read some works on astronomy . . . though his understanding of all that was a joke compared to the knowledge Wynkyn's vader had on the subject . . . He'd known the names of a lot of the stars, at one point . . . in his youth . . . and wished now he could recall a few. It might settle the kid down, hearing some Greek and Latin applied to the confusing heavens.

But that information was gone now, and he also didn't recall there being any that were known to sing or cry . . . So there was maybe only so much you could learn in a book, he guessed . . .

His scientist vader would certainly scoff at all this, Wyn knew, but hadn't his English friend scoffed at science once in a way that made Wyn crow with laughter [and soil himself further, confined as he was back then, in that dark ship's hold, oozing with the miserable gastric sputter of withdrawal]? And the idea of a song of Sirens came to him too, mixed in [like a fragrant stamppot] with tell of a strange but beautiful cry carrying out across the night [signaling that some local fishwife was in the sweet throes of connubial attendance; that her husband was not out in his boat that night].

He had a foggy memory of attempting to lay out the particulars of the native dress of his people for English Van as they were coming through the Suez Canal, trying to get home. Van had then told him [in even further detail] about a rather dour-looking fishwife in his town of Clovelly named Whistling Annie: "She barks and grunts at *everyone*, Whistling Annie does, *but*—! On Saturday nights, for about five minutes only, with the assistance, it's generally assumed, of her saintly husband, Len, she lets out the most beautiful sound ever heard by human ear bones—the heraldry of angels, this sound, I'm telling you, Vinny-boy! Our man the priest, he weeps! Weeps! It's a goddamn scientific phenomenon, is what it is."

"One of the inexplicables of nature . . ."Wyn agreed.

"Ha!" said English Van. "Damn the nature, sir! And damn the science, for that matter. It's the magic of the night does this, my friend! The miraculous and inexplicable!"

This had wound its way into being one of those one-sided conversations he found himself engaged in with the Engelsman [one in which they surely weren't arguing, if you examined it closely, but it rather sounded as if they were]. They were both coming down hard, cranky and crapping themselves, in between the wincing cramps.

"I'm telling you, Dutchman! You think you know all, don't you? We all do—how the earth turns, how the moon beams, how it cajoles the tides . . . You think you waded through that green hell back there, the land where the bong tree grows, your Grong-Grong, your Toba Batok, as you say, hacking away at the undergrowth until you made it through, you survived, and you knew even *half* of what you were hacking at? Don't believe it. Not for a minute, Winky-Wink. You don't know what goes on, me handsome. None of us do."

He remembered all this drivel about their respective home towns, all this time later, because of the way English Van howled, especially at Wyn's description of the standard gold-flaked hairpins that held the local fishwives' drooping bonnets in place [inserted from above, overlapping just a bit of the hem of the white embroidered cap, catching the small expanse of exposed hairline, then jabbing straight down over the brow, the poky ends awfully sharp and awfully close to the eyes, just below]. It was the traditional Scheveningen "village costume" for women.

"I'm imagining knobs on their heads. Like two little doorknobs? Pulls on a cabinet?"

English Van was not far off. They'd always looked to him like a caterpillar emerging from its gauzy cocoon. Two tent caterpillars, maybe a set of perky nipples . . . [only ones that could poke your eyes out].

Van was cackling now. "And the business ends of the pins are jabbing straight down in front . . . ?!"

"So that I . . ." Wyn began. "Well, boys in general . . . They know better than to lean in and try to steal a kiss, see? Too easy to lose an eye."

"Is that on purpose? That's the thinking behind the design?"

Wyn acknowledged that [as far as he knew] there was very little thinking behind it. It was like most things in life, he was finding, as he moved farther into his, now close to three decades into it, about halfway there: there wasn't a lot of rhyme or reason to a lot of it [so you had to pace yourself in terms of looking flabbergasted].

Luuk worked in his song notebook in a lot of places—all around Scheveningen, but lately—roughly since Imke Holt took a job—one of her many, it seemed—at De Haringkoning, he did a lot of scribbling on his verses there. The place had been there since sand, it seemed—and was the perfect setting, as well, to instill in his songs authenticity, having served the saltier locals probably back before most of the chanties he'd first learned were even written. Now the great-great-grandchildren of those early patrons were the wrinkled sea dogs that claimed their positions of honor near the picture of mad King Willy and their favorite spittoon.

The only real change was the hiring of female serving staff—a modernization they counterbalanced with the required uniform—the traditional Scheveningen fishwife costume, with bonnet and gold hairpins.

He liked her in the costume—felt it made her seem like someone attainable—someone who would be out in your kitchen, throwing together a meal of stamppot. And—best of all—it showed off the nape of her neck. He opened his notebook now and scribbled in it:

seabirds overheard
plummet to the ocean
distracted by the nape of your neck

He crossed this out and attempted instead to construct a line about the nape of her neck being like the secret coded message between lovestruck swans—or maybe it would work better the other way round—first set up a verse about lovestruck swans trying to silently communicate, and *then* compare that image to the nape of her neck—?

This got scribbled out too—with even harder lines. It seemed too complicated—too heavy-handed for a lyric you could actually sing. He re-wrote the seabird thing instead.

Ned Nodder heard the song now. It was pretty much the same lullaby his wife sang to their wee ones, charming them into surrender . . . and it *was* probably being sung by the moon.

Sure. Why not?

As They Rocked in the Wooden Shoe:

It was English Van who first made that "wooden shoe" crack. They'd been three days in a pipe den in Rangoon when he'd finally asked him where he was from.

The Netherlands didn't cut it.

"Well, I know *that*, mate, don't I? On account of you seem to have been entrenched down in the Aceh Sultanate with the KNIL, battling the bloody heathen menace. There is a look of that that is like no other, and you, my friend, have that upon you . . . even with the fisherman disguise, even if you hadn't said . . . But *where*, in that mess of dikes and windmills, do you call whatever it is you folks call 'home'? My guess on that, by the way, before you weigh in, is *der haus* or *höom* or *bunkershak*—something along those lines."

The image of the great merchants and bankers and serious-minded men [*grimacers,* he thought of them, much like his father and their kind over at the university] kept Wyn from saying The Hague [or even the general Wassenaar region]. He named the beach area, Scheveningen.

"You don't fish for herring, do you?"

He said he did, though the fact was he'd only done it two seasons.

English Van cackled [the first he'd uttered such a sound in the three sleepy days they'd spent in close contact]. "You crew on those ridiculous great knobby ships, don't you, that look like a wooden shoe?"

[Wyn wasn't sure if he meant the bomschuiten.]

"Our own native herring boat is—ironically—" Van said, "merely the *size* of a shoe, in comparison. But your boats look like those Dutch clogs, right?"

The bomschuiten did have a fairly klomp-like look to them. [Flatbottomed and broad across the beam, both fore and aft, but blunt and bulky in that way of the houten schoen.] He supposed the man could mean a haringbuis [though he'd always equated those huge bastards more with the Chinese junk in terms of their lines]. He'd worked a season on both. [A bomschuit and a haringbuis, of course, not a Chinese junk—although, as of late, given the type of establishment where he'd gotten to know this sassy Engelsman, a Chinese junk *could* make a little sense, too.]

But English Van had moved onto footwear. "It's not enough you people have to squeeze every man, woman, and child into those damn wooden shoes, you have to sail in them too!"

"Do you think *I* wear them?"

"I certainly hope not, mate! It's like donning firewood, isn't it?"

"They're practical," Wyn admitted.

Van gaped.

"The bomschuit, I mean. And the haringbuis."

"So you may think," the Englishman said, taking a moment to steady himself. They were out in the sunlight now, stumbling onto a wharf, peering out at the Indian Ocean. Van leaned back against a piling so he could gesture and remain upright. "But let me describe what we have back home in Clovelly . . ."

Admiring the sound of the picarooner—the sleek ease of it—and the notion of a herring boat that could be handled by two or three men alone, Wyn said, "Nou breekt m'n klomp!"

Van wouldn't let the comment pass, and Wyn managed to translate it for him as *That breaks the wooden shoe!* [explaining it was what you said about something you've never seen before].

The Engelsman said it was ridiculous, and that they'd say, back home, *That takes the cake.* Wyn just stared at him, not sure if he believed this [mentally factoring in the three days in the pipe den]. Eventually they agreed both idioms were equally absurd.

Van described then [and often, on their journey home] the cobblestones and the Red Lion tavern, right down on the harbor floor, and mentioned, more than once, that the author of the swashbuckler adventure book *West-*

ward Ho!, somebody Kingsley, had grown up in the little village churchyard. "*That* story sent a lot of fools like ourselves running off to the nearest ship, I'm sure."

Wyn said he hadn't read it [though he wasn't sure he hadn't].

It was around then that he asked the Engelsman what he was doing in Burma.

"Oh," said English Van. "Did I not mention, then, this other thing about my village back home, Clovelly? It's a steep, pitched, wee town, Clovelly, built right into the cliffs of the cove, and it's lovely, it is, but also nearly *overrun* with donkeys, in my opinion—donkeys to haul the catch up to the village, you see—and so having grown up there, I came to feel there just might be other places out in the world that did not offer quite the surplus of donkeys."

Wyn thought of this often these days, when he found himself thoroughly invested in this project with Nodd and Blenkin [building the picarooner, planning and scheming, and he'd catch himself enjoying it in the moment] and wonder why he planned to keep wandering, to ship off for the States, and he'd tell himself, *So as not to remain among quite so many donkeys.*

By March, Ned could see they were getting close . . . down to the tarring and sealing with pitch and fine-tuning the mast and rigging . . . When they got to picking out a topcoat of paint, the subject of christening her arose. Ned thought of naming her for his wife . . . but it seemed a bit crass since the other two had worked so hard on it, they were essentially partners, and they were bachelors . . . He imagined being in their shoes. Wyn in particular, of course, must certainly be harboring a bitterness . . . Ned didn't want to steer into the very waters . . . their rocky past and that whole barrel of fish . . . which they had both so far managed to avoid . . .

When it came down to it, he didn't want to rub either of the lads' noses in his marital good fortune, so insisted Wyn and the Blenkin boy decide. He would go along with whatever they thought was right.

The boy sat down to puzzle it out. He seemed to do that frequently . . .

to sit down and cogitate over all his options on the subject, as if the act of standing sapped him of energy he could otherwise be using to fire his brain. Luuk's brow furrowed as if he needed a tincture at the apothecary. "Let's see . . ." he said. "Your English friend, he said the term *picarooner* comes from *pirate* or *rogue* or something . . . I like something like that—bold and dramatic and kind of worldly and scoundrelly. *Pirate . . . Rogue . . . The Midnight Pirate . . .*"

"He also mocked our shipbuilding," Wynkyn said. "Said our boats look like wooden shoes. How about we name her *De Klomp?*"

Ned didn't quite get it. This little boat didn't look so much like a klomp, or houten schoen, the sort of wooden clog he and the wife still used in the fields out back . . . But that was young Wynkyn's way . . . to have his private little japes and hide his meaning and generally tickle himself without filling anyone else in . . . Ned was all right with that . . . particularly when it came to things the poor fellow had seen while serving in that brutal jungle. Besides, the men of Scheveningen Beach were apt to guffaw and point at their strangely sleek little boat, regardless if they named it for his darling wife, or named it *De Sterre* . . . Or named it after traditional Dutch footwear.

Luuk Blenkin didn't own a pair of klompen—or houten schoen—the bumpkin clogs of country people. Not even growing up—as a cutesy toddler's getup. Or, rather, he *assumed* he didn't—it was hard to know what he had from that time—he and his mammie had not been able to bring many belongings when they'd moved in with his uncle—who in turn had also moved into a smaller home—the narrow townhouse Uncle Allard once bitterly referred to as the House of Diminished Circumstances—shooting slit eyes Luuk's way, as if it were all his fault. Luuk had insisted on bringing his musical instruments, of course. So there wasn't any trunk of childhood clothes, with or without klompen.

Not that he wanted to put on the clunky clogs and parade around like a fool. The Blenkins just weren't wooden shoe people—or they hadn't been, at least. They well might be now.

The Celestials had klompen they put out as decoration [or a demonstration model, really] to hand a big hint to the thickheaded ang mo, the initiates, that they were to remove their shoes before being escorted downstairs. [Placed on a little Oriental rug, once you'd entered the part that was mostly a front—when you got the nod and stepped back past the counter, granted entry by the bowing lăo băn.]

There were already a couple pipe dens in The Hague, in those streets where you could start to see faces that weren't typically Dutch. [The interesting smells of the more exotic places were down those streets, as well.]

The two he went to were run by Celestials, of course—one downstairs from a noodle shop and one downstairs from a laundry. [He wasn't entirely convinced they weren't part of the same large, smoky den: a dreamy octopus growing nightly under The Hague.] He probably went to the one below the laundry a little more than the one below the restaurant, thinking he was less likely to see familiar faces at the laundry. The folks with families he knew, especially out at Scheveningen Beach, would be too proud to have some Celestial doing their laundry. [Trying Chinese food was more likely.]

Wyn had been there many times before he even knew what to call the place.

The lăo băn slipped out from behind the counter [wound up about something], heading him off, stopping him with a palm to his chest. Forceful enough, but balanced immediately by a withdrawing bow. "Excuseer mij, sailor. I ask you favor?"

It wasn't the first time the proprietor here had greeted him [or even addressed him as "sailor," though Wyn had no idea how this Celestial laundryman could tell he'd served in the navy]. He wasn't even *most recently* a sailor—that was way back, before even the stint in Sumatra. Maybe the proprietor called everyone that [but Wyn kind of felt he didn't, that he knew something about him, somehow]. Maybe he just looked worldly; well-traveled. They probably saw a lot of trade with others who'd been east.

Wyn started to explain that he wasn't there for the laundry, that he was heading downstairs. [Though he thought that seemed pretty obvious. Especially since he'd been there several times.]

"I ask you now, please. *Before*, please. Your head no good when leave, sailor."

The man had *that* right—his head definitely no good when leave.

The láo bán pulled him by the sleeve, back to the door, and pointed at the sign in red Chinese characters that read:

非
常
忙
碌
的
洗
衣
店

"Dūchá come, they say sign no good. We need *your* word sign also. Two sign!" [Seemingly from his silk sleeves] he produced a small slate board and nub of chalk and thrust it at Wyn. "You make how? Show how?"

[Wyn tried his best:] "The inspector's been here, you need a sign in Dutch, too, and you want to know how to write it out?"

[Nodding from the head man.] "You make sign—make your word for sign?"

"What's your name? Can you sound it out?"

"No make my name. Make name we call laundry."

"The name of the laundry. Right. What do you call it?"

He pointed to the Chinese sign. "We call Very Busy Laundry."

[Wyn was delighted.] "*That's* what that says there? The Very Busy Laundry?"

The man nodded again, and Wyn started to write it down as the Celestial began herding him back over to the counter, offering him a little bamboo brush, tipped with ink, and a scroll of linen paper. "You make good one on paper also maybe?"

"I'm no artist," he said, shaking him off. "My hand doesn't always . . . I'll just stick with this, ja?"

Wyn wrote out very carefully in chalk: De Zeer Actieve Wasserij.

He was just handing the lăo băn back his chalk and slate when he caught sight of Imke Holt outside, walking past. [Heading where, though? The *immediate* direction was the Celestial restaurant, but that couldn't be her destination: a bowl of noodles.] The lăo băn, bowing, already had the passthrough counter raised so Wyn could step down to the den downstairs, so he could escape and sleep.

But Imke Holt was right out there—the back of her now [the long nape of her neck, to be precise: she was wearing that traditional onzin getup with her hair up in the bonnet. Probably heading off to that job as a serving girl at The Herring King. Why else would she wear that costume with the dumb gold knobs? She wore it because she was so driven and *busy—very busy*, to borrow a term from the lăo bán waiting to take him downstairs], and something about the sight of her [and her exposed nape with the wisp of one lock trailing down] as she moved with a stride through the street [maybe because she was so industrious, was that it? was that what gave him pause here: some personal shame?] made him [stupidly, he knew; stupidly] change his mind.

And so [ignoring everything that would plague him later: his gut, his head, his bowels] he said, "Not today, I guess," and found himself starting for the front door.

"Today for you on house! One time!"

Wyn hesitated. "Really? Oh, but— Can I maybe—?"

The Celestial was waving him over [encouragingly, like a man calling his dog in from the dooryard]. "No problem! You good! On house! One time!"

Wyn nodded, trying to seem appreciative. "Next time! How about that?"

"No next time! On house *one* time!"

The bell jangled as Wyn yanked open the door and slipped outside. It was bright out, cold, and [the second he was out there, the rush of air scolding his lungs, bringing on thoughts of the bundled older sister, Cokkie, standing there at the end of the strandweg, disapproving] he lost his resolve and flattened himself [like a foreign agent, like the informants that lurked about in the streets of Rangoon and Kutaradja] against the doorway. And if she caught him here, what would she tell her beau, young Luuk, if [despite his seeming woodenheadedness] he had some notion of what went on down below? [They needed Blenkin for the boat, true, but Wyn also simply found undesirable the idea of being demoted in the young oaf's personal estimation.]

He wouldn't step back inside [not today], but he cocked his collar and tilted his head down and waited for Imke Holt to safely pass.

[After he was sure she was gone] he stepped off the stoop and into the street, heading in the other direction, but he didn't feel good about his decision. He thought he'd feel proud of himself [honorable at least or maybe just *fresh*, in some way; *possible*, if that was a thing: he'd feel *possible*], but he just felt low [lost, confused].

Somehow, his head still no good when leave.

AND THE WIND
THAT SPED THEM
ALL NIGHT LONG

Scheveningen Beach *was* wind, to Ned . . . it should've been named Wind Beach, in his mind . . . and as much as he loved it and knew it and had earned a living and life from it for many years, he never stepped out into the howling vastness without a small appreciation that his little home, with his little family, was not right on the beach, but back inland and a little north, past the marshy runs and canals, out where the land could be worked . . . out where his loved ones had some peace from the wind.

One thing that pushed Wyn van Winkel through the night in recent months was the welcome and shelter of some the beach communities . . .

Of Wyn's various bunk spots, one was *too* quiet [or at least devoid of human racket]—one of the tall, tippy-looking netting sheds ranged up among the dunes. A friend, Tad Visser, let him know that he never kept it locked. The wind shook the whole shack, rattling the shutters. And he'd have to stir and go out and inspect. Inside, it felt like a hurricane coming, but outside it was just the beach at night, and he'd stand in the sand-gritted breeze, peppered with bits of beach, his shirttails flapping, wide awake, reinvigorated.

He'd think about America, wondering if it blew like this there, in the heart of the country, along the Mississippi Valley.

The shed was an improvement, surely, over the shelter choices back in Sumatra. [They got a dry wind, the bohorok, along the plains in the north and of course beastly stuff along the western coast—dangerous cyclones, brubru, tidal waves . . . even the island's own eponymous killer squall during the monsoon, the sumatra.] This was nothing, in comparison. [He could sleep through this. He could—by rights, he ought to be able to.]

The winds came up like this that day he helped his pal Cent rush down to Scheveningen Beach to paint the storm. The winds were like this, as well, when he'd been with his old love, sneaking into the dunes and marram grass, lying with her [his girl smiling through the thrash of her corn-tassel hair, bewildering, lying on top of him, looking down at him, the full moon haloing her as she lay on him, all teeth and hair and laughter].

But both of these things were back in those days when recklessness was beauty.

Luuk liked it when the wind blew full and hard like this—particularly on land. When he was heading somewhere, to do something. Lately, his days felt like a string of intentions and errands, all geared toward his goals of building a name as a troubadour—of winning over Imke Holt—of improving his musicianship, taking actual lessons with the Polish lady on Westeinde Street—all of it, all at once—wanting all things, all now, often confusing himself even, just trying to keep track of it—!

So at the times the wind would hit him full force in the back, pushing him forward, there was nothing—no excuse—allowing him to lag and dawdle—just to sneak a break in on himself, a pause in his striving, striving—and manage to get a goose-egg for his daily effort, like Jack and the beanstalk in that fairy tale, taking his cow to market and coming home with only beans.

But when the wind shifted, when it faced him—he had a secret vice. He would hold out his jacket lapels and let the wind cup him like a sail—slow himself down on his strident course—just to be for a few minutes a young boy living seaside, planless but for joy.

The North Sea loved to blow here [really tear loose and liven things up], and so Scheveningen Beach had always been the place for wind. Back in '82 [was it?] when Wyn and Cent [from Groot-Zundert or maybe it was Etten] briefly shared a terrible little room down a seedy side street in the city proper [the year Wyn was in love and having his authentic herring-fisherman adventure with the Nodder brothers on *De Groot Ster*] Cent had been raving [as he did, often, about this and that] about wanting to capture a great sea storm. Wyn was out most nights with Smilin' Ned and the bom [not to mention a few other nights, when he'd managed to sneak off with his girl], and so the times with Cent back at "the bunk" at Schenkweg 136 were more and more rare through that summer [and enlivened by absinthe and arguments and other amusements], and so Wyn considered it good fun to volunteer to be Cent's guide. He would take him, he said, to just the place. "Follow!" Wyn commanded, grabbing up his friend's shabby supplies.

The cobbled streets of The Hague were already churning with litter and sand before they even neared the beach.

Beyond the last building, the wind hit them with a wallop [the swing of a plank, a paddle], and they laughed. Stepping off the board section of the strandweg, they could feel it engulfing their shirts, threatening to lift them off their feet. "Oh ho!" Cent shouted, and they marched straight for the surf. The sky had turned green [as if it had decided to get a jump on evening or compete with the sea]. It was only the end of August, but that sky looked [and felt] like November.

Cent made a quick assessment [his red hair piratical] and pointed to a spot, whereupon Wyn stabbed the easel home and the painter began, nearly mad with it. When the wind roused heavy, Wyn grabbed the easel and held it still, their jackets flapping and grousing with the effort. Cent worked fast, glopping it on, squeezing the titanium straight from the tube to tip the whitecaps [getting sand in it and not caring].

The whole time, they both shook with laughter.

Sometimes [even now, after returning from the jungle, so many years after carousing with the young painter] Wyn would pass the Goupil & Cie art gallery in The Hague and consider going in and asking after his friend Cent. The crazy bastard had mentioned once or twice that he'd worked there [for his uncle] years before Wyn knew him. He thought how he could be there now, well-dressed and perfectly sane [a respected merchant, perhaps supporting a wife and brood, tithing at church]. Or even returned to the clergy [work he claimed to have done, before Wyn's time, in some mining village in Belgium].

All that could be so. [Still, something made him not go in and find out.]

This wind made Ned chuckle with the joke of it: with so many years working the sea, the flap of laundry on the line, on shore, reminded him of the work, of being at sail . . . But now, the sound had been *reversed* in his mind, and it went the other way: the luff of sailcloth now only made him think of the long laundry lines at home . . . the endless linen for the five of them, his love harnessing the wind, the sheets billowing like the great mizzen of the old *Groot Ster*, bulging like his long-stowed, rat-gnawed herring nets . . . providing for their household in this way. His Fenna toiling in their dooryard had long become the more familiar sound of the Lord's simplest bounty being reaped.

Things were different now, that was for sure, when they could twist the meaning of sound . . . When the flap of cloth meant one thing for so many years . . . what was there to do about such a strange change? Nothing, he supposed . . . just go with it, just ride along . . .

When Luuk took his accordion lesson, he had to really concentrate on the bellows work—what she called "the breathing." His teacher, Mevr. Przejrzystość, chastised him—said he made them heave and puff like an asthmatic basset that required putting down—said he grunted and pulled like a butcher stuffing sausage casings—said his breathing form did nothing to ease and hide the hiss and exhalation—that the bellows sounded like a creepy peeper breathing heavy outside the window of a premature widow. His teacher said he wasn't paying attention. Of course he wasn't. It was only that the air pressing through the bellows reminded him of the wind on the beach at Scheveningen, filling the canvas—and of course it would, because he needed the coming fishing work to pay off, to continue with *this*—his music lessons, and presenting his songs—and he needed all *these* things, in turn, to win the heart of his love. And of course *she* made him think of the beach as well—of standing down near the surf, watching her up on the walk, heading toward work at the café, with one hand holding down her apron, the other attending to her white cap, her skirts forming around her petticoat—and the wind bringing back to him her whispered impatience with it—to his delight, she swore—and he found her more wonderful for it.

He wrote in his notebook:

the wind colluding with her skirts
to make the imagination soar—

It was rather kind of some of the barkeeps and merchants along the beach to give Wyn shelter on the colder nights [offering to let him bunk in their cellars and backrooms], and he accepted, but it wasn't practical, really, since he tended to only sleep in the day [if *at all*, since Aceh]. He didn't share this fact with them, and some, like Dirty Ned [an entirely different Ned from Ned Nodder—Agreeable Ned, Smilin' Ned], would slide him the key to his café and tell him he could stretch out in the stockroom after they closed. Wyn would take it and thank him, but he couldn't really start to curl up on the coffee bean sacks and give it a try till nearly dawn, which only allowed him a couple hours sleep before the clang of the front door and the scrape of stools on the floor [Dirty Ned and his staff opening up]. He'd wander out, looking lazy-lidded [a bum], prompting some klootzak to misconstrue and make cracks about how much he slept, that he seemed to always be "sleeping in," and telling him to rise and shine, slug-a-bed. He decided to let them all just think he was lazy, call him sleepybones [not wanting to have to explain that the Acehnese tended to attack at night].

Which was why he preferred sleeping outdoors [when he could, once the winter had passed]. And *both* of those options [stockrooms and the elements] were far superior to the one that involved the saucy Hungarian widow of a carriage-manufacturing tycoon.

[Come to think of it] all the options had their downsides, which is maybe why he rarely slept these days. [And certainly not these nights.]

Of course, the upside to Gert and her "nine-o'clocks" [he told himself] was that it was an efficient exchange she sped them through [never the dreamy languor of all-night-long relations].

And she *was* punctual. [And direct with what she wished. Both admirable traits.]

Another downside: she smelled of roast beets because she ate one every night [unfortunately, it seemed, *moments* before the clock struck nine].

On low nights [after] he was left feeling about as respectable as a nightpiece, fished from a tavern. On better nights, he simply worried about the state of his britches.

Luuk's Uncle Allard—the big blowhard—was forever puffing away, harping on him about how he didn't know what the world was really like and one day his eyes would open wide and he'd get the shock of his puny little life and *then* he'd know, all right—and Luuk wondered now—as they were seemingly flying through the actual heavens, airborne, defying the laws of Newton, jouncing in the spray and wind—if *this* was what his uncle had been going on about all this time—if this was what the world was really like.

Ruffled
THE
Waves of Dew:

☾

None of this would be happening if not for his friend. But leaning on Wynkyn wasn't new to Ned . . . Wynkyn had carried him in his arms. So long ago, it seemed like now . . . one of the last seasons they had *De Groot Ster* . . . The young man was the greatest anchorman and carrier the Nodder brothers had ever known . . . He'd mastered, in only one summer, the strange procedure: once the bomschuit was successfully dragged to the water's edge . . . with cables and winches and teams of draft horses . . . the ablest half-swam, half-walked out into the waves with a big anchor cradled in his arms and dropped it, out the length of a recumbent man. A second, smaller anchor was then lugged to the surf's edge to keep the big anchor from "crabbing". . . meaning inching out, slipping off the coastal shelf, pulling the whole mess into the deep . . . Another cable then ran to an even smaller anchor, placed back on solid sand. Finally, the anchorman fished out the big anchor and again marched it out, even farther, where the waves battered his sinking face, until he had to let go. If he wasn't drowned, he would swim back to the beach and, one by one, carry each of the hands to the stern . . . certainly the funnest part for Wynkyn, in that he made his little jokes as he hauled them to the ladder, unruffled by it all. But when he was gone, that job had fallen to Ned, of course, because even though he was never the youngest or strongest, he was, he knew, seen as Agreeable Ned . . . *Let-Ned-Do-It*—that should've been his nickname, as well . . .

The task never seemed to come without at least one moment of slipping, choking in a wave, certain to die. It was just part of the job. Ned learned to keep a change of clothes on board, so as not to catch his death of cold, sailing out into the gales abruptly, already soaked . . . His wet clothes, once he managed to climb aboard, had to be skinned off him . . . often with the help of his delighted brothers . . .

If he failed to change and got too cold, a nonsensical impulse would take hold of him to curl up, like a puppy on the hearth, right in the bottom of the boat, below the wind . . . and go to sleep. Someone would slap him and get him dry and make him sit up . . . sometimes they rubbed his arms till they were red. It was said you could die falling asleep, wet and cold, like that . . . that your body was shutting down, your mind going first, making bad choices . . .

With his brothers gone, he couldn't really raise enough men to run the bom. It could be done with nine, but not well. The full dozen was needed for a good crew, a sound profit . . . And then yet another storm hit Scheveningen and destroyed several boms on the beach, scattering them halfway to Drempt, and *De Groot Ster* was one of them. Once again people said they were really going to have to build a harbor one day, come up with a new system . . . But even after the loss of his family's bomschuit, Ned saw the traditional ways of life as still manageable, if only barely—he was making do with small logging work, some carpentry, farming his small lot . . . True, his family couldn't live entirely off potatoes and radishes . . . the latter he'd even brought along as provisions on the picarooner, the cause of the occasional crunch and munch and flatulence heard tonight . . . young Luuk politely nibbling, Wynkyn grumbling but tearing through the supply . . .

True, they were wanting . . . but he didn't know any other way to face a hard wind but to smile into it.

His father often accused him of trying to "ruffle feathers" and "make waves" whenever the great professor tried to introduce him to the "stars" of the Leiden faculty. [The latter criticism Wyn found to be ridiculous, given the fact that his father had never, to his knowledge, known anything about waves; had never stepped into a wave in his life—even *without* carrying an anchor. It had always been Wyn's moeder who took him, as a young boy, to bathe at the beach.]

He made sure to attend the last salon in December, with the idea that it would be easier than going to his house for Kerstfeest [and then maybe he could get away with skipping that particular obligation].

At events like this, his father liked to place before him young men relatively close to his age who had done [by his father's measure] much better in life than he had.

One such professor appeared to be nearly infantile—moonfaced, with full suckling lips, and two little eyes [and the iconic Leiden robes did not detract from his appearance as a giant baby]. The man was a colleague of his father's in the practical sciences—he indicated that he was currently studying revolutionary views on many of the alleged foundations of thought in his field [whatever that field was]: "New thinking that questions what we *think* we know . . ." After only a brief pause, Dr. Babyman said, "In America at the moment, there is a man of perhaps Serbia or Hungary named Tesla who was, for a time, collaborating with Meneer Edison. You know who that is, I'm sure—Thomas Edison?"

"He wrote that thing for them . . ." Wyn said, straightfaced. "That Declaration thing."

"He did nothing of the sort. This is the Wizard of Menlo Park of whom I speak."

Wyn nodded grandly. "The electricity man."

"Precisely."

[Wyn was about to top all this with a crack that he often got the one mixed up with the other one—the stout stove-and-kite fellow—but he let it go, excusing himself to go investigate what was happening in terms of beverages.]

One upside to these things was the snacks. There was usually at least the crisp cinnamon speculaas, freshly baked by some unseen plump genius deep in the kitchens of the university. [They never served radishes nor rhubarb there.] And on this occasion the refreshment table was more generous than at other times of the year, and cheerier, with sparkling Advent stars wound among the fare. But hiding by the cider didn't last long. Vader swooped in and steered him toward a spectacled homunculus named Hendrik Lorentz, who was [the elder van Winkel nearly bragged] chair of theoretical physics.

"Meaning physical things that aren't there?" Wyn vaguely recalled meeting this bird at one of these tadoos, way back before he left for the East Indies. His father was getting on now and probably didn't recall this. It was hard to read this fellow: he couldn't tell if Lorentz remembered him too or if he was just being polite, avoiding the recollection that Wyn maybe suggested, back then, that the young phenom studied moonbeams. [Or maybe both Lorentz and his father were simply touched with absentmindedness, like all professors everywhere.]

"Primarily. Ether theories," Lorentz said.

"Either theories," Wyn said, "or what?" [It was a joke.]

The department chair explained it to him: "We propose there exists a medium—call it the *ether*, to borrow the Greek—the 'upper air'—that is an unseen field necessary to the transmission and propagation of electromagnetic and gravitational forces. We have just, unfortunately perhaps, faced some setbacks with the apparent refutation of the theory of 'luminiferous ether'—light-bearing ether—"

"Oh, like moonbeams?" Wyn couldn't help himself. "So they're not a thing anymore?"

Lorentz appeared to be thumbing through something in a mental filing cabinet, double-checking. "If you mean that luminiferous ether is no longer a useful concept, I would concur. Well put, sir. Though I would disagree with the assertion that it's *entirely* no longer viable . . ." He leaned in to whisper [as if he were going to pass along the name of a frisky girl he knew], "I'm thinking more now in terms of *charged particles*."

"But basically" —Wyn pointed at the ceiling— "something's going on up there."

"Indeed! All around us, in fact, but yes—something indeed is 'going on' up there."

Once Wyn managed to beat a retreat from this Hendrik character, his father swooped in again to invite him to an upcoming lecture on these charged particles. [Like the handful of his father's similar invitations Wyn had passed on, he would on this.]

"I feel you may have a lot to learn from him, son."

"About theoretical physics? Light moving through the invisible ether?" Did his father really harbor delusions that he would become an academic— at least one of that order?

"I believe he would present a sobering example for you, son. A role model, if you will. Intellectually, he and I are equals—I'd even daresay he may be my superior, though we are in different fields. But it's the two of you who are actually contemporaries."

Wyn pointed out that he and Lorentz weren't the same age. [He didn't think they were, at least.]

"He has only seven years on you, son. So to be clear, I'm not disappointed that you're not where he is *now*, no—that would be unfair—but seven years ago, at your current age, Hendrik had already been inducted in the Royal Academy and was a respected member in good standing. So . . ."

"Maybe he used some of his moonbeam trickery to science up his time-table."

"Bosh," his father said. "Bosh and fiddle-faddle. More of your slippery evasion, Wynand. You cling to that too dearly, that and your irony and ob-fuscation . . . It is a poor habit that sorely needs mending."

Another winner [this one named Christiaan Hurgronje] was dragged in front of him. Wyn wouldn't have missed this goat-faced fellow. [His ac-ademic robes were notably more Celestial-looking than those of his peers. And he wore a fez.] His father reeled off his pedigree: he was the newest addition to the Leiden faculty, their new professor of Malay [and also a bigwig advisor to the government on colonial affairs, Vader crowed].

"Christiaan here dressed up as a Mahomedan!—rather convincingly, I understand—and went on that walk they take to their 'Mecca,' as they call it."

"The Hajj."

"In fact, he has a magic lantern show he is going to present right after the salon, in a neighboring hall, of the many photographic images he pro-duced while on the Hajj."

Wyn tried to say that was wonderful. [He wasn't sure it came out.]

"He has captured their music, as well," his father said.

"A wax Edison recording I made," Professor Hurgronje said. "Of the call to prayer."

"Oh, I know it," Wyn said. "Very catchy."

This fez-topped newcomer to Leiden seemed duly fascinated that Wyn had been in Aceh [and had traveled much farther into that world than the cakewalk to Mecca, and Wyn could see on his face that he knew it].

"Did you by any chance meet the rebel prophet, Teungku Chik di Tiro?"

"Sure," Wyn said, glancing around for more refreshments. "Saturdays and every other Wednesday for lawn bowls. Hell of a cradle grip, that Chikky."

"My son is being droll," his father said. "I *believe*, at least . . ."

This expert on the Mahomedans went on next about Teungku Umar— the rebel leader who had been brought to their side [with the help of gold and opium and hashish]. This Dr. Fez admitted that military and political science weren't his fields, but wondered if a man who could be bribed to fight against his fellow believers could truly be trusted. Wyn chose not to furnish an answer to this [not really having one]. The whole subject seemed a hell of a lot simpler here [in this beautiful fortress of an institution], on a December afternoon promising snow [snug in that twinkling Advent season between Sinterklass and Kerstfeest], the full arc of meteors distant from the wet jungle heat and the flash of pedangs and klewangs. He'd had these discussions, of course [but only at low volume under the skimpy protection of a rotting canvas bivouac shelter, out on maneuvers or searching, endlessly, for the lost patrol]. So he just shrugged.

"Tell me, sir—the Aceh-mord," Hurgronje said [referring to the locals' infuriating habit of conducting suicide attacks on the Dutch]. "Did you experience this practice firsthand?"

Wyn made a show of placing his palms at various places about his torso, as if checking himself for wounds. "Well . . . I seem to *be* here, so . . ."

"I mean, of course, were you able to witness it? Do you think you could relate it to me so I could set it down in detail?" The tassel on his fez swung as he turned to explain it to Wyn's father. "It's fascinating. The Mahomedan believes so earnestly in his Allah, he will oft-times—"

Wyn interrupted to see if he knew the one about the Sultan, Mahomed, and Teungku Chik di Tiro. "I bet you've heard that one—all your research and all. The one where they're in a boat, I mean."

"I'm sorry—the what now?"

"You were saying, Christiaan?" his father said, ignoring him.

"Oh! Yes! Practicing Aceh-mord, the zealous Mahomedan will oft-times attack a garrison or magazine or powderhouse or gun battery, simply to inflict some damage on the 'infidel,' if you will—on *us*, as it were—with no hope of returning, so great is his devotion and faith that he will be rewarded in the afterlife. Often with honey and oils and various platters of figs! And virgins!"

"Speaking of platters of virgins . . ." Wyn said, excusing himself, pointing to the waiter who had just set down a fresh tray of untouched speculaas.

At most of these salons, it was hard to distinguish who had truly been the *ruffler* and who the *rufflee*.

There were English holiday biscuits among the sweets as well, crystalline with sugar, cut into the shapes of stars and moons [which only served, in Wyn's mind, to bring back the boor's pestering about acts of Aceh-mord and to trot out a little horror of a man with stricken eyes and a crescent shape at the back of his head, a man who waved to him in his dreams]. Wyn would skip the moon cookies and stick with the speculaas, the safer treats of home.

Not long ago, Luuk's mother had used the word *ruffled* to describe him, arriving home at his uncle's—returning from his lesson at Mevr. Przejrzystość's. He'd had to sneak the accordion into the front hall wardrobe, of course—so Uncle Allard wouldn't know what he'd been up to—that his mammie was "wasting" her scant allowance in support of his musical training—but it wasn't the jostling, nerve-wracking arrival that had him flustered—or *ruffled*, as she put it—as if he were some bristly, feathered thing, like the peacocks strolling the lawns of the Malieveld—but the sight of his friend van Winkel in the company of his Imke. Maybe not in her company, exactly— but talking for a moment downtown, in The Hague—in some disreputable side street where the Celestials and the pindas peddled their odd cuisine. It could have been a polite word or two—just passing in the street. It likely meant nothing. Or maybe he hadn't seen things correctly—Luuk had been concerned more than ever lately that he might need some adjustments made to his eyesight.

"Nobody's *ruffled*, Mammie," he hissed back at her, tearing off his overcoat.

THE LITTLE STARS WERE THE HERRING-FISH

Despite the jungle years being something he had to push out of his head and his dreams [despite the nonsense he often spouted about not eating pepper], there were times that nothing would do for him but a bowl of bami goreng, the egg-noodles-and-chili magical mess cooked in a tussle on those big flat pans, hot and sizzling, the way they did, and there was a shop opened now in The Hague, Bistro de Bintang Kecil [The Little Star Café, in the tongue he'd raced away from] that served East Indies cuisine. Of course he wondered if his little trips into the heart of the city were doing him harm. [Hell, he was down there more often for various noodles, it seemed, than he was for the pipe dens.] He wondered, too, what he would say if someone saw him ducking into the tiny café with the greasy window [that he'd gone native, gone over to the side of the savage infidels . . .]. Maybe he could learn to cook it himself. But he wouldn't know where to get the spices. [And he didn't have the special flat pan, the smoky wajan that looked like a coolie hat.] And of course, he didn't have a regular lodging from one night to another, and therefore, no stove.

They served the rendang and the sate here.

If the louts he knew from the beach [Zef Kloet, Harm van Donk, Sem Bongers, and Blan Zylstra—any of those] caught him at it, they'd shake their heads to see him chat and joke the way he did with the owners, Purnama and her man, the nearly toothless Hidayat. Wyn didn't care what those numbskulls thought, but even he had to wonder if it was good for him [for his sanity or his heart] to keep returning to the food of the "heathen rebels" [to smell the cooking of a race of people he'd witnessed running around on fire].

Wyn's policy with fools in general was to simply let them flap their tongues till they tired out, all while holding his own. [But it was one thing, wasn't it, to hold back your response, and another to honestly not know what your response could possibly be?]

He knew women like that: pitiful gals who let their men beat them and still stuck around [even claimed they loved the bastards]. And drunks, of course: those infamous boozers at the beach taverns who claimed to hate the jenever but returned to it every time. [And of course *he* did that same love/hate dance himself with the pipe.]

But this food—it was just plain *tasty*. Wasn't that reason enough?

Besides, these two were his friends. They'd become such the first time he tried their food [not because of the quality of it, which was high, he felt, but because of what followed]. He was about to pay his bill when a couple drunks burst in [he didn't recognize them, but knew the type before the words were out of their mouths], calling sweet Purnama a "pinda slut." [Mush-muscled blowhard college boys from Leiden, full of opinions on the war but no interest in fighting it.] Before Hidayat could appear from the kitchen, wielding the heavy cookware, Wyn was up and snatching a fierce-looking [but purely decorative] golden pedang off the wall, waving it around and clarifying, for his drunk countrymen, that he had killed better men than they. ["Some days, *before* breakfast," he said. "And I have already finished my dinner! So time's a-wasting!"] The statement was short on sense, he realized [upon reflection, after the two dashed off down the street], but the owners were grateful, insisting he would eat for free whenever he wanted. So now [not wishing to abuse their generosity] he tried to limit his visits to The Little Star Café to only a few times a month [usually when he was too starving to sanely turn down a free meal].

He was there sometime back [in January or February], in the days when their little boatbuilding crew gave over easily to the coming night [in no rush, the herring shoals still months off], and so there was only a dirty gray-blue blanket [pre-indigo] descending over the narrow streets of that part of The Hague [the shadows and surplus between, but not quite of, the neighborhoods of Kortenbos, Uilebomen, and Zuidwal] when he slipped into The Little Star to be greeted by the beaming familiar faces and a dignified little hug from Purnama. He was surprised that they didn't offer their best table [just a half-flight up the narrow stairs, where partitions lent it a sense of privacy and gezelligheid], though he would have declined the honor as usual [realizing they actually preferred he sit near the front door where he might once again leap to his feet and defend them from taunters and scoundrels].

The reason for the omission became [somewhat] clearer as he was finishing up and trying to pay Purnama for the meal, and young Imke Holt appeared [tentatively] descending the narrow steps. She stopped one tread shy of the bottom, clearly as surprised to see him as he was to see her.

"Hoi," she said.

"Hoi yourself," he said.

All her attention seemed to be focused downward into her little coin purse as she stepped forward, handing Purnama a silver half guilder with a nod and a thank you and something about it being quite wonderful. He thought the side of her mouth looked raw and flushed and her eyes a bit dewy. [But then, he really didn't know her very well. Maybe she always looked like that.]

He wondered if any of Blenkin's songs were inspired by her and if he described her in them as "dewy-eyed." [He kind of hoped not.]

There was a glimmering, like fireflies . . . sharp pricks of amber and white, floating just off the starboard side . . . But fireflies wouldn't venture out that far from shore . . . it had to be a trick of the light on the water's surface . . . Yet it seemed, as well, as if they were almost floating *above* the boat, dotting the air all around . . . Doffing his cap . . . in a moment when the others were looking away . . . Ned took a swipe at one that seemed to be swooping past, and trapped it quick between his knees . . . When he opened the cap to get a peek, it had slipped away . . . But it sure as shooting had looked like a star . . .

When he wrote his songs, Luuk Blenkin worked in metaphor a lot—but that was songs. This was fishing. This *could* be metaphor—maybe they were herring sparkling like stars—or maybe they were stars glittering like silver herring darting in the moonlit waves—? The problem was, he'd never been to sea, never fished, and so he didn't know what to compare to what. He had no solid basis for metaphor—with metaphor, you had to know *thing A* so you could compare *thing B* to it—something not possible here.

He did his best and tried to act like he knew what he was doing, working the nets. But it sure seemed like metaphor, if you asked him—

He wondered if she noticed that the Sumatrans hadn't let him pay. He hoped she didn't. [And then tried to figure out *why* he hoped that. The couple were his friends, right? Couldn't he have friends, even friends who looked like the people back in Aceh who came at him in narrow jungle paths and in his dreams, running, engulfed in flames? And couldn't friends do kindnesses for each other without the implication that the recipient of the kindness was a vagrant and a bum?]

"I applaud your taste," he said as he held the door for her [jangling the bell, which flew him overhead and back, in an instant, to the small cafés of Kutaradja, the peddler shops of Rangoon], and they stepped out into the sharp air of the clear night [the sky now nearly indigo, the twinkling begun]. "*If* you're actually here. It could be a dream I'm having. Just as likely."

"I *am* rather a dream come true, aren't I?" she said with comic arrogance.

Just then, a put-upon-looking young woman hustled toward them wearing a baby in a sling, despite the hour and the cold. The baby was a tight bundle of cloth, with only his [fat moon] face exposed. He was likely dreaming: his eyes were closed, and he was chuckling. As they passed, the sleeping baby let loose a hearty chortle [just above the huffing mutter of the woman]. Wyn turned to see Imke's reaction [and she was checking to see his reaction], and they both let out a laugh of their own, a cloud of brisk breath exploding between them.

He jerked his head toward the lighter, distant edge of the sky, to the west, where it was still resisting the coming night, over Scheveningen [the last few feet of Dutch native ground, the homeland of his countrymen], said he was heading back toward the beach and asked if he should accompany her again. ["Maybe as far as the point where your sister ambushes me with a harpoon or an eel spear?"]

"She promised me that if she ever saw you again, she would only strike you with something blunt and wooden, like a bung mallet. Nothing metal or sharp."

"Please thank her for that concession. Very kind."

Imke suggested he just escort her as far as the steam tram stop up ahead by the bank, and as they walked on, a laugh bubbled forth from the girl.

"What?" he said. "Come on. Out with it."

She admitted then that her sister [now a pickler's wife, therefore having such articles ready to hand] actually *did* carry a small bung mallet in her coat when she stepped out at night.

Wyn hooted, genuinely taken aback, and told her this was clearly a night of surprises.

Imke shrugged. "You never know, you know? You never know where you'll find yourself, you never know what goes on with people, inside . . ."

He felt he had to explain what he meant about dreaming of seeing her [not wanting to give her the wrong idea about his intentions]. "By the way, earlier—when I saw you there—I just meant I would never have pegged you for a fan of the Sumatran fare."

"My first time," she admitted, and the statement that followed sounded more ardent and earnest than anything in their other exchange along the strandweg. Almost like a confession. "I want to try *everything*. Not just there at that bistro. All the foreign dishes I can. Chinese, Russian—American corn on the cob! I know I'll never actually leave The Hague, and that's fine. I believe you've traveled rather widely—"

"You believe right," he said.

"I don't think I'd particularly care to. I'm curious about the world. And learning things. But I do take comfort in the steady routine. You probably find that silly."

[He couldn't even imagine it, much less manage to find it silly, so he said nothing.]

Then she said, "I want to sleep in a bed that's so familiar, so comfortable and unchanged over all my years, that the woodwork becomes worn—burnished and shiny . . ."

He interrupted to ask if she'd just said she planned to never change her bedsheets.

"Jackanapes," she said, giving him a sharp elbow as she continued. "I'm just going to say this and you're going to refrain from your mockery—"

"Possibly," he said.

"Please do. I want to look up at that moon through that same window and know I'm safe and where I should be, every night, every time. But . . ."

"But?" Wyn asked.

"I don't wish to be bored, either. There's no reason for that. And I don't need to gorge myself on cheeses and herring."

He told her he was trying to think of some way to mock this statement but was stumped.

"Not that I mind gorging myself," she said. "I just want to go beyond the realm of potatoes and cheese. And herring, of course. Always, always, the herring."

He wondered if young Luuk knew this about the center of his universe: that she was so gastronomically curious. Surprising for a slim lass. Her trim figure wouldn't last long with that sort of dare-seeking appetite. [He wouldn't be surprised if such a change in her would dampen his young friend's admiration.]

She smiled then, sardonic with dimples [a smile that would look just great on a plump girl].

Thinking of the dish called "herring in oats," he began to tell her about his friend English Van and the Clovelly picarooner.

"I believe I heard about some flimsy smuggler's dogger or ketch or something you and Meneer Nodder had in the works."

"From Luuk Blenkin," he said.

But she looked momentarily puzzled at his assumption, finally saying, "Oh, right—he's working with you on this too, then—the Blenkin boy?"

This was not a good sign for Luuk. [Granted, she had to be a few years his senior, but the fellow might take less issue, Wyn felt, with being called "boy" and more issue with her seeming lack of familiarity with him.] Then again, Wyn didn't know her much at all, either, other than pleasantries at the tavern, Klaas Vaak's, De Haringkoning, or even the coffee place [where she seemed to be working a few shifts now, too, he noticed, having bumped into her as he crawled out of his makeshift bean-sack bunk one or two mornings], and that half-a-walk-home from the Kurhaus [curtailed rather sternly by her sister Cokkie] when she had addressed him by his first name.

His formal first name, sure, but not as Meneer van Winkel. Wyn *was* a few years older than her, in turn. [Maybe seven—she was roughly twenty, he'd wager.] Of course, the familiarity in his own case perhaps stemmed from a lack of respect, what with his having become somewhat of a local "character."

It struck Wyn [reflecting on it later, shivering far too much to sleep, trying to bunk in Visser's unlocked net shop at the beach, the North Sea wind howling through the tall, rickety storehouse] that he hadn't exerted so much mental attention on anything in a long, long time as he did then in trying to analyze this one meaningless exchange with this curious and frank young lady. [And the realization that he was picking this moment apart to such a degree made him think he should analyze it even further. Because this was not his way. Not lately. This was not shrugging off life's buffeting insults and winking at the moon.]

"I don't know where I heard it," she said. "You hear a lot of things when you're being paid not to be noticed." He thought this was ridiculous [anyone not noticing her], but he supposed these waitresses and hotel maids did overhear things.

[Wanting to change the subject] he steered her toward an intriguing storefront [physically halting in front of the darkened flower shop that seemed to specialize in wicked-looking tropical plants], a little flummoxed that people were already gossiping about their non-code fishing boat. Curious or bored farm kids maybe, farther out, drawn to the lantern and the sawing and pounding, could have peeked into the window of Nodd's shed one evening [he supposed]. And there had been a few supplies they had to purchase, and maybe that had caused some notice in town. [Or—possibly—Old Noddie could be up to his old tricks, walking around town in his sleep, muttering away, right out loud.]

[Pressing up to the glass now] he could make out something with white orbs that might be moon orchids and another with big green leaves with pink veins that also looked familiar. Instinctively, he inhaled, and beside him she did, too.

The fragrance couldn't be coming through the glass. It had to be *her*. It was Imke who'd been drifting through the village with trailing whiffs of far away [the one with the scent of peaceful nights in Burma].

Asking would be overly forward [and she wasn't one for that; not with him, one who smelled of herring]. It wasn't his place to even notice her scent. [Jasmine, probably, but something else, something kitcheny . . . *flour?* Did she really smell of *flowers and flour?*] He knew better than to ask. Instead, he gestured that they continue walking, and he told her of the bunga bangkai.

"The what now?"

"Well, I hesitate to tell you its other name . . ."

"Oh, you're going to try to impress me with some Latin."

"No. Its common name. Well, it's the corpse flower." He explained that it was the largest flower in the world; that he'd seen it in the jungle in Sumatra. Big as a man, caterpillar-green and bulbous, and when it eventually opened, it revealed a deep maroon inside [magical, forbidden, like the interior of a harem tent]. "And it *stinks*. Horribly. I mean, *godverdomme*, you wouldn't believe how it stinks. And all these flies and bugs enter—"

"And the flower eats them! Snap!"

She clapped her hands together, startling him and making him laugh. He could see why young Luuk liked her.

"No," he said. "They do *have* those there, believe me. But this one lets the flies escape. Here's what happens. I read up on it, since I got back. Over at the Leiden library."

"I've always wanted to go in there."

He shrugged and admitted that he sort of snuck in sometimes; that he would sign his father's name. "So, scientists have studied all the chemicals it produces—what goes into making it smell like a corpse. And they broke it down and named the specific Latin elements—which I don't have for you, of course: *not* trying to impress you, Mevrouw Holt—but essentially, it produces, for instance, a chemical that's what you smell in stinky socks."

"Ew."

"It gets worse. Pace yourself. One that imitates onions and limburger, one that's a sulfide like garlic, one part that's basically the ammonias you find in rotting herring . . ."

"You can stop anytime," she suggested.

". . . there's an alcohol in it that you also get in hyacinth and jasmine . . ."

He felt her turn to peer at him. "Those are bad?"

"No. But in combination with the *rest* . . . There's another chemical that smells like medicine and syrup drops, and then indole, which is in mothballs."

"Why are you telling me all this?" She sounded suspicious.

"Hey, I just think it's great how you—how you would never guess what's in there, just looking at it." He pictured it now, stout as the Buddha, immobilized, unswayed by the wind [with seemingly no plan for advancement, no ambition]. "And the thing has real meaning, I think. It's got a message."

"How so?"

He explained how it didn't just smell for the sake of being horrible, or to terrify and repel [though that *did* seem to be the core reason for half the other things he'd seen in Sumatra]. This thing did all this in order to smell *exactly* like a rotting corpse so it would attract flies and other insects that would dive straight into the bull's-eye of it, hoping to find dead material to consume, and then inadvertently help the thing pollinate when they flew away [annoyed and disappointed, wringing their fussy little fly hands over something else]. "It formulates this concoction and pretends to be a big dead horrible mess just so it can go out and be fruitful and multiply."

"And that's the big message."

"No. The big message, I think, is nothing cannot be. *Nothing is impossible.*" He told her he wanted his life to be like a big steaming corpse flower. He said anyone would be crazy not to aspire to that.

"I can see that," she said. "*If* you added some regular bathing to the equation."

Clutching his chest, he tried to appear deeply wounded.

"Not *you,* specifically. I mean, the stench, for anyone in *general,* would not be something to aspire to, I'm sure."

It was kind of her to clarify, but the truth was, living the way he did, finding a bunk here and there, he knew he was likely a bit ripe. The first sunny day of the year, he told himself, he'd start back bathing regularly in the sea. [Sure: nothing was impossible.]

"May you have that, Wyn van Winkel," she said after they'd walked a little more. "I wish for you the life of the . . . bungley . . . ?"

"The bunga bangkai. And I for you, as well," he said.

Ned checked the nets . . . gauging the weight, tugging the netline against the gunwale midships . . . It was odd: it had a lot of give in his hand. He could see the net filling up, silvery and refractive, arcing out like a moon off their beam . . . an illumination that was curious to begin with . . . though the silver darlings could flash and glimmer, true . . . But if it was *really* as full as it seemed, it should be much heavier than this, even groaning where it was secured to the boat. But this catch felt light as a dream . . . a dream of clouds . . . a linen sack of freshly plucked eider, ready for his love to stuff into their duvet . . .

Frankly [the way he was enjoying her company] he felt like he could keep walking halfway to Drempt. And he welcomed an excuse to delay turning in [wherever that was going to be tonight].

But they were at the tram stop now [right in front of the bank], and it would arrive any moment.

Imke Holt seemed genuinely interested in the picarooner, even suggesting he show her [by drawing a map, stepping over to the darkened window of the bank behind them] where Clovelly was. The glass had a layer of condensation; steamy dew [the result, no doubt, of the bankers keeping the furnace stoked even after hours to ensure their precious guilders stayed toasty? It irked him some, thinking he didn't know the location of his next bunk and yet the money was kept cozy, enjoying a fine sense of gezelligheid].

She'd already removed her gloves and drawn with her bare finger [on the right side of the window] the basic line of their own coast and [skipping across the sea] a blob more on Wyn's side that had to be England [with an arbitrary circle she decided was London] while he squiggled out a tail dragging down southwest toward his corner of the glass where Devon was [probably] and added a star [that looked more like an X] at the backside of the tail [Clovelly?].

Her keen interest in all he was telling her seemed genuine [and he liked that], but he was really only going into all this so he could describe the special dish they prepared there [what Van had called "herring in oats"]. They didn't just kipper the "silver darlings" in his little cliffside village, it seemed, but rolled them in oatmeal and pan-fried them. [Wyn could see his assessment was right: she looked like she was off somewhere, mentally trying the herring that way.]

"What's with the grin?" she said. "I didn't say I *never* eat herring." She shot him the elbow again.

"What did you order, anyway?"

Something called . . . *redding*, maybe? It *was* a little spicy. I see why they put the word rescue in the name."

"Rendang. Next time you'll try the bami goreng."

"Oh, I will? Very well, Pappje."

[He recalled her ribbing her sister, the other time he walked with her, calling Cokkie *Moeder*.]

"I plan to marry Purnama simply for her bami goreng alone. Just as soon as Hidayat does the gentlemanly thing and makes her a widow, of course."

"Of course. Very patient of you."

Imke asked him to repeat the name again, and he did, explaining that it meant "full moon."

"*Two* good reasons to steal her away then, I'd say."

"You'll come to my wedding, then?"

"I'll be there," she said.

He heard it before he saw the shimmering light [the steam tram was approaching from the south], and she seemed to stiffen slightly with a tight little smile at its approach, sticking out her hand to shake [so much more formal than the customary kiss on the cheek]. "Thank you for the excellent company, Wynand van Winkel." [He began to correct her again, but she continued.] "I especially enjoyed that we got to see a baby chuckle."

"In his sleep, no less."

"In his sleep, ja. Extra points for that, I imagine, when it comes to good luck."

[In his opinion, neither of them was particularly letting go of the handshake.] The tram dinged and started up, and they turned and continued walking.

As the rear light of the steam tram twinkled out ahead of them in the distance, Imke asked, "Is this supposed to be where I start calling you Winkie?"

He turned, and she had a face so earnest she could act on the stage.

"I'm joking," she said.

Being on the move was the difference—in terms of the herring. He'd seen herring in the market, of course—and on a plate—and spilled out   like a foundry casting, wet and metallic—on the beach from the half-toppled bomschuiten when the catch arrived. But he'd never actually seen shoals of herring before, flitting about in the water—not even in the clarity of daylight, let alone in this confounding moonglint. He pitched in with the other two, hefting the nets the way they'd practiced in back of Old Man Nodd's, following Wyn's work-song lead—heaving when he made the sound for heave—and bracing his feet with some "give," as they put it, especially as they "shot" the nets—that crucial moment at the gunwale when an imbalanced stance could send the caster out into the cast upon—to get entangled in his own net, over the side—to quite easily drown before the others could pull him back to safety. It was a lot to concentrate on—to just get his mind around, let alone his muscles, which had no long-held memory of this task—and so to add a further task—namely to discern whether these were actually fish they were casting for or—Harre Jasses!—it was ridiculous, but *stars*—was not something he was prepared to sort out in that moment.

Plus—aside from their odd, poky-sided look—whatever they were—they seemed to be calling out to him and the fellows. Just as the moon—seemingly—had been doing earlier—chatting away, serenading them. Herring—he guessed at least—didn't generally talk to you. For that matter, neither did stars. So—

Fishing, Luuk decided, was much harder than he ever imagined—especially the part where you're supposed to sort out if you're deranged or not.

Wyn didn't care so much if he was going mad. These days, even kings went mad. [Crazy Willy, for instance, their own brain-defeated king, and Prince Rudolf of Austria, who'd caused such a ruckus across Europe back in January, killing himself and his mistress in the great hunting lodge at Mayerling.]

Madness was life. Craziness was everywhere these days. And it seemed to blend in even better at night. Unflinching as they shot the nets, he told himself that either way, he was out of there soon. [Bound for America, jiggety-jig.] So either this was happening [meaning this was *not* a shoal of herring but actually a constellation, a school of stars], in which case his coming unglued would amount to little help, or he was hallucinating [for which he had ample excuse]. Either way, he would keep his guesses to himself, brace his legs the way he'd learned from Noddie himself [a decade ago, was it?], and cast the nets from their peculiar little picarooner, out into whatever that silvery mass was [whether herring or stars or dreams or delusions]. Either way, he'd fish it. He'd drag it into the boat and haul it back to shore and sell it for whatever the going price was. And then he would move on [past Britain and Ireland], farther out across that black night all the way to the other side of it, to America, where maybe things behaved the way they were supposed to [maybe boats stayed in the water and stars in the sky], or maybe they didn't. But he wasn't going to jump up and down about it now [and capsize their piddly little boat]. He'd seen too much [smoked too much opium] to even raise an eyebrow.

[Though some of them did look like stars.]

Of course, his father [the great professor] would have it that stars were large balls of flaming gas [as large as the moon or a small planet]. Fine, then these were not stars. These were herring [silver and would fit in his hand]. Except they were sparkly with jagged, radiating points.

He imagined taking some of this mystery catch over to the Leiden observatory and hanging a few of them up in the planetarium with fishing line. [*See the pretty herring, father? See what you've been missing?*]

THAT LIVED IN THE BEAUTIFUL SEA:

There was one thing Luuk really didn't like about the moonlight tonight: the way the sparkling path it made reminded him of his uncle—the last person he wanted to think about, out here on the sea—or *over* it. Uncle Allard—and his clear plans and paths—!

Luuk's uncle—his guardian now—insisted a boy of seventeen was no boy, but a man, and as such should have a fair grip on a plan. He should know exactly where his path lay and be well upon it. "Trim the sails," he'd growl. "Overboard with the excess jetsam!"

His mother, on the other hand, quietly counseled him not to panic—to take his time and carefully find his way. "There's nothing worse than being stuck in something," she said—"Something you realize is not the place for you."

That was a hard thing to figure out—a place for yourself. If you were like Luuk—lately—no place felt comfortable. There was an unspoken shame—he felt—that he had to bear around town like a cumbersome haversack—something he felt everyone was secretly thinking or even whispering behind his back: that his father—in his role as a principal in the family's whaling company—and as the one overseeing the shipbuilding—had been responsible for the disaster that befell *De Droom Schat*—and ultimately the disaster that befell the company itself—by not only being responsible in a number of ways, but—most importantly—for the shoddiness of *De Droom*

Schat's design, that it never should have risked the tricky waters of the Southern Ocean, let alone the icy South Bay of the Antipodes.

His uncle made it very clear that he blamed his dead brother—though Uncle Allard never admitted that he was dead. It was as if he wouldn't even give poor Pappje that much. Maybe to concede that he certainly must have been lost along with the ship was to concede that he should grieve for him—and Uncle Allard was just too stingy, it seemed, to do even that.

There were many shareholders in The Hague who had lost money on the Baas, Bos & Blenkin Walvisvangst Compagnie—and so Luuk knew the Blenkin name was not always a welcome one. He considered changing his name—at least when he performed as a troubadour—maybe chop off the last name and appear simply as *Luuk*, if he could only get big enough to merit that familiarity. Or a new last name, better fit with the world of his songs—*Ruis*, the sound of wind and water—or *van der Zee*, by the sea—Or *Zanger* or *Speelman*, to bluntly identify his trade. Maybe *Luuk Scheveningen*—if he was going to do that: just invent a name that wasn't really a name—and just adorn himself in the humble mantle of the fishing community there—sing songs of the tiller and net.

It was one reason he sought work among the humble folks of Scheveningen: unlike the neighbors on his former street—where they'd lost his childhood home—the folks on the beach were less likely to have invested in his father's fiasco.

Maybe that's what his moeder meant by a place for him—down at the beach with the real people—the real men like Vagabond Wyn and Agreeable Ned.

At sea. That's how he felt. He'd heard that term and thought it ridiculous, but yes [moving on past the tram stop by the bank, now clearly at stroll with Imke—Luuk's Imke—or *was* she?], as they continued on from the Bistro de Bintang Kecil, wandering with a clever, lively maiden, there was no other way to describe it: *at sea.*

Lightheaded, he dismissed. [*Undernourished*, in general, sure, but he'd just wolfed down a bowl of the lovely, smiling Purnama's bami goreng.] The effects of the pipe, perhaps [or lack of the pipe?—was it time to slink down another of these nearby streets]?

Maybe he was [legitimately] ill. It still felt like winter, and he'd been forced to bunk in a few drafty, wet places of late.

She told him how she had moved out of her parents' house [despite the gossip that might cause] because her father was not well and she saw no reason to be a burden to them while they waited for her to wed. [Especially if she did not want to become a "barrel girl," brining herring all day for Jaap Bunk. Turning down work with her brother-in-law meant, she felt, that she had to offset the insult to Jaap by bringing in a lot more in wages.] She pitched in with the household expenses, she said, in her sister's home, and worked several jobs, including at De Haringkoning, where she had to don the Scheveningen fishwife getup he'd seen her in passing the Very Busy Laundry [the day he'd curtailed his visit to the pipe den downstairs]. And tonight she was heading back to the rich people's holiday masjid, where she sometimes worked in housekeeping but did extra duty several nights assisting the baker [in the basement, in the wee hours, seeing in the dawn].

The head baker now, she told him, was Lammie Elzinga, whom the Kurhaus hired away from the Elzinga family bakery. The Kurhaus management was willing to hire the best baker for the job, regardless of the employee's sexhood.

"Novel," he admitted.

"She can outbake all the Elzinga men," Imke said, "but they'd never put her in charge there, give her any real say in the family operation . . . And so ja," Imke said, "Lammie has chosen the resort over her family, who did not choose *her*, after all."

Wyn thought he could picture her [from long ago]; big girl, ruddy-faced with a quiet smile, in the back of the Elzinga shop. [And apparently the talent behind the operation.]

"They're letting women into Leiden University now," he blurted out. It hardly seemed relevant [*We're talking about baking here, idioot*], but he didn't know what else to say and he wanted to say *something,* at least. His father had mentioned it at one of Wyn's recent stops in on campus [at one of his salons, perhaps]: it came off as an intended enticement, as if it might draw Wyn in, cause him to enroll. The female student population, his father claimed, was now up to two percent. [Wyn hardly thought he would meet a smart college girl given those odds, if that's what the brilliant Professor van Winkel actually had in mind.]

All Wyn could say at that time was "Very modern." [And that's what he said now: "Very modern."]

"There should be a lot more enrolled there," she said, and he laughed at her outrageousness. This was obviously one of the things his young friend admired in her.

He offered up a joke—the one about a dog, a cat, and a turtle in a boat.

She didn't *not* laugh. The loose tendrils of her hair [a curtain to her profile] bobbed slightly as she walked along beside him, and when she turned to face him there *was* a smile there.

[And getting more at sea, he was.]

True, sometime his mevrouw made a little extra pin money tatting the traditional Scheveningen bonnet of the local fishwife costume used for all community festivities . . . which wasn't the same as sewing heavy sailcloth. But they couldn't afford a new sail . . . custom-made to fit the sleeker needs of the Clovelly pleasonier. Ned still had serviceable sections of the much larger bomschuit sheets, salvaged from his family's wreck, *De Groot Ster* . . . They could cut out what they needed, working around the mouse holes and tears . . .

It was a bit tricky, since no one on this side of the North Sea had full-size templates for cutting that sort of a sail . . . so they had to do their best at sketching it larger, freehand, with grease pencil, right on the salvaged bom sails. This was committee work . . . the three of them eyeballing it against the small outline of the sail in the drawings sent them by Wyn's Engelsman . . . One held the drawings . . . another stood with a wide stance over the old sails, laid out on the ground, charcoal or grease pencil in hand . . . and the third contradicted the decisions, frantic that they were making a mistake . . . If they couldn't agree on what the sail should be, then they couldn't get a sail . . . and if they couldn't get a sail, it hardly mattered if they succeeded in building something *to* sail . . .

Mevr. Nodder and her younger sister took on the task of stitching the scraps together. Luuk couldn't quite picture what the end result would be, based on the Engelsman's drawings alone, but he felt that if Ned's wife was involved, the level of work would certainly be more than competent—she did the tatting on a lot of local costumes, and what he'd seen on Imke Holt had always looked just about perfect.

All the times they met up to work at Ned's shed—after the sailmaking had been assigned to the ladies—when updates on its status came up—it sure seemed as if Old Man Nodd was going out of his way to make mention of how pretty the Mevrouw's kid sister was, as if Luuk might have some interest there. And Luuk would feel as if he had to explain—once again, it seemed—that he had big plans with someone else.

Here's what's happening, Wyn told himself: I'm simply impressed with this person [and he thought of her as that now: *this person*], the way he'd felt suddenly thrown in with English Van, for example—a sense that he could see vivid glimpses of this person's life, in intimate detail, and it was something he could understand and grasp. This wasn't skirt-chasing, sparking, trifling for favor [after all, she was his young friend's love]. He just felt at ease and fascinated, in a way he hadn't in so long—way back before Aceh, maybe, when you could have a friend, and invest in conversation and care for him [or in this case, *her*] without worrying that the friend's head might be cut off with a klewang or blown to bits in an act of Aceh-mord. [Before you thought you knew who you were and were worthy of such friendships and then found your own hand raising a torch to the thatched eave of a native hut. Before *that*.]

And this business of striking off on her own [and not waiting out her maiden years in her parents' home until her nuptials]: why, it was nearly as bold as running off to fight in the Aceh War. [Maybe bolder, since she had to stick around and face the consequences of her actions, while he had not.]

For not the first time that evening, he stopped and scanned the narrowed shaft of skyline overhead [between the buildings, searching for the moon, trying to get his bearings], wondering if this was part of a dream. In dreams, often, people shifted into each other, become joined and captured by one another. Maybe he'd dreamed this young love of Luuk's into the memory of his stowaway friend [or even the memory of himself, back in his reckless days].

Probably not. Probably she was just kind of great [and so he felt he should hit her with another joke before it all drifted away].

"Let's see if you know this one . . ." he said.

"I like to laugh," she announced, "but you tell too many jokes."

He would've taken it as a rebuff, if not for the gentle touch of her hand on his, reassuring, and the simple smile. She held his gaze, and he tried to chuckle, shrug it off, turn to take in Schoenmaker's creaking klomp-shaped sign just across the street . . . but her other hand came up to his cheek, turning his face back to hers, keeping it there. Relentless, this girl's gaze.

He could barely get it out, his words shriveled and unembellished with false boldness [nearly unrecognizable to him]: "I'm just trying to pass the time."

"Time passes with no help from us, I find." She rubbed his arm reassuringly, as if she were breaking some hard news to a small boy.

He could hardly take it. He could hardly breathe. [And went, for a moment, to all the pitifully small recent newspaper items of the sudden heart attacks visited upon even young men who abused the pipe.] But then he did: he breathed.

"You've seen a little too much of the world, haven't you?" She was peering *into* him.

[Making him glass. Making him the dusty window of a sad little shop where they sold only slightly dented things.]

"Csavargó!"

He turned to a carriage braking alongside them, with the dowager Rademaker [Gert] in the back, mushrooming half out the window, calling to him.

"Now cast your nets
wherever you wish.—

When they were at full sail and first approaching the fishing grounds of the great haringbuis companies, Wyn thought he should throw out a few jokes to calm the boy. Good ol' Nodd had felt it only fair that they admit, back when they went through [on dry land] what they hoped amounted to a training session for Luuk [as best they could with the lack of water and the lack of any obvious natural aptitude on the lad's part], that there was a possibility that the haringbuizen [if they felt encroached upon] might send out some of their crew in a small dogger or even swing over in a ventjager and capsize them. [Wyn was reminded of his choice not to ride back to shore that summer back in '83 in the brimming ventjager, to dump the barreled catch and check on his girl, though he didn't like to think about that.] Or they might snag their nets with a grapple and tear them away. They could conceivably do anything to them [especially out there, with no one to witness].

The men Wyn crewed with his one summer on a herring buss had been only a notch below the men he'd later served with in the Royal Navy [and then the KNIL, fighting the Acehnese] in terms of violence and ferociousness. [And general beastliness.] As much as you could quantify such a thing, they'd likely been even more unhinged and lawless on the haringbuis, in fact, because at least in the war there had been a modicum of discipline. Whereas on the haringbuis, the scuttlebutt was if you set off the wrong maniac, you could disappear over the side one moonless night, never to be seen again.

[Unless you lucked out and your pruney corpse became entangled in the drag nets. Well, perhaps you didn't luck out in that situation, but your parents would, in a way, if they were hoping to have something to bury.]

So he threw out the one about a teacher, a priest, and the village idiot in a boat, then followed it up with the one about a haringbuis, a ventjager, and a bomschuit in a doctor's office.

Young Blenkin [with his head on a swivel like an owl] just stared back at him [as if accusing him of some outrageous deception].

Ned had heard the local tavern trash and their gossip about Wynkyn . . . *Wyn van Winkel cast a wide net,* they said . . . *even when not fishing* . . . Ned always smiled and moved on . . . or pretended he was asleep . . . It was best to ignore this talk, he felt . . . He wasn't the sort to knock back his chair, rising to his feet, fists flying . . . He didn't need to defend anyone's honor . . . cause a ruckus, pop a blood vessel . . . Just smile and nod.

Luuk admired van Winkel's roaming spirit—he really did. But the man never seemed to put it to good use. Boy, if *he'd* had all those roaming years, belting the planet—well, maybe he hadn't roamed quite *that* far, but no one really knew, did they?—which was his point: Wyn never went into it as much as he might—not really . . . But if it was *him*—if Luuk had been through all that himself—he'd have so many tales and songs—and boy, Imke would fawn and bat her lashes his way until it would be nearly sickening. At least that's how Luuk hoped she'd react—and it seemed real and possible, when he thought about it in his bed at night, half asleep. In the flesh, he'd never seen her even remotely bat her lashes, even at other men—she seemed like she could walk through a cobweb and not bat one single lash.

They were waiting for the first nets to fill—a part they'd schooled him on, but the practical part of it—the waiting patiently—was harder than any of the physical labor had been—and while the other two seemed content to gaze at the stars—stars that now seemed to not only form a shroud overhead in the standard night canopy but encircle the boat—Luuk saw them only as reminders of all the places he'd never seen—places this world traveler van Winkel surely *had*, and he thought what he ought to do was attempt to write a series of songs based on Wyn's point of view—to make a list of all the places he'd been—if he would spill such information—and attempt to write a song from each, as if in his shoes—from A to Z.

One reason Wyn had his heart set on America for his big exit [specifically the heart of it, where it opened up toward the West, the range] was the curiosity of his mother. She'd always been one to wonder about the un-known, even when it came to simple recipes. When he was a boy, a rich merchant in the area returned from the East Indies with a new wife—a Javanese beauty—and the mevrouws of Wassenaar [hissing like civets] were horrified [except for dear Moeder, who baked up a plate of cookies she'd learned about in an American magazine with coconut and oats—and took them over to the merchant's manor house and made friends with the new neighbor from Djokjakarta]. Afterward, his vader teased her that she'd only wanted to get a peek at the "Celestial." She countered his jab with the ad-mission that she'd mostly been looking for an excuse to try out the strange cookie recipe. [Though now, looking back, Wyn felt pretty sure his mother's inquisitiveness about the world around her was a kindness; the result of her enormous, moon-sized heart.]

He later remembered they were called "ranger cookies" [for some reason], and he thought of the wide-open range [like a green dry sea, full of possi-bility; the vastness waving back at him like marram grass].

And so Luuk began, while they waited for the nets to fill—half hoping, as well, that a little conversation might drown out that hushed lullaby or perhaps rowing song he could swear was coming from out there somewhere in the pooling moonlight—he suggested, as if playing a parlor game, that Wyn had been to faraway places for every letter of the alphabet.

There was a *humph* from the bow, where Wyn was lounging like a cat.

"*A* would be easy," Ned agreed, stretched out in the stern. "Places like Africa, Australia . . . America . . ."

"Never got quite as far south as Australia," Wyn said. "But Aceh counts. And I'm heading to America."

"Amsterdam begins with an A," Ned said. "And it's not nearly as far away."

"*I've* been to Amsterdam," Luuk said.

"No, you haven't." Wyn laughed. "Have you?"

He felt like an ass. "No, I haven't. But I've *thought* of going. And I've seen a picture postcard— And written some lines about it— Plus—" Now he laughed, too. "No. I haven't."

"Wandering doesn't take a mess of courage," Wyn said quietly. "Doesn't make you some big brave hero. Throwing down the anchor, now . . . well . . ."

Old Man Nodd groaned, bending to gather up the anchor. He looked like he'd just been roused and reminded of a pressing chore. Luuk hoped he'd realize—it might do something rather drastic to the boat if they were actually—

"Noddie," Wyn said. "Not now, Noddie. Don't throw that thing over, buddy."

And this confirmed for Luuk that his first take on this anchor business had been right—Wyn was talking about staying in one place being the tougher choice than moving on.

"Very recently," Wyn said, "a certain very bright young person nearly set me straight on this very matter."

Luuk wasn't sure whom he was talking about. And if it was true about staying put, he asked, why didn't Wyn cancel the plans for the States—why was he so set on roaming?

"You're right," Wyn said, shrugging. "Everyone knows me around here, they make great speculaas . . , I hardly ever feel compelled here to run someone through with my bayonet or spoil their foodstores."

He was clowning around now.

"Seriously," Luuk said. "Why travel to the States?"

Wyn's face and voice turned hard. "Because I suspect I'd feel even *less* compelled to do those last few things I mentioned if I kept going. If I got even farther away from *there*." He must have recognized that he needed to clarify where *there* was. "From where the bong tree grows," he added.

"NEVER AFEARD ARE WE!"

Don't show your fear, he told himself, wanting to turn and run.

[He couldn't yet smell the beets, but still] it was Gert, calling from her private carriage ["Csavargó!"], interrupting his stroll back to Scheveningen Beach with Imke Holt.

Gert wore the tired widow's weeds, as usual, with the impressively engineered décolletage [a contradictory message, he felt: grief and flesh], that she claimed, variously, was considered perfectly fine in either Paris or Budapest or Naples [depending on where she claimed she'd had it made].

He thought he might ignore her [blame it on his bum ear], but knowing the burly dowager [and her strange Hungarian ways], she would likely disembark and come after him, so he stepped closer [hoping to avoid feeling obligated to make introductions].

"You are behind on nine o'clock, mosódeszka. Two, three nights now, no nine o'clock." [She said it with cheer, but way, way too loudly.] "You are now owing Gert two, three nine o'clocks."

[Not unlike a sailor sidled up to the bar] she was now leaning out of her carriage window with one elbow. And behind him [damn it] Imke Holt was stepping closer.

"You are out exercising the leg muscles, ja? No tram for you, you walk and build up the muscles so good!" With a hoot [like a goddamn owl] Gert extended her beefy arm, swinging it low, and slapped him right on the thigh. "We catch up soon, mosódeszka."

Luuk was still concerned—crouched in *De Klomp*, waiting for word that they could pull in the nets—that they should be afraid of the retribution of the haringbuis bloc—afraid of violating some subsection of the North Seas Fisheries Convention of 1882. The notion of divvying up the sea into assigned territories—*waters,* plural—now that they were out there—seemed ludicrous enough—in the dark, with no landmarks on shore visible—let alone divvying up the *heavens*—!

He strained to see out there. "Is this something we should worry about, fellas? I mean, there's so much that's unclear here, I—"

"This'll be the same as *any* work, son," Nodd said. "You just put your head down and do the task before you each day. Everything else will work itself out."

It didn't feel like an answer. He asked van Winkel if *he* was worried about it. He was resting back against the bow, with his arms along the gunwales—head tipped back, eyes closed, even as he announced, "I'm probably more worried about where I'm going to sleep next."

"Seriously—no jokes."

With a deep inhalation, Wyn hopped up, breathing deeply, stretching. "Just counting my blessings I'm back somewhere I *can* keep my head down and don't have to worry about someone whacking it off with a goddamn klewang." The moon appeared again from behind the clouds, and Wyn spun around as if to address it directly: "Any work that stirs up less of a threat than a beheading, that's all dessert. Fruittaart! Just a sweet, zingy, flaky, refreshing treat. Powdered sugar and cream, my friend!"

It was not the sort of talk—frankly—that left Luuk feeling any less fearful. And then the man started pulling in the nets, and it was—apparently—time for the real work.

"I'm afraid," Imke said [in a voice he hardly recognized, as the rich Hungarian's carriage pulled away], "that I'm going to be late, actually. I better get going . . ."

He knew this wasn't true. But she turned and was gone, effectively side-stepping debate [at best, over the hours of her work schedule or, at worst, the perils of the elements in winter versus the perils of Gert Rademaker's so-called nine o'clocks].

Wyn was afraid he didn't really know that much about the dowager Rademaker [and also was just generally afraid of her, to be honest]. The old girl was from Budapest. [Or Prague?] She seemed to change it sometimes. Though maybe it was his fault: maybe he just didn't hear her right. [He tried to keep his bad ear aimed in her direction as much as possible.] And then one night, she was going on about a little village called Virt, and he was pretty sure she was saying she was from there. And though he doubted he had that exactly right, she became, in his mind, from then on, Gert from Virt.

After the Mayerling Affair, as it was being called [that nasty business at the end of January, when Crown Prince Rudolf, heir to the throne of the Austro-Hungarian Empire, and his mistress pulled off a suicide pact at his hunting villa], the scandal was everywhere. Even the old herring men at Scheveningen were chewing that one down to a soft mash, and to Wyn's surprise, he knew who all the fuss was about: the fop on the wall with the red sash and the sword.

[The fellow looked a good deal like his old friend Cent, the painter. Same narrow head, pointy beard, sad forehead.]

At first, she veiled the portrait with black crepe, but still fixed her focus on the covered square on the wall [perhaps out of a sense of observing a proper period of mourning, perhaps because she didn't know where else to look]. A little later [the next time it was just too cold to sleep out and the guest cottage seemed too warm and inviting to resist], she'd replaced the picture with one of a horse—*his* horse, Gert claimed: the regal charger of the crown prince.

Wyn had kind of been holding out hope that she would frame and hang the photos from the newspapers, which included one of the young mistress, Baroness Mary something or other. It would be a small improvement, but at least he'd have something a little more pleasant to look at than Gert's great, galloping back. He liked a healthy-sized woman, and the unfortunate young baroness had been that, but there was a limit to the volume of displacement [as it was phrased in the shipbuilding books he'd been perusing], and Gert from Virt had moved beyond that some years back.

Rumor was she'd been on the stage in Budapest. [Wyn's imagination failed to stretch that far. He'd once responded to this overflattering assertion, thrown out by some lout in the taverns, by suggesting that *was* possible if perhaps she'd once been a grand piano.] And then [after this rumored stint on the stage] she landed some nabob heir to the Rademaker carriage-making dynasty, who left her a plush, rolling estate between The Hague and Wassenaar. Wyn had never been inside the manor proper, but he had spent more nights than he'd care to admit in the guest cottage, dispensing her "nine o'clocks."

As they hauled in the nets—hand over hand, spilling them into the shallow hold—Luuk wondered—*if* he was hearing right—why the stars would feel they had to reassure three lousy fishermen—two and a half, really—tonight would constitute his first night at such an occupation—so he was about a half—and he wasn't convinced what they were putting in the boat was technically fish—but why would *stars*—lava-hot balls of gas, weren't they?— possibly be afraid of *them*? True, the notorious Vagabond Wyn could be a little intimidating, but Luuk felt pretty sure that was mostly just the cryptic nature of him, the sense of mystery he cultivated by never giving a goddamn straight answer. But for the most part, the three of them certainly were nothing to intimidate actual elements of the cosmos.

Harre Jasses!—if he had that kind of ability to intimidate—to cow the very stars—he certainly wouldn't ever tiptoe around his uncle the way he did. He'd have no fear around him—or Imke, for that matter—or anyone else.

They shook out the nets in the cramped space between thwarts midships . . . and then Ned waved a lamp over the catch . . . to show the jittery boy it was only the silver darlings, lively and sparkling . . . They went back to looking like stars . . . some of them . . . once he withdrew the light . . . as if they'd been afraid of it, or shy at first . . . and the boy seemed to calm a bit and was ready to try again. They had room for more . . . even in this funny little boat.

If the choice came down to letting the people of Scheveningen think he was a coward now [or afraid of the night or afraid to go to sleep], Wyn preferred to let them think he was a drunk and a vagrant. [Or both.]

He heard them discussing him sometimes, and it often roused him, stealing forty winks out in public, in the daytime. Maybe in the shade of the boardwalk portion of the strandweg, where a small cavity in the banking dunes allowed just enough headroom to tuck under it and bunk [lullabied by the shush of the marram grass]. Or sprawled across an empty booth at one of the taverns or cafés when there was an afternoon lull [as he'd been not long ago at Klaas Vaak's when he stirred to the murmur of the bomschuit crew of the *Dromenvanger* discussing him over lunch].

"He's changed, of course, our Winkel there . . ."

[Even half asleep, Wyn felt fairly certain they didn't mean *there*, as in *right there*, hidden by the high booth. They hadn't spotted him.]

"Not hardly. Have you talked to him much since his return? He's about the same. Still cracking wise, keeping his cards to his chest."

"More so now. You kill and it changes you."

"Van Winkel? You think he's killed?"

"Please! Where he was?"

"But a lot?"

"He came back upright, didn't he? Must have."

"No white men, though. Just your brown infidels. You reckon *that* changes you, or would you have to kill a good Christian man for it to change you?"

It was mostly a fog, his kills in Sumatra. But he did know there'd been at least one Christian. A *real* Christian too, twice over, in that his Christian name was *Christiaan*—Korporaal Christiaan DeWitt of the 5th Brigade— who'd macheted the tail off a macaque racing through his tent, just for the keepsake. Wyn waited for his chance in a skirmish in the thick cover of towering red meranti trees and strangler fig, on a pointless march to

Gunung Abong Abong, and ran DeWitt through with his bayonet. A white Christian. [He'd been astonishingly white, in fact, in that moment, rolling over among the rhododendron leaves, staring up into the treetops, at the gibbons and leaf monkeys hiding there.]

The fellows talking about him stared at their shirtsleeves and mugs [once they realized he was standing there at their booth], but they seemed to relax immediately when he said, "I know what you fellows are trying to do. You're trying to tell the one about the three old maids in the lifeboat, aren't you?" And he grinned, selling it.

"*Trying* to," the one who'd claimed he'd changed said. "But no one has it right. You tell it, Winkel."

And so he pulled up a chair and did.

Van Winkel had this annoying thing he said in the shed—granted, Luuk wasn't bringing a lot of shipbuilding knowledge or skills to the operation—he knew that—but still. It was annoying. Winkel would say, "If there's time to lean, there's time to clean"—meaning Luuk was not being helpful, just standing around gawking while the two older men did stuff—and he'd hand him a broom or a dustpan.

Then one time—while he was distracted momentarily by the curl of wood left by Meneer Nodder's old plane—thin and wispy as a pretty girl's locks—and sure, he was tugging on it a little, making it spring back into his palm—van Winkel said, "If you've got nothing better to do . . ."

It wasn't his standard chestnut, but Luuk got the drift—he dropped the wood shaving and reached for the broom. Wyn nodded, declaring, "Any free time should be spent searching for the lost patrol."

Luuk couldn't read the man's face—it looked like it was a joke he wasn't supposed to get.

Then Old Nodd said—while drawing his plane along the gunwale—"Look no further, boys. For certain, we must be the lost patrol . . . Doomed, at any rate . . ."

This seemed to focus Wyn's attention. "No, Ned. We're not the lost patrol. We're at least that blessed."

Even Nodder—who seemed to go along with everything—appeared drawn up short by this comment. He looked up at van Winkel with a puzzled frown—but the man had already stepped outside.

Luuk honestly had no idea *what* was really going on.

It was always like that with these two.

Privately, what Ned Nodder was most afraid of was just getting lost. It could happen too easily, if he kept to himself. Which was why he always did everything these days with someone along who would notice if he wandered off. He could never be like his friend young Wynkyn, bouncing around from one ill-considered venture to another, wandering the globe . . . even wandering The Hague . . . He loved that about him, sure, but he could never do that himself . . . Hadn't Wynkyn told him something . . . maybe a few times . . . about some "lost patrol" they could never find, back in the jungle . . . a terrifying notion . . .

Ned was less fearful out there in the picarooner because he had the two young fellows with him . . . They wouldn't let him get lost. They'd take him back to his tiny, crowded farmhouse with amber light of his mevrouw's lamp, waiting up for him . . . He wasn't afraid.

Sometimes . . . not always . . . Ned's love still tied him to the bed. She seemed to know when the walking sleeps would take him, though they were rare. For the most part, it was the nodding . . . the sudden sleep in the midst of even the whirl of the day. But he never forgot how they had first come to be bound together, and she stood, at times, as his sentry . . . monitoring the sound of his breath or maybe some muttering that signaled a stirring to come . . . And she would tie his ankle, with a soft woolen noose she'd knitted just for that, to the bedpost, and she'd place eggshells on the floor and a bell on the doorknob. Every now and again, he still made it out of their little house, but he never went far . . . The doctor, Goedkoop, thought he was growing out of it, that the sleepwalking part of his malady had been something wrong with his younger brain, but Ned knew any improvement wasn't aging or luck but the keen care of his better half. And her bonds . . .

[As much as he was able to bring himself to worry about anything at all] Wyn worried sometimes [or was *curious* about] his status in terms of the king's service. [In terms of how much time he might still owe.] Going strictly by the calendar now, he was safely past the end of his official stint in the service. The catch was, however, the sloppiness of his separation from that service. Chances were good he was down in their files as a deserter—that label might even have been put on him way back when he was pressed into serving in the KNIL in Aceh, conscripted from the navy in a manner as perfunctory as a British press gang of Nelson's day. [There was a steamy jungle country with hopped-up Mahomedans to get to—what were the odds someone bothered stamping and blotting all the forms and then sent them off in triplicate?] And *leaving*, finally, to get himself back home, had definitely not been done by the book.

Lately, he wondered if [when he finally scraped together the money to purchase his liner ticket to cross the Atlantic] it might trip some alarm. Some officious agent for the steamship company [or at the moment of boarding—some ship's junior officer, not much more than a paper-pusher] might actually do his job and check the passenger list against a list of deserters and men wanted for questioning, and America would be out. Not just America, but any of this. He'd be swept into a cell, where he'd *wish* he could have a job that even rivaled wading into the chilly sea, cradling an anchor . . .

Luuk ate the rhubarb—mostly to try to feel normal. Normal people ate rhubarb—maybe not at night in a small boat in the North Sea, but they ate it. And so if he did this thing that normal people did, then maybe what was happening was *also* normal and he had nothing to fear.

But maybe these things they were seeing and hearing—maybe this was one good reason herring season didn't traditionally start quite yet—so fishermen could avoid seeing some things out here they'd rather not see—could that be it? Like fish that glowed like stars? And seeing them was one thing—*acknowledging* them another—but should they be pulling such creatures into the picarooner? Maybe they'd just been lucky, that first haul. Couldn't they—potentially—scorch right through the hull with their cosmic molten heat? They were living in the modern age, no doubt about it—*less than a dozen years from the twentieth century!*—to phrase it in the terms Uncle Allard kept spouting when objecting to Luuk's interests in so-called peasant music and in the people who lived by the sea—and really, *any* of his interests at all—but still, there were men in the taverns back in Schevenin-gen Beach that had sea monsters tattooed on their arms—and the ballads he'd been learning to perform were full of strange things at sea—inexplicable menace.

The wind picked up, and the moonlight sparkled still more as the dark surface out there grew even more choppy—certainly that had to be what they were seeing as stars? Science and logic could account for it all.

He sat with his knees up, in a ball—in the bow by the mast, trying to stay out of the way—and take a little break—he'd provided the muscle they needed, hadn't he?—and eat some damn rhubarb and just think about this for one godverdomme minute. He looked down again—though tried not to look too closely—at the creatures wriggling darkly in the bottom of the boat, just a few feet distant—a small sea of single, accusatory eyes—plain ol' fisheyes. The other two, working on getting the nets ready again, actually had their backs to the catch—that took nerves!—though Luuk reminded himself that once they shook out the nets, it all looked just like herring—*most* of it looked like herring. He'd purposefully not looked *too* closely.

But there was still the singing—shouldn't that alone be worrisome?—reason to turn around and head back to shore? "Those sounds—" Luuk said— "Can we at least agree it's a haringbuis out on the shoals? I know we thought we were getting the jump on the season, the first boat out, but—And then can we further agree that the crew of that buss is pulling some sort of prank on us, tossing out maybe some Advent decorations or starfish or India rubber toys or—"

Nodd said, "Sure. That's fine, son."

"Listen to you two!" Wyn hooted. "You both sound crazy, boys! Cracked as the king!" And he halloed out to the moon—with a great hearty *ho!*—as if there was nothing to fear in the least.

The night they applied the last of the pine pitch [a tedious job], they'd had to keep a small fire going, just outside Ned's shed, to keep the pitch running smooth, and it took so long that by the time they were done [or decided, to the best of their collective meager knowledge, that they were done] all three of them were too tired to move. And so they threw a few more logs on the fire, and Noddie brought out three mugs of cider. "Nearest she'll get to a real christening," he said as a toast [each of them quietly wondering, no doubt, if they'd truly sealed the hull properly; if, on their shakedown voyage, they'd drown in the North Sea].

They sat in silence, staring into the fire. Things were happening in there, in the prancing flames.

Such sights, since Sumatra, had become humdrum.

At first there were three competing maestros [blond and bulbous-headed, top-heavy with their conductor's mane], each one popping out from under the face of a split log, licking up under the blackened bottom edge, against the grain [vying for the podium as if in some contest to see who would conduct the symphony of the fire circle. In the end, the bigger two disappeared, leaving only the tiny contender, bopping in time to the unheard sonata].

Then three goblins chased each other round and round a stick of kindling—a scrap of 1-by molding it looked like [the kind of refuse scrounged by Cent, to cobble together stretchers for his sad canvases]—and again this wispy trio lost a member, one and then the next, until only the smallest ghost-flame remained.

Wyn supposed it might have something to do with the nature of gas escaping, depleting to meager capacity, the final flicker making one last stab at putting on a show. [Scientifically, sure, but what it looked like was the meek inheriting the what-have-you.]

Then the flames poked up under a barky quarter-round piece [the dregs of the lumberyard, the rough outer log that's tossed aside in making planks and beams]. It had one thicker, sawn end, and a narrow, splintery end [it must have been cedar or oak], and as the flames rounded the hull of it, spiking up from under, they became fangs and maybe even flames [a redundancy here now, but flames as *flames*], emitting from the knotholes that served as nostrils, the log turning reptilian.

"I can't decide," said Blenkin, "If that one looks like an alligator . . . or maybe a dragon."

Having been bitten by a Komodo [and wanting never again to have a small actual dragon attached to his arm as he screamed and shook to fling it off], and planning as he was to book passage soon to New Orleans, USA, where they likely had alligators [perhaps in more abundance even than Komodos back in that prehistoric land where insurgents also lurked], Wyn felt, personally, the log certainly looked more like an alligator than a dragon. But he preferred to keep some things to himself. "Just looks like a flaming log to me," he said, kicking it back in the fire.

He'd seen plenty of strange things since. He didn't even need the opium to see these visions. These were free.

The night before *De Klomp*'s shakedown cruise, Ned had tried to let his fear of getting spotted keep him alert and awake . . . All the while, pulling it to the beach, through the wet grass, dragging it by draft horse . . . he had not been quite ready to let everyone in The Hague in on their foolishness. Any second, he told himself, someone will call out to us . . . Just one isolated *Hoi!* or *Smilin' Ned!*

He didn't care so much what word spread around about *him* personally, but he had a family to think of now . . .

And mostly it was enough to keep him alert and awake. Mostly.

Right before Kerstfeest, at the observatory, Wyn had tried to make an [unseen] exit from that solstice faculty-student salon [fleeing Dr. Fez], but his vader caught up with him in the stairwell [looking nearly as thrown by the ridiculousness upstairs as he felt himself]. So Wyn was forced to linger, just outside, at the top of the steps, in the lee of the white columns, while his father tried to light his pipe in the wind [and they had to make small talk without the convenient baffling effect of the academic chatter]. It was just bright enough out to see a little past the winter-barren river trees that lined the Nieuwe Rijn.

He was rather surprised the old man wasn't back upstairs, taking in his [fez-wearing pet colleague] pal's travel talk on his adventures as a fake Mahomedan on the Hajj. [Even outside, he could make out the first strains of the call to prayer on Edison cylinder, leaking out from the lecture hall.]

A broadside, flapping loose from the portico column where it had been plastered, announced a performance on campus of Bizet's Nocturne in D Major. The sound brought the chill wind to mind and in turn the issue of where he might sleep next. This time of year, indoors was becoming more of a necessity, which limited the choices, and meant [possibly] the Rademaker guest cottage.

Tonight, he wasn't sure he could take the weight. He'd walked half the way to the university [catching the spoorwagon for only part of the trip]. The muscles in his legs ached already, and Gert was a big lady. [Which wasn't always a bad thing. But the sudden climbing aboard!] She didn't seem even remotely invested in working any wiles on him. This was clearly a system that she'd worked out for herself, and he had to admire her straightforwardness. Once, early on, he'd attempted to caress her massive bosom [having assumed he was expected to make some attempt to engage], but she swatted his hand away like it was some small lap dog attempting to sneak snacks from the dinner table.

"A man your age, Wynand," his father said, "you should smoke a pipe. Put aside childish things and all. Might endow you with a modicum of respectability, son. You really never took it up?"

"Never," he lied. [His was of course a different sort of pipe; a water pipe; not what his father had in mind.]

Feeling suddenly that he didn't know what to do with his hands, Wyn considered pulling out his knife and whittling—it was what he used to do as a boy when he was just sitting reading and his father would enter the room, wanting [perversely, perhaps] the old man to think he was a lout and not bookish in the least. He'd slip the book under his buttocks and whittle away or pretend he was playing mumbley-peg [usually with his hand resting on some precious end table], carelessly pricking away with the penknife.

[After a short time at the widow's] he began to notice the presence of more doilies [other than the one she put on his leg] on the end table or the dresser or under the cheese she left for him in the pie safe. The first one he spotted under food *really* threw him. That simple hand-tatted circle began to grow to the size of the moon as he eyed it with an unnerving and mounting sense of dread and wonder. [Was it one of *those* doilies, reused, and if so, had she at least laundered it?] *That* [the question of the doilies] was something that had been giving him the shivers [even before they'd seen the deepest chill of winter].

His vader [puffing away on his pipe now] studied the vividly setting sun.

"There must be a reason, I suppose, that nature has given us a sunset that can often rather resemble a bloody wound across the sky."

Sailor's delight, Wyn thought. *Red skies at night.*

His father continued. "It *is* the time of day we often sit and reflect—perhaps on life's little wounds. Perhaps that's part of it."

"That's rather poetic, Vader." [Especially coming from him.]

"Yeah, and a lot of bunk, I suppose . . ." He tapped out his pipe to head back in, giving Wyn a single pat on the shoulder in passing, as a goede-navond, before stepping back inside.

It was too much—Luuk needed an answer. And from the man who never seemed to give one—van Winkel, who was making some adjustment to a net they'd just emptied aboard, repairing a small hole in it or something, not looking up. He laid his hand on Wyn's chest to get his attention. He'd never touched him before—he realized as soon as he did it. The look Wyn gave him was grave. Luuk asked him, "Yes or no, are you hearing those things calling out to us?"

But Wyn just shrugged and smirked. "Bum ear. Ever since the Ma-homedans blew up the powderhouse. I told you about that, didn't I?"

Luuk mustered a nod.

Sorting out the nets, getting them lined up on the starboard side to go again . . . Ned overheard the grilling the boy was giving Wynkyn about the talking stars . . . and subsequently heard Wynkyn refer to the powderhouse explosion back in Aceh. The way he phrased it, though . . . That didn't quite fit what Ned remembered Wynkyn saying about it that one night, planking the hull in the shed, when he'd spoken rather frankly about his actions there . . .

But Ned wasn't about to stir those waters now . . . Why should he? What business was it of his how or why some KNIL arms depot blew to bits and dust halfway around this planet?

But moments later, as Wynkyn scooted around closer to him . . . keeping low to balance, and bowlegged so as not to trample the first haul of their catch, shiny and silver in the bottom of the boat . . . and then squeezed past to help lay out the net along the gunwale, Wyn allowed him a private peek at his unguarded face . . . and breathed, in a quick, low rush, "Godverdomme, Noddie!" which was enough for Ned to take as a confirmation on the issue of hearing the voices . . .

On the way back from the East Indies [stowed away with English Van], they slept in the cargo hold in the day, snuck topside at night and sat in the lifeboat [studying the moon and life, gazing out at the dark unknown]. But one day he woke to flesh against his mouth. English Van was clamping it shut, whispering to him that he'd been "yelping." [Wyn had no idea what that meant.] "Carrying on," Van said. "Acting the fool. And loudly." Despite the rude crack, Van was patting him, and he realized the touching, the jostling, had not been manhandling on the part of one of the old chiefs of Batak that he'd been dreaming of [lowering him to their stone chopping blocks, with his head about to join all the others on nearby pikes]. The nightmare was [partly] set there, in that ancient mountain village of blood sacrifice, way back in time, but then it shifted to followers of a more recent religion and to other loose heads [those of the lost patrol] lined up along the road, and at some point in the dream, he'd been playing cards with four of these heads. [The game of boonaken, to be precise.]

"I was screaming?"

"Yelping."

There was a clatter in the companionway; some hand coming below deck. Van rushed toward his hiding spot. [Wyn got himself covered, but Van couldn't make it back in time.] Much yelling followed, and they were dragging the Engelsman topside to see the captain.

Wyn kept hidden, knowing it was his fault. The limey fool had just been looking out for him.

He crawled out of his spot, taking the large square package that he hadn't yet let out of his sight. It was his opium.

The captain accepted the trade: Wyn's opium for continuing passage for the two of them.

English Van told him he felt terrible about the whole thing. [Not as terrible, Wyn knew, as they'd both feel if he didn't make it home.]

Fortunately, when he finally made it back to the Netherlands, he found opium's arrival had preceded his own.

So Cried
the Stars

This was back some time in the colder months . . . before the sap would weep and run and make a mess . . . when they were out gathering dead pine branches for the pitch they'd soon need for the hull . . . Wynkyn told him he knew of a copse . . . in among the oak . . . in the Haagse Bos . . . that no one would notice they'd reduced "just a touch". . . especially if they took a "short cut" he claimed to know that would arch up around the north of the public forest, toward Wassenaar and along a long hedge that bordered the estate, Ned was pretty sure, of the late carriage magnate, Gerolf Rademaker III . . . The wheels on his patched-up cart were creaking away . . . a steady weeping sound from the axle on the driver's side . . . The stars had returned for the night, and it began to sound like they were crying up there, and it all began to lull him, the fluttering coming over him . . . Lotte never gave Wyn any trouble, so Ned was able to surrender the reins and flop in the bed of the cart . . . hoping the cold would continue to stanch the sap . . . hoping his love would not scold him for gunking up his clothes . . .

It *was* the stars crying overhead . . . it was . . . and he was gone for a time as the hedge rolled past and he floated along, his breath a sparkling constellation before him and then the dark blanket descending . . . And then, after a time, the crying grew stronger, nagging now . . . and the rocking ebbed and he felt he was awake . . . that this part was not a dream . . .

Wynkyn was saying something about how he wanted to propose that he pay actual guilders for the "bérlés." Ned didn't know what bérlés was, only that it sounded a bit Hungarian.

He stole a peek through slitted lids . . . The crying was a goat bleating. They were stopped at a break in the hedge that ran along the Rademaker estate . . . and the widow was there . . . that eccentric foreigner . . . atop an elaborate, gilded goatcart on the other side of the hedge. The great manor house sparkled and glowed far back on the grounds, many rods away . . . framing her solid physique . . . The goat looked perturbed, overburdened . . . the snack he was momentarily allowed to make of the hedge was likely all that kept him tolerant of his mistress and the unreasonable load . . .

His young friend was afoot now, standing right in the break in the hedge, and she was answering him . . .

"Listen, csavargó," she said. "Here is something I am hearing in England when I am visiting there with the late Meneer Rademaker on business. I am told it is a thing about how you want something. They saying, 'If fishes were horses, then beggars were flies.' And I saying that to you now, mosódeszka: If fishes were horses, beggars were flies. Simple, simple!"

"Can't argue with *that* math," Wynkyn said with a sigh, climbing back in the cart. "In theory, it sounds like a fair exchange, fishes being horses and all things being equal . . ."

Ned tried to will himself back to sleep, and Wynkyn gently cracked the reins.

It wasn't the pain that made him cry out. [The pain came after.] Wyn cried out with the idea of it [step one], and in his excitement, roused from his nap [step two], bumped his head on the low stairs overhead [step three]. It was the stars [tiny as tears] painted, against a cerulean swash, along the underside of one tread in the stairs close above [probably by some small child former occupant who had once slept or played or hid here] in this spiderwebbed staircase cupboard. Wyn figured it out: he and the stars were in the hovel currently called home by Maas Bruss [who had taken pity on him outside of his tavern, Klaas Vaak's], and the late afternoon now lit up the stars as it snuck in through a crack in the clapboard siding. It was the stars [bringing to mind the observatory at Leiden], coming not long after the run-in with Gert [his embarrassment in front of Luuk's love, Imke], and then another run-in yesterday, with Imke alone, that made Wyn hit on an idea [and then cry out and then hit his head]—an idea for a plan that might better help him get through the nights: childhood things.

It was true he didn't have a place of his own, but he wondered now if that was partly because [even if he did have a place] he would feel restless there anyway [out of place, trapped] and maybe he could stand such a thing [a room of his own; a responsibility] if he just had a simple [familiar] bed. [Or bedding—just the bedding.] Like the one he'd known back when he still felt safe [and good and one of God's children].

He knew getting the childhood bedding wasn't any kind of answer to the actual problem [the question of *where* he was going to bunk], but he felt somehow that if he could just get *that* same old small featherbed [that safe, knowable nest of down and familiar, days-gone-by must], he could then make all the rest of it work. He'd *find* a place to bunk. And he'd feel safe enough to sleep at night, not wander around under the stars like a hedgehog, footloose, waiting for the sun to show itself. And maybe that would open up more opportunities [just getting on an "acceptable" sleep routine]. There would be more friends' spare rooms offered up, perhaps, where he wouldn't be underfoot, if it was more during so-called normal hours [the time when the happy folk slept, safe from anything like his leafy jungle dreams].

There were kids who needed the comfort of the same blanky every night, weren't there? [There *had been*, at least, before he went off to the jungle. Kids couldn't change that much in six years. He suspected good ol' Nodd's kids were like that. He imagined. He hadn't actually met them yet, as he was always out in the shed or it was past their bedtimes.]

Therefore, dear professor-vader . . . we are dealing here with a precedent . . . Granted, the subject has never before been twenty-nine years old . . . This will be the variable against the control in this experiment, professor . . .

He'd considered the bunk issue before [a little], but it had never seemed important enough [until Gert had come along the other night and talked about her stupid "nine o'clocks" in front of Imke Holt].

And then, to make things worse, he'd run into Imke again, yesterday, while she was working. Luuk had talked them into bitterballen and a bowl of snert at The Herring King to celebrate completion of the keel and stems: the ribs, transom, and beams. [The skeleton was in place, and they were ready to begin the planking.] She hadn't waited on their table, but he caught Luuk stealing looks at her. She seemed to be ignoring all three of them, busy with her own section and helping at the bar. But when Wyn could no longer ignore the cramping [symptomatic of his Celestial practices], he ran into her on the way to relieve himself at the rear [De Haringkoning being possibly the only establishment left in Scheveningen that hadn't updated, while he was off fighting the Aceh War, to proper modern water closets, still only offering an indoor privy in back with ancient chamberpots. Men had expired in there. He'd even known a few of them—old herring men; spent.]

She looked different, of course, because she was in the traditional Scheveningen fishwife getup, but she was different beyond that. The chill was evident in the way she addressed him: "Meneer van Winkel."

"So formal! What happened to Wyn?"

She whispered, "There's a Hungarian girl works with me in the laundry at the Kurhaus, you know. So I *know* what mo—mos— That word means."

He decided not to pretend. "Mosódeszka."

"It means *rub-board. Washboard.* She says it all the time at work. I didn't ask her about the other one."

"Csavargó."

"Mm. I didn't want to know what *that* meant."

"I think I know. It's not as bad. It's just kind of . . . who I am now."

She looked at him levelly [and maybe not unkindly]. "But *is* it?"

Somehow, that had been the final bit that fueled his need to settle this bunk issue. It would be uncomfortable, doing what he would have to do to acquire this thing, but now something about the way he'd felt standing there, under Imke's gaze [all of it starting with the sad look she had given him when they'd run into Gert, Imke glancing away finally, as if distracted by something across the street], had settled it for him: he needed a more regular and reliable bunk situation.

And now, the next day, hitting his head here in Maas's staircase cubby, seeing the toddler's stars, he thought he knew how to do it.

If the other two were able to keep working in the face of this—paying out the nets again, then Nodd, with his oar back in the sculling notch, maneuvering the boat so the net trailed in an arc just so—and van Winkel, the worldly cynic, now—like a butterfly collector on the beach—swatting and dipping with a handnet, whooping, scooping up the occasional glowing passerby—some *overhead*—(the silvery catch hauled aboard so far, squirming at their feet, still smelled to Luuk like fish, and yet he was now more certain that there *were* actual stars among them)—then *he* was determined he could put his head down, as well, as Nodd had instructed, and do the work without knowing what the hell was happening or why. To tune out the disturbing cries of the stars, he repeated—in his head—the verses of one of his own songs—one he'd done at his debut at Dirty Ned's the other night—the part he liked that went:

> *She tells her secrets to the marram grass*
> *that follows her down to the shore*
> *She lets the sun in on the punchline*
> *to the jokes no one's ever heard before*
>
> *She does her crying in the daytime*
> *She does her thinking in the night*
> *All the stars she's yet to touch*
> *they only pray she might.*

It had been inspired by Imke, of course—watching her walk along the beach, alone. He'd been sitting on a broken piece of shipwreck—using a bomschuit's rudder as a chair—squinting to work in his notebook, when he'd looked up to see she'd just passed. She likely hadn't noticed him there, squatting among the broken wood. Passing by, she'd been just a blur and the whisper of skirt—and he'd been lost in the arrangement of his own words—it was only once she'd moved on that he realized it was her. And it was only when she got far enough away that he could see she was crying.

Part of his farsightedness, he feared—wondering again about the spectacles. He didn't want to be one of those fellas who needed spectacles—even for just the close-up stuff. What he wanted to be was one of those fellas who could walk down there and know what to say to her—some gentle joke or soothing word.

There were Advent stars, just after Kerstfeest, back in December, decorating the front of Goupil & Cie at Plaats 20. Tasteful, elegant stars, bunting the showcase window, feigning incandescence in the streetlamp gaslight, and Wyn stopped to appreciate them for just a second, still wobbly from his last visit to the pipe den, and remembering that this was the gallery where his friend claimed to have clerked before taking up the brushes himself. As Wyn stood there [wobbling and wondering], the decorative stars seemed to tinkle with sound. It was the shop bell of course, just jangling.

A trim, elderly man stepped out, saying, "I know you . . ."

He looked, at first, as if he *didn't* quite know Wyn. [Not entirely.] Nor did Wyn know him [entirely]. He took in the long, wind-rudded face, the pipe, the vest and ascot. It was the dune painter, Weissenbruch. He'd been balding and ancient back then, when Wyn often visited his studio with Cent. Over on Kazernestraat, he thought it was, living with his sisters. A jolly family man, with real talent, according to Wyn's friend—and a real man of The Hague, not running off like all the other painters who came through for the scenery, to learn about how the sky really works, what light looks like . . .

"Do you know about our friend?"

"Cent? Is he well? Are his paintings selling?"

"Ja, Vincent. You haven't heard then?" The old painter eyed him suspiciously.

What came to mind was that shipwreck of an entanglement the crazy fellow had had here in The Hague with that Sien [Cent's drunk night-piece, pregnant at the time he befriended her on the street], with whom he'd moved into his rooms at Schenkweg 136. [*Their* rooms—they were supposedly, for a brief part of that wild summer, the painter's *and* Wyn's, the two hardly getting in each other's way, what with him heading out every sundown for his first herring season in the Nodder bom.] The last he saw of the lunatic, Cent's parents and uncles had succeeded in getting him to leave her, threatening to cut off financial support, and he set off traveling, supposedly to Drenthe [to "ramble and create," to take in the land and the people].

"I received the most awful news from his brother, just after the new year. Theo's taken a few of my seascapes at the Paris branch of this gallery, and has been kind enough to include in our correspondence information about the state of our mutual friend. Vincent is not well. Not well at all. And at Kerstfeest, this was!" He shook his head as he spoke. "He's done something rash and—*grotesque* . . ."

Grotesque, being such an odd descriptor [and one he likely wouldn't even use to describe his own more fringe behavior], left Wyn very curious for an elaboration [yet at the same time loath to ask for one].

Weissenbruch sighed. "He's harmed himself. Cut himself. He's being looked after now. That's the main thing. You haven't been mixed up with him then?"

"I haven't seen him in *years*. I mean . . . *seven* years, maybe?"

"He *is* painting, Theo says. To answer your question. I consider that much a solace—" He removed his pipe to jab toward the gallery behind him. [Wyn caught a whiff of its contents and hoped the man couldn't smell on his own person the contents of the pipe *he'd* just left.] "His work should be filling the walls in there! Though I understand there are those who consider his work the *source* of his problems. He is . . . troubled."

"Yes." Wyn nodded politely, as a farewell, but the dune painter seemed to be looking him over finally, assessing him.

When Weissenbruch spoke, it was hushed and held back through his clenched pipe. "What is it with you young men? Why do you get so unraveled? Why do you come so undone?" [He looked as if he might start weeping.]

TO THE
FISHERMEN THREE.

☾

When dear, well-meaning Wynkyn showed up with this Blenkin boy back in the start of winter, Ned struggled to hide his concern . . . He couldn't expect to get an experienced herring crew . . . that was one of the forfeits of the position in which he found himself. "Beggars can't be choosers," his love reminded him . . . though she hadn't yet seen this boy, van Winkel's idea of the third man. Perhaps she'd made an assessment of him across the back field, leaving the shed . . . watching from their bedroom window as she nursed the babe . . . It was possible she knew the talk of the elder Blenkin and the shady speculations . . . that was men talk, beach talk . . . Or perhaps she already knew Luuk Blenkin from around the village . . . they were, after all, much closer to the same age . . . she twenty-two then, and the boy insisted he was seventeen, as though this were a great accomplishment. He hadn't expected Wynkyn to scrounge up age or experience . . . but he at least expected muscle, if not the first two . . . Granted, the boy had a walleyed oafishness to him, but he was hardly a big lug . . . unless compared exclusively to Wynkyn's current scrawny state. One had to have *build* to rate the designation of a true oaf . . . Still, he was young, and youth came with the resilience of India rubber. And he seemed to need any form of work.

His attendance at their evening meetings in the shed, slowly building this odd little boat, was sporadic at first . . . he possessed the unreliability and tardiness of the young. The first night, Ned assumed he might genuinely be simpleminded. He said little and had to have his hands physically placed where they instructed . . . holding down in exactly the right spot a plank to be sawn or planed . . . But by his third evening with them, he chatted away like a parakeet . . . new subjects popping out of him in bursts like a cuckoo clock, rattling on about a girl he clearly adored . . . Ned grew concerned the boy would, in his verbose self-distraction, make some fatal error or at least injure himself terribly . . . so he did what he knew was the best way to steer him: he spoke to the boy calmly . . . smiling all the time, like they were just chewing the rag . . . but describing each step of the work several times so it was clear as a winter sky.

When he reported the evening's progress to his wife one startlingly chilly night in early February, she asked, "And with Luuk Blenkin? Still have all his fingers?"

She was giggling, one of his favorite things that ever happened in that feather bed . . . Ned took the cue and laughed along, too. "All these hardy lads you see out there on the canals, playing ijscolf, swatting that ball around with their heavy clubs . . . and *we* settle for the moody kid who writes love songs?"

"Obviously," she said, "your partner, the famously practical Meneer van Winkel, chose the *one* boy who wasn't too busy playing IJscolf all winter!"

Her laughter was the sound of the astonishing songbirds he'd once seen as a boy. His mother told him, later, that he must have dreamt it . . . that he couldn't possibly remember anything from that toddling age, barely able to stand on his own . . . and besides, she told him, nothing like that ever passed through their simple cottage life. But they'd passed overhead . . . bright blue and chipper . . . swooping down low over the hedge and sneaking just a sip, on the fly, from the canal, heading somewhere warm . . . like the Mediterranean, Africa, Madagascar, Sumatra . . . She laughed like that . . . like those blue birds nipping past.

Ned Nodder had wed so late in life, but he had wed so very well.

The night Wyn felt Imke Holt was short with him at De Haringkoning, she spoke to him once more, as he was leaving, pulling him aside at the door as he was following the other two out. [They were well ahead now, Luuk grilling Noddie about lifesaving measures in the case of a man overboard.] She didn't look to Wyn as if her disposition toward him had changed, but she did put him onto some potential work. Her brother-in-law needed some help storing a big load of new barrels. [They were untreated and needed to get out of the elements quickly and stacked in his warehouse.]

He asked if they were talking about *empty* barrels.

She frowned at him [even more than she had been]. "Ja. Empty. Like your head. Is it easy enough for you?" The sharp, spiked ends of the gold hairpins in her bonnet moved as she spoke [menacing him]. "I thought you could make a few guilders and maybe earn your passage to America sooner and be gone—not have to deal with your strange little boat and . . . well, not have to do any *other* things you don't really want to be doing."

He wanted her to reach out and brush her hand against his face [the way she had in that moment walking back from The Little Star Café], but she didn't do that now. He also wanted to do the same to her face [but he didn't].

So he went to Jaap Bunk's pickling operation just north of the beach the next morning and stacked his hundred green oak barrels for him, the close air heavy with brine all day. Somewhere in the process, he started thinking about Blenkin and ol' Nodd: he couldn't leave them in the lurch just yet. He needed to see the picarooner through; see it properly launched and underway. [It couldn't be done with only two men.] So he took the few guilders Jaap gave him [gave him almost reluctantly, it felt like] and took his pay instead to the Very Busy Laundry and the safety down below, where he dreamt, all through the night and well into the next, on silken pillows and damask and to the attenuating threads of a twanging snakeskin banjo, of flying safely above the green jungle [floating and cloud-darting well out of razory reach of the slashing rentjong], but also of the two fellows back at Nodder's [working on the hull planking without him, getting *De Klomp* ready], and of sly, smiling English Van and gold hairpins like caterpillars [and maiden scolds bold-tongued as mothers].

Luuk was unclear—from the start—how three men could ever operate a herring boat. His mother—whom he kept the secret from for some time—

was even more unclear about this, when he finally fessed up to what he'd been working on.

"*Three men?*" she nearly shouted. "And *you* barely a man!"

He was seventeen—how much more of a man did she expect?

"You're my baby, Luukie! You know that. I just want you safe. You've much more important things ahead of you, not to be drowned in the North Sea some dimwitted scheme with that Vagabond van Winkel and Ned the Cradle Robber!"

He told her he wasn't about to make it his life's work. It was just step one in a grander plan.

"It better be," she said, headed toward the stairs, carrying her skimpy taper to light the way. This was well past her bedtime—and the fact that she'd stayed up to question him upon his return from Ned's shed spoke to her level of concern. "My one and only son I expect to have nothing less than a grand plan." His mother—who had perfected clucking to the level of musicianship—let him hear her stern tongue *tuck-tuck* all the way from upstairs.

The plan, of course, was to marry Imke Holt. But to do that he'd need success and money—and an impressive career as a troubadour and showman—and to do that he'd need more lessons, because he certainly could never afford to go to a musical academy and earn a proper degree—*that* couldn't be part of the plan now, unfortunately—but this would still work. It would. And he'd need a better instrument . . . and his songs—he'd need those, too, of course—but more of them and maybe some better ones. And also maybe—why not?—he'd need to develop a manly side, a *can-do, step-aside-I-got-this!* side, and maybe a stronger connection to the traditions of Scheveningen—maybe more hands-on work with the simple people—the peasants and laborers—to give him real-world topics to sing about—

Sure, there were a lot of parts to the plan—it was a complex plan, with several subheadings to each step—the kind of plan where a big chalkboard would come in handy—but it remained a plan. Even a grand plan.

The plan was to make her *see* him—really *see* who he was. Simple.

But before that, he'd have to make himself into somebody, of course—somebody worth seeing.

Also—

WYNKEN, BLYNKEN, AND NOD

Ned could tell, from the rare mention the Blenkin boy gave the circumstances of his father's vanishing, that Luuk believed the fishermen of Scheveningen would hold no ill will toward Ludovicus Blenkin, but . . . Ned didn't think that was actually the case. He'd heard them grumble . . . how the Blenkin brothers had skimped on everything, including the hiring of a whaling crew with any real seamanship . . . They'd doomed *De Droom Schat* with their lack of care. And though the men who worked a simple bomschuit may not have had the scrimpage to gamble on a whaling company . . . even one measly share . . . they were sailors, all the same, and had that maritime bond with even the poor souls of a whaler lost somewhere between New Zealand and Antarctica.

Wyn was a bit surprised that the Blenkin boy wanted to join them. He said he needed any kind of work he could find. His uncle—whom Wyn thought had been a financier on the board of directors of a string of haringbuizen [the year Wyn had tried his hand with the big ships]—claimed to no longer be in a position [according to the boy] to do more than cover the basic upkeep of his nephew and sister-in-law.

Wyn couldn't quite puzzle out if Luuk really believed his father was dead, that the ship had foundered with all souls lost [and by no fault of his own], or if deep down he subscribed to the version that nearly everyone else who knew about it did [including, Wyn assumed, Luuk's own uncle]—that Ludo Blenkin had worked the whole thing; that he'd finagled massive subsidies from King William for the venture, then, under the ruse of accompanying the ship to the Antipodes in a supervisory capacity, as an observer for the board of trustees, paid off the whole crew to fake a wreck on the icy shore. All that was recovered [according to reports from a Russian whaling fleet] were two whaleboats, branded with *De Droom Schat*; some loose, splintered planking [which could have been anything really—scrap from the ship's carpenter]; and a dozen empty casks bearing the brand B3WCo. that could have been from the ship's hold.

Of course nothing was ever as simple as it seemed [even when it came to shipwrecks]. There were four distinct designations [flotsam, jetsam, lagan, and derelict], each with different legal consequences. Wyn never pointed this out, but instead let the varied stories of Luuk's missing father pass over him like a breeze. [*Huh*, he'd give it, at the most: *How about that?*]

Some Frisian whaling men, traveling through South Holland at one point, swore up and down they'd seen *De Droom Schat*, rechristened *The Dream Treasure*, anchored in New Bedford harbor under American colors, with two local fellas, born in Scheveningen, still working on board.

Ned told him that despite the loss that bankrupted the company, there existed a separate, personal life insurance policy that was allegedly paid out to an unknown bank account somewhere in the States. [Ned claimed folks talked loose around him when they thought he'd nodded off, but he was often, Wyn had noticed, just awake enough to hear.]

Of course, Luuk didn't know either of them as well as they knew each other—going way back, well before van Winkel left to join up, when Luuk himself was roughly ten or so . . . And so they never got into what the man

did there or how he'd come to return—Wyn didn't strike him as a war stories kind of fellow. But one night—back in the winter—they were steaming
and warping the planks to the hull—the process taking what seemed like
historical epochs—when van Winkel started talking about it, and it was as if
the wind had whipped the cloud cover off the moonlight, so sudden and full
was it, blazing with the most illuminating personal things he'd ever heard
from him. He wondered if maybe he was a little tipsy—he was speaking
that evening in the lulled, drowsy tones that Old Man Nodder often did.

It started when Luuk made some comment about how difficult and
time-consuming it was, burning thatch over the soaked wood, bending the
heavy planks.

"This is light housework compared to what they had us doing in Aceh,"
Wyn said.

He doubted it. "In the navy, they have you constructing your own ships?"

"This was with the KNIL, after the navy." Wyn said. "And no, they do
not. That would be easy. Comparatively. They send the grunts marching
through the jungle, trying to find insurgents and trying to bend them to
their will. You can't find the rebel groups in the jungle, of course—that's
why they're in the jungle. They find *you* if they want, but not the other way
around. So then the brass orders you to just find whoever you can. Even if
they're not really a rebel group."

And when Wyn got near to him, moving around the plank, he smelled
noticeably of syrup-heavy stroopwafel and flowers.

Or—more like American maple syrup—he wondered if this had something to do with the man's yearning to keep traveling, onward to America—
and he wondered where he would have found such a thing. Though maybe it
wasn't syrup— And maybe it wasn't coming off of him—off his clothes—but
rather was just the burning thatch.

"It's like this," he said, holding up the smoldering bundle and a swab brush
they were using to douse the planks. "The whole jungle's as wet as a baby fish's
nappy, but still—entire fields of crops, fruit trees, storehouses, whole villages,
the roofs of rumahs . . . these great big houses that almost look seaworthy—
built like an ark in Aceh, but swoopy like our picarooner in Batak—and
their rice barns, the sopos . . ." The words were rolling forward, oozing out
of him thickly, like treacle, like he was currently dreaming, relaying it. "It's
all damp and steamy, but still, you can get 'em lit, no problem."

Smiling Ned wasn't smiling, eyeing van Winkel. "You all right tonight, Wynk?"

Van Winkel waved him off, and Ned went back to shaping the long dowels with his froe, making what he called treenails.

Wyn wasn't done.

"See, the earlier expeditions were too punitive and only managed to run confused and frightened civilians deep into the mountain jungle, into the ranks of the rebels. Greatest recruiting campaign the Mahomedans ever saw. And we just handed it to them. Rebel numbers grew. But the smart boys in charge, the best strategy they can manage is a name change. The brass started calling it the 'tuchtiging' policy. *Chastisement,* right? Sounds like mild discipline, doesn't it? Like correcting bad manners. And also calling it 'exemplary action.' You know what that means?"

"You'd think . . . actions that are very, very good, wouldn't you?" Old Ned asked, and Luuk was surprised he hadn't nodded off—even though he was working the clamps now, bending the planks around the hull, bunging in the treenails.

"Hardly," Wyn said. "Actions meant to serve as an example. Extreme punishment. A real 'above and beyond' response. Burning them out, destroying camps, villages, down to the ashes—all the same killing and destruction, really, we just weren't supposed to call it raids or massacres or revenge anymore. But that's what it came down to: they do something small, we do something big, indiscriminately, against the easiest target we happen upon. The natives called it siksaan, which more or less means torture. It's as a good a word as any, siksaan."

Ned pounded the treenails home, pegging the plank in place, but Wyn kept on, just raising his voice to be heard over the hammering.

"And the natives that *did* fall in line, that we *could* manage to bend, we weren't any kind of friend to them, kid. Not the kind of friend *I'd* want to be. When the attacks from the rebels got bad, we stayed in the garrison and held the line. Every night, they'd take potshots at the wall—just harassing us, keeping up the pressure."

At his own mention of pressure, van Winkel gestured for Luuk to lean into the plank more, to bend it just a hair more.

"So this little village of allies—friendlies, set up by our garrison—they get attacked by the rebel forces one night—just outside our wall—we can *see* them down there—*that* close, running out of burning rumahs, getting hacked to bits by the rebels—we're ordered to stand down and not join in. Not get involved, just watch them destroy these allies' village all for being in cahoots with *us*."

His words grew even thicker, and Luuk picked up that smell of syrup again.

"I was fed up at that point, already, but then, to top it off, orders came down that we were supposed to march into the jungle and burn the first village we found where they bowed to Allah—more exemplary action. Just to make an example. Make big siksaan. I was in the general briefing, and the new commander, this real klootzak—as a kid, he probably caught fireflies but didn't let them go, just smeared them on his face for war paint—that kind of a klootzak? He thought it would be fun to get out a big map of the province and throw a dart at it, and wherever it landed, we were going to head there and give it the tuchtiging treatment. And he did. He threw a dart."

Even Ned was visibly listening now—his hammer stilled.

But van Winkel's story had jammed. He was glancing over to his left—studying the glowing embers of the small fire they'd built just outside the shed door, to keep the thatch lit—and drumming the swab brush against the planks, and when he spoke again, it seemed to Luuk his tone had changed—some of the complaint was gone—the anger—but to his ear, Wyn's voice had modulated from roughly B minor to C sharp major, his words now clipped—pizzicato through the teeth.

"So I built a little explosive—mostly bang and smoke—and contrived to make it appear as if some Mahomedan guerrilliacs were performing a suicide attack on our gunpowder magazine. Aceh-mord, they call it. But that's all that happened. No actual Mahomedans were injured or killed in the attack. No Dutch, no Acehnese, not even a dog."

"You faked it?"

Wyn winked, pointing the smoking thatch Luuk's way. "Just set a long fuse and slipped away, heading for the coast."

Luuk didn't *think* he said anything, but some oath must have slipped from his lips.

Wyn said, "Don't put any of that in one of your ballads, please."

"Ja," Old Ned said. "I don't need one-third of our little crew hauled away by military police or something, some tribunal . . . We're too shorthanded for that . . ."

Luuk realized then that these two had, of course, never heard his songs—he had yet to perform in public. "Most of my songs are— They're about other things."

He left it at that—feeling a little silly in the moment that none of his inspiration came from important things, like what van Winkel had seen. But Luuk couldn't help it—his muse was his muse.

Ned munched on a handful of radishes from his dooryard garden, and they tasted a little rubbery, from the inside pocket of his slicker . . . These weren't from the supply his dear wife had packed for the whole crew . . . these were extras hidden in there . . . as a special message . . . from his oldest daughter . . .

These rubbery-tasting radishes were the best of all of them . . .

The one thing that survived the *Droom Schat* disaster—the business end of it, not the actual wreck—were the stacks of surplus record books—bound and blank, embossed with the corporate seal of Baas, Bos & Blenkin Walvisvangst Compagnie—for which Uncle Allard said some better use should be found—and so Luuk took a stack to use for scribbling his songs.

Back in the late-summer days of the previous year—1888—pondering what sort of world he should write about—Luuk Blenkin sat in the natural saddle of a dune, in the marram grass, holding down the flapping pages of his journal—tugging against the wind like a wild waterfowl—and he tried a line: *ruffling the waves*—then struck it—running a line like the horizon— what must be the far herring shoals and unseen England—right through it. *Ruffled* hardly seemed right. The pages ruffled in the wind. Water didn't ruffle, did it?

He needed to get in a boat—like his father before him—and know what the water did and what the wind did. It was the only way to make the song sound right. He couldn't go serenading his love with the wind doing things it shouldn't be doing and the water completely confused as to what it was.

And then he caught sight of her—stepping off the strandweg—moving down to the shore. He watched her—hidden as he was in the swaying marram—and felt she was speaking to the sea. She moved like someone who had things to do, but this was one of them.

She has things to do
Moving through her day
She has things to do
But this is one of them
This is also one of them
Speaking now to you
Speaking so only you
And the ancient sea can hear.

Opening his notebook again, the lines came in now—long and steady—like breakers in the surf—

Wyn wasn't ruffled by much, but going to see his father [as he had to, finally, soon after the stroll home from the Bistro de Bintang Kecil] was one of those things that got to him. [He made a distinction between going to campus explicitly to see Vader versus casually appearing at a salon. The man seemed to harbor an uncanny knack for telling when he was there for a reason.]

It was twilight when he arrived on campus. Wyn envied his father his schedule [allowing, as it did, the man to function in practice as a night person yet retain all the dignity of his field; his seminars *had* to be held in the evening, so they could culminate in an observation of the night sky].

In the front atrium of Leiden's famed observatory, Wyn kept alert, scanning each approaching figure in academic robes. [It was a sea of looseness and flapping. The students here wore those ridiculous Oriental pajamas while on campus—a tradition that made it easy to confuse them, at first glance, with professors, and rendered a trespassing working man like himself inordinately aware of his britches.]

His father was now ancient [fifty-three], but that wasn't special here: these men of learning at the university seemed to live a lot longer than the men Wyn had known in the decade of his adult years. There were old salts out in the haringbuizen [weathered codgers who snarled more than spoke in the course of dispensing any allotment of wisdom], but looks were misleading. Those "old salts" were men no older than Old Ned Nodder, Wyn was convinced. [Most of them younger. They'd lived a wind-burnt, sun-dried life full of mistakes one wore on one's hands and face—each scar or ache or mishealed joint a memory, a tale.] Granted, the men the great Prof. van Winkel worked alongside did suffer from a lack of fresh air. They were consumptive, no doubt [catarrhal from hovering over the dust and spores of ancient books], and the men of the applied sciences [the chemists and physicists and that bunch] likely dyspeptic and liver-grown [from working with elements and material they had yet to fully understand]. But they lived on and on. They didn't get knocked overboard by an unexpected jibe, the boom coming around, uncontrolled [or drown marching an anchor into the sea].

He couldn't recall when he'd last seen the old man in the classroom setting. Probably not since he got back from the jungle. But it felt easier doing it here [than in the awkward privacy of his father's home—*his* home—in Wassenaar]. So [even including his appearance at the holiday salon] it had probably been closer to a decade since he'd seen his father out of his academic robes. There were radical young professors now, he heard, who skipped the pomp [other than for graduation or other official ceremonies], dressing instead in a suit and tie and perhaps just the black beret [no bib or toga]. He knew what his old man would think of this ["troublemakers"], so Wyn didn't raise the subject. The tradition did seem a lot like wearing your nightshirt to work, and he wondered if, once the old man's mind began to squeeze itself and suffer [somewhat the way Wyn's had, back in Sumatra], the noted Professor van Winkel would possibly confuse himself and look up one day from the podium [long since devoid of any lecture notes] and wonder, peering at the young faces in the gallery seating, staring back at him, how they had snuck into his bedchamber.

There was a bulletin by the door that announced the astronomy department's next regular salon, open to the public. Wyn considered if that might be a better time to approach his vader [when he was already prepared to grimace his way through the personal interactions that came unnaturally to him]. But he slipped into the lecture hall just before his father announced the break [leading into the laboratory section of the seminar, which would take place upstairs in one of the domes]. As the students filed out past him, Wyn gave them all smiles, working his way, a step at a time, against the foot traffic, down to the rostrum [where he waited a few more minutes for straggler students to step up and ask the great scholar for some clarification on one point or another]. After the last, his father took a step forward before stopping, his case in his hand.

"Oh, dear," were his first words. Then: "Son. Of course." He clutched Wyn's forearm. "Forgive me. I thought you were just one of the thicker students, Wynand."

[Whether he meant a student who was so often absent that his father didn't recognize him or a student so hopeless he wore regular street clothes, Wyn couldn't be certain—only that his father had not recognized him.]

"I'm sure I'd be your thickest," Wyn said, and they embraced awkwardly the way they always did, his father standing to his side [as if fearful their groins might touch].

Vader toddled to the low slope of shallow steps, indicating that they must walk and talk. "You would be much sharper at this than you pretend." [The old man was as skilled as ever at making a compliment feel like scolding.] "If you applied yourself, of course. I never believed you didn't have a mind for science."

"Well . . ." Wyn told him, "if your supply line is cut off, say, due to unrest among the Mahomedan horde, I can mill you up a batch of homemade black powder. Fifteen parts potash, three parts charcoal, two parts brimstone."

"Lovely," his father said. "I suppose you can transform a potato into a stomachable offering of stamppot, as well."

Wyn shrugged. "It's all heat and chemicals, pappje . . . all science."

"You have the learning to make peasant grub and blow things up."

[The man wasn't chuckling, but Wyn felt he couldn't rule out that he was at least a *little* amused.]

The one thing that his father had succeeded in teaching him [the constellations] had never left him. In fact, he'd increased his knowledge of the stars in Sumatra [trapped as he was under a different stellar realm, in another hemisphere]. But he felt no impulse to hand his father this information [which could either please or annoy the man—it was hard to predict].

"Are you working as a cook then . . . or something?"

"Something," Wyn said.

His father studied him harder, frowning. "I shan't be giving you money, Wynand."

Wyn laughed at this. He'd never asked his father for money. He might *look* like a panhandler, but the implication was so lacking in historical context, he wasn't even going to address it. Instead he told him what he wanted: his old bed.

This got the old man's attention. [He stood and goggled slightly, half twisted around to study him further, in mid-step on the sloped stairs.]

Wyn had been thinking he could take the small feather bed off his boyhood bedframe and curl up on that, maybe in the storage room at Dirty Ned's, maybe finally let a room. It might be just the thing to compel him to find a place of his own, possibly start sleeping more at night. It could be because he was hanging around so much these days with Noddie [who seemed to remarkably just *know things* sometimes], but Wyn just knew this: the old bed would help him. [He also knew he hated how it had felt, standing in the street with Imke and Gert, knowing he was going to have to endure the Hungarian widow's nine o'clocks just to eke out a little peace and shelter.]

But his father didn't get it. "Your baby bed? The trundle?"

"No, the one *after* that. The boyhood bed. The single feather bed. Not the trundle bed. The one I left in my room."

His father resumed his climb [*sighing*]. "You couldn't fit in that thing now, Wynand. Look at you. Lanky as a Gunter's chain . . . Besides, I've long since converted your old room into a study."

"A study? You've already got a study in the house. Plus your office here is a study, isn't it? Plus the department lounge. How many studies do you—?"

"Do *not*," said his father, "make a scene."

Wyn hadn't realized he'd raised his voice. [And he likely hadn't.] He tried a grin. "I'm only joshing you, Vader. I'm not upset in the least." [He *was*, of course, but there was no reason to give the old man that.]

"You're far from boyhood, Wynand. Kindly do yourself the dignity of comporting yourself as an upstanding adult with the maturation your years *seemingly* insinuate."

Wyn didn't get that. What did maturity have to do with it? There was one thing everyone did the same way, no matter their age, and it was something everyone needed to do and no one else could do it for them. That was sleep.

He didn't say this to his old man, of course. He considered asking if he'd ever heard the one about the three fishermen who had to spend the night sharing a bed, but he knew that even the implication of such a joke would horrify his father [especially in the sanctity of his hallowed university]. And besides, his adoring students were waiting for him in the atrium, ready to ascend to view the heavens.

III.

ALL NIGHT LONG THEIR NETS THEY THREW TO THE STARS IN THE TWINKLING FOAM.—

The normal manner of business . . . when a man needed to make dirt, away from the catch . . . was to perch on the transom and draw down the britches. Ned knew few men on a first-name basis that he hadn't witnessed performing this business at sea . . . the prodigal Wynkyn included . . . So shyness certainly couldn't be why the fellow failed to do so now, while they were working the nets. Considering they'd been out here for hours . . . Ned wondered if this was more of the silent changes in the lad. Because if what his eyes were telling him had happened had *actually* happened . . . if they were truly fishing, somehow, in some unearthly way, up in the actual *heavens* . . . that might conceivably account for Wyn choosing not to move his bowels at the stern. Meanwhile, the Blenkin youth had been astraddle the transom several times already . . . though Ned would have guessed the boy would be the one too jittered to hang his duff over the edge . . . Maybe the fright was running the scumber straight through his innards, yet having the opposite effect on Wyn . . . perhaps constricting his evacuation . . . Or maybe he'd actually grown up and no longer sought the neck-breaking chances he used to, when he was a terror . . . back before he went off to fight in the Sultanate . . . If that was the case, Ned would welcome the change in him. He was free to live his own life, of course . . . he was not Wynkyn's father . . . and there was no question the lad had long seasoned and aged into a man . . . he had to be bounding toward thirty at this point.

Whatever the mystery of Wyn's restraint, it was gladdening to know at least one of them wouldn't go overboard while at stool and possibly fall a mile or two to his death . . . For besides his strong affection for the rascal and the fact that they had ties that went back . . . and besides the fact they were now business partners in this sleek and strange little boat, he also wouldn't want to have to be the one to explain this unusual death to the villagers, to the folks of Scheveningen Beach . . . many of whom also loved Wyn van Winkel and his jokes . . . his easygoing way of entering a tavern and somehow bringing in more lamplight, dragging a glow in with him . . . They would blame Ned. Even if he and the boy survived to tell it, they would find their account more than a mouthful . . . a hatful . . . of shit, ironically . . .

Ned trimmed the mainsheet and pondered more on the fate of his young, flawed friend. Bracing the tiller, he set a new tack, to try a little to starboard . . . whether that still lay to the north, he could no longer gauge, being so close to the moon . . .

The folks around the beach loved Wynkyn, true, and yet he didn't really have anyone now, did he? Sure, there'd always been girls . . . plural, definitely . . . He did still have some family . . . over at the university. His father, the great professor, was still breathing, Ned believed . . . he'd seen him in person about a year ago . . . Certainly, *he'd* care if his son fell miles to earth with his trousers around his ankles.

But thinking of this business of evacuation, it struck Ned now that all through the winter . . . as they worked on the boat, this picarooner . . . he'd never seen Wyn head off to the privy. His stomach seemed to irk him . . . He'd seen him grab at his sides more than once. Ned had nearly come out and asked him . . . *Where are you going? And when do you go?*

Young Blenkin moved to the stern yet again, and Ned reminded him to be careful . . . and he sure hoped the moon didn't take offense at the boy crapping away among the stars, and let *De Klomp* drop and shatter somewhere high over the ocean . . . But Ned decided he would simply will it so: that the moon smile kindly on these necessary easements.

Of course, the more evidence he saw that this all was a dream, the more susceptible he was to dozing off . . .

He told himself not to . . . Normally, they wouldn't pull the nets till dawn, but with the bounty tonight, they'd filled in a wink, and yet the little boat could still take more . . . and so he had to keep up with these strong young men and pull his weight, grunting the bulging nets over the gunwales, spilling it out into the hold, shaking the catch. Glinting, piling over the transoms now, there were countless stars . . . or magic herring: they could work that out back on shore, weighing and sorting their night's catch . . . But either way, he had to stay alert. And if he needed to . . . stop and crap over the stern.

Wyn hadn't visited the head for a week. He had the cramps. [And the sweats would soon follow.] But he'd been trying to hold off [on getting himself to a pipe den]. At least till they got their new fishing boat up and running and brought in their first load and started to settle their accounts.

[He was pretty sure the other two couldn't tell. He was holding it together just fine.]

Ned thought he'd try something: when one of the ones that sure as hell looked more like a star than a herring flitted close . . . with his back to the boys . . . he reached out and scooped it into his bare hands . . . thinking it would startle . . . even terrify or burn him . . . But it did none of those things . . . It was an agreeable thing, cradled in the palm of his hand. It sparkled and glowed . . . with only the warmth of perfectly toasted bread. He'd have to say it was a star. But he said nothing, slipping it into the wide pocket of his slicker.

Luuk told the older two men—back at the end of last year—that he was doing this to earn enough to buy a better accordion—to raise the level of his performance, once he started up as a troubadour. And that was true. True enough. In fact, when he told them that—in his mind—that was the only reason there. That's how it felt sometimes—one thing would shine bright and clear right in the peachpit center of his mind—and the next minute, something else in there would fire up and twinkle and he'd stand gaping at that, like the village simpleton out on the beach on a moonless night, stunned by the stars.

Like right now—that big dazzler grabbing his eye on the starboard side of their boat—

Starboard, he thought. Maybe that's the trick to this whatever-it-is that's happening. Maybe we need to fish only on the starboard side—

All he could do here was try to narrow his thoughts—concentrate on doing only the task before him, not injure himself, not fall out of the boat, not panic or go insane because—*boven de hemel, were those stars?!* And not disappoint Wyn van Winkel, whom he'd admired since he was a boy, or Meneer Nodder, who was the kindest elder he knew—or kindest old fool, to maybe be more accurate.

Possibly being up in the clouds and stars—*possibly*—in the dead of night, did not help him keep things straight.

He thought for a while how one would assume such an event, theoretically, would really concentrate the mind, but in practice—*mijn hemel*—it did not.

Ned didn't exactly spread it around about the nature of his dreams . . . the ones that often appeared to come true . . . Even to a good egg like Wynkyn, he downplayed the rare and inexplicable quality his dreams sometimes held. But there was one he'd had recently . . . while helping his mevrouw with the soapmaking, churning the lard and lye into lather . . . the upshot of which, he felt, he should share. Ned had been waiting for a good moment . . . a time when he felt he could casually insert what he knew now about Wynk's friend from his war adventures. The opportunity arose, Ned felt, when they were . . . up in the air, and they'd been up there a while and were almost used to it . . . and young Blenkin had even eased away from the mast, and was starting to look around, to get his bearings, and the two young men were pointing out

what they thought was even just the barest insinuation of the English coast
. . . a thing they would normally never see with the unglassed eye, but given
the height now . . . what *felt* like height, at least . . . maybe they *could* see
it—a low dark mass to the west—and Luuk Blenkin said, "Is that England
. . . ?" Ned took this moment to bring up the contents of that dream . . .

"Say, Wynkyn," he said. "Been thinking about your Engelsman . . .
Maybe I'll have Fenna whip up some of her smart baby booties to send
along next time you write him. I have a feeling he's settled down with a
woman and she's with child."

"My friend in Clovelly?"

Ned nodded. "And maybe we can scrape together a small purse from our
catch to send along as a christening present . . ."

"Van? You sure, Nodd? That crazy Engelsman was more unglued than me."

"Things work out, mostly, Wynkyn . . . Folks find a way."

That's all he said. He didn't tell him the dream: a steep, rocky path in
the cliffside, scuttling down to a narrow strip of gravel beach . . . the jangly,
loose-boned young scarecrow pushing off in an odd boat that looked just
like the one they'd built in his own shed, this thing they were working right
now, possibly high above the night sea . . . and a dark, plain woman, who'd
be judged a spinster if not for the round belly, standing there by the harbor
wall, one hand up in farewell for the evening, the sunset bringing out her
freckles and a freshness that belied her age . . .

It had been a peaceful dream. Ned didn't know any of the people in it,
but he was certain one was the fellow who'd sent them the picarooner plans.
The man had friends with him, working the herring boat . . . possibly family
. . . and the woman on shore was round with *his* child.

He'd even seen how the two got together. The woman's family had a pe-
culiarity in the design of their home . . . a small wing had been added to the
building that enclosed what was for centuries a public pump, a community
well . . . and so neighbors now quietly slipped in and out of that part of their
home at all hours, to get water. The woman was the schoolmarm and stayed
up late, having no husband, grading papers. The man known to his friend
as English Van had reason, it seemed, for not sleeping much . . . like poor
Wynkyn, Ned suspected . . . and the two took to chatting when he'd come
through for water in the later evenings, when her family was tucked in . . .
and he made her laugh in ways she'd given up, and found delightful his rec-

itation of a bit of fluff about an owl strumming a guitar, courting a pussycat
. . . and the man sketched it out for her, in illustrations she then kept in her
bureau drawer, including the odd little boat the mismatched pair took to a
palmtree-lined isle . . . It was Ned's favorite part of the dream, and he knew
it was all true. All of it. It was one of those . . . the dreams of certainty . . .
But he didn't tell young Wynkyn all that. He just told him enough so that
he'd know that his English friend was all right. Safe . . .

And maybe Wynk would take the hint and do right by himself in the
same regard. The fisherman in the dream seemed like a scrawny, scurvy
specimen—even gaunt young Wynkyn seemed hale and vigorous in comparison . . . If that fellow could do it, so could dear Wynkyn.

It wasn't his first night with the nets. During the boat-building months, as
days grew warmer and longer, they not only worked on the picarooner but
took a little time—when they remembered to—to give him some net practice.
Luuk, having never done any work in a herring boat, needed—somehow—
to get handy with the nets—and fast. So they'd set him up on a stump by
the massive woodpile beside Ned's shed and have him "shoot" the net, was
how they put it—pulling it and casting it out onto the woodchip-strewn,
thaw-muddied ground.

"Invest in a larger accordion!" van Winkel hooted. "It'll build up your
muscles!"

From his perch on the stump, Luuk could see just past these two—
the older one wasted away, the younger lean with weathered muscle—
like the wince-making torso of Jezus Christus on the cross that Mevr.
Przejrzystość—being a Catholic Pole—had displayed on her parlor wall,
where it snagged his gaze and distracted him at each accordion lesson. And
beyond them—for it was his vision up close that was giving him trouble,
not that from a distance—just inside the small copse of woods from which
Old Ned eked out this life here, Luuk could make out the tiny wooden grave
marker he'd spotted at the start of this crazed scheme, then half-hidden in
the snow—the bas relief carving of a sleeping, nightcapped moon, with apple cheekbones and a dreamy grin—the sort of moon carved on a baby's crib.

"I'm performing tomorrow." [Wyn had heard him say this, back in the shed, less than a week before the launch.]

"In public."

That night, they were trying out an efficient way to fold and store the nets under the thwarts, to compensate for the much smaller capacity of the picarooner. And they'd been so intent on this business of building and training the kid to shoot nets and tutoring him on all things herring that Wyn had sort of forgotten what the kid's interest in all this was. Of course: he was a balladeer, or intended to be, at least. [Wyn glanced at Ned: had they been remiss in not showing curiosity toward their young partner here about some *earlier* performances they'd missed?]

But then Ned smiled and said, "Congratulations, son." [So there'd been nothing previous to overlook.]

The boy blushed. "It's my first ever. My big break."

"Tomorrow? And this is where?" Wyn pictured a recital at the university [having to travel over to Leiden, dreading running into his father on campus . . . He'd have to make an excuse].

"At Dirty Ned's."

"There's music at the café?" Ned asked.

"He said if business is slow, if there aren't too many customers—" [the kid interrupted himself to chuckle] "—*to annoy*, he said—he's such a kidder— then he's fine with me playing a few songs out on the back terrace."

"Dirty Ned's has a terrace?" Ned asked.

"Sure. Out in back there. . . They open the doors sometimes. Next to the little room where he keeps the sacks of beans."

"You mean those rear doors?" Wyn asked. "That's an alley, isn't it? They open them to haul out the rubbish sometimes?"

"It's a terrace. Or a patio, then—whatever . . . It's a little wider than a regular alley."

"So if no one's around, he'll let you sing outside in the alley?"

"He doesn't want me disturbing—*distracting*, he meant— You know, he doesn't want to impede the customer service and the staff having to move in and out—changing out the empty coffee urns—and just slowing it all down— If everyone's focused on *me* too closely, it might really slow down the flow of coffee sales."

"I'm sure that's it," Ned said.

"So you'll be there, right? Both of you?"

"I think . . ." Wyn said, " . . . I have something with my vader." [Which was ridiculous, of course. Why would he go out of his way to see the old man?] "But if I can squeeze out of that . . ."

[Regardless] the kid was beaming. "Well, I hope at least Imke will be there. I have a good feeling about it, because I sent her a letter in the evening post to tell her and another one this morning. But I only just booked the engagement yesterday, so it's kind of last-minute. I mean, I'll understand if she can't make it."

Wyn made eye contact with Nodd for a moment over the net they were [once again] folding, just for a heartbeat.

"But you fellas—what excuses do you two have? What the hell are you up to—other than building a new kind of boat that's taking up all your free time?"

[He seemed so happy, Wyn felt he had to give him a big grin back.]

Luuk was there when they took the pine for the mast—"a great, lone bastard," as Wyn called it, far at the end of a vast estate up toward Wassenaar. He said they had permission to take it for the heartwood—but they did go the long away around, not through the gates—instead leading Nodder's lumbering old Lotte—at twilight—through the snowy woods that ran alongside a high hedge on the property line—and coming through the back—and then they waited there a while, stamping their feet to keep warm, Ned gentling the draft horse—van Winkel out on the edge of the clearing, watching from the shadow of the hedge. The great house was all lit up like a faerie parade, and he thought they might be waiting for dark—that this was not on the up and up—but then the full dark fell and they were still waiting.

Ned's horse had rags—it looked like nappies—lashed to her hooves— Wyn explained that old mares like Lotte did better in the snow with a little protection. Until recently—since the setbacks with his family had lowered his station—Luuk had led such a different life—and it sometimes felt as if he would never learn all the little practical methods of this world—the tricks of the trade—not even if he lived to be as old as the sea and the stars.

It was only when music started up—brass and strings and the murmur and chatter of a grand ball—that Wyn signaled to begin with the crosscut saw.

"The widow knows we're here," he assured them. "I just promised I wouldn't disturb her fancy party."

Luuk looked to the elder of the group for some guidance here, but Meneer Nodder was just nodding as usual—Agreeable Ned.

Quickly, in the cover of the adjacent woods, they lopped free its limbs—which the old man had him scurry around and collect, to add to what they'd previously collected for the pitch pot they'd have to boil for sealing the hull.

Once they got the fallen pine trunk home to the Nodders'—and after eventually removing all but the oily heartwood—the two older men marveled at the beauty of it: "Straight and upright as a clergyman!" Wyn beamed—as if he were in love.

Wyn knew that even though Ned had agreed to go see Luuk play, he'd have to go over and collect the old man. [Not that Ned knowingly agreed to things with the intention of not following through, but simply because Ned Nodder could easily turn in early, or just slump over while engaged in the routine of another long day: sharpening tools, reading, repairing nets, entangled in conjugal bliss with his wife . . . godverdomme.]

Wyn walked to the little farm and retrieved him, whistling from the road [even though he knew no one but the baby girl would likely be turned in just yet]. It sounded lively in there, the candlelight glowing warmly through intricate lace. [She'd made those, he could tell. She'd always had a keen hand for tatting, embroidery, crocheting . . . all manner of fancywork.]

The whistle he used was the one he referred to as his meteor call [developed with his squadron in the jungle, when they drew the bad luck of forward patrol]. It started up high and light, a shrill whistle, growing deeper and louder as it continued, like a great star falling to earth. So his men, mostly alert, one would hope, would hear it first [*before* it caught the attention of the enemy out there]. He liked doing the meteor call because it reminded him of his father, and how annoyed he would get whenever he tried to develop in his son an interest in the observatory telescope. Whenever he'd plunked him down in front of it, when he was a boy, Wyn would attempt to find shooting stars. [His father would tell him to knock off the trumpery and pay attention, stressing the importance of learning the constellations and the names and positions of the planets.]

"A shooting star might seem more important," Wyn told him once, "if you were standing right where it was falling." And he was paddled for it.

Wyn watched from the garden gate as the door yawned open [all that happy yellow light leaking out into the night like poured gold], and there was Mevr. Nodder, snagging her husband round the neck with a muffler, pulling him in closer for a kiss.

"Goedenavond!" She waved from the door, and there was nothing to do but wave back.

They talked [on the walk to Dirty Ned's little coffee joint] about the logistics of getting the picarooner to the beach.

There was still only lantern light on the streets at Scheveningen, unlike the gaslight back in the downtown of the city center. But it was enough to see, as they approached the beachside café, that Ned was already half asleep.

Out on the small "terrace" [if that was really what Dirty Ned insisted on calling it] the music hadn't started yet. Their entrance didn't go unnoticed by Luuk, over in the alcove [by an old cask Wyn assumed was for garbage] shuffling his notes. Wyn had hoped they could grab a spot in a dark corner, so Luuk wouldn't really notice Ned sleeping or his own unguarded reaction to the boy's songs. But there were only three others there [an old married couple and Luuk's mother], so he felt they had to sit a little closer, not hide in the shadows [to help fill out the *room*, such as it was].

Wyn was overcome with unease: why did he feel compelled to be here? He'd avoided these sorts of entanglements for most of his twenties. What was the point of avoiding having kids, family, friends, if you couldn't squirm out of one godverdomme social commitment?

On the other hand, if they hadn't shown up, the audience would have been reduced by forty percent. He resented feeling good about his decision to come support the kid. [Like it was some sort of moral imperative.] But he *did* feel good about it [damn it].

Ned smiled through the performance, focusing on the words . . . or trying to. If he listened only to the lyrics, it was . . . bearable. He could raise a smile. If he listened to the boy's voice, though, he thought of milk cows lowing, the need to get to chore and milk them . . . And the boy had a fiddle with him for some of his songs, and the combination made him think of the old book his wife read to their wee ones at bedtime . . . *Histories or Tales of Past Times, Told by Mother Goose* . . . based on an earlier French text, his wife claimed . . . and the one about the cat and the fiddle and the cow jumping over the moon . . . and he would surely nod off . . . thinking about his oldest, the three-year-old, struggling against sleep in the bed she shared with the boy . . . and it wasn't just the thought of bedtime that made Ned drift away . . . it was something more, he'd felt . . . it was his quiet concern for them, his stifled fretting that they were all much too young for him to oversee and protect much longer . . . that he might be gone soon or just not be able to provide for them in his advancing age . . . and he thought sometimes that it was this sort of anxiety that made him fall asleep, check out like a daffodil made limp by a buffeting wind . . . And so, not wanting to do that to young Blenkin, to slump over noticeably during his earnest performance, he tried instead to concentrate on Luuk's perfectly admirable lyrics and not the tone of his voice . . . which was indeed the uncertain lowing of a cow jumping over the moon, belting out that same bovine utterance that was at once surprise and crowing at her sense of accomplishment . . . to have made oneself lighter than air, to have arced up into the night, udders wobbling, hooves kicking free . . .

"The words are good . . ." Ned muttered out loud . . . more to himself, to keep himself alert, than to anyone else.

[There was a lot of fussing around with his gear between songs; lots of stops and starts.]

The boy's lack of poise was painful. [But not as painful as the singing.] Wyn decided to concentrate instead on the lyrics themselves:

Holding back her smirk
by the towering sunflower fence
with her hair like dark honey
with her hair like disdain
Far down the beach there's a muffled laugh
Sneaking out to dance
Sneaking out to sail away
And tantalize my heart

Wyn clapped, hoping Ned would wake and help with the meager applause [from just him and Mevr. Blenkin]. He did, lifting his head, smiling, clapping automatically, nodding, mumbling to Wyn, "He's terrible, isn't he?"

It was true. He was. He couldn't sing.

Tonight—out in the boat—this wasn't his first night with the twinkling foam, either.

It had been just a few nights back that he had his big debut at Dirty Ned's—not quite his *debut*, technically—and not quite *big* in any way he could really tell, one way or the other. Van Winkel was there, and even Meneer Nodder—more or less. They applauded and smiled—though that hardly counted so much coming from the man known around town as Smilin' Ned—other than it showed he was awake at those specific moments. His mother came too and managed to somehow both smile and furrow her brow—*what* she was fretting over, Luuk couldn't imagine—possibly the absence of his Uncle Allard. Luuk hadn't expected him to show—not for something his uncle termed *fiddle-faddle.*

Calling the turnout *modest* was a stretcher. *Meager* was a more fitting description and, well—maybe that was for the better. He couldn't be *certain* about the quality of his performance—he'd had a lot of original material to get through—to get straight in his mind and concentrate on doing right—and worry over—and so he rode out the couple hours or so that evening—mentally, that is—back in a dark, high corner of the interior of the establishment, through the open door that led out to the terrace, through the clatter and steam of the small kitchen inside—off away from himself, as if floating—high somewhere over the auxiliary coffee urns in back of the café, and the dusty chalkboard where the other Ned organized his business, far from the husk of himself—from the nervous kid singing his ballads, working his inadequate accordion and bowstring, trying not to look directly at the supportive faces so close—the familiar and few.

Now *that* was flying—! *That* was a dream—! Not joyful flying, necessarily. Not glee. But a disconnection—an escape to a safe remove. A winging away.

He simply didn't know— He expected to get a clearer sense of how it went over—at least by the very end of his show—but when he said his final bedankt and goedenavond, he was so overpowered by his mother—descending on him with kisses and effusion—that all he could get from his partners in the picarooner project was a smile and weak wave from van Winkel—coupled with a gesture toward the drowsing older man—indicating that Wyn was going to have to herd Nodder out of there before he collapsed.

And the next day, at the shed—checking the pine tar coating on the boat—after a few basic remarks about his show, they seemed preoccupied with planning the launch. Old Ned moved along the hull with a lantern, close to the shine of the hardened pitch. Van Winkel trailed behind, poking it with a broomstick when the old man questioned a spot. If they really weren't sure, Luuk was supposed to toss a ladle of water on it to get a better sense. Wyn made an X with a greasemarker on the spots that needed another application of pine tar. Luuk knew he should do more to help, but it was hard to pay attention when he was still thinking about the night before—so it was startling when van Winkel abruptly stood, facing him, grabbed him by both shoulders and launched into a word-for-word rendition of his verse about hearing Imke laugh far down at the other end of the beach.

"You remembered that one?"

Wyn thumped him on the chest—not exactly gently, either. "You *made* it memorable," he said. "You make something that sticks in someone's head, even for a little bit, that's a gift, kid."

And then he gave him that wink—he never knew what to make of that wink.

Moments like this, Luuk Blenkin found difficult to manage—it was one thing to wonder what people were thinking most of the time—but he had to add on the time he spent wondering if *everyone* wondered such things—or *anyone*—or if he was unusual in this excessive wondering. It made for a hell of a lot of wondering.

Not to mention wondering why Imke Holt had not shown up.

But the twinkling foam— The whole night of the show, Dirty Ned would come out that narrow back door with a spent coffee urn and upend the thing into an open cask not far from where Luuk had set up—it would slosh and catch him with coffee spittle, misting his boots—and the slosh bucket would settle, bubble and steam, frothy and dark and catching glints from the lanterns, twinkling.

This—tonight—swaying and gliding over the starlit North Sea—smelled a little better, at least. He wasn't sure which brought him a deeper sense of fear—a night like this or a night like that—playing his tunes at Dirty Ned's.

[With the sky murking up, dawn not far off now] Wyn had the rhythm of that Lear nonsense verse in his arms as he hauled in the last of the nets: *Pussy said to the Owl* [heave], *"You elegant fowl!* [heave] *How charmingly sweet* [heave] *you sing!"* all the while thinking of this poor foolish boy the other night and his squalid little debut at Dirty Ned's. And the debates that he and English Van had, back in the hold [over that same foamy bit of blather], after the Engelsman had launched into the thing for roughly the eighteenth time:

"You realize, of course, that's absurd," he told Van somewhere around Tunisia. "He'd devour the cat halfway through the boat trip."

"Not to mention the guitar-playing," Van said. "You couldn't very well finger the fretboard with a wing— You'd be rubbish at it, with only a *wing*."

"It clearly never happened," Wyn agreed.

After a time, Van said, "We're assuming it's a big owl. Now, a *little* owl . . ."

"Like a member of the genus *Athene*—" Wyn suggested, "—the burrowing owl, the forest owlet, the so-called Little Owl . . . ?"

"Fancy! Wink-Wink knows his owls."

"I read a lot. Don't ever let my father know. I prefer he think me the uneducated dolt."

"Mum's the word, mate . . . And then you toss into the equation a grand bastard of a cat—your Siberian, your Burmese, maybe a Persian what's been overfed by some duchess on Park Lane—the cat might eat the owl."

"It's a big owl," Wyn countered. "He's the groom in this scenario."

"That's unclear," Van said.

After a meal of stale uncooked noodles, then crowding around the one small porthole to peer out at the moonlight and quietly debating it still further, they agreed that no one could ever be certain about the owl and the pussycat.

"Red skies at morn . . ." Ned muttered, noting the thin rosy fissure, starting to crack the night, all across the east . . . He completed to himself: *sailors take warn* . . . Not his favorite bit of verse, that one. And the boys, pulling in what would be the last net, looked up and out that way.

Luuk Blenkin didn't know what was true anymore.

Wyn van Winkel didn't care anymore what was true.

Ned Nodder knew that sometimes things were made true just by knowing them to be so.

THEN DOWN FROM THE SKIES CAME THE WOODEN SHOE.

Luuk felt it as a tingle—a rising tightening clamorous hubbub in the center of him, just below his ribcage—and he thought of breathing, of the exercises with the accordion—but he could *feel* it—it was the feeling he'd had riding the glittery giant zweefmolen when his pappje took him to the fair—as the calliope petered out, and the lines holding the swing chairs began to slacken—and so he knew it was true: they were coming down now. They were moving—as a group, as three friends, as a crew, *in tutti*, as the maestra had put it—and rather suddenly—to an elevation lower than the one they'd recently occupied. They'd been right about him in the past—he knew now, thanks to that rising gasp in his center, his stomach moving up into his chest—along with Mevr. Nodder's radishes and rhubarb—the speed of it rushing against his neck, his face, his jawline clenching, peppery and sour. He had never had clarity like this before, and now he had it—like a fog lifting: they *were* up in the air or *had* been *because*—simple logic—they were now coming down—fast—and now he had yet another new, equally clear thought—gripping the gunwale, locking one foot against the mast: they really should brace themselves.

Wyn generally liked to keep things to himself [to feel out a room or a situation and get a good impression of things before sticking his neck out] and then maybe throw out a wry hint or two and see how things went. That was not the way to go here: "Brace yourselves, boys!" he yelled into the wind.

Ned took his purchase at the halyard, twisting his hand in the line to let it bite into his palm . . . less to secure himself and more as a way to prod himself alert, to make sure he didn't nod off and miss this moment . . . the downward rush, like falling, like the gannet or kittiwake must feel, piercing the surf from on high . . . the water stirring against the hull with only the shush of a vigorous shaking of sheets in a freshly made bed, rising in the morning and throwing them back, greeting it all, bounding toward the sun.

Bringing the Fishermen Home:

Of course the first thing he did when he got home from the jungle the previous year was check up on his old love. Of course, the ondertrouw [the public notice of intention] had been registered and posted and widely discussed even before he ran off [before he collected his pay from the haringhuis and stamped around the beach], outraged [at both of them, Ned included]. But he'd never had it confirmed, all those years [being far off in the land where the bong tree grows], that the wedding rites had been completed [not until he got back home and saw for himself]. But ja, she'd done it, all right. They were indeed married [of course they were! of course!], with kids and a home. Clearly, her hasty choice had blossomed into something more [beyond whim or retaliation]. She was no longer a girl, but happy as a busy mevrouw [as far as he could tell, from a distance]. Unless he could do something magical, that was it then. That was just how it would be. The only magic *he* knew was a trick he could do with a pipe.

And so he set about finding something else to do [making other plans, mainly to move on, to keep roaming, to head back out into the void].

They were yelling "heave!" as they came ashore, struggling to pull the fully-laden *Klomp* through the crashing surf—and that's what Luuk did as the other two handled it—he heaved. It went unnoticed—his vomiting—as he tumbled over the side to join them, crumpled in the sandy wash, the smell of brine returned. He had to stand—he had to or drown—and this wobbling must be what they called sea legs—the whole world tilted and crashing—the laughing whoops from Ned and Wyn not helping him stay level. But he knew somehow that this wasn't a part of the normal initiation—this unsteadiness had more to do, he was sure, with what they had just done and seen—the impossibility of it—and now that he was safe on firm land—or at least *sand*—he felt he had to tell someone.

When Wynkyn was away . . . in the later years of his absence . . . Ned had one of his prescient dreams . . . *Knew* the lad was coming back home, that he was safe. It was strong enough that his dear wife . . . well-meaning as she was . . . insisted he travel over to the Leiden campus to inform the elder van Winkel . . . to comfort the lad's father, he'd hoped.

The great learned man squinted, as if straining to just barely recognize his name: "Nodder . . . Fisherman, perhaps?"

"Not for some time," he said. "Changing industry, you know, sir . . . I farm a little now . . . Some logging . . ."

But he wasn't there to make chitchat or describe his own simple life. Instead, he launched into a description of all he'd seen. He told him his son had safely departed the jungle with the tigers and monkeys and the infidels with long knives and was currently in the hold of a ship, quietly playing cards with a friend who knew something about herring . . . and he was on his way home.

The professor looked confused. "Do you have some letter or telegram to this effect?"

When he explained how he knew this, Professor van Winkel looked suddenly tired. "Sir, I thank you for the trouble you took in coming here, and do appreciate the goodwill with which it was intended, but this is a place of science, sir. I deeply respect your faith. I do. Indeed, I have a great fondness for the uncomplicated beliefs of all those good folks over there, working the sea and the farmland, their dedication to simple rustic traditions that must needs lead to a certain . . . crude mysticism, if you will. Well, and it's not just those of your station, granted— I have friends among my many learned colleagues working in the realm of divinity, but, sir . . . theological studies are conducted in an entirely different building."

It wasn't *faith* . . . not the way the professor meant it. For all Ned knew, these dreams could be coming from a malevolent source, no part of the holy trinity . . . But he knew, somehow, they were true. When he said it to himself . . . or to his love . . . it sounded plain and fine and simple enough to under stand. But here . . . surrounded by all this marble and dust and grand wood paneling . . . it sounded like the ravings of an Icelander . . . Some witchy crackpot with a reindeer skull for a mask, casting entrails in the snow . . .

Now he could see, just as that stern darkness descended over the poor man's face, that what he was attempting to do was an unkindness . . . Ned backed out of the scholar's suite in shame . . . apologizing for bothering him with his foolishness. And as he left the grounds, crossing the lawn along the river and glancing back, he could see a panel in the great dome of the observatory sliding aside . . . the famed telescope tipping into position to study something seemingly real and far, far away . . .

Upon his return to The Hague and specifically the beach last year [regardless of how they'd left things and the names he'd called the older man his last night there], Wyn began spending time with Old Ned Nodder, because frankly, Ned was the only man in Scheveningen he could sit with for more than one ale or jenever and not be pestered with questions about the war. [Perhaps it was their unspoken agreement to skirt all serious topics, like Sumatra and Fenna, that kept it mostly chitchat and boat talk.] And because Ned asked nothing about it, sometimes, when it was just the two of them, Wyn found himself offering up bits and pieces about the steamy little island. It was only when Ned admitted he wasn't sure he could even find the right part of the globe, let alone pick out Sumatra on a map, that Wyn realized he hadn't exactly been offering a magic lantern show or lecturing before the geographical society.

"You know how to picture it?" he finally came up with. "It's like in the Bible, when they say 'the Land of Nod.'" [That was it. Because they're in the garden, they're told it's the only place on earth, there are no other people, *you two are it and this is it,* and then when they get hauled out of there, they go to live in the Land of Nod.] "Picture a place that's this other place that's entirely *different* from the *only* place on Earth. And everything there makes about as much sense."

He had the strange feeling that ol' Ned could picture it, that he could see things sometimes that others couldn't.

Young Wynkyn joined him . . . walking part way home with him . . . after the lad's performance at the café. Ned felt he could barely manage the walk home . . . that he was perhaps in yet another dream . . .

They waited till they were past the boardwalk portion of the strandweg and beyond the beach before either of them broached the obvious subject.

"The lyrics were very fine . . ." he began. "Stunning, even."

"That's how I'd put it," Wynkyn said. "Young Luuk can write some fine ballads."

They moved on toward the farmland, past the glow of it all . . . even the massive Kurhaus now a tiny firefly flicker far to the south . . .

"Someone needs to tell him he can't sing," Wynkyn said finally.

He told Wynkyn if he thought that was something important that the boy should know, then maybe Wynkyn should tell him.

That kept him quiet for the length of another field. "Likely someone else will, soon enough," Wynkyn supposed. "Not sure why it should be me . . ."

They paused where they got to the fork toward the Haagse Bos. Wynkyn hadn't said it out loud, but Ned got the clear impression he was planning to walk into those public lands running north of the beach and bunk in the forest for the night. He felt a little guilty not speaking up and offering him some proper shelter . . . but this was already so late to be returning home . . . even by himself, let alone with a surprise houseguest . . . let alone with Wynkyn van Winkel, of all people, sleeping in their house . . . The wave across the dooryard, earlier, had been civil enough.

They stood in the crossroads, shaking hands. Ned could feel himself swaying, wobbly-kneed. And he'd had nothing to drink . . . other than a mug of chocolate. "You going to be all right?" he asked.

Wynkyn grinned and pointed to the crisp waxing moon. "Clear as an eye chart, Noddie. And I've always got a contingency plan, but I don't like to bunk there if I can help it. It's complicated. Strings attached . . . I'll be all right!" he added with cheer. "I'm a csavargó!"

"Which is what?"

"I think it means vagabond or vagrant or something?"

The idea of his own kids . . . years from now, grown . . . ever being as displaced and lost as this, filled Ned with something as close as he ever got to panic . . . The middle child, the boy, could easily be caught up, as a young man, in something like his friend here was, and he'd be helpless to assist . . . He'd be gone by then, surely . . . abandoning them to the cruelties of their dumb wild youth.

They shook hands again. Wynkyn waved and started off for the Haagse Bos . . . Ned watched him go until the rascal turned and called back to him, "Someone should tell him he's wasting his time with that Imke, too, while they're at it!"

Stumbling back to his cottage . . . bone-tired . . . half the fatigue was the weight of wanting the impossible: some peace in knowing that those he loved would fare well . . . would manage and laugh and get by . . . Just to see them settled, a little, content . . . certainly not sleeping out in the forest of the Haagse Bos but also just not making even fairly terrible decisions . . . No father . . . to varying degrees . . . ever really knew this, of course; had any guarantee . . . But it would be more the case with him . . . given his age, given theirs . . . and it pained him to know there wasn't really anything he could do to change this . . .

As the sun rose higher and the moon slunk away, all around them, Wyn saw the locals were beginning to gather on the beach. Harm Van Donk [pretty much king of the local oafs and klootzakken] drew close, demanding an explanation: "What are you two idioots doing?"

"Keeping busy!" Wyn tried his best to beam. "Secret of my vast success!"

This wasn't untrue. It *was* idle time that did it; that sent him right back to Aceh. [And the missing shoe and the horrible man with the little moon on his head, that last night there.]

On the journey home, English Van had always followed up any mention of the Aceh War with the phrase, "Back Aceh . . ." [Wyn didn't get it for a while. He'd smirk, figuring it was a joke of some sort, but he didn't get it.] By the time they were into the Red Sea, passing the horn of Africa, the Devon scamp knew him well enough to grasp when he was bluffing and deigned to explain.

"Like *at-cha.*" Van raised his hand as if cupping a glass. "*At* you. Aceh."

"Back Aceh," Wyn agreed, hoisting his own invisible drink [his was jenever].

"*Same to you,* it means."

He told English Van that ja, ja, he got it [and that time he did]. It was like a toast, though they didn't have glasses and were days from any tavern [traveling past still more Mahomedan lands, where drink was forbidden]. He liked the toast because it helped erase the other phrase he had in his head, whenever he heard the name of that province, the term *Aceh-mord.*

As for the idle time back in Aceh [down time, they called it there], that was spent out looking for the lost patrol. His friend Lammert was in that patrol [and carried an outstanding debt of ten guilders, owed to Wyn for a game of boonaken, yet Wyn still rather hoped, for his friend's sake, that they'd deserted and were long gone and that he would never see Lammert or his ten guilders again].

About a week before Wyn left Sumatra entirely, they finally found the lost patrol, nearly to Pulau Samosir. Their bodies were lined up neatly on one side of the road [their heads on the other]. But even that gory display he could understand [being similar to their own ideas of war, to payback and no quarter]. It just wasn't the same horror as Aceh-mord.

Luuk was stunned, the way Wyn handled the nosy louts.

"I got shoes bigger'n this puny boat!"

"You should have that looked at, Harm." Wyn played the concerned chum. "Could be gout."

"Not even big enough to piss in!" another said.

"Oh, good," Wyn said. "So you'll find some other place to do that, then, Zef?"

He wasn't even on his feet, ready, defending himself. Luuk could hardly believe what he was seeing. Wyn remained stretched out in the shadow of *De Klomp*, in the sand by the hull, eyes closed, arms folded, all settled in for a nap—yet effectively sailing out retorts and putdowns to these klootzakken— nonchalant as a baby in his cradle.

Luuk would've given anything to fit in here like that—to be so at home with these common men of the sea— And yet van Winkel didn't seem to see it—the degree to which he was at home here. No, he was heading out to the States as soon as he could, Luuk guessed—and much sooner, he was just now starting to realize, than Luuk himself would personally prefer. If they worked together just a little longer—maybe some of *this* could rub off on him—being more of Scheveningen than The Hague. The one called Zef had the edge of the tarp up, grunting at the empty picarooner. "What kind of tiny catch could you idiots pull in? Two or three herring, maybe?"

"Ja, we are proud of both of our herrings," Wyn said, the sun washing over his half-smiling face. "But we already hauled our catch back to Jaap Bunk's with a pair of tweezers, so . . ."

The laugh that Wyn got topped the laugh provided by the lout Zef.

"Actually," Luuk chimed in, "we did quite well. Much better than you could imagine."

"And who's this? This green kid is your *crew*, Winkel?" They turned on him and examined his hands before he could react. "Soft!" they all agreed. The one called Harm sniffed his fingers.

"Blenkin did great," Wyn murmured. He could be asleep, for all Luuk could tell.

"Blenkin? From the whaling company Blenkins? Oh ho! This is your financier, Winkel? This kid's backing this fiasco? You're doomed, Vagabond Wyn!"

The thing was, this could all be avoided— he and van Winkel weren't waiting for Smiling Ned or anything. Old Nodd had already been back with the barrel man, Jaap Bunk, and his cart—and they'd filled it. Later on, they would meet up for their cut of the money, out at the fisherman's home, and the boat was already secured and covered up. He'd only lingered in the hopes that Imke would happen by on the strandweg, leaving her night job at the Kurhaus—but he could—and would—just head home now and meander off a little in that direction, just happen by the hotel and hopefully run into her.

All the times he'd been to the older fisherman's home, and yet [for the longest stretch, working on the picarooner through the winter months] he had never really been there [managing to avoid setting foot in the house itself]. Most evenings they worked, it was past the kids' bedtime, according to Ned. "The mevrouw just put them down," he'd say. Or during the afternoon, he'd often just missed her—"Off to market with all three of them in tow," Ned would explain. Or they were lying down for an afternoon nap.

So Wyn was able to get pretty far along with the boat-building, which they'd succeeded in containing in Ned's little shed in back [well within earshot of the dinner bell, his cottage being just at the other end of the short plowfield], without actually crossing the Nodder threshold.

Wyn gracefully repelled all dinner invitations for most of the duration of the project. When finally Wyn saw no out but to cave, Ned asked, "Is there anything you won't eat?"

"Anything with pepper," he told him. "I won't eat black pepper." Back with the KNIL, he had developed a standard witticism he'd dust off when ever a fellow grunt would bemoan their presence in that distant jungle region. [*What are we doing here?!* someone would ask, and he'd say, *We came for the pepper, stayed for the opium, and will die for religion.*]

It didn't help [and wasn't that witty], but he'd say it anyway. [Mostly just to keep it straight in his mind.] He didn't bother explaining to his friend Ned that pepper reminded him of the war in Aceh. It seemed like a thing no one could cook without, and so he'd assumed the invitations to Noddie's hearth would stop if he said no pepper. It just seemed easier than saying he didn't wish to come up to the house for dinner.

But Ned pushed and pushed. ["Keep it up," he told him, "and they're going to stop calling you Agreeable Ned."] They settled on a night [in mid-April] and started the boat work early so they could knock off for dinner. Except on the day, while working on the rigging, Blenkin announced he'd forgotten, but he had to get his accordion tuned. [It was the only evening the maestra had free.] Wyn advised him he'd better at least come up to the house with them and square it with their hostess. Luuk straggled behind, uncertain as ever, so Wyn found himself alone with Noddie entering the cottage [and there was the little family, tearing around the crowded room with glee, with Mevrouw Nodder standing in front of the small table, wait-ing to greet them].

Fenna glowed [as he completely expected her to]. Everything about her looked like home.

"Thank you for having me," he said. And Ned smiled, nodding, reaching out to put his hand on both of their shoulders, tipping his head forward as if he wanted them to touch their three heads together. [They did not, but it felt like it all the same.] And then he called for the kids to settle down and come to the table.

Luuk was still there, lurking in the dooryard. Wyn stepped out and jerked him inside. Already Ned was explaining to Fenna that he would be the only one joining them.

"Sorry about the mix-up," Blenkin said again.

"Luuk Blenkin," Fenna said. "Don't be a goose. Stay as long as you can, eat what you can."

The kid had a little round pocket watch with a smiling moon on the cover [all he had left, he'd once told Wyn, from his pappje, and though Luuk didn't spell it out, Wyn took it to mean it was also all he had left from his family's former prosperous days]. He flipped it out and said he didn't want to be rude and bolt halfway through, so maybe they shouldn't set him a place.

"Just sit," Wyn told him [and tried to give him a look that said, *If I have to do this, you better stay as long as you can, kiddo*].

The occasion was also the first good look he got at their little ones [other than the oldest occasionally running around outside the shed while they worked, sing-songing nonsense and rhymes, or squatting on the edge of the small copse of trees to pee]. The oldest was three, the boy was two, and the little girl was still an infant, whom Fenna wore in a sling of cloth as she served the meal [the two little eyes, in and out of sleep—closed, blinking, wide—studying him], carried much in the way of the women of Sumatra [and in the way of that laughing baby he and Imke Holt had passed that cold night at the start of the year, walking home from The Little Star]. She was more peasant now than perambulator-pusher. Even if the Nodders could afford such a thing [which they certainly couldn't], there was no place here, in their muddy dooryard, to push one of the more modern prams of Wassenaar. [He'd ridden in one of those, he believed.]

She served stamppot. [This could be either good news or bad news, depending on how it was prepared. Wyn was assuming it was good news: a shrewd cook could keep it simple and yet as potentially complex as the fancy of the maker]. Along with a few feeble shreds of klapstuk [an extra ingredient that made him feel a little guilty: having him to dinner had meant a lot to them, or they wouldn't have splurged for even this stingy, stringy bit of meat] that Fenna had stretched to give it a hint of beefy flavor, she'd included something else crunchy to husband the celery and radishes . . . apple? She admitted they had a healthy surplus [along with the potatoes and turnips] in their root cellar, "Hence dessert tonight . . ." [an easily decipherable hint: that likely meant one thing, fortunately].

As she dished out the stamppot, Ned reminded her, "Now you didn't pepper any of this, did you, love? Meneer van Winkel here hates the taste of pepper."

"Well, that's not quite it," he said.

"There's radish instead," she said. "Oh, but they're a little peppery tasting. Should—?"

"It's not the taste." He dismissed this with a wave. "Don't worry." Ned shouldn't have said anything. "I *like* it fine, I just don't care to eat it. Black pepper, I mean. Since Aceh. Sumatra." [And even that wasn't true, he knew: pepper was required in irresistibles like the novelty-shaped ginger cookies, speculaas, and certainly all those spicy noodle dishes he wolfed down at Bistro de Bintang Kecil—The Little Star—right there in The Hague.] He just felt he should take a stand against it [officially, that is—out loud—a show of protest] if it was being openly applied in front of him [especially by Dutch mevrouw, safe in their kitchens, far from the fighting]. The true East Indies folks, they of course had to use it. But it did bother him, if he were being honest, when he saw people here back home throwing it around with no thought of how it had journeyed to their kitchens.

"That's right," Ned said. "I guess that is how we got entangled there, isn't it? I'd forgotten about the fighting being over pepper."

"At first," Wyn said. "Way back at the start of it."

Fenna clucked. "What a ridiculous thing to start an entire war over!"

Wyn had never heard her make a sound like that cluck, back when he knew her. It sounded more like her mother. [In his memory, that woman had clucked at him left and right. He'd had moments far away in Aceh where he'd wondered if Fenna's mother was clucking still.]

"I guess," Ned said, "you don't get entangled in something by *thinking* you'll get entangled. You get entangled because it looks simple—like, *I'll just stretch out this drag net here . . .*" [He aped awkwardly working a net, rising from his seat, making the little ones giggle.] Wyn couldn't remember when he'd ever seen him so animated.

The food was wonderful [just enough turnip, the way he liked his stamppot], and the little girl across from him turned red with fits of giggles every time he looked her way. Fenna asked about the picarooner, and it was obvious she'd been out to the shed many times [when they weren't working on it, to get the tour from Ned]. Most of her questions were about handling such a small craft out there in the rough sea, safety issues. She didn't ask much about the capacity of the little thing, or how successful they expected their experiment to be [how much of a haul].

Luuk kept flipping up the moon on his pocket watch, keeping it low below the table [as if that made it less rude]. Wyn hoped he would just skip the accordion-tuning. And he tried to keep pace with the young fool's shoveling, thinking that if he was also done eating when Luuk was, it might be easier to take their leave together.

With another apology, Luuk was suddenly rushing from the table, red and flustered. "Lieve hemel! My mammie didn't raise me to exit in such a rude manner— I'm terribly sorry—"

But Ned, grinning, waved him away. "Go, son! 't geeft niet!"

"You're running off to see your sweetheart, aren't you?" Fenna teased.

Wyn was beginning to doubt the situation with the girl Luuk adored was quite what they'd thought it was, but he said it anyway: "It's that Imke Holt." [And got a big, beautiful *ha!* from Fenna, startling the baby she held.]

"Hush, Wyn! Jeetje! It's the *accordion* thing—I told you!"

Shuffling in his seat, folding his napkin, Wyn gave going with him his best shot, saying maybe he'd better walk back to town with him, but Luuk said, "No, no. You stay. We can't both be rude to the Nodders."

"Besides," Fenna said, "I made appeltaart."

Ned waggled a finger at Luuk. "That's your punishment, son. You'll miss out on the appeltaart. But you'll get your priorities set with age, don't worry.

Now, Wynkyn here, being wiser, and a few years older than yourself . . . I know *Wynkyn's* planning to stay for *that*."

"Of course he is," Fenna said. "Give my regards to Imke! I quite like that girl."

At the door, sighing, Luuk looked defeated as he tugged on his hat. "I *told* you—it's my *accordion!*"

Everyone laughed at him [even the kids, joining in like mynas] as he thanked them again and let himself out.

Fenna announced that it was time to tuck the wee ones in. As she carried the baby and whisked the other two ahead of her like chicks, she stepped back a moment, leaning jarringly close, and whispered to him and Ned, "Leaving more dessert for us, boys!" The eldest, the three-year-old, whined a moment about wanting the appeltaart, but Fenna convinced her somehow that "a kiss from Pappje would be just as sweet," and the girl circled the table to get her kiss and then Fenna had them out of there and into the meager anteroom, where he could hear her running through lullabies.

[There was peace here, in this cramped little home, and it was hard now to conceive of all the worries he'd harbored at the prospect of the fisherman bringing him home.]

Just as he was beginning to feel at ease [thinking he could complete this dandy little meal and make his exit in the manner of any other dinner guest, devoid of any and all awkwardness and anxiety], he glanced up to see good ol' Noddie had fallen asleep, right there at the table, his head rolling nearly into his plate.

Fenna stepped back into the room, the infant asleep in the sling she wore. [The baby must still share the bed with them, he figured.] She stopped when she saw Ned, though she honestly didn't appear that surprised.

"It just happened," Wyn said. "Just now. I didn't know what I should . . ."

The first thing she did was ease his plate away from his head [a precaution it appeared she'd taken more than once in the past] and picked a few small fluffs of potato from his thinning hair.

Wyn offered to help move him [before realizing how awkward that would be—to take him into where they lay together as Meneer and Mevrouw Nodder].

She thanked him but declined, fetching a pillow for the poor fellow. "He would just wake halfway there," she said, "and that's startling. He'll wake in a little bit and retire on his own."

He watched her work the pillow under her husband's head, prizing his face from the table. "You wait up for him, don't you?"

She blushed in a manner [sliding back the strands of her hair, away from her face] that brought so much back, all in a rush. "Of course," she said, smiling with it, then quelled the smile [with her lips pressed tight, in the way she did when they first met], and she stroked the old man's back.

It was wrong to stay, to be alone [or something near alone] with her now. Though it also seemed wrong to tear out of there and leave her like this. And so he lingered, and they just looked at each other [across the table] for quite a long time [smiling with it], as if taking in a view they knew they would never visit again.

He got up to serve the dessert, so she could remain in attendance to her husband and the sleeping baby. As he cut into the appeltaart, she said, "I want to try it with glazed lemon instead someday."

He said he'd never heard of that.

She shrugged. "I haven't either, but it's possible, isn't it?"

He tried to think of things he could tell her [*would* tell her]. He asked her if she remembered old Weissenbruch, the dune painter. She'd been with them a few times when Cent dragged them to the older man's studio on Kazernestraat, but he didn't know how much she'd bothered recalling about those days. [That good summer, '82.] Back when recklessness was beauty.

"Of course," she said. "He's still around. Out painting, in the sun and wind. Always."

"*En plein air,* Cent called it," he said.

"Most times I get to the beach, I see him out there. That ruddy, smiling face, still the gentleman. And still as cheery as ever."

[Wyn didn't quite think so. He'd struck him as sadder, older.] "He said Cent hurt himself. It sounds like he's been acting mad." [He left out the part about him cutting himself; he skipped the word *grotesque*.]

"Lieve hemel . . ."

"Ja," he said.

She touched Ned's head while they talked, playing with his hair. The baby, in her arms, was asleep, all lashes and milk-swollen lips.

He just said it out loud: "Peace is the new beauty."

Her mouth fell open a little [enough to put him back on the beach, in the sun and wind and marram grass and the swirl of her hair]. And her hair fell forward a little now [or she caused it to do so] to cover whatever was happening there.

As he rose to leave, she reached out and took his wrist, stopping him, whispering, "One thing."

He waited.

"When you left . . . Did you leave because of . . . some *gossip* you heard?"

"About you marrying Ned?" He looked down at the man. The top of his head was staring right back at him right there on the table. It looked little, like a small boy's.

"No, before that."

"No." He wasn't sure what other rumor she could be referring to. "I'm sorry." He tried not to say it with a question mark [which would be there only because he didn't know what "before that" could be referring to], because there was no question that he felt sorry about leaving her back then. So he would let the phrase sit out there as a general sort of apology, that might just magically cover all of it [for making her wait the next summer, '83, while he stayed out on the buss *Het Zilveren Fortuin*; for the countless hours she likely spent on the beach, staring out toward the shoals, her hair seaweeding in the wind; and also for running off and joining up].

Plus [despite the muttering and consternation that characterized his last night in Scheveningen and any ill words that might have spiked his rants, boggled and fuming as he was over her sudden vows with the old man, much of his sulk steeped in at least half a keg of ale and a boatload of jenever at Klaas Vaak's before stamping off to join the Koninklijke Marine; despite the hurling of her name, repeatedly, out into the blackness of the North Sea, after finally being tossed from the taverns], he *hadn't* truly been thinking of her but thinking mostly of his own battered pride [mostly just that], if thinking at all, and he *was* sorry for that. No, he hadn't truly been thinking of the humiliation she'd feel when hearing of the public scene he made so much as thinking of himself [in that way the stupidly young do, he saw now, six years too late], and it was a horrible thing, to not factor someone in [and it felt like more of a horrible thing pushing thirty than it did at twenty-three].

"It was my father. Mostly. I mean, more than I let on. I left because of things he said. Thought I'd show him. Somehow."

It was true about his father, of course. That was *some* of it. [Or seemed like it after he left, once he found himself grinding through small-arms drills on an open deck in the bastard sun of the Arabian Sea.]

'TWAS ALL SO PRETTY A SAIL, IT SEEMED AS IF IT COULD NOT BE:

☾

Back home the morning after the first sail, he watched her for a moment through the window . . . Fenna was getting lunch for the children, as pretty and nearly impossible as ever she was, even in this simple task . . . As he came through the door . . . in one motion, having seen him . . . she set her cutting board and knife up high on a shelf, away from little fingers, the lunch-making interrupted. His sore body ached even more when she lunged at him for a hug. He supposed she was just glad to learn he hadn't nodded off and fallen overboard . . . not that she'd yet understood the outcome of their maiden voyage . . . But then she must have gotten a whiff of him. She pulled him close, her eyes wide, taking the meaning of it: "You smell of fish!"

"A *lot* of fish," he corrected her as she scooted the kids out of the way to fetch the washtub and prepare him a bath. "Herring galore and something else . . ."

She dragged out the heavy copper tub and began unbuttoning his shirt while he swayed in place, barely stable . . . and the two eldest danced around, unsure what they were celebrating. He wanted to tell her she needn't bother; he could fall asleep right on the floor if they just moved out of the way . . . or out on the woodpile, if she wanted him to air out a little . . . He wanted to tell her she needn't do *anything* for him: just being there in their home, just being that wondrous face that looked into his in the manner she had just then . . . that was more peace than he ever thought would come his way.

She leaned in and sniffed him again. "I smell something else . . . Something metallic . . . ? No, wait . . . you smell like lightning."

"Do I maybe smell like starlight?"

The kids cheered. He was sure no one knew what this meant, but they knew to cheer.

He was home . . . with them . . . and he smelled of starlight.

AND SOME FOLK THOUGHT 'TWAS A DREAM THEY'D DREAMED OF SAILING THAT BEAUTIFUL SEA:

It was hard for Luuk to keep it straight. And he wasn't sure where to begin. But of all the people he could tell about what they'd seen out there—as soon as he got ashore—just after the puking—it was Imke he wanted to tell.

He couldn't do it straight away—first, they had to cover the catch from prying eyes and the rising sun till Ned returned with Jaap, and—Luuk held out faint hope—possibly the assistance of Jaap's mevrouw Cokkie and, most importantly, her sister, Imke. Except Jaap didn't bring the ladies along to haul it back, of course, because Jaap highly doubted what Old Man Nodder had told him—about the success of their trip—this early in the season— such a small, strange boat. Then they had to get all the fish into Jaap's cart, then all four of them—even Jaap Bunk joining in—feeling sheepish, it seemed, for doubting Ned—grabbed the gunwales and heaved the pica- rooner up higher onto the dunes. There he and Wyn saw to the rudder, stowed the rigging, battened it down with the tarps. Wyn gave him a wink as they heard the curious beachgoers drawing close—even a strolling moeder with her pram up on the strandweg could be overheard chattering to the baby tucked inside: "Ooh, look at the funny little boat, darling."

And that was when van Donk and his band of useless taunters came by and told them they were dreamers and fools if they thought they could make a serious go of the herring trade in essentially a child's bath toy.

And it wasn't till then—when he realized Wyn was likely going to just curl up by the hull—right on the sand—and dream away the midday—that Luuk decided to set off toward the Kurhaus and hopefully intercept Imke Holt heading home from the night shift.

She was coming out of a side door on the lower level used by the staff. The evidence of her work assisting the baker was all over her in a light dusting of flour and the weary set of her frame, but she greeted him with a pleasant enough hoi, and he fell in alongside her, the whole adventure spilling out of him—he just went ahead and said it all—they'd had a successful sail—and same with the catch, but possibly they'd caught stars, because they seemed to have left the surface of the sea at some point and sailed up into the air—and the moon or something out there was serenading them— And— And—

He thought he knew her silhouette like he knew the bouts of his fiddle. He thought he'd seen the full range of weather—every passing expression she could produce with the movement of her body—at more of a remove, usually, it was true— But he'd never witnessed this gesture before, where she appeared almost to be sinking to one side, her shoulder and chin—and her hip, though he blushed to consider such intimate geography—slightly tipped and out of joint. He couldn't swear an oath that the stance was a new one for her, but he felt a rare sense of clarity that it was a stance that did not bode well. She inhaled deeply, clamped her mouth shut, her eyes saucered and alert.

Even a breath or so before she actually spoke, it struck him—given the way she was suddenly locked in on him—that she had never been more so in addressing him—that in comparison—all those times they'd spoken—she'd barely been paying attention—what little he'd said in the past had hardly made more than a ripple on the surface of her consciousness. In a panic, he wanted to take back everything he'd just told her—no, of course he hadn't thought they'd been up in the sky! Of course he didn't think the boat could fly! But it was too late. She was not taking it well.

"I know what you want me to say, Luuk Blenkin. You want me to say this sort of labor is not for you. Right? You're not made for man's work: you should never go back to the sea, you're going to say, because you have finer things to do with your life. Let me be even more bold and frank: you want me to say that frittering away your days with your minstrelling does not detract from your eligibility as a potential suitor. That it doesn't disqualify you. You want me to say I'm the kind of woman who can live on music and moonbeams. *That's* why you spin this fairy tale."

"No, no," he said. "It's just it really was—" He had to look down—away from her fuming gaze—and realized his britches were still soaked and sandy from dragging the boat ashore. He couldn't remember the rest of his thought—but it really *had* been something—the night before . . . "Van Winkel— You can ask Wyn about it. He was there, so—" Some of that mud on his britches—he could see now—was perhaps not mud but his own upchuck. "I'm perhaps a little unclear on what happened last night, Imke, and I apologize. But I'm not unclear how I feel about you."

"You fell asleep, then," she said, as if even this much was a large concession. "Maybe? No flying boats, no singing moon, all right? It's none of my business, I'm sure, all this onzin you're spouting, but *that's* what happened. Simple."

She told him again that she had to go. "Now I need to get some sleep myself, all right?"

It was true that once they had hit the beach, in the light of dawn, what was visible—crowding the bottom of the little boat—sure looked like plain old herring. A pretty large catch for an undersized boat and crew—but herring all the same. Yet that didn't mean they hadn't been up in the air—or that he hadn't found stars, lingering among the wriggling herring—a handful of stars, silver and gold, that he stuffed in his pocket. They were surely worth *something*—at the least, a sign—a personal omen, telling him what he should do with his life.

His uncle always called him scatterbrained, but his moeder said his head was just too full of ideas—this debate came to him as he watched Imke reach the end of the strandweg—she slipped away through the dunes to the north, to her home at Jaap Bunk's—and he realized he should have just shown her the stars.

He got a whiff of that singular combination and had a moment's dream of a young maiden baker, preparing exotic varieties of fruit taarten in a great glass hothouse mobbed by tropical flowers and elephantine, heart-shaped leaves, burning with sunlight, and knew it was her and stirred himself even before she prodded him with her shoe.

"Not sleeping," he told her, blinded by the sun. Imke was a silhouette in the blaze of it, hugging herself, squinting at the boat. "I was just lying here for a second," he lied. "Checking the hull. Not sleeping away the day."

"I'm hearing various reports . . . How'd she fare last night?" She stepped closer, running her hand along the low gunwale of the covered picarooner.

"Like a star," he said. Scrambling to his feet, he stood and squinted at it just as she was doing, wondering if he should undo the tarps and let her take a better look.

"Someone said she flew."

"Oh, she *really* flew. Just took off! You get down to something this size, there's no holding her back. It's the shallow draft. She's a racer. Just *flies*." Gauging that he knew her well enough now to give her a friendly wink, he did. "Like lightning unleashed. Took off like a rocket." [He wasn't sure what she wanted to hear.] "Like a shooting star."

[She did something funny with her eyebrows.] "What you're saying, then, is she's fast?"

"Ja."

"All right. *That* I believe." Nodding goodbye, she continued on down the beach [turning to call back that he should try not to get burned sleeping out in the sun].

Today of all days, his uncle insisted on his participating in a meeting—in Rotterdam, to make it worse—with the many stockholders who were pressing legal suits against the bankrupt company—to give him "a taste of the blood-rich soil that is this real world the rest of us, the uncoddled, tread upon!"

Luuk insisted he needed a nap first, that he'd been up all night working— "doing this real-world work you seem so interested in."

"Bunkum!" Uncle Allard's face did a brief impression of a pomegranate. "Fible-fable and moonshine!"

Uncle allowed him only enough time to fire off a quick letter—by the afternoon mail, to Smiling Ned—saying he'd been delayed, and asking if he could meet them later that evening to collect his cut—and just enough time to squeeze his weary bones into his Sunday best, laid out and waiting by his mother.

[Fingering the stars in his pocket] Wyn felt that he might want to tell someone about this [someday; show them to someone]. It surprised him a little, this sense of wanting to share what had happened.

When he first arrived back home last year, his pal [good ol' Nodd] was the only person in all of the Netherlands to whom he admitted the habit he'd picked up in the East. [Certainly half The Hague guessed it soon enough, but Ned was the only one he knew who would leave off with the *tsk-tsk-tsking* and dragging him off to see the clergy] and so he laid it out for him one day while helping him rethatch his roof. [Femna was away with the kids till it was done, and they were collecting seagrass at the dunes.] Neddie seemed to be deeply considering what he was saying, and it struck Wyn that his friend might be able to benefit medically from the pipe. [If Ned had the solid sort of stuporous sleep that one obtained down on those silken, subterranean pillows, he might then feel more fully rested and might no longer sag over in a heap in the middle of a task or conversation.] When he proposed it, to his surprise, Ned grunted assent and dropped his bundle and sickle, all set to go try it [with vim!]. Wyn grabbed his hat, and they hopped the steam tram into the city section, to the Kortenbos district. He insisted on treating, and the old man just nodded, grinning. Downstairs, Noddie took the pipe with no hesitation, following his instruction, and drew it in [like a regal maharaja, like a dream, not a blink or a yelp through the whole process].

Afterward, Wyn realized that his friend had been asleep the whole time—from the discussion in the dunes onward [one of his legendary somnambulant rallies] and decided he would never tell the poor chump that he'd once [unknowingly] smoked opium in a Celestial's cellar.

But sitting on that secret was a little different than sitting on a pocketful of stars.

Ned dreamt one night of Fenna . . . and that young Imke lass, and another, not so young . . . Three women, in the market, in the traditional Scheveningen costume . . . the gold hairpins and bonnet . . . looking over their fresh catch . . . one strange fish in particular . . . not your standard little herring, your silver darling . . . They all seemed to want to take it home at first . . . but Fenna ended up patting it and saying no, she wasn't interested anymore . . . and young Imke Holt . . . who had been standing off to the side . . . stepped up and said she was. She would possibly want the fish . . . Meanwhile the dowager Rademaker, that woman from Virt, with the grand estate and hedge, rubbed her big hand along its scales . . . rather roughly and with a sniff . . . as if considering it as a treat for her cat . . .

There were three stacks of guilder banknotes lined up and waiting on the small kitchen table when Wyn got to his friend's. The late-afternoon sun was streaming in, and Wyn could see straight away his cut was already more than enough to pay for his ticket to America.

Ned removed the dishcloth from his lunch pail. He'd stored some stars in there. [The ones that seemed to glow silver.] "I didn't show these to Jaap."

Wyn opened his coat pocket. [His were glowing, too.]

"Four of them, we're going to keep . . . just for decoration." Ned pointed to the overhead beam, just under the sleeping loft.

There was one above each of four sets of tiny klompen, nailed there. Wyn hadn't noticed the tiny klompen the only other time he'd been in the house, for dinner that night. Probably they'd been lost in the shadows. *Four* . . . [But they had three kids; the two girls with the boy in the middle.]

He squinted at the one on the far-left side. It read *Ma. 26.*

Noddie was talking about the boat. "We'll go back out in a couple nights—inspect it bow to stern, see how it's faring."

Wyn didn't comment. [He'd already told him he'd see out the maiden voyage and beyond if he still needed to raise his ship fare, which he clearly didn't now.]

There'd been afternoon mail, with a letter from Luuk, saying he couldn't make it, but he would be playing again at the tavern [Klaas Vaak's] that evening if they wanted to drop in and give him his cut.

"I will likely be asleep." Ned put the third pile of money in the envelope with the note from Blenkin. "Dragging me to see that *once* was what I'd call a miraculous event."

"So that means *I* have to face that ordeal twice. Fine!" He snatched the envelope and money from his friend, who patted him on the shoulder, chuckling, as he turned to go.

Outside, he slipped around back, where there was the familiar shed and the copse of trees beyond it.

[And it was there.]

The gravemarker was a beauty [well-oiled cedar, still holding a hint of its golden shine against the silver of weathering]. The carving was of a sleeping moon, but the name, Sterre, seemed contradictory. And there was no last name, just—

26 Maart 1884–24 Mei 1884

He checked the dates Ned had carved there. So the girl had lived for two months, and he could picture [with a clarity he hadn't felt in years] every single day of those two months. They were suddenly some of the most important days of his life, and he'd spent them in training exercises, cruising around the Strait of Malacca, and then ashore running close-arms and cutlass drills and assisting the KNIL in putting down a small rebellion by the followers of Teungku Chik di Tiro [his first interaction with the ground forces there, hacking away at the jungle and the crops, spotting his first orang-utan], and then back to the ship to stop over in Singapore and visit his first pipe den [and other sorts of dens in Batavia, where two of those days were spent in a jail cell]. *Those* had been the days he'd shared the planet with this Sterre.

He stole a glance back at the house as he stepped from behind the shed. [No sight of the man who carefully crafted this marker.] Such a solid fellow, his friend Noddie [in the way that so often goes unnoticed in the kindhearted].

They'd been on the beach one moonless night, he and dear Fenna [in June of 1883, right before he went off to work on that horrible haringbuis], staring up at the perforated sky, and one of those twinkling dots overhead had jumped and leapt, rambunctious, and they'd agreed if they ever had a daughter, her name would be Sterre.

He could perhaps nap right there [right now, just for a bit], knowing the line of sight from the house was blocked by the shed. He tried to nudge himself to get up and get himself over to the Very Busy Laundry and smoke a big pipe and sleep away all of this. But he pushed that aside and stayed a while, wanting [more than even the delirium of the pipe den] to spend just a little time with little Sterre.

"Some folks," Uncle Allard said—not for the first time—"thought I should let you and your moeder founder, you know." With his uncle haranguing him, right there in the street, there was no way he'd nod off—though otherwise, he felt like he could—just drift off, right on his feet, in the bright midday sun. But not with the man yanking on his collar, straightening his clothes for him—straightening his whole body for him. It was a good ways to Rotterdam, so Luuk wasn't sure why he couldn't just slouch till he got there—and close his eyes at least till their ride arrived.

"I wouldn't dream of such a thing, of course. Responsibility!" Allard spat in his handkerchief and used it to wipe away at Luuk's face—the way his moeder—not all that long ago—had done to him Sunday mornings before church. "But the least you can do today, nephew, is comport yourself as someone worthy of entering the offices of the most respected maritime concern in South Holland, and not like someone who has spent the night in a boat!"

Wyn woke from his graveside nap surprisingly rested, knowing it was real [that he could touch the splintery cedar of this infant grave and the pointy tines of the miraculous objects in his pocket, which gave out a shimmery, fluty sound like a glass harmonica when his fingertips grazed across them].

The sky over toward the beach was just pinking up now [*sailor's delight*] as he got to his feet, dusted himself off, and [staying in the growing shadow on the edge of the copse of trees until he was well away from the Nodder homestead] he continued walking north to his father's house in Wassenaar.

The urge was strong to tell the great astronomer about the adventure they'd had in the night skies—and perhaps also share the news that the man had briefly been a grandfather. [Wyn wasn't sure which story his father would find less believable.] But for the first time in his memory, he felt compelled to seek out his father's company [disapproval and all] and unburden himself to him.

They took an omnibus, pulled by two fine Gelderlanders—slow and lurchy compared to the ride he'd taken last night. The rocking seemed to be lulling the baby held by a dour nursemaid seated across from him—Luuk envied him the rest he was getting, the sunshine sparkling in the babe's long lashes. When Luuk tried to do the same, it earned him an elbow in his ribs— Uncle Allard grousing that soon there would be a proper spoorweg running between The Hague and Rotterdam, for daily business commuters, and if his damnable brother hadn't scuttled the company, that's where they'd be putting their money.

Luuk's one satisfaction—at the offices in Rotterdam—as they closed the doors in the airless boardroom with the dark walnut paneling—was knowing he still bore on his boots the smudge of stargrass from the beach and—from the sniffles and nose wrinkles of the ruffled investors seated around him—that he still stank of the sea and the herring.

Some folks thought, Ned's brothers reported, that Wyn van Winkel had made their brother his babysitter . . . And they continued to say it, even after the cough took little Sterre . . . the meaning being that Ned was also babysitting the scamp's beautiful girlfriend, waiting for him to reappear from his roving . . . Ned told his brothers to leave it alone . . . that they didn't need to question everything. Some things, he said, just were.

Ned had always known Wynkyn was the father . . . she'd been straight with him from the start When she told him, well before the ondertrouw was made public . . . he pictured, finally, the summer before that one, when Wynkyn had worked *De Groot Ster* with them . . . and scared off the fish with his chatter of rowdy fun the night before, with a redheaded painter friend and his girl . . . Some days, she'd come to the edge of the beach to greet the lad, her hair swirled in the wind . . . no bonnet that summer. And that . . . the past . . . was fine with him, because he was fond of Wynkyn, as everyone was . . . and though Wynkyn was the vader of the baby . . . Ned would always be Sterre's pappje . . .

Sometimes they felt they'd dreamed her, she'd been with them so briefly . . . She'd only seen two full moons. He'd held her by the window every night, showing her the night sky . . . He'd never dreamt he'd ever feel like that . . . like he was holding the universe in his cradled arms.

And he secretly dreamt of having another . . . more . . . though how that would happen . . . considering the way they were with each other . . . he had no idea. He tried not to question it though: life had a way of just happening . . . Life was a vast sea full of beautiful things . . .

Ushered into the boardroom in Rotterdam, Luuk deliberately took the seat most pelted by sunshafts from the window, knowing full well it would make him even drowsier—that it would lull him to sleep, along with the blather and concern of these stuffy men of money and soft hands, rolling over him like a lullaby—at times stern, at times high-pitched and whiny, and all the incomprehensia of commerce, of their graphs and charts, provided far more fible-fable and nonsense than any baby's bedtime song of twinkle-twinkle and hi-diddle-diddle.

Because he wanted it settled, he decided. He wanted to make his own bed—wanted to seal the deal, as Uncle Allard would say. He wanted the avuncular fuming to simmer to a final white-hot silence on the way back— the clarity of knowing he had doomed himself from ever being pulled further into the family enterprise—that he was now free to roam. None of those company men—though making livelihoods from the big, beautiful sea—had *ever*—he was sure—put one day or night into doing anything real—at sail, out in a boat, or even wading into the shallows, casting nets, or pulling clams, oysters, crabs from the mud—nothing to wrest that living from its waters—nor would they ever dream of it—and knowing that—after having put just one night—one twisted dream of a night—into such work—Luuk knew they had nothing to offer him that he couldn't find himself.

BUT I SHALL NAME YOU THE FISHERMEN THREE: WYNKEN. BLYNKEN. AND NOD.

"Let me lay out the entire roster of our illustrious herring crew," Ned said one night to his love, after a couple slugs of jenever . . . and after they'd lost several days of work, the night before, when the Caucasian wingnut wood they'd been drying to cut into thwarts started to exhibit disappointing checking along the grain . . .

She was changing the boy as he took stock of the state of the wild-eyed project they were up to out in his shed. He took the youngest and rocked her mid-grouse, being the resident expert at putting them down, according to Fenna.

"Three, in total. Count 'em, dear. First, good ol' Noddie, whom no one will fish with on account of he slips off to slumberland if the wind blows steady . . ." She shot him the *look*, but he kept going. "Wynkyn van Winkel, who fished for herring for all of *two* seasons, six years back, and now seems to be receiving ongoing updates of military movements in Aceh in his head, as well as some other demons, probably . . . Young Luuk Blenkin, who's green as they come and whose family name's considered sullied by everyone at Scheveningen whose occupation is the sea . . . though that doesn't stop him from writing songs about the sea . . . So in case you're wondering how I think we'll fare, I think that's your answer."

"Hush," she said. "I don't believe that's how you really feel."

"Just in case you're wondering . . ." he said, tossing into the stove a hunk of timber . . . the wingnut wood they'd abandoned last night . . . careful so as not to stir the baby girl now deep asleep in the crook of his other arm. "Or in case you need all the names for an obituary notice . . ."

She flared. "Stop it, Ned Nodder. That Wynkyn is rubbing off on you—hiding how you really feel like that. I know you secretly have high hopes."

He gave her his *own* look.

"Well," she conceded, "medium-height hopes then. But enough with the Wynkyn-style wisecracks. I'm not telling you *not* to work with the man. I think you both can help each other. But you're not him. You don't hide behind sarcasm and grumbling. You're the man who decides something is fine and right and will be so, and you put on a smile and it is so."

She had him hand her the sleeping baby, so he could work his magic on the boy.

"I need you to keep being that man," she told him. "*We* need you to be that man."

iV.

WYNKEN AND BLYNKEN ARE TWO LITTLE EYES, AND NOD IS A LITTLE HEAD.

It was times like this that Ned Nodder chose, deliberately, to see his life as a mere dream . . .

And not a dream *he* was having, either. This one . . . he decided at some point back on *De Klomp* . . . was being dreamt by the small son of a poet . . . a writer of children's verses living far off where the sun dipped down into the inky blue . . . far over the Atlantic, deep, deep into the New World. America . . . St. Louis . . . That's where the versifier would live, right alongside his own vivid waterway. St. Louis always sounded like a kind place, named for a saint, after all. And a near miss, muttered, to the English word *lose*, but kinder, saintlier . . . Ned believed it lay somewhere in the middle of that vast landmass, and he imagined it as a place that rested nicely at night; that turned off the gaslight and . . . twinkling only with dew and the occasional candle . . . allowed the moon to rock the sleepy dwellers there well into slumber . . .

It was a vision that steeped him in content.

This wasn't the same thing as dreaming what was to be . . . This was telling himself, for the moment, that *this life* wasn't real . . . that maybe it was just a dream being dreamt by a smart little lad, an ocean away . . . Some place he'd never been . . . as far off and fabled as America's St. Louis. So ja, it was just a boy dreaming up the three of them . . . dreaming up even their odd little boat . . . and knowing nothing of what it was . . . the Clovelly picaroamer . . . but thinking of it as a great wooden shoe, afloat, drifting out into the moonlight . . . And the gathering of stars as fish and the whole lot of it: ja, all of this was just stardust whirring around in the head of a small American boy. It had to be . . . . A boy sleeping so peacefully that when his father peeks in to check on him, the father is inspired to descend to his study on the first floor of the house, sidestepping the tread that always creaks, and sit at his desk with the wick turned low and compose a romp in verse about the boy asleep upstairs, tucked in in his trundle-bed . . . Concocting a beautiful dream in four stanzas about three silly herring fishermen, somewhere far away like the Netherlands . . . and how, all along, it wasn't really them; the three of *them*, whether real or imagined . . . but merely the features of the poet's beloved son, his nod-heavy noggin, with the heaven-bound journey taking place inside . . .

A fellow . . . a simple fellow who knew when to smile and nod . . . could convince himself of almost anything, he well knew . . .

For nearly the first two years of his married life, he'd merely watched his young wife sleep . . . He made do with that. According to the records they'd signed in the little church in Scheveningen, they'd been man and wife since September 1883, but it had been more than two years before they'd truly been joined in marital union . . . He hadn't wished to press it. It was bliss ever after, but his real marriage, he saw now, started in roughly the last week of October 1885 . . . Fenna stirred beside him, breathing heavily in the moonlight . . . she'd thrown back the blankets in a sudden flurry of motion, opening her nightdress, pulling him over onto her, frantic with it . . . as if they hadn't lain in that very bed . . . one he'd built for them, including the carved headboard . . . for two years, like nothing more than siblings . . . It was sometime around the full moon . . . around the same time he'd heard word, from some young men in town closer to Wynkyn's age, that Wyn van Winkel had somehow left the Royal Navy and was instead fighting murderous heathens in the jungles of Sumatra. Ned wept when he told his wife, and Fenna's concern at this news was plain to see . . . And though that look in her eyes rattled him, it was a fear he could manage . . . and nothing compared to the sense of unrest he felt at the thought he might never hear the careless young man's laugh cut across a crowded tavern again . . . At least nowhere but in his head, in his dreams . . .

When they'd come ashore that morning [after Luuk heaved up the radishes and rhubarb], the kid had been laughing a little, too [from relief, perhaps, that whatever *that* had been out there was now over], and Wyn watched him let out a couple whoops [low-key whoops, more appropriate to the early hour and the public setting].

"How about that!" Luuk rubbed the back of his head, eyes wide. Behind him, the moon remained, faint in the morning sky, not yet set. But just a plain, run-of-the mill moon [not a moon currently up for singing and interrogations].

"I remain unconvinced, gentlemen," Wyn joked, "that any of that complied with the North Seas Fisheries Convention of 1882."

It brought a hearty laugh from Luuk and Ned, and Luuk declared, "That had to be the craziest sight you've ever seen!"

"One of them," Wyn said. [He didn't say which previous, crazier sight wasn't quite topped by fishing for stars in the sky, but witnessing the magazine going up, at the garrison in Kutaradja, was still hard to beat.] He just nodded a little and winked and left it at that.

He'd told the story the *way* he told it in the hopes he would then be spared the dreams [when he next found a place to bunk] of the missing shoe, the wide-eyed man, the little moon on the top of his head.

Because of course he hadn't faked the attack, as he'd once told the two of them. All that was a story. [Sure, he'd been hoping for a diversion to come along and cause to be canceled the order to move out at dawn, to march into the jungle to inflict reprisals on a randomly chosen village, but he hadn't actively schemed to stop it; hadn't whipped up a diversion with his own bang and smoke.] The push, with the new leadership, to inflict more brutal and more frequent exemplary actions [like the one set for the following day, selected by a dart flung at the map of Aceh]: that was happening. But despite the fairy tale he'd told some since, the attack on the garrison had been real. [A textbook demonstration of Aceh-mord, the likes of which young

Professor Hurgronje would drool over; a proper, bona fide act of fevered self-destruction in the name of Allah, suitable for framing on a microscope slide for that insufferable fez-topped colleague of his vader.]

He'd been on the wall and had seen the whole thing. It was after the call to prayer over at the masjid, the sunset nearly inked away. All day, they'd been letting local suppliers and peddlers in through the gate, laying on pro visions for the big retaliatory push the next day, when the brass would get their gesture of tuchtiging, their "siksaan." [His comrades in the KNIL had to be well-fed and well-watered to properly demolish Acehnese homes and farmland and poison wells—and climb on their women, like that monkey-slasher Korporaal DeWitt was wont to do before he vanished one day on the march to Gunung Abong Abong.]

It wasn't Wyn's fault the rebel got in. Another man working sentry duty waved him through, with his cart of [what they assumed was] fruit. But once past the gate, it happened [right in front of him] so close, looking down from the wall, that Wyn could see the man had a bald spot [in the shape of a waxing gibbous moon], premature for a man who appeared rather young. He stopped [to readjust his grip on his handcart, perhaps], but he was tossing back the tarp and revealing a row of large cans and overturning one over his head and the smell assaulted, unmistakable [coal oil], and then he was ignited, running straight into the little blockhouse that served as the garrison's magazine.

It seemed as if it couldn't be: the silhouette of that shriveling, blackened body, turned inhuman in a flash, unrecognizable [but moving forward, on-ward, toward the gunpowder stores].

He kept seeing that little head [the man's lopsided bald spot, that im-perfect moon, glimpsed seconds before he went up in flames]. The bald spot had struck him as sad, as something that might [in another time, another part of the world] be charmingly revealed, in private, by an insecure friend who shyly wanted Wyn to weigh in on his appearance [to answer his *What do you think—is this something I can work with? How bad is it? Give it to me straight, Wyn: should I pack it in? Is it all downhill from here?*] And the little burning man had left one shoe behind [fallen away in the effort, somehow uncharred].

It rocked him. In that moment and after. In that moment, he nearly fell off the wall, staring down at the lost shoe [the screams and rolling explosions were there too, but like a distant dream remembered in snatches from way back, childhood even]. And later on, in that time and place he got to eventually [somehow creating space and distance between himself and that act of Aceh-mord], it shook him like nothing else he had seen on that steamy jungle island. And behind it all was a conviction he had no way to properly recognize. He'd seen nothing like that in himself, ever—that kind of dedication [to anything, really]. He hadn't known a single thing that would make him want to set himself on fire and charge toward explosives. [And it wasn't as if Wyn yearned to *do* such a thing, but he thought it would be rather nice to care about *something*—anything, really—as much as all that.]

The rest was more of a blur [a blur he was now working on: he'd decided he should work on it], but he did know he'd bribed some native fishermen [the blue-eyed Puteh who lived along the coast, it had to be], and he'd dressed like one of them and traveled north across the Andaman Sea to Rangoon and, once there, inhaled as much opium as he possibly could.

AND THE WOODEN SHOE THAT SAILED THE SKIES IS A WEE ONE'S TRUNDLE-BED:

Wyn set off walking on the Army Road, north to Wassenaar, where his father lived, closer to the Leiden campus. [It was his boyhood home, of course, though he usually didn't think of it in that way as of late. Some would say his home, wouldn't they?]

It *had been* his mother's home, in a lot of ways. [Meaning Wyn's home, too.] Now it was just his father's *house* [period], convenient to both the university and The Hague, surrounded by big fancy homes owned by big important people.

It was a few miles, but he'd made it in two hours in the past. [Of course he wasn't in dire need of a pipe den those other times—or exhausted from whatever that crazy adventure was the night before.] It felt unusual [this impulse to seek out his father]. But if anyone in South Holland might know what happened in the sky last night, it would be Vader. Wyn *probably* wouldn't ask him [but *maybe* he would].

And if he couldn't bring himself to open up about this strange fishing trip [if it seemed, in the moment, too ethereal to reveal to the man of science and reason who was his stern, disapproving father], he imagined that maybe instead he would reveal something else. He'd sit him down and tell him

[. . . well, *something*] about Sumatra. Not just a joke or a brushoff or a news report the old man might just as easily have read in the papers, but some idea of what it was really like, what he saw and felt [how scared he was; how enchanted by the strangeness and beauty of it all]. He might ask him for help with the pipe [kicking it, that is] or admit that he'd been planning to run off to America, that he likely would never see him again. Any of that, he supposed, would be a start. [Maybe not start with *Looks like you were a grootvader . . .*]

The sun [though lingering languidly these days, now that it was summer] had set sometime during the march up the Army Road to Wassenaar, so that [by the time he reached that quiet, stolid neighborhood of respectable homes] the lamps were lit along the lane. And when he got to the front door and tried it, lightly [and got no answer], Wyn left it at a *scritch-scratch*, declining to do those things he might have in his younger years [throw pebbles at the upper window or cup his mouth and bellow, waking the lane]. He'd pictured his father still up, in his study, reading or working on a lecture, but now Wyn suspected he was in bed, and if that were the case, he didn't want to disturb him. [Or his housekeeper, old Mevr. Schenck, mostly because Wyn did not wish to confirm his mounting suspicion that their arrangement had become something more familiar. *Better to leave that a mystery, Pappje.*]

The stillness of the house, though, tinged him with doubt. He began to consider that perhaps his father had no interest in any information he might impart [whether about Sumatra or about this impossible night sail they possibly took among the stars—or about the short-lived infant daughter, Sterre]. After all, the great astronomer had given him no sign that those recent run-ins, in which he seemed impatient [the times Wyn stopped in on campus], had anything truly to do with the preoccupations of his busy lecture schedule and weren't simply what they seemed: signs that his vader had washed his hands of his son.

It was then that he remembered the bedding he'd asked for and [with some little hope of being proven correct in his suspicion] slipped through the hedges, skirting the house, unlocked the side gate, and snuck around back to peer in at his old room. [Or rather, what would be his vader's new superfluous study, likely filled with important-looking books, maybe a small telescope and star charts.]

His room was unlit from within; the leaded glass wavy and imperfect.

[He wondered how his father, accustomed to the meticulously ground lenses of his famed observatory's telescopes, could stand having these windows in his own home.] But by moonlight, the curtains left open, he could make out enough to see, straight away, that the featherbed of his later adolescence he'd left there, with the bedding he'd asked for, was gone. And the room hadn't, in fact, been converted into a study, but rather appeared now as his room was long ago when he was a toddler: the hobby horse, the globe, the balsa-wood bomschuit high on a shelf, where the small hands of an enthralled boy wouldn't snap it. It was all restored to when the world had been a wee one.

There was his small trundle-bed, which had preceded the featherbed.

His *vader* had done this. He'd put it all back exactly the way it used to be, laid out like a museum of his childhood.

It was really more difficult to believe than the sights they'd seen the night before, and a long moment passed before he could pull himself away, and then he was halfway through the hedge when he thought better of it and backtracked to his old window. Rummaging in his coat pocket, he pulled out a good-sized star [this one glowing gold] and set it on the brick sill.

He would hang onto the rest [for now], thinking he'd like to be more thoughtful and far-sighted with his resources, and not squander it all. [For once in his life.]

On the return trip from Rotterdam that afternoon, his uncle seemed even more disgusted with him—if that were possible—probably because Luuk hadn't been able to follow any of the meeting with the board of directors.

Seated on the other side of him, once again, was a baby—held by, this time, a young mevrouw overburdened with elaborate curls—the woman younger, possibly, than Luuk himself. He knew better than to stare at a young married woman, was loath to turn toward his uncle, so he focused on the baby—which he figured had to be her first—and the thought struck him that he wouldn't even know how to build a cradle—and he'd have to, with Imke. Because they'd keep a pennywise little home, he had no doubt—at least at first. Even after he saw some success, though, he suspected she'd insist they still live like that—like Old Ned. She was too practical and hardworking not to. Only unlike Old Ned, he was witless as to how to make things—other than verses, of course—the scribbling in his notebook. It was the only thing he did know how to do.

Did they *have* to have a real cradle, then a crib, then a trundle-bed—?

The baby opened its eyes and smiled at him—the baby was daunting as hell. Where would a baby even sleep?

After what he'd seen in his father's window, he felt himself hedging, losing faith in the plan, but he went forward with it [setting off for The Hague proper, before he would go to find Luuk and give him his cut].

Ahead of him, to the south, church steeples speared the starry night beyond. Just the previous evening, out on the beach, the old dune painter had preached the importance of [literally] looking up; the vital nature of the skies.

Just yesterday, he'd woken [late, as the day was wrapping it up] in the broken hull of a storm-wrecked bomschuit, not far from where they'd stored the picarooner in the dark of the night [after that marathon drag from the Nodders']. He'd picked this spot to bunk through the day because of the proximity to *De Klomp*, needing to be on time for its maiden voyage. He woke and peered out through the splintered side at the darkening sky [the blue hour, his artist friends had called it] and recognized the figure down by the surf as old Jan Weissenbruch, folding up his easel, boxing up his paints and brushes and canvas. By the time Wyn crawled from the bom and staggered over to their much smaller boat up in the dunes, Blenkin was there already, removing the tarps, getting it ready for the launch. And the old dune painter was stopped there, talking to him as he worked. As Wyn approached, he could hear the artist speaking with admiration of how unusual it was.

"I've seen many, many boats here in my life, but never one quite like that. Nou breekt m'n klomp!" [The expression that his fellow stowaway, English Van, loved so to rag him about.] "Another time," the old man said, "when you have it uncovered again, in the better light, perhaps I could do a study?"

Luuk told him sure.

By this time Wyn had reached the far side of the picarooner to work on the tarp lines on that side, nodding hoi to Weissenbruch and muttering some agreement. Weissenbruch thanked them and returned to toting his easel and supplies toward the strandweg.

"Excuseer mij. Young man—"

Luuk looked up, and the old man struggled back down the dune. [But he was addressing Wyn.]

"I'm sorry. You're Vincent's friend, ja? We spoke, I believe, during the holidays, about his recent . . . downturn?"

"Wyn van Winkel." [He could smell the paints on him as he shook his hand.]

"I've received further word from his brother Theo."

Wyn braced himself. [Here would be news of more recklessness, swinging back into his life with a hard thud.]

"Word is that he is working. He's . . . in attendance, at a place where he's getting care . . . but he is working again and feels buoyed by a canvas he just began of the starry heavens, the view from the window of the room where he sleeps. I don't know if the work's any good, of course, but the main thing is, he sounds hopeful again."

"Hopeful is good," Wyn said.

"Apparently he's been doing a few nocturnes. Theo said he also wrote that he has been feeling a real need for religion lately—a 'tremendous need,' according to Theo—and so he finds that he is looking up at the sky at night and painting the stars."

Reflexively, they both looked up at the sky for a moment. [He didn't know about dragging religion into it, but wherever this asylum was, they probably didn't let you keep a crazy pregnant night-piece in your room, and that was probably as great a help as a person needed.]

"Bedankt, sir," Wyn said. "I'm very glad for this news."

After a few more seconds, swaying awkwardly in the sea wind, the old man turned hearty and joyful, the way Wyn remembered him. "Ja, it's a good thing, what Vincent is up to! The sky in a painting, that is what is most important! Sky and light are the great magicians. The *sky* determines what is. We can never pay too much attention to the sky!"

Wyn knew it was true. Weissenbruch's work could be described as landscapes and seascapes, and yet it was all almost entirely the sky. He lived on the edge of a wet, wet land, by a sea where the sun slept for the night, and yet his life's work was the sky.

Honestly, Luuk was envious—Wyn van Winkel seemed to know everyone in the community. Of course Luuk knew who the dune painter was—but the dune painter would never know him.

His moeder had taken him—when he was little—to a gallery show that included many of his watercolors—she even owned one of his seascapes—a wee one, not much bigger than his song notebook—or did own it, before their *unfortunate reversals*, as she put it.

They were chatting like old shipmates, Wyn getting a peek at his wet canvas and praising him for still keeping at it—for staying fascinated with the sea and the sky and finding new things to say about it—Weissenbruch admitting that he would be turning seventy next year and planned to go to the forest—"Just to paint some trees, just to say I did it!"

The two men laughed, and Wyn told him he was planning something similar—in a way—heading off to America next.

For some time now, Luuk had thought of this old dune painter as a personal role model—a painter version of what he wanted to be—*of* one area like this, all his life, synonymous with the place and how it reflected in his art—in Luuk's case, it would be his ballads. Those ballads, that is, that wouldn't be about his love. And even a lot of those that would be about her—they would also be about this place—in a way.

A musical version of Jan Weissenbruch—one whom folks in Scheveningen would point to and say, *Do you know who that is? That's the great troubadour Blenkin. Why, that old man and his songs are part of this place like the sand and the marram grass are part of the dunes—like the silver darlings are part of the sea and part of us.*

Thinking of the wee ones . . . and thinking of that unknown, red-cheeked tyke in his dream, his lashy, surrendering eyes winking and blinking, his head nodding into his pillow . . . thinking that what remained at home was what sent men to sea . . . that morning, after collecting their pay from Jaap Bunk for their extraordinary catch—the actual fish portion of the catch, that is . . .

Ned purchased a hunk of klapstuk and a small sausage at the butcher and some spices at the grocer . . . He stopped at Elzinga's and splurged on store-bought rolls and chocolate bread . . . and heard the news . . . not news to him, of course . . . that the shoals were running, that someone had returned with a massive catch that morning . . . it was *massive* by now: that made him smile . . . and so all the crews were scrambling to gear up for the season . . . Ned then returned to the grocer and purchased hazelnuts and dates and even, to tantalize the wee ones, three real lemons from far across the sea.

With growing misgivings, Wyn headed into the Kortenbos neighborhood and the so-called Very Busy Laundry.

The lăo băn came around the counter to greet him. "Sailor! Finally! And not too soon, it look like. You look no good like bowel movement not person—you feel like that also, yes, no good? We fix you up no time, no problem."

The headman took hold of both of his arms like a wheelbarrow and pulled him backward toward the cellar stairs. [Wyn could smell it from the top step, wafting up, hear the chiming trill of that small Oriental guitar thingy—the one he pictured the owl playing in those verses English Van liked to recite. One of those kind, smiling ladies cradling it, no doubt, kneeling on a pillow, near enough to assist if he dropped back too clumsily, if the pipe overcame him too fast . . .] His whole body wanted to follow along.

"No." He grabbed the railing, twisting away from the cellar stairs. "*No.* I'm not here for that. *I'm not.* I need a steamship—"

"Pipe no good, sailor?"

"Pipe no good. Steamship ticket! Me needy ticky" Wyn stopped himself. [Why did he fall into that sort of jibber-jabber? It couldn't actually help anything.] And he was really doubting he had his information right [that you could purchase a transatlantic liner passage here from this half laundry, half pipe den . . . half travel bureau?].

But the fellow then produced a brass skeleton key from his elaborate silken sleeves and, turning to a door beside the cellar stairs [which Wyn would have assumed was a broom closet if he'd even ever noticed it before], unlocked the door, stepped inside, and closed the bottom half [which was braced with a narrow countersill, like a box-office window]. There was gas-light in there, and he turned it up, revealing a space no bigger than a closet. Officiously, the lăo băn slipped a teller's shade over his perfectly pomaded hair, and arranged a few clipboards along the wall, heavy with the Celestial chickenscratch pictographs. Behind him hung maps of the world, with lines swooping across them, routes like bunting.

"Which lines? You name!"

"The . . . Holland America Line?"

The lăo băn plucked one of several lapel pins from a narrow shelf beside him and attached it prominently on his high collar, displaying the logo for the Nederlandsch-Amerikaansche Stoomvaart Maatschappij. "Official steamship agent, N.A.S.M. Goedenavond, sir."

"Hoi yourself." [Now he was *sir*? It must depend on what you were there to buy.]

"Where you go, please?"

"America."

"No problem. You leave Amsterdam, direct to New York, seven day, no problem, you good."

"No. I mean— Sorry. New Orleans."

He only glanced at his charts; it was as if he could do this in his sleep.

"Two boat, then. You leave Rotterdam, take Holland America Line for Mexico, get off Florida, second boat to New Orleans, eight day, no problem, you good."

It *was* a broom closet. He could see a mop handle leaning in the corner and some spare gongs and dragon statues. The Celestial held several small rubber stamps, ready to construct his ticket. [This was how he managed it, Wyn saw now; how the same man who couldn't write out the name of his own laundry could produce an official ticket for him.]

"Why you look at me like I fairy tale, sailor? Give money, take ticket. Go."

He wasn't sure anymore. The idea of never speaking to his father again, after what he'd seen in the window earlier—it made him hesitate. [That and a few other things.]

But he could always cash it in or unload it somehow. So he handed over the money and took the ticket and, as he turned to leave, passed a big brass gong with two little mallet marks that caught the light in such a way they were like smiling eyes, like the moon smiling at him all over again.

Luuk headed to Klaas Vaak's early enough to set up in the corner—he thought—but even from far down the strandweg, he could hear it was already lively and jumping—buzzing with laughter, strained voices, the clink of glass. His big inhalation—he wasn't sure—was either for fear or excitement. This was going to be different than the other night at Dirty Ned's. A coffeehouse was one thing—a full-house tavern another.

But the owner, Maas Bruss, stepped out and clamped a hand on his shoulder. "Hold up, kiddo. Listen . . . Sorry. I have to say no—not a good idea, you entertaining. Not tonight. Too many folks here right now, and we're doing real good business."

"That's great— So—"

"More of a drinking crowd. Rowdy. I don't want to run them off."

Luuk tried to peek in around him, and caught the barmaid Hilly's eye—the way she looked down at her tray suddenly, he could see that she had probably said something about his debut at Dirty Ned's—which, granted, had not been the stuff of legend, but still—

Maas slipped a couple guilders in his pocket and slapped him on the back like he was just a stupid kid—the village simpleton. Luuk edged over to regroup by the big sign—the one of a long-whiskered Klaas Vaak flying on his owl over a sleepy town—a half-assed Scheveningen, given the silhouette of the Kurhaus—sifting his moon sand from a sack—the upturn of wing ruffled in the night wind. This was supposed to be the big show here. Dirty Ned's had been rehearsal for tonight.

The door sailed open and a jumble of men burst out, hooting and talking over each other—Harm van Donk and Zef Kloet, who'd taunted them about their boat on the beach that morning—even made fun of his hands—only now they had more of the *Dromenvanger* crew with them. And Wyn wasn't there—damn him.

Luuk tried to gather his instruments—but the hoots increased once they spotted him.

"Kid! It's you! Mr. Butter Hands! Remember me?"

It was Zef, getting right up close.

"Hey, you know, all them klootzakken in there right now, they're in there talking about your puny little boat. Spreading lies." He rapped him on the chest with the back of his hand. "We had to get out of there. Couldn't listen to no more of that onzin . . ."

Sem Bongers gave Luuk a hard look. "Never happened, you know. Bunch of liars."

"Maybe it did, now, lads," said Harm van Donk. "Maybe it was some devilish magical spell van Winkel picked up in the Orient."

More hooting followed—meant to be laughter—but more like the owl on the sign beside him. Impatient now, Luuk asked if he was inside.

"Didn't see him," said Harm.

"Probably with the Celestials." Bongers made a sucking sound like he was drawing on a long pipe.

"Maybe he's up in the sky again!" Zef bent way back, searching the heavens, barely able to maintain his balance. "Wheeeeee! I'm flying!"

They thought they were hilarious, and when Zef straightened again, he chucked Luuk under the chin—like he was five.

He almost didn't catch it over the laughter—but it was the weedy one—Blan Zylstra piping up with his own theory. "Bet he's with that Holt girl. Cokkie's little sister. I seen them together."

Zef asked what Luuk wanted to ask. "When?"

Blan shrugged. "Couple of times."

"Then he's probably somewhere working his magic on her!" Zef grabbed his crotch. "His magic *wand!*"

Luuk wanted—so badly—to ball up his soft, butter hands into fists and let them have it. *They* were the liars. He busied himself rearranging his instrument cases—until van Donk eventually shifted his *band of liars* in another direction. But Luuk still had to wait for Wyn—who probably thought he'd be playing till late and could take his sweet Asiatic time about it like the careless dope fiend he was—

He moved down the strandweg a skosh—sat on his accordion case like a camp stool—and dropped his head in his hands.

Even with the herring crew gone—Luuk could still hear the men roaring inside—even make out snippets and whole phrases—and it was clear there was an exciting rumor riling them up tonight—whether they had it straight or not, he couldn't tell, but they were definitely talking about "Vagabond

Winkel" and "Agreeable Ned" and "what Bunk said"—and some contraption that likely defied the North Seas Fisheries Convention and possibly gravity itself—and still others were shouting them down, declaring it all horsecrap.

No one was including him in the tale. No one was even saying, *Where's that youngster was supposed to sing here tonight?*

He got up and dragged his accordion and fiddle to a spot still farther down the strandweg.

His body was telling him now that he'd made a mistake back at the Celestial's [multi-tiered business enterprise]. Just for the sake of maintaining, he probably should have gone downstairs. It had been far too long between visits to the pipe den. He could really feel it now. [He could feel *everything* now.]

But he recognized the form of the boy, framed in the glow of the Kurhaus just down the strandweg, sitting on some sort of case. [Was it luggage? Was he going somewhere? *He should,* Wyn realized. *He really should.*] He moved toward him as best he could, cramped like never before, his whole body like a fist now [yet ready to come apart at the seams].

"Luuk! Luuky, Luuky . . . How strange is this: last time I saw you, you were retching at the start of the day, now it's midnight and I may just be doing that myself any second now—look out! *If* I'm lucky and it comes out of *that* end, that is. Lucky, lucky Luuky . . ." Wyn fished out the kid's envelope. "We did all right, kid. Maybe *you* were the good luck. Not a bad haul for your first run. Here you go, lucky."

He handed it over, and the kid said "Bedankt" [but not very loudly], and Wyn felt *he* hadn't said enough either. There had to be more he could give him. [He saw then that they were instrument cases and knew he hadn't been allowed to play.] He wasn't sure how to say this [or if he should say it]. He clamped his hand on the boy's shoulder. "I want to leave you with something else," he began.

Luuk seemed distracted, thumbing through the cash in his repurposed envelope. "More than generous, splitting it three ways—" he interrupted. "I mean, I didn't even invest in the boat like you two—"

"Let me give you something more in the way of advice . . ." This was painful. But it almost felt as if the stars in his coat pocket were making him brave, giving him the courage to be honest and straight-ahead [for once]. He tried to hold a sigh in but failed [this not being the sort of thing he normally got entangled in]. "Listen, you're very . . . You've got a lot of great spirit, Blenkin . . . a helluva spirit . . . and it's easy at your age to run off in a dozen different directions, helter-skelter . . ."

"It is?" The lad grinned. "I know we saw some impossible things out in the boat, but *that* really sounds—just *physically*—"

"I'm saying I'd hate to see you do what I did, spending years frittered away in the wrong direction. I mean . . ." Wyn stopped himself. [Why was he doing this? Life went so much smoother if you just kept things to yourself unless really pressed. The kid wasn't even fishing for his opinion on his talents. And yet here he was walking right into the subject of his own free will. What the hell had happened to him?]

"I'm saying, it may seem like you've got all the time in the world to try a lot of things, run down the wrong alleys—and you're young—you are, but—"

Luuk dropped the smile. "I know where you're going with this."

"Well, then I'm not the first to suggest this, but "

The kid jerked his shoulder out of his grasp, standing to face him. "They told me what you were up to, you know. The crew from the *Dromenvanger*."

Wyn was trying to remember the night of the Dirty Ned performance [more specifically, after] and who the hell might have overheard him and Smilin' Ned discussing Luuk's caterwauling [he didn't recall any herring crew] when Luuk hauled back with what looked like a fiddle case and caught him in the side of the head.

Wyn's legs buckled. One knee hit the boardwalk planking, and he was half in the sand, his bad ear and shoulder gouging into the dewy beach, and Luuk was snarling something about Imke: "They said you were working your *magic* on her is what they said! That dimwit Zef Kloet—he said—"

"Kloet's an oaf . . ." Wyn said to the sand [or just thought to himself—he wasn't sure now].

"Well, he said you were sparking her, out on a stroll! Making time behind my back—the great Casanova, returned to The Hague! So I don't guess I'm just going to take your advice, am I? Go ahead! Say it: *Oh, she's not for you, kid. You're just wasting your time, kid.* Gonna hand me that *plenty of fish in the sea* line? Nice try, you—you fucking weasel!"

"What?" His head was ringing from the fiddle case, and it felt wet and warm just under his ear. He wanted to get back up [where he at least had a little height on the kid], but everything was spinning. Craning his neck [his hair mashed into the wet sand], he was trying to get Luuk in his view, but all he could see was the sky above—a couple stars, which he addressed: "The hell are you talking about, Luuk? I'm talking about your *singing*, you ungrateful little shit!"

There was a silence in which he could hear the surf.

"What *about* my singing?" Luuk barked at him.

"It's the sound of an ill-fitting oarlock, Luuk. *That* part of it . . . You're great at writing verse—really great—and you ought to put everything into *that* and . . ."

It was too late. He wasn't listening. Wyn continued to try to twist around so he could see the boy, but his body wasn't cooperating and his legs remained higher than his head [still hanging over the edge of the strandweg, ground into the sand and marram and stargrass]. But he could hear footsteps retreating.

Then he heard them growing louder, returning, and the lad was standing over him again. "Keep your opinions to yourself, you derelict." Luuk kicked him in the side. "Meneer van *Weasel*." Then he was gone.

"Oh, here's something else . . ." Wyn said to himself [but right out loud, having realized in that moment, piling on to the blows from Luuk, his recent neglect of the pipe was kicking in with a wave of cramps and a stirring that might herald a rumbling in his bowels], but he had to chuckle. He couldn't help it: had the kid just called him *van Weasel*? It was possible he was dying [or at least crapping his pants, out in the elements, in public], but at least he'd been left with a good laugh.

And how nice to hear his mother singing . . .

He'd known—

There was a hulk left on the beach—the wreck of *De Zilveren Schat*—one of the many boms busted up in the last great storm—and Luuk had poked his head in there one time—maybe a year ago—some time before Wyn van

Winkel—with his addled swagger and biting remarks—had even returned to Scheveningen. Inside, he heard an echo—an unerring reverberation—and—checking first to see if anyone was just outside, strolling past on the beach—and finding no one there—he stepped back into the shadows, faced the great upturned hull, and let loose. He gave it his best one—the ballad he'd written about the fine day he would marry Imke Holt—the one that began:

Berries needlepointed
On her blouse of blue and white.
You can tell by the moon
She's out walking in the night.

He got about two verses in, and he heard it. He knew that now, a year later—he'd heard it back then. The sound coming back to him was flat, the note not quite right, troubled.

At the time, he'd told himself it was the wind—some acoustical warp to this sea-tossed monster, this inadequate ruin—or the disharmony of the breakers out there, polluting his tone—but he'd known. He'd heard it then: *he couldn't sing.*

And it stung—the clarity of this stung—the way sometimes his eyes stung when he opened them too wide on the beach, when a low howler picked up, cutting along the sand—and it stung more than any other world-shifting fact he would ever have to face—he was sure of that.

And there was the taste of brass in his mouth now—beyond the bilious bite of his own retching [either blood, Wyn imagined, or possibly he'd somehow taken a big chomp out of a moon-shaped gong? No, that didn't sound right].

Running home, back toward the city center—in a rage, too upset to stomach being goggled at on the steam tram—it struck Luuk that when he'd thought Wyn was reaching up, trying to push him away or poke at him, he was shoving something at him. When he came upon the shoe store where he'd first laid eyes on Wyn, he slowed to check in his satchel and found the money inside—plus a second envelope, crumpled.

He felt even more certain he must reek now when she was able to slip up on him [without him smelling that scent he'd come to think of as Imke Holt]. There was no jasmine or flour or whatever it was, just her voice, hovering over him, saying, "Wynkyn? Is that you?"

It struck him as far too difficult a question. "Korporaal van Weasel, commandant, sir," he mumbled, "reporting for duty . . ."

She knelt on the edge of the strandweg, and he could confirm now [through the syrupy thickness stinging his eyes] that it was indeed Imke Holt [though maybe with a cumulus cloud on her head? No, a baker's cap.]

"Lieve hemel. You're bleeding."

"And that's actually the *best* part of it. You're only getting half of the story, I assure you." He hoped she couldn't smell him. [At least before he got a chance to do a personal inspection and survey for possible seepage in his breeches.] "Don't get too close, sweetheart . . ." Maybe the smell of last night's catch was still strong on him and would cover the conflagration down below. He was just glad that Luuk's brief return [to kick him in the side] had jarred him completely off the strandweg [so he no longer lay half on and half off, the lower half slightly on the uphill side].

She was ignoring his warning, he realized [though he couldn't force his eyes to focus]. He could feel her taking his weight [her breath on his cheek, her baker's hat crushed against his neck] as she strained to try to help him to his feet.

Then she seemed to be letting go of him, easing him back down to the strandweg. [Giving up, probably: she should. Maybe she'd finally gotten a whiff of him.] "Hold on." She sounded like an annoyed mother. "Your *shoe* . . ."

She was right [one boot had come loose in the scuffle]. Wyn stared at it for a time. [Tipped sideways, reckless-looking, alone just down the strandweg, the sad little clump of leather looked rather like the lost shoe he'd seen his last night in Aceh, when the garrison was attacked.]

Fetching the loose boot, wedging it into the wide pocket of her apron, she returned, wrapped herself around him again and, with a heave, helped hoist him [more or less] upright. The strandweg seemed to tilt [along with the glowing masjid, as he called it, the whole dark North Sea beyond, wriggling with silver darlings, no doubt].

He was pretty sure that he'd slipped into a delirium [whether from want of the pipe, from getting thrashed by the kid, or maybe both]. But in this dream, at least, he was draped all over her, and then she was making him walk [taking his wobbly weight, made wobbly herself with it].

"Who did this to you, Wynkyn?"

"Orang-utans. A band of the beasts emerged from the trees . . . a great orange hairy wave of them . . ." [With his mouth awash in blood, he was sure she couldn't understand him.] "Also, the rebel band of Teungku Chik di Tiro. They're in cahoots. Couldn't be stopped . . ."

"Enough with the onzin." Somehow, the way she said it sounded like more than an admonition to cut the sarcasm. [It sounded like an official announcement of great import, like an armistice; a cessation of hostilities; the commencement of a new era whose time had come: the End of Nonsense.]

So Shut Your Eyes
While Mother Sings
Of Wonderful
Sights That Be.

His mammie had always said he sang like an "angel baby." Luuk wondered if this meant he sang like a dead infant—but that couldn't be what she meant.

—Could it?

Kicking off his shoes, he tiptoed into his uncle's house—the House of Diminished Circumstances. Luuk's moeder kept a photo of his father there, in the small vestibule—which he figured Uncle Allard only tolerated because it remained shrouded in black mourning crepe.

Luuk found her sleeping in his small bed—like the story of the three bears, from that English book back in his old room—the room that had been twice as big as this one, with two whole walls lined with such books.

She never did this—though he had a feeling she'd moved in here the night before as well—while he was out on his crazy herring adventure on the sea—or high *above* it. She likely didn't sleep that night—worried about her only son. True, back when he was quite small—in their old house, in their old life—she'd often sung him to sleep and then blown out the taper and snuggled alongside him till sometimes she'd fall asleep—accidentally—and have to rouse herself and navigate back to her own bed. He couldn't recall now what songs she sang, but she sang to him back then. With a beautiful voice—he was sure of it. Not a voice like an ill-fitting oarlock.

He was glad she was asleep—she'd look him over and know he'd just done something ugly and unfair—and to a friend.

Withdrawing from his satchel all but two of the stars—if that's what they were—the things that seemed not to be fish—guided by the snore from his uncle's room, he arranged them on the Persian at the foot of Uncle's four-poster bed—making an *L* that glowed silvery bright—an *L* for *Luuk* or maybe *Ludovicus*—that would burn in his uncle's mind—and then turned to flee.

In the vestibule, grabbing his shoes, he whisked away the black mourning crepe, shoving it in his satchel, leaving his father's photo exposed for Uncle Allard to see—to acknowledge his *vader* and recognize he *was* out there, somewhere—still upright—in all ways.

Out on the cobbles, he took one last look back at the House of Diminished Circumstances—his uncle's bedroom windows stood out in the dark—a magnesium sheen leaking past the edge of the blinds—burning madly with starlight.

There were stairs at the side entrance of the Kurhaus, and she eased him back down and told him to wait right there. He had nowhere to go, of course, and [so it would appear] no great degree of muscle coördination at the moment to make himself go there. He heard her scrambling down the stairs and through a service door, into the basement, and then there were the stars overhead [and his mother singing about three men in a boat], and then she was breathing close to him again, putting her arms around him, trying to get him back up.

"Lammie's here," she said. "Lammie will help."

The big baker girl, Lammie Elzinga, took hold of one side of him, and the two of them half led, half dragged him down into the lower level of the Kurhaus.

It smelled of bread and appeltaart [and laundry].

Now that Imke had help, this part was like floating [the sultan on his gaudy palanquin, with this hulking mistress of the loaves practically carrying him down the steps, toward the warm smell of yeast].

Once in the basement corridor, he tried to help more [to support more of his own weight], but the careening feeling grew worse. Here he could make out the lines and right angles of the walls more distinctly than he had up on the strandweg, and so it was clear the whole world was indeed tilting. It was as if he were pitching forward, over and over, without actually falling. [If he didn't have the two women to hang onto, he wasn't sure what would happen. Something that defied gravity, likely.]

"At sea," he said [out loud, he was pretty sure].

Imke groaned with the weight of him. "Heard the whole fairy tale this morning from Luuk Blenkin—*I wasn't sure if we were up in the* air . . . *or at* sea . . . *It was so* confusing, *Imke*—all that. So you can save it for now."

"*Me*," he said. "*I'm* kind of . . . *at sea* . . ."

"He's ripe, but I don't smell jenever or ale on him," Lammie Elzinga said, as if he wasn't there [and Wyn wasn't entirely sure he was]. "You better check his head. He looks drunk, but　"

"Ja, his ear's bleeding," Imke said. "Blow to the head, I'd say."

Lammie told her to be sure to check his pupils. [Probably what made her such a good baker, he figured: those little details; not skipping anything on the list.]

"Bedankt," he told them. "There's a star in it for you—both of you." [What he meant to say, of course, was *I've got stars in my pocket.*]

In a room at the end of the corridor, they eased him down onto a chair against the wall by a bathtub. "Leave the gas off," Imke told her friend, lighting an oil lamp instead.

He still felt like a human baby rattle, but a little was coming into focus— there were lighting fixtures [a sconce by the door, which she wasn't turning on] and a footstool by the tub [for climbing in] and a Japanese screen and shelves of linen and towels, and on the other side of the room, in the shadows, cots.

The big lady baker patted his shoulder [bull's-eye on a direct hit from Luuk] and heaved a deep sigh, as if they'd just hauled in a shipment of large flour sacks for the week's dough. "No more wandering for you, Wandering Wyn. At least not tonight, ja?"

He didn't argue. [Though it did strike him as a bit forthy. He didn't really know the Elzinga girl, and here she was treating him like some sort of local character, the tolerated Tom Fool.]

"I'll sit right here," he said [or thought he did, and also thought *in my own filth*].

Imke thanked the baker gal, who went back to work [putting something on the doorknob, it seemed like, before closing the door behind her].

Taking a washcloth from the shelf, Imke ran it under the tap [ah, the modern miracles of the Kurhaus, even in its dark underbelly, where the common folk toil!] and brought it over, along with the oil lamp.

He managed to make some muttering sounds meant to convey the idea that she should just get back to work [that he wouldn't want her to lose even one of her many jobs on his account].

She said she was on a break anyway. ["The three hours the dough rises, I'm supposed to clock out, just leave Lammie to it."] She'd been starting for home when she ran into him, she explained, though it was hardly worth going home for such a short stretch [which was why the staff kept this "bunk" in the basement, handy to the big ovens where they did the night's baking].

They were down the hall from the ovens now, by his estimate, based on the echo of a woman [Lammie, he decided] singing a husky lullaby.

Ned Nodder had a long-held theory about his friend . . . He could see that one of the things Wynkyn was punishing himself for was not being back before his moeder passed . . . but Ned knew that may have been for the better. Ned had known Mevrouw van Winkel . . . As Hendrikje Vandroogenbroeck, Hennie had been a few years ahead of him in school. She never seemed to take on airs after becoming a professor's wife and moving to Wassenaar . . . and she was the reason, Ned felt, that her son had a sense of humor and why he'd behaved, in his youth, like he was from Scheveningen all his life . . . and not at all like he'd grown up closer to Leiden in a fine brick home with a high hedge . . . She'd come out to see her son off, back in '82, the year Wyn crewed with him and his brothers in *De Groot Ster*. She walked down along the wet sand of the tidal flats and greeted Ned with that smile of hers, like they were old friends . . . and asked them informed questions about the state of the bom and the prospects for the season, and she asked Ned, personally, to please take care of her only boy.

She'd shown up at the house, too, with a plate of coconut cookies, when the first one, little Sterre, hadn't survived . . . She didn't linger or intrude . . . but this gesture was deeply felt . . . long after the cookies were gone.

If she'd still been alive when Wyn returned home, it would have been sad. She was the only person, Ned was sure, that Wyn had ever always been straight with. Hennie and her son joked as they spoke . . . but beneath it all, he knew, Wynkyn always came clean with her.

And so what would her Winkie have said to her, had he made it back in time: "Guess what I did, Mammie? I killed people, for the crazy king, for pepper and oil and religion . . . burned crops and villages, spoiled wells, deserted, picked up an opium habit . . ."

Imke Holt was tut-tutting, mother-henning, shifting his head under the glow of the oil lamp, working her way around in his greasy hair, probing [likely checking if there were more or deeper wounds].

"What, exactly," she wanted to know, "happened out there?"

"Ah, your basic siksaan."

"There were six of them? Was this a herring crew who did this?"

"It's siksaan. The word is *siksaan.*"

"I need you to try to be clear and direct," she said, abandoning the search through his dirty locks. "Did they hit you hard on the head, maybe? Your ear and eye look the worst, but you sound like they may have cracked your skull. Are you slurring?"

"You know—punishment. Retaliation. The ol' tuchtiging policy. Siksaan. That'll teach the natives a lesson, boy . . ."

"Whatever you fellows call it, it's unacceptable. You upset the other fishermen with your little experimental foreign boat, didn't you?" Dabbing at his tender eye with the cloth, she moved the lamp closer, side to side [the wick in the globe a moon that close]. "You strike me as a trouble-stirrer. Jeetje! Still, they can't do this." She cupped her hand over one of his eyes and waggled some fingers. [He didn't follow what was going on.]

"Come on," she huffed. "How many fingers?"

"Two?" he guessed, and asked what she was doing.

"*Trying* to check your sight."

"I'm probably a sight," he said, "if that's what you're asking."

"You are," she said, straightening herself, "and I'm not."

At the tub, she set the drain plug and squeaked the big knobs, and with a great beastly grunt, the famed modern plumbing of the Kurhaus heaved into action, gushing water into the tub. Unfolding the Oriental privacy screen, she arced it around the chair where he sat slumped, shielding, also, the view of much of the tub. He peered around it, eyeing her. From a cupboard, she produced a box of little votive candles and arranged a mass of them at the foot of the tub, on the floor. As she lit them, the shadows flickered in shafts up the wall. [He thought of that winter night at Noddie's shed, when they'd watched the northern lights, the three of them.]

"You'll need a little light. But we might as well keep it discreet, right? Besides," she said, "fellow staff peeking in is one thing, management another."

"You don't have to . . ." [He couldn't finish the thought even. And he couldn't quite get to his feet.]

"Sit."

"I can hardly just sit here and watch while you draw me a bath and—"

"So close your eyes," she said.

He closed his eyes [but only because his eyes were insisting]. When he opened them, she'd moved back around to his side of the screen and was removing his remaining boot and his socks. [At first, this felt pathetic, but he was soon glad she had: when she got up and retreated behind the scrim again, he bent to remove his trousers, and that bit of bending alone made him wince. On his own, he never would have made it down to his socks.]

"Most of them wouldn't make a fuss, finding you here," she said, "but we don't need to light you up like a stage show."

Unbuttoning the sleeve of her uniform, she tested the temperature of the water with her elbow, the way a mother might. With the bath drawn, she repositioned much of her army of candles to the rim, nearer the water, rounding the tub with them [and the flickering gold brought him back to that moon the night before, strung out ahead of them, filling their nets.]

Stripped, he eased up out of the chair, groaning, and peeked over the scrim, down at her handiwork. The candlelight was the glimmer of the music of the Toba Batak [gongs, finger cymbals, the clack of wood blocks, the steady dong-dong and withered old lady wailing], all playing across the water and the walls, shimmering, ancient.

She peered up at him now, from the other side of the screen. "Now, I *would* leave, but frankly, you seem pretty foggy. I'm rather afraid you'll slip getting in and get even further banged up— Are you sure you—?"

"*I'm* not foggy."

"Dizzy then."

"It's the night that's dizzy, dancing around. The night is a misty sea, sweet Imke . . ."

"Of course it is." She tapped the top of the screen, as if it were his shoulder. [Or maybe his head, like a little boy's, patronizing him?] "I'm concerned about leaving you here alone. Besides, Lammie will cover for me and tell anyone who asks that I'm using the room right now, but if I'm waiting out in the hall, or back by the ovens, some might assume it's empty and barge right in and . . . well . . ."

"So close your eyes," he said.

And she gave him such a look [long and piercing], he didn't know what to make of her.

"Stay," he said. "Please?"

Finally, keeping to the "safe" side of the scrim, she retreated to the far end of the room, took a chair and turned it around and sat, facing the dark wall, as if to study the flickering of the shadows cast from his candles on the water [though in truth, they barely reached that far]. But what was illuminated was the nape of her neck. He edged the screen around a little [keeping it between her line of view and the tub] to cover him as he climbed in.

"Don't fall," she suggested.

"So very helpful," he said. [He felt like explaining that he'd been up in the *sky* all night in a small untested boat only marginally larger than a shoe and he'd managed to not fall to his death, so . . .]

Gripping the rim for support, he eased himself in. The stomach cramps were bad, but the shakes and chills he could imagine dissipating already at the prospect of the warm tub. [Here was the liquid warmth, the peaceful sea, of the pipe he'd gone without for too long now.]

"Luuk Blenkin," he said [a little delayed in offering up this non-orang-utan answer, he realized, but she *had* asked].

"What about him?"

Wyn changed his mind in that moment, taking her in [what he could see of her, that is, across the dim room: that neck, the turn of her back]. No [on second thought], she didn't need to hear it had been Luuk out there.

"Just— He's written a lot of songs that appear to be about you. Some are actually good."

"Good for him."

"He only *looks* like a big oaf, you know."

[She had no response to this.]

"He has a clever one about the nape of your neck."

He felt for a second [based on something in her shoulders, the stiffness of her back] that she might turn around and address him directly, but she seemed to stop herself, taking a deep breath instead. "All my life, men have tried to impress me with how clever they are, how large their brain . . . They're too clever by half."

Wyn closed his eyes, focusing on her voice [trying to block out a rising wave of cramps].

"It's all so unnecessary," she said.

He waited for more [hoping she couldn't hear his teeth clattering or his stomach gurgling in the gray silence].

"*You* used to impress me," she said, "and with very little effort. By doing basically nothing."

He didn't know what she was talking about. Maybe he was imagining it. Or maybe she meant before tonight [*before* he'd embarrassed himself out on the strandweg, knocked senseless, just a mess]. Before he needed a young woman to help him up and remove his shoes and stockings for him.

"As a girl," she said, still to the wall. "I saw you, you know. The way you'd sling your bundle over your shoulder and kind of ease down the strandweg, a little lopsided, loose in your bones . . . It was probably the most I've ever been impressed by a man, then or since."

Even in the dim candlelight, he could see the sudden blush rise along her neck, the move her hand made to reach up and capture it like a moth, or hide it, and then a scattering motion, as if to cast the blush away. [Or his gaze.] She fluttered her hand [as if shooing the moth, not just this brash confession].

"And I can't begin to tell you why."

She told him she'd even seen him walking out into the ocean with an anchor.

"Cradling it in your arms like a baby. I've seen the bomschuit men doing it, of course, but I never understood why."

"That's just standard practice," he told her, not sure how else to respond. [He didn't think she needed a whole lecture on the peculiar practices of sailing off Scheveningen Beach; of fishermen having had to come up with a way to moor there without being pulled into the sea.]

"There was something nonstandard about your attitude, Meneer van Winkel—marching out into the waves, big grin on your dopey face . . . And another time—the same summer, when I was thirteen—I watched you going out to the water's edge, helping a shabby painter. Not the dune painter, the cheery old one . . . I've never seen him since, this redheaded one. There was a storm coming in, and the two of you were moving out *toward* it, toward the beach, and he was kind of wound-up and nervous. Everyone was leaving the beach, but you stayed. You stayed *for* the storm. Jabbering nonstop, the two of you, likely up to some deviltry. But you just—"

"Did you think I painted too?"

"No."

"Because I don't. Sorry."

"No, no. It wasn't about you *doing* something, some talents. I'm telling you, I'm not impressed by all that! It was just the way you carried the easel, braced it for him. It was the way you moved."

"You should have seen the way I moved in Aceh," he said. "In Sumatra. *That* was impressive."

He could hear her frowning [or it was something about the tilt of her head, the way she stiffened in her chair, a flicker of a headshake]. "Big heroic man deeds, all that—wading into battle— I don't—"

"I mean how I *avoided* bullets and pedangs. Very impressive."

"Oh."

There came then a swell of cramps, rolling through like breakers, and he did his best to breathe through it, resisting the attending wave of dizzy disorder—like he'd taken another whack to the head with Blenkin's fiddle case. He tried to be quiet about it, hoping it would pass [and hoping she would keep talking].

"You stopped the wind," she said, soft as the shushing ocean outside. [He wasn't sure he heard right.] He waited, and there was [finally] more: "Heading out onto the beach that time, I mean. You kind of . . . stopped the wind."

He tried to picture just saying something like that to someone, with no jokey spin to it. [Just putting it right out there.] She was braver than anyone he'd run into in the jungle, on either side.

It struck him for some reason [in that way his brain felt awash at times, sloshing in the lack of his peace pipe] that here was perhaps the first person he'd met who would not be flustered by his father [or dumbfounded that this father could have a son like him]. An irrelevant thought [like something on the sea, heaving in sight out of the mist], followed by an equally unrelated thought: he might really need to heave, and soon.

Earlier in the evening, Ned had watched the gleeful mayhem overtake their little cottage . . . the kids dancing round in their nightclothes, each one with their star over their head. Fenna had taken down each of these marvels he'd plucked from the dark to let them examine them yet again . . . after Ned assured her repeatedly, and demonstrated . . . that they would not burn his flesh or blind him, but would simply glow and give off that small, soothing hum . . .

He let them play with these three . . . but he'd kept more of these wonders, and if they proved valuable, he would use them to further provide for this little troop, his marvelous wife . . .

Fenna clapped and laughed with delight . . . "My family! I'm raising a string of Advent ornaments!" . . . and launched into the first verse of "Zie Ginds Komt de Stoomboot" and the one that went *See, the moon shining through the trees* . . .

The three-year-old, caught up in it all . . . confused and excited and forgetting it was June . . . brought out one of her little shoes and carefully placed it on the hearth for Sinterklaas.

Being unaccustomed to the sounds common to the belly of this massive masjid [with its modern plumbing and heating and engineering], he wasn't sure if someone was at the door or it was some other negligible tapping [a steam valve, a stoked boiler, dumbwaiters engaging gears and throttles] until Imke hopped up and answered it. [He watched through the slim space between the Japanese screen and the wall, sinking down in the tub to spy on her.]

"It's just Lammie," she assured him.

He could tell as much, though, from the heft of her arm [the baker not having opened the door more than its girth required], reaching in blindly to her assistant with a small basket, covered in cloth.

Imke thanked her and closed the door and brought it to him, squeezing the basket around the screen. The smell gave it away even before she flipped back the dishtowel: hot fresh bread [the first batch of the night, she said], and he took it [knowing it might even make the cramps and nausea worse]. She'd helped make it, after all, and it was warm and good and he wanted it in him. And maybe if he stuffed more of that sort of thing in, there would be less room for the bad stuff.

[Besides, if the heaving started up, he currently had nothing in him to expel.]

"Godverdomme!" He tried to tell her, through a bread-crammed mouthful, how impressive *she* was; that the bread was exceptional.

"It's all Lammie," she said. "I just help out."

"No," he insisted. "I made sure to only eat the parts that you made . . . And I say *godverdomme*."

"You sound chilled." She sounded genuinely surprised. "You have the shivers?"

Rising up, he poked his head around the screen and told her no, the water was plenty hot. She picked up her oil lamp and shone it in his face again [as if she were trying to warm him that way], frowned at him a moment, and headed back to the door.

"Where are you going? Don't—" he called after her, but she was gone. He could hear her moving quickly down the hall and returning moments later, carrying a bucket [additional hot water, he was sure]. Averting her eyes once again, unable to see where she stepped, she edged cautiously toward the tub, set the bucket down, and stepped back into the shadows. Leaning over the edge of the tub, he could see that it was empty [for a moment], before promptly throwing up in it.

Her hand appeared around the screen with a fresh washcloth. Wiping his face, he then rinsed it again, resettling in the tub.

"You can see the future," he said, steadying his breath, feeling the dizziness ebbing. "Witchery, but an admirable talent."

"I'm just not colorblind," she said. "You were pea-green."

He closed his eyes [trying not to huff and puff like an expectant mother] and draped the damp cloth across his brow.

Ned woke to Fenna softly singing to the youngest. The lullaby trailed off. "Only one feeding a night," she whispered, shaking him gently with her free hand. "She's down to only once. So maybe, now that the boat is finished . . . You've got all that planked lumber left over . . . Maybe you start thinking about building that little bed for her, and just about the time you're oiling the wood, we should have this one all to ourselves."

He marveled at her, knowing her meaning . . . Still, as he pointed out, the baby wouldn't be ready for a trundle, off sleeping beside the other two in their bed, as quickly as it would take him to go out to the shed and build such a thing . . . Not really . . .

"Well," she said. "I'm sure making it will take longer than you imagine."

"Because I'll fall asleep out there, working by myself," he conceded.

"No," she said. "I'm figuring in the limited time you'll have for furniture-building, given you'll be out running your new herring boat till the fall."

She was right. She was always right. It was a wonder he'd made it all those years without her there, alongside him, being right . . . And the fact that it hadn't just been a lark, an experiment, but would serve as an ongoing enterprise through the new herring season, even at his age, even without his brothers . . . and even with the need for recruiting a new crew member, with only the inexperienced boy left and Wyn running off to America . . . all those iffy factors were swept away when Fenna said it was so . . . that he would be back out there with the picarooner . . . with the silly little, surprisingly successful, *Klomp*.

"You think so, dear? Even with . . ."

"I can see it, Neddie."

She hadn't covered herself after the nursing, simply moving the baby girl aside, burping and shushing her . . . and he kept his eyes on the ridiculously lovely Mevrouw Nodder . . . on the rise and fall of her swollen breast, knowing she was watching him . . . After a time, she murmured, "Close your eyes and back to sleep, lover."

Imke was back with a glass of what looked like water.

"No way," he said. "You expect me to drink that mess? Then I'll *really* throw up."

"You need something in you. It's just water."

"But spa water, right? Sulfury or salty or something?"

"What are you talking about? It's *water* water."

"But don't folks come here for the saltwater cure?"

"To *bathe* in, yes. Not to drink. You did injure your head, didn't you?"

"Or for the hot springs or something?"

"You're *from* here, Wynand van Winkel. You know there isn't a hot spring! And even at those other kurhauses that have natural springs, I hardly think they make them *drink* it, silly. They throw away a fortune on some ridiculous follies here, all in the name of health, but *that* isn't one of them."

"Don't you have jenever or ale?"

"Try it." She sang out with the brass of a strandweg barker, calling to the seagazers taking in the sights: "The famed Kurhaus, ladies and gents, has *the* finest, cleanest drinking water, bar none. It's a modern wonder!"

He took a sip.

"Give it a try, folks! Step up and see!"

[*Water's water*, he recalled telling Luuk.] He drank it slowly, pausing only to chime in with her sales pitch: "Nothing but the best at the masjid."

While he drank, his hand trembling [concentrating on not losing his grip on the glass], she retreated to the shelves in the shadows and announced she had something that might be gentler than the washcloth on his injuries, and he really ought to clean them properly. "More health from the sea!" she declared, tossing something high, over the scrim. He squinted up at something bloblike that bounced back off an overhead pipe and landed just shy of the tub. In the gap at the bottom of the screen, below the fabric, lay a mustard-colored sponge.

Reaching, shaking, he tried for it [and wasn't surprised when he dropped it]. Of course his body was reacting [and rather sternly] to the choice to *not* go downstairs at the Very Busy Laundry earlier that evening. But it was something else, beyond the trembling: his hands were swollen and bloody, he saw now, as if he'd been the one punching away [recalling now holding them up, trying to protect himself from the kicking, and also something else—trying to hand the stupid kid something; his cut of the catch in the envelope? or maybe his steamship passage, rubber-stamped for America?]

"I'm a bit stub-fingered," he said.

She scooped up the sponge and reached around to pass it to him through the crack between the wall and the screen. When he took hold of it, she touched his hand for a moment, tentatively. "Can you move them? Are they broken?"

"Ask me in a day," he told her.

She pulled his hand closer to examine it, stooped over, half crouched there at the narrow crack in the screen, then sat on the edge of the chair he'd used earlier to undress. She was still holding his hand, squinting down at his fingers, clearly having trouble seeing in the shadows there.

"Just stubbed, probably," he said. "I'll heal. Always do."

Her hair in her face, annoying her, she inched the screen back just a little to allow her to move down onto the low footstool at the head of the tub, pivoting so that she was facing away from him, but still holding his hand, lightly, examining it, now able to catch some of the candlelight there. Finally she released it, saying, "Hopefully they're just stubbed, as you say, and you should be back fishing again in a day or two."

He didn't contradict her, but he wondered if she'd forgotten about the steamer to the States. Withdrawing his hand, still minus the sponge, he settled back into the tub with a groan, muttering, "My whole body is stubbed."

"You," she said, "are ridiculous."

She did settle in there now, not retreating back to her shadowy chair but remaining on the footstool, and in the small space allowed by the screen on the edge of the tub, rested her head not far from his [aiming her gaze back at her well-studied wall across the room]. From her apron, she fished out a peppermint candy [she said the maids put on pillows upstairs when they turned down the beds]. Unwrapping it, she crooked her arm around [toward the nape of her neck], waiting for him to take it. He thought that peppermint might be a little rough on his stomach right now [but said nothing], awkwardly nibbling it from her fingers, unsure his own could manage. Sweet and strong, it opened his eyes and filled his head.

"I can help you, if you're— I shouldn't be such a ragheaded schoolgirl about this and just . . . I should help you."

"A lullaby would help," he said. "Could you sing to me?"

"Ja," she said. "But I won't. You're welcome to just shut your eyes and *imagine* I'm singing to you."

"Great."

"The Kurhaus is not a geisha bath, you know."

He asked her how she knew of such things.

"I *do* read, you know? Remember our walk back from the Binty—the Bittag—"

"The Bintang Kecil. The Little Star Café. I wasn't sure that wasn't one of my dreams."

"So you know I don't care to drag myself around the world like you, but I do enjoy reading about the wonders and sights."

"Geishas?" He reminded her he hadn't actually traveled to Japan. And anyway, she was the one with the Japanese screen.

She had the sponge in hand now, holding it up as if she wanted him to acknowledge it; take it seriously. "So on the lullaby request, how about you just use your imagination there, pal . . . But we need to get those wounds clean, and you—"

"We're pals now?" he said. "*Those are silver; these are gold . . .*"

"You're babbling. And you need help."

She hopped up again, announcing she was going to first try covering him a little. "I'm not looking," she said as she scooted the screen more toward the foot of the tub.

"Certainly none of this," he said, "complies with the North Seas Fisheries Convention of 1882." He wasn't sure how she would do this, but watched as she produced a clean, folded bedsheet from one of the shelves, opened it lengthwise [with her head craned around like an owl, chin jutting toward the overhead pipes, straining as if to exaggerate her discretion], and draped it over the middle of the tub [covering the sights a young maiden like her had no business seeing]. She scooted some of the candles aside, to avoid the flames touching the sheet, then plopped back down on the footstool, sponge in hand.

"It may take more than a bedsheet to render me decent," he said.

"In addition, I'm also planning to not look."

"Good plan," he said.

"It's my favorite plan," she said. "Not looking."

"Not gazing upon my ravaged and abused form?"

"Well, now that you've described it," she said, "looking seems unnecessary."

She was making him laugh [and nervous]. He closed his eyes and tried to think of her as a sort of medic. [Except the medic that came to mind was a goofy jimber-jawed korporaal from Drempt named Houtkooper, and that did not serve at all.]

He assumed she was still averting her eyes . . . till he felt her hand on his left bicep [his arm having slipped over the edge of the tub, his limbs too sore to cooperate entirely] and she twisted it toward her slightly, trying to read his tattoo [from the navy portion of his service—the anchor and *Moeder*].

"I'm surprised," she said, pushing his arm off the rim, letting it slip back over into the tub.

"Shouldn't be. It would be surprising to serve all that time, especially out there, and come away with no artwork on you."

She reached in now with the sponge, just behind his shoulder, tipping him forward just enough to dip it in the water first. "I'm surprised it's for your mother." Starting in with the sponge, she dabbed gently just above the waterline [at the bruises forming where he was pretty sure he had a busted rib]. "I was expecting another name there."

Even in this fog, he knew she meant Fenna.

He'd probably considered having it put on there, at one point. [But not truly. If he'd really meant to do that, he wouldn't have left in the first place.] "No," he said. "No one else."

"Good choice," Imke said. "Your wife'll respect that choice one day."

"Especially since she won't be competing with my mother in person. She's passed."

"It's hard to compete with folks from the past," Imke said.

"I'm sure she won't have to . . . my wife, I mean. When and if I ever get around to such a thing."

"You may never," Imke said. "There are men who just aren't the sort. Marrying, I mean. I understand you're the sort in plenty of other ways, of course. No question there. But you may never."

"Sure I will. I don't aim to wait as long as Old Ned did."

Imke stopped soaping his wounds and turned toward the door, on alert. Wyn had the bad ear from the garrison explosion, so maybe there was something out there, but he'd swear he hadn't heard a thing.

"Do you hear that, Wynkyn van Winkel? Why, it's the sound of all the lasses of Scheveningen letting out a great whoosh of relief!"

He nearly pulled her into the tub with him [hooking his arm around her neck, kissing her hard], and the ticklish sound of her laughing against his teeth was something he hoped to know on his deathbed.

AND YOU SHALL SEE THE BEAUTIFUL THINGS AS YOU ROCK IN THE MISTY SEA

Earlier still, at supper, watching him bustling around their little home, lifting the kids from their bench at the table . . . and the little one from her stool . . . and flying them around the room, hoisting them high to admire the stars he'd placed at each of their names . . . and confirming to each of them that they were such beautiful, beautiful things . . . Fenna remarked, "*You* sure seem wide awake."

It was true, he'd had no sleep the night before, in the boat . . . and nothing approaching what he would consider a proper nap during the day, what with dealing with Jaap Bunk and settling up with Wyn and all the rest of it . . . yet he felt as rested as if he'd just risen from a long, full night of sleep. Winter sleep, even. She said she hadn't seen him like this since back when his brothers were around.

"Please don't tell me you're now on Wynkyn's foolish sleep schedule," she teased. "You're going to buzz around all night and flop somewhere during the day? Harre Jasses."

But when she blew out the candle for bed, Ned closed his eyes and knew he would sleep just fine . . . and right in his bed as he was supposed to . . .

It was fuzzy [how much time had passed?], but Imke was telling him she had to slip out and go down the hall and help Lammie.

"Try to nod off if you can," she suggested, "if you can manage it without drowning."

He told her not to worry, that he surely wouldn't sleep. [Unless of course he already *was* asleep: he couldn't tell anymore.] "Not for all the fish in the heavens . . ." he thought he was saying. "Not for all the stars in the sea . . ."

But to his surprise, he did. And he dreamt of the rocking motion of the blue-eyed Putehs' fishing boat, smuggling him up to Rangoon. It all came back now, but it was fine: the scramble to hide among the orang-utans in the peat swamps of Rawa Tripa, then hiring the strange blue-eyed fishermen, sailing north. The Andaman Sea had been misty, he recalled, some of it like gliding through a cloud, and the Puteh fishermen made it clear [with hand signs and pidgin] that it was happening because of great distant storms, but those were far enough behind them not to do them any harm.

He dreamt of the low green line of mangrove forests and seagrass meadows along the coastline of a necklace of small islands to the west—how they fished for snapper and octopus, escorted by leatherback turtles and the hideously beautiful, flipping and flapping dugong, the lady of the sea.

[And he dreamt of Imke Holt, coming back down the hall, with something wonderful and warm from the oven.]

Fleeing The Hague, Luuk Blenkin took the omnibus again—a chillier ride this time—sitting near the driver, who told him he'd charge him half fare if he sat up there and let the man yammer away—so he wouldn't drift off and tumble off the box.

"The rocking motion up here," the old man said. "Godverdomme if it don't feel like a cradle some nights!"

"Or like we're at sea," Luuk said—as if he were now some great expert at seafaring.

"That too!" The driver gave him a pull from his flask. "The cradle and the boat—both far superior to these brutes!" He cracked the reins over the team—to insult, it seemed like, more than to drive them on.

The drink was stronger than anything Luuk had ever sipped—it burned and left him teary-eyed—made misty the dark road ahead.

"Word at the station, at the turnaround," the driver jerked his head back behind them, indicating—Luuk assumed—the omnibus stop—"Did you hear, lad? Word's spreading halfway to Drempt: the shoals are running! The silver harvest! The boms at Scheveningen are being righted and untarped as we speak, everyone a-scramble." The driver grinned, but sounded wistful. "Wish I were young again, like yourself, back in one of them . . . Back in *either* one, actually—a boat *or* a cradle!" He laughed at his joke.

The three of them had singlehandedly started the herring season. Luuk knew the others might be catching plenty of the silver darlings soon, but they wouldn't snare in their nets any of the beautiful things *they* had—they wouldn't sail off into the miraculous.

He'd painted all three of their names on the boat, under the name *De Klomp* . . . *van Winkel, Blenkin,* and *Nodder* . . . to announce who owned her once the curious began to poke and peek at her moored in the high dunes on the beach, dragged back farther, not further inland than those bulky bom-schuiten could ever be budged. He chose to put his last name . . . though everyone would know it from Ned alone . . . but he wanted to have his brothers' name on the boat, and so it was.

He knew, too, that only two of those named on the hull would be returning for the next voyage . . . but he wanted all three listed, to make it official.

The idea for trying the strange little boat design had come in the previous year . . . soon after Wynkyn's return home . . . while the dazed-seeming young man helped him with some much-needed rethatching. They'd cut mats of stargrass, on the marshy side of the dunes . . . hauling it up in loads with Lotte and the hay cart . . . His wife and kids, away at her folks, missed seeing the beams exposed to the heavens . . .

Up on the ladder, they admired the strip of blue that was the sea beyond. "We have such bounty all around us, Wynkyn . . . The sea itself so close! If only we could find other work that we could manage with just a small crew like this You and me, maybe one other . . ."

It was a fine job they did, and he thanked his friend Wynkyn for the peaceful dreams he would have under his new stargrass roof. And Wynk told him then what he'd heard of the strange little boat . . . told to him while rocking along in the cargo hold of yet another vessel, far off somewhere else in the sea . . .

WHERE THE OLD SHOE
ROCKED THE
FISHERMEN THREE:—
WYNKEN.
BLYNKEN.
AND NOD.

"She's trying to rock the boat, as usual. Lammie's trying some strange American cookie recipe," Imke announced upon her return [part of one already obscuring her words, he could tell]. "Coconut and rolled oats." She held a couple lumps in her hand [sweet-smelling as she brought them near].

He sank back down into the tub [unsure], pulling back from the coconut that [especially in this darkened room and at this late hour] could take him back painfully to his last night in Aceh and the witnessing of the act of Aceh-mord, when the explosion rocked him [rocked him nearly as much as the subsequent sight of that native-made sandal blown clear of what shredded blackened flesh was left of the Mahomedan, the lone shoe tipped on its side in the dirt]. The possibility of sudden transport didn't scare him anymore. It just wasn't a land he cared to journey to right now.

[Plus, he hadn't kept even that delicious bread down.]

But this was a different Imke Holt than he'd imagined before. This was an Imke who had kissed him and cradled him, nearly tipping into the tub with him, nearly joining him in the bath with a fine audacity. [Hell, he could easily imagine her being one of those bold young women attending university at Leiden, if she so chose.] She was an Imke who could and would disrupt personal plans and life plans and the fate of the stars, even, and subvert the official timetables of spoorweg and steam tram and oceanliners and the course of all forms of travel and transport, by foot, by rail, by sea or even air [by imagination or insanity or dreams]. With another *tut-tut* [a sound he was swiftly getting used to], she brushed past the feeble blockade of the Japanese screen and slipped the cookie right in his mouth.

It was chewy and salty and sweet [so many things, all at once].

But it didn't take him there. It didn't taste of Aceh, of jungle terror. It tasted, first, of her lovely fingers, and the coconut and oats tasted like a memory of his mother, making this very cookie—could that be?

"*I* could make these," Imke said, examining one. "If you like them. I'm pretty capable, you know."

"You certainly seem capable," he said. He didn't know her well [he was only starting to realize—even more the more he got to know her]. He would need to linger here, to better determine how capable she was. [She was certainly capable of joy; capable of a laugh that might draw in the moon.]

He tipped her head to his, over the edge of the tub, and he had nothing clever to say, so he just said, "Hoi."

"Hoi yourself," she said.

At dawn—back in Rotterdam for the second time in twenty-four hours—Luuk Blenkin stood on the passenger dock, ready to board the liner.

His passage was paid already, the boarding pass safe in his pocket. (Thanks to Wyn—already he was softening toward the foolish klootzak.) He would sail to New Orleans and then—if he could earn some small wage with which to journey on—or maybe pawn his slightly damaged fiddle or one of the small glowing wonders still in his possession, wrapped in the black mourning cloth to hide the glow—he might just steam up the Mighty Mississippi to the fabled city of St. Louis—or just look for towns mentioned in the songs of Stephen Foster and go ashore there and try his luck. He would find *some* work, anyhow—perhaps in a songmill or newspaper—

hopefully apprenticing with an established master in the business of light verse.

And with the goal now of setting them out in print, not loose in the air—he would see how many of his hand-crafted words he could place out into the wide-open world, like tiny stars, burning on.

While tilling his garden one day, with the bright sun high overhead, just after lunch, Ned found himself on the edge of a makeshift dance floor . . . planks set out under the twinkling night sky, girdled with lanterns like a child's sparkly necklace and laughter nearly drowning the music as he watched the last wee one, now grown, weightless in a reel with a beaming young man who was her groom . . .

Wynkyn was a guest, with some gray of his own . . . and dancing with a gal who looked a lot like the Holt girl, only wide as a German brewer . . . And it was clear somehow, just by the wink Wynkyn gave him, that they were partners still, in several fine boats working out of a new man-made harbor . . . a real harbor, built after yet another storm destroyed the boms on the beach at Scheveningen . . . He could tell, in that way of knowing in dreams, just by watching the lean, silvered jackass and his patient wife dance out of joy for his friend's family, Wynk chanting, "They danced by the light of the moon, the moon . . . they danced by the light of the moon!"

Ned was seated on the edge of the wedding party, beside his love, holding her hand.

And then she was bent over him, the babe mewing in her arms, too young for a wedding gown . . . Fenna bringing him a dipper of water, gently rubbing his sun-stung shoulder blade, rousing him . . . He'd been leaning against the arms of the tiller. His hat was at his feet. He dusted it off, feeling the fool, as she poured a little of the water on her kerchief and dabbed his brow, asking him, "Do you know where you are, love?"

"Always," he said.

It was a foolish dream, of course, that moonlit dance . . . yet all the same it nearly made him weep. If only it could be true . . . to live to see that celebration. But he'd be something like seventy, which was ridiculous to expect

. . . the withered age of a great-grandfather, not a father, not the host of a wedding feast.

Still, it felt real. He'd felt the chill night air . . . heard the band . . . tasted the glazed lemon taarten made with real lemons . . . He was there . . .

Einde

Acknowledgments

A BOATLOAD OF THANKS TO . . . Huck Lightning Amick, Mel Anderson, Richard Bausch, Charles Baxter, Barbara Neely Bourgoyne, Benjamin Busch, Peter Ho Davis, Marein de Jong, Joe DeMatio, DTE Energy, Erik Esckilsen, The Field House Museum of St. Louis, Dr. David Freiband, Deborah Garrison, Steve Gibb, Michael Griffith, Julie Gu, Sam Hiser, Roger Holloway, Felicia Krol, Josyln Layne, Chistopher J. Magson, Nicola Mason, Gregory Dean McIntosh, Michael Mungiello, Chuck Pfarrer, Richard Scullin, Joe Snapp, Jon Soto, Jack Spack, and the students and fellow faculty of Pacific University MFA in Creative Writing.